THE GHOSTS OF YESTERYEAR

ALSO BY BETHANY HELWIG

International Monster Slayers:
The Curse of Moose Lake
The Bite of Winter

~

Darkest Light

INTERNATIONAL MONSTER SLAYERS
BOOK THREE

THE GHOSTS OF YESTERYEAR

BETHANY HELWIG

BRIGHTWAY BOOKS

Copyright © 2017 by Bethany Helwig
Published by Brightway Books, LLC

Cover Illustration: Bethany Helwig

First Edition: October 2017

ISBN-10: 0-9981247-6-1
ISBN-13: 978-0-9981247-6-6

For the lost, for the found,
for those still searching,
and those still waiting.

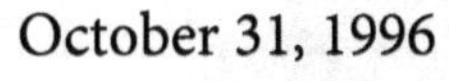

October 31, 1996

She doesn't know where she is. Wherever she's ended up, it's dark, cold, and smells like dirt. Moonlight turns the tall, daunting silhouettes of the trees around her into the creaking fingers of the boogeyman come to gobble her up. She shivers and wraps her arms around her legs, tucking her knees in to her chest to stave off the chill. Her hands and feet are covered in drying mud and her fingers ache as she clenches onto her jeans.

It feels like she's been running for days even though it's only been tonight. She didn't want to go. She wanted to stay with her father, but she just *had* to run. She couldn't stop herself. So she ran and ran and kept running. Now she's in this strange place and can't remember how she got here.

Her father must be so worried. If only he had been there when it happened. He could have stopped her, but he said he had to go help the Masons. He left her with the babysitter and hurried out the door. He left her alone.

The sitter didn't know what to do when she transformed in front of her.

She shivers again. She loves dogs. She loves wolves. She never thought she could *become* one. But it hurts. It hurts every time it takes over. She can't control it and doesn't know how. Something dark inside her decides when the change happens and when she becomes a seven-year-old girl again.

She's always known about werewolves. Her dad taught her. His job is hunting monsters. He'll come find her. He has to.

But what if she ran too far? What if she's not even in Moose Lake anymore? She puts her chin on her knees and start to rock back and forth.

Humming quietly to herself, it makes her feel better. Her mom sings all the time.

Mom *used* to sing.

She continues to hum while tears roll down her cheeks.

She misses her mother's smiles, braiding her hair, and singing her songs. She misses helping her in the garden. She squeezes her eyes shut tight and pictures everything about her mother—long dark hair, warm hands, the smell of earth about her, the way she made the plants dance, her songs, her nicknames for those around her. Mom called her squirt in the dirt and would rub a streak of dirt on her nose when she said it.

She keeps rocking back and forth but stops humming.

The image of Mom in her head always changes to how she looked that night. The night everything changed. Wolves came into their home while Dad was away. Mom had her hide under the bed while she tried to fight them off.

One of the wolves bit Mom and when she went to protect her mother, they bit her too.

She wraps a hand around her right wrist where the bite is nearly healed but is still wrapped in a thick bandage. Dad told her what a bite does. She knew what would happen.

She survived. She changed. Mom didn't.

She was the one that called the Masons and got Dad to come home to help. Mom said she loved her and it would be okay. But it wasn't okay. Mom was in pain. So was she. Only Mom didn't change like she did. She—

A branch snaps nearby. She freezes to listen and *smells* something. She sniffs a few times and wipes the tears off her face. Shuffling footsteps come far too close for comfort. She uncoils a little and plants her hands on the ground so she can leap away in a hurry if she needs to. She holds her breath and listens to those footsteps come closer. Could it be Dad?

"Hello?" she calls. "Is someone there?"

"Who's there?" a boy responds.

Disappointment settles in her chest. Not Dad. Through the darkness a pale yellow light appears. It comes closer a little at a time. It's shaped weird like a small airplane.

"Where are you?" the boy calls.

"Over here," she says louder. He doesn't sound like a grown-up. He sounds like a kid like her.

The glowing airplane comes closer until she realizes it's a glow-in-the-dark shirt the boy is wearing. She holds up a hand to wave and he finally sees her. He comes within a few feet and then stops. She can hardly make him out at all but he's short, probably about her height. He's got shaggy hair and white shoes but that's all she can see.

"Where are we?" he asks.

"I don't know. How did *you* get here?"

"I ran."

"Me too."

He comes over and takes a seat next to her. He smells foul and dirty.

"Really?" he asks.

"Yeah." She brings her hands together in her lap and tries to act polite as her mom taught her. "What's your name?"

"James."

"I'm Genna," she says. "So we're both lost?"

"I guess." He sniffles loudly. "Can I . . . can I hold your hand?"

She reaches across the space between them and their hands fumble about until they find each other. Holding his hand makes her not so afraid of the strange woods around them. "Are you okay? Are you hurt?"

"I'm scared."

"Me too." She scoots across the dirt towards him until their knees are touching. "At least we're not alone anymore." Saying it out loud makes her feel better. She is *not* alone.

"I want to go home," James says, a tremor in his voice like he might cry.

"Then we'll go home. My dad will find us."

"But—" When he starts to sob, she squeezes his hand. Eventually he takes a deep breath and says, "I don't know where my house is."

"It's okay," she says, lifting up her shoe to pull back the tongue, and tries to show him what's on the inside even though it's too dark to see. She feels so clever. "I have my address written in my shoe. If we can get there then we can find someone who knows where you live. We're going to get home, James. You and me."

"How?"

"My dad will save us. Or we'll just have to get there ourselves. We can do it. Once it's light again, we'll figure out where we are." She holds up her other hand. "Pinky swear, okay? I pinky swear I'm going to get us both home."

He holds out his pinky and she gives it a good shake with her own.

"See? We're going to be okay."

He nods and they sit together holding hands as they wait for the sun to come up. Genna will wait for it all night if she has to, but waiting takes a long time and the sun doesn't want to rise. She waits and waits and James ends up curled up next to her with his head on her shoulder. She stays awake to keep him safe. That's what her father does for others. That's what she's going to do for him.

Creatures move nearby in the darkness, crumpling leaves and rustling grass, so she keeps very still and quiet. When a squirrel starts chirping at them, she nearly jumps but James sleeps on.

Her eyelids grow heavy as the night wears on and her head nods. She's about to fall asleep with her head resting against the boy's when she sees light in the distance. A flashlight. She prods James awake with her elbow and they watch the light come closer. James lurches to his feet but Genna grabs the back of his pants and pulls him down. Dad taught her to be careful.

"We don't know who that is," she hisses at James.

Then she hears it. A man calling their names along with a bunch of other kids echoing his words. If there's a bunch of kids with him, he must be okay, right?

"Come on," she says and hauls James to his feet.

"Over here!" he yells.

The flashlight turns in their direction. They wave their hands and walk towards their rescuer through tall grass and bushes.

"Kids!" the man calls. "I'm so glad I found you!"

Struggling through a tangle of nettles, they at last reach the man and find seven other kids with him—all dirty, scared, and huddled together. Did they run off like her and James? Are they all werewolves?

The man kneels so he's at their level and tilts the flashlight to illuminate his face. There's something familiar about him. Genna feels like she knows those bright blue eyes, the wild dark hair, that dimpled smile.

"Hey, it's okay," he says and gives each of them a pat on the shoulder. "I'm going to take care of you. I know you're scared but everything's going to be all right. I've got you."

He keeps on smiling and the other kids bunch up around him, watching her and James.

"How do you know our names?" she asks. "Did my dad send you?"

His smile fades and he takes her hand. "I know your name, Genevieve, because I'm like you. I know what you are. And I'm going to take care of you."

"We want to go home," she says and points between James and herself.

"I know, sweetheart, but it's dangerous right now."

"Why?"

"Because *you* are dangerous. Think about it, Genevieve. You couldn't stop yourself from running all the way out here. You couldn't control changing into a wolf. If you go back home, what if you can't stop yourself from attacking your father? Do you want that?"

Her throat feels tight and her lower lip starts to tremble. "No."

"Then let me help you. I can teach you to control it."

She's not supposed to trust strangers but part of her knows that she should. That feeling grows stronger and stronger until there is no fear, no worry, no doubt. She will trust this man. She must.

"Okay," she says and wraps her hand around James's again. "What's your name?"

His smile returns. "You can call me Dasc."

14 Years, 4 Months, 25 Days Later

1

I can hardly remember a time when my biggest concern was making sure I didn't insult a centaur by mistake or show up late for agent training. In the last five months, I've nearly been killed at least three times, took on *the* alpha werewolf and won, stopped vampires from waging a war, and survived an attack by not one but two lamia. I'm sure the name "Phoenix Mason" is edging near the top of the monsters' hit list given the amount of times I've ticked them off—or killed them.

Despite facing all those monsters and the horrors that came with them, this last month has been the hardest of my life.

Jefferson and I and our Scotland-based team have been showing the locals a digitally rendered photo of what Genna might look like today—olive skin, black hair, dark eyes like Jefferson. After splashing through puddles and combing the small town along the shores of Loch Duich most of the day, we decide to try talking to those on the tour bus waiting to head to a nearby historical attraction. Rain drums on the roof of the bus as Jefferson and I crowd the stairwell. Mist wraps around the landscape outside shrouding it from view but every so often I can see the water of the loch as the fog parts. At last, the driver of the tour bus tells us exactly what we want to hear.

"Yeah, I've seen her," he says, his Scottish accent thicker than any member of the small team we've been working with. "Short hair though."

"Where was she going?" Jefferson asks and bears down on the man like he'll beat him to a pulp if he doesn't answer. We've been on his daughter's trail for a solid month and Jefferson hasn't let up a single second. It's do or die. His intensity has been wearing me thin, but I can't blame him. I can only help him.

The man leans back and his newsies cap almost falls off his sprig of curly hair. "I dunno! She wanted to know when the visitin' hours for the castle of Eilean Donan ended and then she vanished."

"That's it?" Jefferson growls. "You've got to know more than just that. What was she wearing? What was she doing? Did she look injured? Tell me!"

I lay a hand on Jefferson's arm. He doesn't shrug me off. The last time he tried, I held on tighter until it hurt. He hasn't done it since. Instead, he gets the message and takes a step back. I move to fill in the gap left open in the stairwell as the man leans away from us in his seat.

"Look, she's a missing person and every detail, no matter how small, will help us find her," I say. "Please, is there anything else you can tell us?"

After a frightful glance at Jefferson, he gives us a rough description of what Genna was wearing—a dark-colored rain jacket, hiking boots, and jeans—and where he thinks she was heading next.

"She kept wanting more information on the castle," he says. "The hours, the most crowded visiting times, when the exterior lights come on. I'm pretty sure you'll find her at the castle."

"And, umm, what exactly *are* the visiting hours?"

After he provides us with the times, we let him go. We step off the bus and into the rain that's been nonstop for the last week. The driver pulls away and nearly splashes us as the tires slosh through massive puddles. We quickly walk off the quaint country road, through a gate in a stone wall, and across a muddy gravel parking lot. The white walls of the lodge we're currently staying at look ghostly wrapped in the fog creeping inland off Loch Duich. Everything in Scotland has this otherworldly beauty to it, and the rain and fog are no exception.

Although I've been in the country for a month, there's been no time to truly enjoy it. Searching for Jefferson's daughter and other missing werewolves has turned my focus into tunnel vision. Jefferson's been even worse. He would have starved by now if not for my reminders to eat.

This is the closest we've ever been to catching up to Genna Barnes. She's been moving across the country and evading us—which isn't at all what I expected when Dasc told us he could lead us right to her. Some naive part of me believed Genna and the other missing people had been held captive somewhere this entire time, but Dasc wouldn't waste werewolf talent. Of course he wouldn't. Once we actually got here and discovered the first location Dasc gave us was empty, we found clues for where Genna went next but apparently only Dasc could decipher them. Figures. He always has to be the one with all the cards, doesn't he?

Jefferson stomps through the downpour and leads the way into the lodge. I stop to shake out my raincoat but he doesn't bother. The floorboards creak under our steps as we move past the front counter and hurry to the three rooms our company has rented out. Jefferson doesn't even knock at the first door we come to. He throws it open and the door hits the wall behind it from the force.

Four heads turn in our direction. Sinclair, Ross, and Thane are all poised around one of the two beds putting together their packs. Ross and Thane are the burly muscle of our group and also the most soft-spoken. Sinclair is a string-bean compared to the others and is nearly lost in the folds of his plaid shirt. Past them on the floor, pausing in the middle of a push-up, is Tawnee McDonnell. While unassuming compared to the three men, she's actually the most lethal of the bunch and by far the most friendly. A map marking our progress through Scotland lays on the floor in front of her so she can continue to study it while working out.

"News?" she asks and jumps to her feet, her extremely long, curly carrot hair bouncing around her shoulders.

"We think she's heading for a castle at Eilean Donan."

Tawnee cracks her neck and stretches her arms. "Odd. Why go there?"

"Why has she been going anywhere?" Jefferson grumbles and stalks over to help finish loading the packs with the other men.

I shuffle inside the small room so I can close the door. Tawnee does an acrobatic backflip over the map and returns to her previous position of doing push-ups while studying the map.

"Phoenix, fire up the laptop," Tawnee says and nods to me. "I think we need to confer on this."

Quick to obey, I navigate around her to the second bed and pull the laptop out of my bag. While I get it up and running, Jefferson scowls at me before continuing to fold up a shirt and tuck it into his pack. I know he doesn't like this part. I certainly don't. This is the last thing I want to do on any given day. I make the connection to the encrypted IMS network and dial in to the Minncapolis Division in the States. At a nod from me, Tawnee orders Ross and Sinclair out into the hallway to guard it while she moves to the window and checks to make sure no one is close nearby. Jefferson sits on the bed opposite me and stares at the back of the laptop while Thane gathers the packs and sets them in order by the door so we can move out as soon as possible.

The video chat connects and I come face to face with Director Knox. As usual, he's sitting in his office with a row of dead presidents framed on the wall behind him.

"Mason," he says. "ID."

"0919-32."

"Code in."

"Auribus teneo lupum."

He nods and asks, "What do you have for me?"

"A possible lead at the castle of Eilean Donan. We need to talk to Dasc to see what he knows and make sure we're not heading into a trap."

"I'll have the techs patch you through. Good luck, Mason."

"Thank you, sir."

The director vanishes and a message asking me to please wait takes his place. I clench my hands and focus on controlling my breathing with exercises I learned from a book Charlie lent me. It's easier to calm an emotional reaction by controlling the physical half of it.

A countdown appears on my screen and in five seconds another face appears. Devilish blue eyes, wild black hair, and a smile that says "I like burning the world down." He wears his mandatory white penitent clothes and folds his cuffed hands calmly on the tabletop in the interrogation room.

Dasc.

"Is it time to chat already?" he says. "You know, I always look forward to our discussions."

"Shove it," I say calmly. "We followed the last clue at the previous campsite we uncovered."

He inspects his fingernails as if this bores him. "And?"

I really wish I could punch him through the screen. I hate this. I hate having to rely on his information to keep tracking Genna. Whatever Dasc did with those missing people, apparently part of it was training them with secret codes he designed himself. Each time we've had a lead on someplace Genna has stayed or camped, she's left behind random clues that only seem to make sense to Dasc. She's always gone by the time we reach the next destination though, and no one knows where she's heading—until now. The castle is the first time we've had a clue without Dasc's assistance.

"We headed due west as you said," I say, trying not to grit my teeth. "A local saw her. She was asking all sorts of questions about Eilean Donan. What's there, Lycaon?"

He instantly forgoes examining his fingernails to glare at me. I've discovered he doesn't like the name most commonly used with his origin story, so I've formed a habit of using it as often as possible.

"The castle has a long and bloody history," he says and feigns disinterest again. "Clans fought over it. It was almost completely demolished at one point and then rebuilt again. Like the rest of Scotland, it has a history as red as—"

"Get to the point."

He leans in towards the camera. "Such a point of interest attracts certain creatures. One in particular is drawn to locations with bloody histories or are supposedly haunted. If I'm correct, Genna is looking for this creature."

I can only imagine that if I had been kidnapped, I would do everything in my power to escape. If Genna's had this much freedom and has been expertly avoiding us and the authorities for over fourteen years, it throws everything I thought about finding her out the window. Not for the first time, I wonder if she's free, why hasn't she tried going home? I glance at Jefferson. He's staring stone-faced at the floor.

I massage my forehead. "You're telling me she's off hunting some monster? Why?"

"Who ever said she was hunting it?" Dasc says. "You IMS agents are all the same. Seek and destroy. You don't see the benefit in *learning*."

"Okay, fine. Then if she's not hunting it, what is she doing? What monster are we talking about here?"

"Not a monster. A bean nighe."

"A what now?"

It isn't Dasc but Tawnee who answers. "The washer woman." She keeps her vigil near the window but cocks her head in my direction. "Native Scotland creature. Extremely rare."

"Well, bravo to your mystery friend," Dasc says sounding annoyed that he was interrupted. "And what else does she know about it?"

"They're said to know who will die and when," Tawnee says. "And if you're nice to them, manage to get on their good side, they'll tell you the fates of three people."

"*Or*," Dasc says, "if a person is extremely persuasive, one might even tell you the specifics of when, where, and how someone will die. I imagine you can see how finding a bean nighe would be particularly opportunistic."

Yeah, I can imagine. I wouldn't mind talking to one myself in order to ask it about Dasc. I can only hope that's the same reason Genna is going after it and not on Dasc's command.

"Should we expect a trap?" I ask. Unfortunately, when we first tried this hunt without Dasc's input, one of Genna's camps had a surprise waiting for us—a trip wire connected to a loaded shotgun. I guess she was worried the wrong people were following her.

"Genevieve will be extra cautious. You should also expect company. If anyone else has gotten wind that a bean nighe is still alive, she won't be the only one after it. If that's all . . ."

"For now."

"Take care of yourself out—"

I close the feed and the transmission automatically returns to Director Knox who's been watching our little chat like he does every time.

"Sir?"

"Head to the castle and see what you can find. Obviously, finding Genna is our mission here, but if there's a bean nighe it sounds like it's going to need our protection. And Dasc does have a point. Being able to talk to one could be incredibly beneficial." He adjusts his tie and pulls his lapels straight. "Have Spartan McDonnell call in some backup. If this ends up turning into a battle for the bean nighe with our missing people caught in the middle, I want you to be prepared."

"Yes, sir."

"Good hunting."

The transmission ends so I close the laptop and stuff it into my bag. I chew on Dasc's words for a moment and worry my lower lip. Something isn't sitting right with me on this as usual.

Tawnee pulls out a cell phone and makes a call to Edinburgh Division per the director's orders. Bulky-man Thane starts picking up the packs and tells the others outside to get our van loaded. Jefferson stands and slings his pack over his shoulder, waiting for Tawnee to finish her call. I feel like I should say something to him but like every other time, the words dry up in my mouth. He doesn't want the same platitudes from me that everyone else gives him, those empty reassurances that everything is going to be all right and Genna will be safe and sound. He needs me to power through and actually get the job done. Pointless chitchat isn't going to achieve that.

Not for the first time I wish Hawk was here to help me and say the right things when I can't. There's a twist in my stomach every time I think of him back home in Moose Lake working with a fill-in agent to monitor the city. We've never been apart this long before. Not ever. Before, we always stuck together like glue because that's just who we are. Now, it's become alarmingly plain that he needs me—more accurately, he needs the power in my veins to keep his werewolf disease in check. I'm the walking, talking cure for it but my power isn't ready yet to get rid of it. At least every time we've done video chats when I'm able, he seems fine thanks to the pendant Scholar put together with a little of my blood as the secret ingredient. She said it would need to be refreshed, though. I'm not sure how much longer we can stay an ocean apart before the power of the pendant fades.

But apart from knowing he's okay, I could really use him here for moral support. I'm terrified I'm going to mess this all up somehow and Jefferson's daughter will disappear like a ghost again. I can't let that happen.

Tawnee finally finishes her phone call and faces us. "There's a nearby selkie squad working the waters in Loch Carron. They'll meet us at the castle in an hour or so. For now, we should head down there and check the place out ourselves."

"Then what are we waiting for?" Jefferson says and hurries out the door.

I make to follow after but Tawnee grabs my arm. Although several inches shorter than me, she's a lean, mean, fighting machine and can be incredibly intimidating when she levels that dark gaze of hers. She was born a fighter, I can tell.

"How is he?" she asks quietly.

"Hanging in there," I say. "But we need this to end. If we don't find Genna soon, I don't know what he'll do."

"And if there's a fight?"

"We can count on him. He's good for it."

She purses her lips and lets me go. "Well, then we best get to it, lass."

We meet the group out in the van. Ross and Thane sit in the back row, Jefferson and I take the middle, and Sinclair drives while Tawnee sits shotgun to navigate. We work well as a team after spending a month together chasing ghost leads. Ross and Thane are our front assaulters when we clear through areas while Jefferson and I work as support. Sinclair covers from a distance and Tawnee leads. Everyone respects Tawnee. While the team's medic, she's also the only Spartan class agent—an IMS super agent—while the rest apart from me are regular field agents. The only reason she's here is because the rest of her team is recovering from a leviathan attack. In fact, it was the same leviathan that drew Draco away when we needed him most during the lamia's attack in Minnesota. When we came to Scotland and required a team of local agents, Tawnee volunteered in order to keep herself busy. We couldn't have asked for better.

The drive to Eilean Donan is short. We're quiet in the van with the rain drumming on the roof and windows as white noise.

A thought I've been mulling over since the lodge keeps me on edge. "If bean nighe are so rare, how would Dasc know that's what Genna is going after?" I say aloud.

"My thought?" Tawnee says from the front. "That's probably the real reason Genna is in Scotland in the first place. Dasc sent her to find it."

I hold back my next comment for the sake of Jefferson beside me. If Genna is here on orders from Dasc and he's locked up, why is she still following through? Not for the first time, I question what kind of person we're going to find at the end of this long journey. Jefferson's grip on the armrests tighten until he's white-knuckling them.

Not ten minutes into our drive, the castle appears through the fog and rain—a real castle, not some insert in a movie. I press up against the side window and gaze at it. A single bridge stretches across the water of the three lochs that merge around the island where the castle sits. It looms stories tall made of weathered stone and glistening with a coat of rain. Eerie and majestic, appearing and disappearing in the shifting mist, it looks like the perfect place for a creature with supernatural knowledge to hide.

We park in a lot on the mainland in front of a row of white-washed cottages and wait in the van as we check out our surroundings. Despite the weather, there's a steady stream of people moving to and from the castle across the stone bridge.

Tawnee starts giving out orders. "Ross and Sinclair, check the cottages and flash Genna's picture. Maybe someone's seen her. Thane, scout the castle with the Jefferson. Phoenix, you're with me. Don't spook anybody. Let's go."

We pile out of the van and split into groups of two to head to our assigned destinations. Tawnee and I keep a good distance away from Jefferson and Thane as they make for the stone bridge. The way is gated and we each pay for admission to enter the castle, which apparently is a popular tourist destination.

As Tawnee and I walk across the bridge together, I ask under my breath, "What does a bean nighe look like?"

"The stories say she's an old woman who washes the shrouds of those about to die while singing a dirge." She gives me a crooked smile. "So keep an eye out for anyone washing and singing while we're here."

"Got it."

Her expression sombers and she tosses her voluminous curls over her shoulder. She didn't bother putting up the hood of her jacket against the rain so flecks of water fly off the strands to pelt me in the face. "If there truly is a bean nighe, I think it might be a wee bit cautious and we probably won't see it at all."

"Do you think it can really do it?" I ask. "Tell you who's going to die and when?"

"Aye, I believe it."

We reach the end of the bridge just as Thane and Jefferson walk out of sight through the courtyard and into the first of two conjoined buildings that make up the castle. When we reach the courtyard we join a group of strangers with cameras bunched up for a guided tour. While the guide begins to talk us through the history of this place, we scan the people around us. A lot of them have hoods up, ponchos on, or hats so it's difficult to make out specifics but there's at least five young women in the group. Genna could be here right now.

I focus on keeping my breathing level again. I'd like to rush between them and take a good look at everyone's faces but I'm not supposed to spook anyone. I have to be patient. I hate being patient.

Together we move through the castle and stop in each of the splendid rooms. I catch glimpses of elegantly carved mantels, suits of armor in corners, and antique sitting chairs, but I'm not paying close attention to the decor. I'm watching the people.

No one jumps out at me as being peculiar or out of place. It's your normal ragtag bunch of tourists with their cameras and phones taking pictures of themselves in front of crested shields and mannequins dressed in old Scottish regalia. At least once out of the rain the majority pull off their hoods so I can get a better look at them all. Two of the girls have short dark hair but after passing near them under the pretense of getting a closer look at a suit of armor, I realize neither of them looks like our rendered photo of Genna. We complete the circuit through the castle and end up at the end of the bridge where we started. The tourists take a few more pictures on the edges of the island and slowly walk back to the mainland across the bridge.

"The bus driver said she specifically wanted to know when visiting hours ended," I say as I loiter with Tawnee near the courtyard. "Chances are she'll be coming here after the place is closed."

"Well, at least we got a good look at the layout of the buildings."

"Which are huge," I grumble. "Unless we see someone come in and follow them, they could hide anywhere in there and slip right past us."

"Well, backup will be—ah! Here they are now."

She gestures towards something over my shoulder. I turn around as a group of tall, tan, athletic women strut down the bridge just as the guide calls last admission for the day. Tawnee pulls on my arm to bring us inside the front entrance of the castle so when we meet our back up we aren't out in the open for all eyes to see. We wait as the group comes to us and when they turn the corner, the first face that greets me is a familiar one.

Nessa, a selkie with impressive combat skills that I first met in Minnesota, gives me a mischievous smirk and puts her hands on her hips. "Look who it is. Need our help again, Phoenix?"

We shake hands and the rest of her band crowds around behind her. I spot her sister Gillian there as well who dips her head respectfully. I return the gesture as Nessa shakes hands with Tawnee.

"Spartan McDonnell. It's been a while," Nessa says. "What can we do to help?"

"We need eyes, preferably hidden, all over the castle and on the outskirts." As Tawnee describes what we're dealing with, Thane and Jefferson show up to join our crowded little party in the front entrance. I look to them but they both shake their heads—they've had no luck either. We're briefed about our assignments and then split off to our designated locations. The selkies go on their tour of the castle while Thane and I head out of the castle to meet Ross and Sinclair by the van. Tawnee and Jefferson will stay in the castle for the time being and continue to scout until visiting hours end.

Then we wait. I sit with Sinclair inside the van while Thane and Ross discreetly patrol the roads around the castle. The light starts to wane but I know it'll be a good long while until it's truly dark. Daylight hours are prolonged in Scotland. I'm supposed to sit on the sidelines because, as Tawnee put it, I'm too valuable to have in the open. Meaning, I'm the only person Dasc will talk to and we still need that source of information. Stupid Dasc.

After visiting hours end, bright floodlights come on to

turn the castle into a beacon in the growing darkness. Sinclair and I continue to watch the castle from a safe distance with pairs of binoculars. Out there I know some of the selkies will be watching from the water in their seal forms, while others will be sneaking into the castle to back up Tawnee and Jefferson who both announced on our comms that they managed to evade the security check and are now hidden in a bedroom.

"You look anxious, lass," Sinclair whispers as he takes a brief moment off his binoculars.

"I should be in there with them," I whisper back. "I don't like being on the sidelines."

"I've noticed, but think of it this way—if there is a battle and it goes south, we'll be able to rush in to be the heroes of the day."

I give a single laugh. "Yeah, I guess. I hate being too late, though."

"Aye, me as well."

We return to silence and the boring job of watching from a distance. The last stragglers on the roads return to their homes and a local tavern becomes the hotspot of the evening not far behind us. I'm listening to a rather rambunctious Scottish drinking song when I catch movement near our end of the stone bridge. I nudge Sinclair and we both focus on a lone figure crouching to hide in the shadows on the bridge. There's no mistaking it. This mysterious figure is a girl, but there isn't enough light to get the specifics on her appearance.

Sinclair grabs the radio beside us and sends out two vibrating bursts over the line to signal an incoming message before he hits the talk button. "We've got a single female at the end of the bridge on the mainland. No confirmation on identity, but she's sneaking out to the castle."

A series of checks come back from those in and around the island. I keep my eyes glued to the young woman as she crouches low and makes a stealthy dash across the bridge to the other side and then pauses again before the area illuminated by the floodlights.

Moments later Ross comes over the line. "I've got movement by the—ugh!"

There's an audible thud and then Ross cuts out.

We wait for two breaths of silence for him to say something else before Tawnee speaks up. "Ross? . . . Come in, Ross. Thane, go check on his last location." No response from Thane either. "Thane? Someone talk to me."

Sinclair hits the talk button on the radio. "Phoenix and I can go check."

"Then go," Tawnee says.

We drop our binoculars in a hurry, my heart up in my throat. Sinclair clips the radio to the front of his jacket, we snatch up our bio-mech guns, make sure our retractable blades are secured on our belts, then burst out of the van to another round of drinking songs spilling out from the tavern behind us. The rain has lessened somewhat but thunder rumbles in the distance ominously. Sinclair leads the way and I race after him, our flashlight beams bobbing across the ground.

"This way," Sinclair says and takes the road heading south from the castle. We don't meet anyone else along the way and nearly stumble across Ross lying prone on the side of the pavement. We come to an abrupt halt and while Sinclair turns his friend over, I stand guard with my bio-mech gun trained on our surroundings. We're in deep twilight and someone—or something—could be hiding anywhere in the rolling hills or lapping waters of the loch.

Sinclair patches through the radio. "Ross is down but alive. No sign of Thane."

"Any sign of a culprit?" Tawnee asks.

"Not yet. Hold on."

He does a once over of Ross's body with the flashlight to find any noticeable injuries or clues left behind from his attacker. My eyes are on the landscape when Sinclair makes a curious sound and I turn around to find him inspecting a bite wound on Ross's neck.

"I don't know what this is," he says. "It's not vampire. It's nothing I recognize."

"Let me see," I say and we swap positions.

I pin the injury with my flashlight and recognize the teeth marks instantly. I've got a matching set on my own neck that still gives me trouble if I stretch the wrong way. Adrenaline, my old friend, quickly makes an appearance and flushes my veins.

"We've got a big problem," I say and quickly pull out the small first aid kit strapped to the inside of my jacket to smooth a large bandage over the bite. "Get Tawnee back on."

"What is it?" Sinclair says and pauses with his finger hovering over the talk button. "What do I tell her?"

"That I hope everyone is carrying swords or machetes or we're screwed." I haul Ross up into a fireman's carry over my shoulders. He's a little awkward to hold with his bulk but his weight feels like nothing with the combination of magical strength and adrenaline in me.

"There's a lamia here."

2

Sinclair calls in our emergency as I carry Ross across my shoulders. Ross should be fine but the lamia's poison in its bite will leave him knocked out for a while. There's a loud static pop over the radio and then nothing. No one replies in response to our report of a lamia on the loose. He tries a few more times but it's no use.

"I think someone's jamming our radios," he says. "I don't even know if they heard me."

"Think it's about time for that swooping in part you mentioned earlier?" I say.

"We still don't know where Thane is."

I pause and sweep the sides of the road with my flashlight. "Yes, we do."

We rush to another prone body that we first missed on our way to find Ross. Thane is propped up on the rocks beneath the stone bridge. Sinclair rushes down to assist as I stay at the top of the slope leading down to the water to watch our backs. We're alone out here with two teammates to look after and a lamia in the wind. If we don't take care of things soon and warn the others, I fear what kind of bloodbath this could turn into.

Could it be Epsilon, the lamia that got away? If it is, I have a terrible feeling she's here because of me. Or maybe there are more out in the world that no one knows about. Either way, if a lamia is here, we have to be prepared for anything. Undoubtedly this lamia has brought a supply of blood with her—she can temporarily gain the power of any magical blood to use against us.

"Phoenix," Sinclair calls and walks away from Thane. "He's gone."

I swallow. "Are you sure?"

"He . . . his throat's been ripped out. There's nothing we can do for him." He coughs into his hand and runs a hand through his hair before waving me along up the road. "Come on. We have to warn the others."

"What about Ross?"

"We can't leave him behind and we shouldn't split up. Can you keep carrying him?"

"Yeah, but that leaves both of us vulnerable," I say. "Can't we hide him on the floor of the van out of sight? He'll be all right once he wakes up but that's not going to be for a while at least."

"Umm, yeah. Yeah, okay."

Sinclair is visibly shaken and I get it. I'm trying not to think of Thane's fate myself. I didn't know him well on the account of him hardly ever speaking, but he was kind to me. He didn't deserve to go out like that. No one does.

We run back to the van, my strides somewhat awkward with Ross slung across my shoulders, and lay him on the floor behind the front seats. Sinclair throws a blanket over him as well so he's hardly even noticeable. We make sure to lock the doors and then book it over to the bridge. Sinclair tries the radio again out of desperation but the signal is still being jammed. So, without any sort of communication with our teammates, we run across the bridge.

When we're halfway across, the floodlights illuminating the castle go out, throwing us into darkness. My eyes adjust but I've got the ghost of the bright lights in my vision. I blink quickly trying to clear it away. Sinclair and I share an anxious look. We don't have a clue who just shut off the lights but my guess is—whether it be the lamia or Genna or someone else—they don't want to be seen approaching the castle. Hopefully it will at least signal the others that something is wrong.

We enter the courtyard and take aim as we run into a group of three women dripping water onto the flagstones. Selkies.

Nessa holds a hand out towards us and we quickly bunch together into a staggered formation, three of us facing outwards and watching the surroundings while Nessa and Sinclair group in the middle to have a fast whispered discussion of what's going on. The selkies came up as soon as radio contact was lost. The other half of their team is inside somewhere with Tawnee and Jefferson while two other selkies remain out in the water in case anything else tries to approach.

"Blades out," Nessa whispers. There's a chorus of chimes as the selkies unsheathe thick sabers from their backs and

Sinclair and I drop down the segments of our retractable swords until they form solid blades.

"Phoenix, you're on point with me," Sinclair says and the selkies fall in behind us as we enter the first building at ground floor level. We clear through the billiard room under an arched stone ceiling and around a solid wood table, our flashlights sweeping across antiques and displays, before we check the parlor next and then take the stairs to the next level. Halfway up the stairs we hear voices. Sinclair signals us to slow and keep quiet.

We move cautiously up one step at a time and turn off our flashlights as we approach the open doorway to the banquet hall. Silent as shadows, we take up positions on either side of the doorway as the selkies crouch in the darkness of the stairwell. Inching forward, I get a look at one side of the banquet room. Tawnee stands beside a couple of selkies with her bio-mech gun drawn facing someone further in the room.

Jefferson's voice echoes out to us. "We just want to know who you are and what you're doing here. We aren't going to hurt you."

"Then why does she have a gun on me?" a girl responds with an American accent.

"We lost contact with our people on the outside," Tawnee says. "I don't know who you are or why you're here. Until I get some answers, I'm not letting my guard down."

"Fine," the girl says in a long sort of drawl that makes it sound like she's bored.

It seems the situation is under control by our side. Sinclair nods to me and I signal to the selkies to move forward. We walk into the banquet hall together to back up the rest of our team, and I get my first good look at the young woman I had first spotted at the bridge. She's lean and there's a mean look to her heart-shaped face. Her light brown hair falls in a wet, tangled twist over one shoulder. It's long—not like our description from the bus driver and she doesn't fit the photo we have of Genna. But if not her, then who is this girl?

When Jefferson turns about to see us enter, his eyebrows shoot up.

"What are you two doing here?" he asks sharply. "You're supposed to be—"

"Thane's dead and Ross is down," I say. I don't have time to say it more delicately. "A lamia's here."

Tawnee immediately pulls a retractable blade from her belt and the selkies around her draw their peculiar swords as well. The girl they have cornered in the room doesn't seem confused or fazed by this at all. Annoyed maybe, but that's it.

"We need to do a shapeshifter check in case that lamia's got ahold of their blood," Tawnee says. "Hands out everyone."

We each obediently move to Tawnee one by one and let her give us an unpleasant electric shock. If any of us is a shapeshifter or a lamia with shapeshifter blood, the shock will momentarily destabilize a false appearance. Thankfully, we all pass the test. We spread out to cover each of the entrances and exits of the hall while a few selkies head to the upper level to get a better view of the castle. I stand by a window and keep guard over the courtyard.

Tawnee moves towards the girl. "Hand out."

The girl glares at her unafraid. "No."

"I'm sorry but I'm going to test you whether you want me to or not."

"Why?"

"Because you're an unknown entity and dangerous. You clearly know who we are and you didn't even flinch at the word lamia, so you know our world. Question is which side of the spectrum you fall on."

The girl cocks her head to the side and lets her arms hang loose at her sides. "You mean monster or just *in the know*?"

"Basically."

Tawnee gestures to Jefferson and he keeps his bio-mech gun trained on the girl as Tawnee moves forward with the stun gun. The girl doesn't hold out a hand for the test or move at all but watches everyone in the room very, very closely. I'm getting a real bad vibe from her, whoever she is. We still don't know who or what she is and why she's here. And where is Genna? Have we missed her?

The rain picks up in intensity outside and drums on the windows. Lightning flashes across the sky and thunder rumbles in the distance like a backdrop for a horror movie. Except this is real and there are monsters very much alive waiting out in that darkness.

"You aren't going to touch me and I'm not going to go with you," the girl says as Tawnee comes within a few feet. "As much as you don't know me, I don't know you. Why should I tell you anything or let you come any closer, hmm? You could be working under her orders for all I know."

Her orders? At the same time, Jefferson and I ask, "Whose orders?"

The girl's eyes rake us. "Are you stupid? Or are you play acting? I can't tell."

Wow, she's a real gem.

"We're looking for another girl who's been missing for years," Jefferson says, desperation coloring his voice. "Do you know a Genevieve Barnes?"

Tawnee shoots him a sharp look. "*Jefferson.*"

"Please," he continues, ignoring our leader. "We thought she'd be here but we found you instead. Do you know her?"

She focuses her attention on Jefferson and smirks. Oh, I want to punch her.

"Yeah, I know Genna."

My breath catches and I glance to the others in the room, exchanging our surprise. Tawnee, however, never takes her eyes off the girl. Thunder rumbles and draws my gaze back to the window. Is this girl playing us along, using Jefferson to gain some upper hand? Or does she really know the target of our search?

"Where is she?" Jefferson asks more forcefully. "Is she okay?"

She laughs and, despite how much I'd like to pummel her myself, I jump to hold Jefferson back as he starts to charge the girl.

"Touchy, aren't you?" the girl says with a smile.

Holding onto Jefferson with both hands, I glare at the girl over my shoulder.

"Moose Lake," I say and her expression slips into a dark frown. "You're from there, aren't you? Taken at the same time as Genna?"

"You don't know what you're—"

"You seem about the same age Genna should be," I say,

fighting her jerky attitude with interruptions. "Brown hair, blue eyes. Let me guess, Samantha? No? Then you must be Rosalyn." A muscle in her jaw twitches. "Rosalyn Graham. That's your name, isn't it?"

"No one's called me that in a long time," she snarls.

What did Dasc do to her to make her react like this? Shouldn't she be relieved to be identified with a chance of rescue?

"I know your brother," I say. Tawnee and Jefferson don't stop me from talking so I keep on going. I eventually drop my grip on Jefferson as he relaxes for the moment. "Jared. He's a good guy, a good friend."

"Stop."

"He's been looking for you since you went missing," I continue and take a step towards her. "He even became a deputy in your honor. He wanted to help other people to make sure what happened to you never happened to anyone else."

"*Stop*," she says through gritted teeth.

I take a few steps closer. "We stopped him, Rosalyn."

"Don't say my name!"

"We stopped Dasc."

She sucks in a sharp breath and her eyes go wide. There, I've gotten through a crack in her armor. Her eyes begin to water.

"It's over," I say. "You can go home. You can see your brother and your parents again. They've been looking for you all this time. You're not alone anymore."

I get even closer and hold out a hand for Tawnee to pass me the stun gun. She places it in my palm and I come within arm's length of Rosalyn.

"It's a trick," she whispers.

"It's the truth." I reach out with the stun gun. "Just this one test and we can get you out of here, okay?"

She nods and lets me press the stun gun to the back of her hand. She doesn't even wince at the pain but it's obvious she's no shapeshifter.

"We need to get moving," Sinclair says from the other side of the room. "That lamia's still out there."

"How?" Rosalyn says, ignoring his comment. "How did you stop him?"

"Plugged him full of wolfsbane bullets," I say, rather proud that I can deliver this bit of good news.

She lifts her eyes full of fury to mine and her lips curl in a snarl.

The stun gun is twisted out of my hand before I can react and it's jammed into my throat. The shocks bring tears to my eyes and my teeth clench together painfully as my teammates yell and a bio-mech pulse slips right past us. I bring up my own gun but my fingers loss their grip as the shocks numb my mind. The next second it's in Rosalyn's hand and aimed over my shoulder at Tawnee. I manage to grab her arm and pull the stun gun away from my throat but my muscles are seizing and I don't have the control I need to throw her to the floor. Instead I'm used as a human shield to stop the pulse from Jefferson's gun.

The shot hits me square in the back and I crumple to the floor. Rosalyn slips around me and I'm lost with my face pressed against the cold, hard floor of the banquet hall. The sounds of the fight around me dull and disconnect. My body shuts down but what's in my blood fights it and keeps fighting until I'm able to push myself up onto my hands and knees. I don't know how long I've been down but Tawnee's somehow managed to get Rosalyn in a headlock. I sway as I rise to my feet as our only Spartan agent puts Rosalyn on the floor and starts to bind her hands with zip ties.

I stagger to the table and brace my hands on the back of a chair. Jefferson comes to my side and roughly grabs my shoulder. I wave him off to let him know I'm okay as I hang my head but it takes me some time to even out my breathing. He gives me two solid pats on the back then hustles over to where Tawnee hauls Rosalyn to her feet, Sinclair covering them from behind.

"Where's Genna?" Jefferson thunders. "I'm her father. I have to find her."

"Well, you haven't so far, have you?" Rosalyn snaps. "How hard were you really trying?"

Jefferson grabs the front of her jacket and shakes her.

"Where is my daughter?!"

"Stop!" Tawnee shouts at him and pulls Rosalyn out of his reach.

Catching my breath, I jog around the table and insert myself between them again. At the same time the selkies rush down the stairs from the upper level.

"We've got to go," Nessa says and waves us over. "There's a lamia in the courtyard and I think she's got leviathan blood. Our sentries dropped as soon as she was in range. She's heading for the stairs."

A hush falls over the room and we all race for the stairs on the other side of the room. Tawnee pulls Rosalyn along but the girl has suddenly found a desire to work with us and follows along without fuss. The selkies lead the way up to the walkway on top of the sea wall which leads to the second building and escape. We can't face a lamia with leviathan blood on our own. We aren't prepared.

"Genna could still be here," Jefferson huffs in front of me as we continue to run.

"We can't go back!" Tawnee shouts at him. "We need backup. We need dragons!"

I bring up the rear along with Sinclair and glance over my shoulder constantly while keeping my bio-mech gun at the ready, although it'll probably be little more than a nuisance to a lamia. I flashback to fighting those two lamia in Scholar's labs. Back then we had a dragon on our side and we still almost died.

I gotta keep running.

The selkies reach the door to the other building and find it locked. We bunch up behind them as they kick it open but we've halted too long. Sinclair falls first and I know what's coming the second before searing pain rips through my skull and I let out a cry as I fall to my knees. I can hardly see through the agony wrenched through my mind as a shrill screech obliterates all other sound and I try to cover my ears, but the sound is coming from inside my head.

Ahead of me the others fall one by one, yelling and writhing in pain. This is why the leviathans are so deadly. Not only are they enormous sea monsters capable of tearing a battleship in half, they can incapacitate their enemies with a deadly psychic scream. Suffer it long enough and you can end up with brain damage—or die.

Warmth trickles between my fingers and I bring up a hand to find it coated with blood. My freakin' ears are bleeding it's so bad. I can't concentrate. I can't think, but somehow I manage to flip onto my back so I can at least see the lamia coming at us. Sinclair moans beside me and isn't going to be of any use whatsoever.

A silhouette appears at the end of the walkway we just came from and lightening strobes the woman's features into light. Slit eyes, clawed hands, and hair so pale she's like a ghost. Not Epsilon. A different lamia. The rain continues to fall and drips into my eyes. I blink it away and keep a hand pressed to one of my bleeding ears as I fumble for my sword. As far as I can tell, I'm the only one able to move, even if it's not by much. It's going to be up to me to stop her from slaughtering us all.

"Where's the bean nighe?" the lamia shouts as she stalks forward at a leisurely pace, knowing full well that none of us are going anywhere or are able to fight back. "I know she was here. Where are you hiding her? Tell me and I'll make all your pain go away."

Her wicked smile, full of shark teeth, tells me her version of taking away our pain is by ending our ability to suffer permanently.

"Up yours," I croak and struggle to push myself into a sitting position. I grab the stone parapet with one hand and drag myself up onto wobbly feet. A second later I almost collapse again but brace myself against the parapet to hold my ground.

She pauses. "A challenger? Interesting."

I have to stop that scream. Fire. I need fire. It's a leviathan's weakness and I have to neutralize that before I can chop off her head. I think I have a lighter in my pocket but that's useless unless the lamia will dry off for me first and then wait patiently as I set her clothes on fire. We're trapped and, with no weapon that can stop that scream, we're doomed.

I keep my sword at the ready in my hand anyway. If I'm going down, then I'll go down swinging.

"Wait, it's you, isn't it?" the lamia says and proceeds to give me a slow clap. "Well done. You killed Zeta and managed to frighten Epsilon off. The demon's pet."

"I didn't know . . . you guys . . . send out . . . a newsletter." Each word is a struggle to form. My legs are shaking terribly and I'm pretty sure I'm bleeding not only from my ears but my nose and eyes as well.

She laughs. "What can I say? We're a tight bunch. Now tell me where the bean nighe is."

"Why? Who . . . who are . . ."

The lamia comes closer and crouches with her hands braced on her knees to smile up at me like my slow death is great entertainment. "Keep going. You've almost made a full sentence."

I try to glare at her but have to keep blinking water and blood out of my eyes.

"Are you . . . working for?" I manage to finish.

She frowns and straightens. "Well, that's an anticlimactic question. The answer is—who cares? You're about to die anyway. Unless you tell me where the bean nighe is."

Unfortunately, I've reached my limit of trying to fight this off. I slowly sink against the wall but keep the sword propped up in my hand. Maybe I'll at least be able to stick her if she gets a little closer. It won't do much but if I can tick her off on my way out, it'll be worth something. The moans and cries around me are beginning to fade, meaning the others have either fallen unconscious or are dead. I get why leviathans are classified as level five monsters. They really ought to boost the lamia's rating as well.

"Poor, sad little pet," the lamia says as she looms near, water dripping off her claws. "To have accomplished so much, only to die here without even being able to say goodbye to that brother of yours."

Hawk. Sweet majestics, no. How does she even know I have a brother?

She sighs and pouts. "I guess I'll have to bring him the bad news and put him out of his misery too."

She flashes her teeth and raises her clawed hand, ready to strike me down. I angle the sword in the hope I can chop off her hand as my small parting gift.

But she never gets the chance to gut me.

A flaming arrow flies sizzling through the rain and embeds in the lamia's chest right through the heart. The arrow must be coated in some kind of oil because the rain doesn't put the fire out and it spreads out from the point of impact.

The lamia's screeches fill the night as the power of the leviathan's scream fades and clears from my head. There's no time to consider who shot that arrow. She's close enough. I can end it. I bring up my shaking sword hand and swing at her. She stumbles away from the blow and takes it in the shoulder instead, cleaving open flesh and releasing a torrent of black blood. I'm not fast enough to try a second time. She roars at me, ducks beneath another flaming arrow, and then does a backflip off the walkway.

With the wretched screaming gone, I'm able to haul myself up and look over the stone parapet to the darkness far below. The lamia disappears beneath the waves of the loch.

Turning back around, I keep myself braced on the stone wall as half of my teammates stir. The other half are still unconscious or worse. I peer through the rain in the direction the arrows came from but there's no one on the walkway above the main gate that I can see. Where did our mystery good Samaritan go?

I help Sinclair to his feet and nod to Jefferson as he struggles upright still pressing a hand to his ear. The rain washes away the blood on our faces but not our confusion or the lingering pain. The leviathan scream may be gone but my head continues to pound with the worst headache of my life.

"I never wanted to go through that again," Tawnee says, sways, then vomits over the side of the walkway.

"What happened?" Jefferson asks.

"Someone else was here," I say and hold a hand to my forehead with a grimace. "They saved us. Shot the lamia with a flaming arrow."

"Who the heck?"

He freezes as he spots something over my shoulder. I spin about to find a crossbow pointed at me from the other end of the walkway. The woman holding it marches forward, her hiking boots splash through the puddles, and once she's within ten feet she draws back the hood of her dark rain jacket.

Short, wavy black hair. Dark eyes. Olive skin. A fierce expression with the face of our photo.

Jefferson lets out a shuddering breath. "Genna?"

3

Genna. The elusive captive who's not really a captive at all. There's steel in her cold expression, the unrelenting way she holds the crossbow aimed at my chest, the solid stance she takes, and unflinching gaze despite the rain dripping into her eyes. The way she carries herself reminds me of the few dragons I've met, how they can draw every eye to them in a room.

And she's still aiming a crossbow bolt at my chest. I raise my hands weakly to the sides to show I don't mean any harm.

"Who are you?" she demands.

Jefferson stumbles forward to brace himself with one hand on the parapet and one on my shoulder as he comes to stand beside me.

"Genna." He breathes her name like the word is life itself. "My Genna."

She doesn't relent but her eyes narrow slightly. "Who are you?"

"It's me," he says and takes another uneasy step forward. The others remain behind us, silent and watchful. "I'm your father. Jefferson. God, you look just like your mother."

Her aim switches to his chest. I tense. If she's anything like Rosalyn, I don't doubt she'll pull that trigger.

"What did she used to call me?" she snarls. "What was her nickname for me?"

He shakes his head and continues to stagger towards her, one hand touching the parapet. Stop, Jefferson. Don't push her, I want to say but I'm afraid saying anything will set her off.

"I . . ." Jefferson mumbles in a daze. Did he even hear her question?

"*What was her nickname for me?*" she shouts at him.

"Squirt," he says at last, his voice breaking. "She called you her little squirt in the dirt."

Her eyes widen and her finger moves off the trigger. The world slows and even the rain seems to stop. She lowers the crossbow and lets it hang at her side. It's enough for me to relax and I slouch against the parapet completely drained.

"Is it really you?" Genna whispers.

"It's me, Squirt. It's me."

She rushes forward and they wrap their arms around each other, holding on tight. Genna holds the crossbow loosely at her side but her other hand clenches onto the back of Jefferson's jacket like if she doesn't hold on hard enough he'll disappear. He does the same and whispers over and over again into her hair, "I've got you, baby girl. I've got you."

A huge bubble of relief swells in my chest and I feel like I could sleep for about a week. We did it. We found her.

"I'm sorry, but we need to move," Tawnee wheezes behind us. "We can't stay here. I've no doubt we'll have company soon enough and we need to let headquarters know there's a lamia on the loose."

Jefferson and Genna don't seem to hear a word of it. I let them have their moment of bliss in finding each other and move to help the others to their feet. Some are still out of it and I worry they have serious internal damage. I sling a selkie over my shoulder and Nessa wraps an arm around Sinclair to help him down the stairs.

"Jefferson," I call. "We have to go."

He ever so slowly draws away from the hug with his daughter but keeps an arm around her shoulders. Together they follow everyone off the walkway and I bring up the rear. It's a long, plodding walk through the second building of the castle, out to the bridge, and back to our van. The party at the tavern is still in full swing, completely oblivious to what happened out on Eilean Donan. Once at the van, Tawnee makes a few calls for transportation and medical assistance before getting to work on everyone, bringing her medical training to bear. After settling the selkie on my shoulders into one of the seats, I go with Nessa for the awful job of retrieving Thane's body from beneath the bridge. We carry him back with the utmost respect and return to the van as an undercover IMS ambulance arrives.

Those still unconscious are loaded up, along with Thane, and are quickly sent on their way for treatment. The rest of us loiter around the van, leaning against its frame and keeping our eyes open for the lamia as we wait for another transport to arrive. We don't want to dwindle our numbers by one van load leaving the rest behind to the mercy of the lamia or any other lurking monsters. So, instead we wait together.

Jefferson and Genna sit side by side on the back bumper in the open hatch of the van. I keep guard near them feeling that it's my personal duty to ensure Jefferson and his daughter can have a moment to themselves. I try not to eavesdrop or even turn their way, but I'm drawn in watching a parent reconnect with their child. Some deep, hidden, torn part of me wants it so badly for myself even though I can never have it. My parents are dead. I'll never get my happy reunion. Not on this earth.

"But you're sure you're not hurt?" Jefferson murmurs. "The leviathan scream—"

"I was far enough away. I shot from the walkway on the opposite side of the courtyard," Genna says. "I was close enough but out of range."

"You're amazing you know that?" he says and looks at his daughter like the sun is radiating out of her and he's been living in darkness for fourteen years. "I never stopped looking for you, Genna. Not once. I can't believe—I can't believe you're actually here after all this time."

Jefferson's in tears but Genna just looks so very tired. She rests her head on his shoulder and closes her eyes. I look away.

I sway where I stand and occasionally dab a wade of gauze at my ears, nose, and corners of my eyes where traces of blood linger. While Jefferson continues to dote on his daughter, I consider a few unsettling things. Genna's clearly a very capable woman as she demonstrated tonight. She's fierce, and is displaying a very strong affection for her father. That's all fine. It's great really. We were worried she'd be a tortured soul but all I can think is—if she's so capable and fierce and loves her father, why has she never tried to go home? To me, it seems she certainly could have.

I hang my head and dab at my nose again. I shouldn't be over thinking this. We've only managed to find her. We don't know a thing yet of what her life has been or what she's endured. It's very possible Dasc has some hold over her or blackmail or something I haven't considered. I should be giving her the benefit of the doubt, not suspecting her.

But after Rosalyn's reaction, can I really blame myself?

I pace towards the front of the van where Rosalyn sits. Tawnee keeps a hand on her arm from the driver's seat. Rosalyn looks annoyed again and occasionally rubs her ears on her shoulders that probably feel itchy with dried blood.

"How much longer do you think?" I ask Tawnee.

"Not long." She swivels in her seat to look through the van to the back. "How are they?"

"Good. They're real good."

Rosalyn makes an odd strangled sound and her eyes narrow at nothing in particular as she stares straight ahead and ignores everyone around her. She makes me uncomfortable.

We wait another ten minutes before I hear a helicopter in the distance. Tawnee glances at her watch and then starts to rally everyone.

"Okay, ride's here," she says. "Let's go everyone. They're going to meet us further south on the road. Pack in."

The selkies take the seats while the rest of us sit in the open doors and hatch with our feet dangling over the road.

Tawnee takes the wheel and drives slowly past the castle—a looming shadow without the floodlights to illuminate it—and around a bend to head south along the empty country road. I keep a hand wrapped around a strap dangling from the front passenger seat and sway with the movement of the van on the bumpy road. Over the rumble of the tires the sound of the helicopter grows steadily louder.

We come to a stop on the shoulder and Tawnee throws chemlights onto the pavement to guide down the helicopter. The rest of us pile out of the van with our gear packs and hunker in the ditch until we're clear to approach. Two agents disembark to meet us and have us board one by one through the open side door. I take a seat next to Jefferson along the wall and strap in. The others fill in the rest of the space, strap our gear in a cargo net in the rear of the helicopter, and take seats on the floor. Tawnee readjusts Rosalyn's restraints so they can strap her in safely opposite me.

As soon as Tawnee gives the all clear to the pilot, we begin to rise and the road sinks away into darkness. I keep a firm grip on the straps over my chest and enjoy the ride. I've never actually been in a helicopter before. This is fantastic. But I can't enjoy it as much as I'd like to with Rosalyn shooting daggers at me and everyone else on board. There's a nasty knot of anxiety in my stomach I can't seem to shake with her around. How am I going to explain Rosalyn to her brother? It's going to break his heart seeing his little sister act like some psychopath.

I try to ignore her and stare out the windows. Another helicopter takes the spot we vacated. I can't see what happens next but I can only assume it's a cleanup crew moving in to make sure there's no evidence of a battle at the castle and maybe coordinate the beginning of a search for the lamia.

We stay in the air for at least an hour. Some of the others start to nod off by the time we reach our destination. We ease out of the sky and are given a slight jolt as the helicopter touches down. The rotors slow as we clamber out of our seats and through the big side doors onto the landing pad. Another agent, a man I swear is seven feet tall, bends down almost in half beneath the rotors and ushers us off the pad, along the tarmac, and to a nondescript tour bus waiting for us. All tired and aching from the lamia's attack and long helicopter flight, we stagger up the steps with our gear in tow and slump into the seats.

Our giant liaison agent takes the wheel and drives us away from the sleepy airport. I sit with my forehead pressed against the cold glass, letting it freeze my brain. Some pain medication and a nap sounds mighty fine.

We pass through the slumbering streets of Edinburgh that are mostly deserted at this time of night except for the few heading home from a late night at a tavern. The buildings and lampposts look like they belong in a different century or another world. Scotland has buildings older than the creation of the United States. There's nothing quite so majestic and ancient back home. The buildings here are all made of intricate stonework and everywhere you can see a spire rising from someplace in the city.

And in the heart of it all, up on a hill overlooking this beautiful city lies the castle of Edinburgh. As the bus passes beneath, I gaze up at the massive stone walls dotted with light. This was our first stop when we came to Scotland, but I haven't had a chance to explore it yet. Maybe after tonight

I'll get a break and have a little fun seeing the sights. For now, the bus stops in a park in the shadow of the castle's walls and we pile out. The place is empty so late at night. Visiting hours for the castle ended hours ago, but we don't make for the castle itself. We make for the Vaults.

Our guide leads the way to a locked wrought iron fence. After opening the gate, it doesn't look like it leads to much of anything at all. The steep hillside and rocky cliffs upon which the castle sits face us along with some trees and bushes that look a bit scraggly since they haven't started to bloom yet. But get close enough and a hidden walkway suddenly appears. You have to be looking at it right up against the side of the cliff face or it disappears. An optical illusion. We walk down into the earth in single file to another illusion that opens into a stone archway leading to the Vaults.

Fifteen feet along a dark tunnel, glowing sconces start to line the moisture slick walls. It's a little creepy here but I've been told that's sort of the point. In fact, the part of the Vaults that was opened up to the public some years ago—much further away from the hidden base beneath the castle, obviously—they played up the creepy factor to scare people away. Of course, that also drew in ghost hunters and whatever. But every now and again, if someone gets too close, an air sprite will turn the air suddenly cold and an illusion appears of a creepy little drummer boy, a ghost, who plays his haunting song to drive people away.

We walk for what feels like an eternity until we reach the central hub of the Vaults. The stone ceilings rise to fifteen feet at the pinnacle of their arch and slope far to the sides of the main area. It's fairly active at night since that's when the real nasty monsters come out so that's when the agents are up too. In the very center are vendor carts with food being sold by centaurs and elves. Agents mingle and pick up supplies before rushing down one of the many pathways branching out from this hub. In the dark corners and under the carts preparing food or cleaning are fairies—pardon me, brownies. Or are they urisks? I've been getting them confused and made several of them angry because of my lack of distinction between the English and Scottish fairies. Small, wrinkly creatures the size of my forearm in brown clothes tinker and help tidy the place up but don't like to talk to anyone directly. I've learned to give them their space and not interfere with the work they always seem to be doing.

The Vaults is a combination of new and familiar things to me, but I wonder how Rosalyn and Genna are receiving this place. I watch them both and neither of them seem too surprised by what's before and around them. In fact, they look more interested in marking each entrance and exit and stealing glances over their shoulders to the path leading to the surface. Neither of them make a move to escape but that could also be because Jefferson is holding onto Genna and Tawnee has a hand on Rosalyn's shoulder.

Our guide beckons us down a hallway on the left and we follow, our footsteps echoing against the stone floor and walls. We pass another hub, take another hallway, and then end up in the medical suite. High end medical scanners and equipment sit in contrast to the ancient stone that makes up this place. Rows of beds line the long room and more rooms branch off for surgical wards, infectious quarantines, and recovery rooms.

While there are a few human doctors and nurses, the head physician in the Vaults is a wulver. He hurries towards us in a white lab coat and midnight blue scrubs. Although he walks upright like a man and his body is human in shape, his head is that of a wolf. The gray fur of his head recedes into soft hair all over his body and the hand he stretches towards me has pads like a wolf's paw on his fingertips. A pair of glasses sit partway down his muzzle and he peers at us through them. I'm used to werewolves, sure, but Dr. Lyall is bizarre even to me. He's also the only one I'll ever see. Most of the wulvers are dead. He's one of the few left of his kind.

"What do we have here?" he asks and ushers everyone further into the room. His voice is deep but not guttural by any means and with the usual Scottish accent. As I'm one of the first ones in the room, he gently takes my hand, sets it in the crook of his arm he holds aloft, and guides me to a nearby hospital bed. A gentleman wolf.

"I heard we have leviathan scream trauma?" he asks Tawnee over his shoulder before bending down so he's at eye level with me. He pulls out a pen flashlight to whisk across my eyes and gauge my ocular reflexes.

"Everyone except Genna," Tawnee says and takes a seat nearby as a nurse comes to check her over as well.

Dr. Lyall straightens and whips off his glasses. "Genna? *The* Genna?" He sniffs at the air and focuses in on Rosalyn and Genna standing next to each other. Can he pick out werewolves in a crowd? "My gracious, it is a pleasure indeed. Please take seats, all of you. Each will be tended to in turn."

The others spread out, unload the gear near the door, and Tawnee keeps a grip on Rosalyn. Dr. Lyall checks my eyes, ears, runs me through simple motor control tests, and has me answer a few questions to see if there is any apparent brain trauma.

"I do believe you'll be perfectly fine after some rest," the doc announces and gives me a sharp smile. "We'll run you through a CT scan just to be sure. Nurse Stewart can help you and give you some medication for the pain. Right through there." He holds out a hand to gesture the way and helps me off the bed.

Nurse Stewart, a short plump woman, leads me into another room to get a CT scan. Once I'm finished, I wait in a chair in the main medical hub as everyone else goes through the same procedure. The lab quickly sorts out the scans and everyone in our group is cleared. Only the people that were taken by ambulance at Eilean Donan have some internal bleeding from what Tawnee tells us after talking to the hospital there run by a band of selkie healers. As soon as they're stabilized, they'll be flown in to the Vaults to be monitored.

"And there . . . there'll be a memorial for Thane in a day or so," she says and silence falls over us. Poor Thane. I wish I had gotten to know him better. "A perimeter has been established around Eilean Donan but there's been no sign of the lamia. It's been a long day."

The selkies and agents disperse, going their separate ways into the Vaults. I remain where I am and Tawnee returns to overseeing Rosalyn getting a physical. On the opposite side Genna is going through her own with Jefferson waiting outside the closed curtain. He paces back and forth and eventually spots me sitting by myself. Turning midstride, he comes over to slump into the chair next to me.

Despite the shadows under his eyes and scraggly beard that's seen better days, he looks more alive than I've ever seen him. He can't seem to stay still and starts tapping his foot on the floor and shifts between sitting upright and bending over with his elbows braced against his knees. I sit silently and watch him, hypnotized by his movements in my tired and pain medication induced state.

"I never said thank you, did I?" he says at last and manages to hold himself in one attitude long enough to fix his gaze on me. "I never would have found my baby girl without you, Phoenix. I owe you everything." He reaches over and squeezes my hand. "So, thank you. *Thank you.*"

I blink back moisture building in my eyes and give him a warm smile. I squeeze his hand in return but I have no words for this moment. I'm too tired, too drawn. And as happy as I am for Jefferson, I can't help thinking about the others still missing from Moose Lake and elsewhere. We've only found two of the hundreds lost under Dasc's control. Where are they? Will they be as difficult to find as Rosalyn and Genna were? A dark hole is forming in my chest as I let such trying thoughts consume me. I can still feel the weight of Thane's lifeless body across my shoulders. It's too much. I need to talk to Hawk. He helps me get through times like this.

We sit in silence until Dr. Lyall comes over, his hands clasped in front of him. Jefferson instantly rises and I take a moment longer to follow suit.

"How is she?" Jefferson asks.

"All and all, she's in far better shape than any of us expected," Dr. Lyall says quietly and his ears twitch, swiveling backwards for a brief moment before facing forward again.

"Typically in a case like this there's an expectation of malnourishment, physical abuse, and a low level of educational competency due to being held captive for an extended period of time since childhood. Such a child clearly wouldn't have access to means of education so his or her writing and speech skills are stunted."

"Just give it to me straight, doc," Jefferson says and closes his eyes as if the next bit of news is going to be more painful than he can bear.

"She's surprisingly well-adjusted. In fact, I'd go so far as to say she's exceedingly intelligent and shows no indication of prolonged physical abuse or limited mental capacity. She has a few scars which she said she received from various fights abroad but none from the hands of her captors. When I briefly asked her about her situation, she was very forthcoming with information and gives me no reason to suspect that recovery will be an issue with her. She was, however, insistent that you remain nearby. She said she didn't want to lose track of you."

Jefferson runs a hand down his face to wipe away a few tears before laughing quietly to himself in relief. He grips both mine and the doctor's shoulder, gives us a good shake, and says, "Thank you," before jogging to where Genna is waiting.

"That's the best news I've heard in a long time," I say and heave a sigh, watching Jefferson hug his daughter again, how she leans into him and closes her eyes with a smile on her face.

"Yes, I wish I had better for our other young captive," Dr. Lyall says and takes off his glasses to wipe them with a handkerchief from his coat pocket.

"What's the word?" I ask quietly and my focus shifts to where Tawnee stands over Rosalyn. Both have their arms crossed with hard expressions as they talk.

"From my examination of Rosalyn, and what Spartan McDonnell told me happened at the castle, I fear she is showing impassioned symptoms of Stockholm Syndrome."

I nod and massage my forehead. "I figured."

I had read up on kidnapping victims—more books courtesy of Charlie—so I would have some idea what to expect when we finally found Genna. I read about the bank hostages in Stockholm where they bonded with the robbers and even went so far as to protect them. Stockholm Syndrome was coined after that fiasco to identify the strange bond sometimes formed between captives and their captors. I had been so worried that with Dasc's powers of persuasion, Genna would be experiencing the same thing. It seems that won't be an issue for her but Rosalyn on the other hand . . .

"She's clearly just as educated and capable as Miss Genna Barnes," the doctor continues, "but I fear her recovery will be much more hostile and lengthy."

"Thanks, doc," I murmur.

"Thank *you*. I hear you did some great work out there today. Get some rest. Doctor's orders."

"Yes, sir."

He moves away to speak with one of the nurses. For some reason I feel like I need to stay here and guard Jefferson, protect his happiness to make sure it isn't broken again. But no one comes over to me again or says I'm of any use here. I stand awkwardly by the chairs for another minute before wandering through the hallways. My feet take me to the main hub where I inspect a batch of fresh Scotch pies from a centaur vendor. I pick one and while I sluggishly see what money I have, a tall shadow falls over me.

"It's on the house," Sinclair says and pays the centaur for my pie and another for himself. He jerks his head towards a hallway that leads to a bustling underground tavern called Drummer Boy. I find Ross and all of the selkies that travelled with us at a table together. Sinclair and I sit at the end and he calls over a round of whiskey. They don't talk or even attempt to start up a conversation, but when the whiskey is brought over, we all raise our glasses and say in unison, "To Thane."

I take a courtesy sip, twist up my face, and then gobble my meat pie, not realizing how hungry I am. Sinclair pats me on the back every so often as everyone eats their own preferred meal. I eventually grab his wrist to glance at his watch and do some math in my head to figure out what time it would be in Moose Lake at this hour. It'll be early in the evening. I'm sure Hawk won't mind having his supper interrupted.

I say my goodbyes to everyone and make my way through the Vaults to a room stuffed with electronic equipment, surveillance video monitors, screens streaming the news, and rows upon rows of IMS servers tucked into a room separated by glass panels where air sprites move the hot air up and out through overhead vents. I make for a row of land line phones screwed to the wall. There's no cell signal down here so it's the only place I can make a call. Five agents operate the surveillance feeds and don't turn in my direction in order to give me some semblance of privacy as I dial my brother and take a seat in the wooden chair directly beneath the phone.

He doesn't pick up on the first round of rings and I get his voicemail. I dial the number again and hunch over, propping my forehead up with my hand.

"Hello?" he says when he finally picks up.

"Hey, it's me."

There's a sound of silverware clinking and a chair scrapping across a hard floor in the background. "Phoenix? Hey, how's it going? What time is it there?"

I glance at a clock on the wall. "Midnight."

"You're up late."

"Yeah, long day. Just finished. Well, I think I'm finished for now." I take a long deep breath. "We found her, Hawk. We found Genna."

There's a beat of silence. "Is she okay?"

"Yeah. Yeah, she's great. Accordingly to the doc she's a prime specimen of intelligence and capability." I massage my forehead with the heel of my hand. "It was hell getting her though."

"What happened?" he says sharply. "Are you okay?"

"Getting there. Feels like I might still be bleeding from my ears though."

"*What?*"

I explain losing Thane, finding Rosalyn at the castle, and the ensuing fight with both her and the lamia. My throat starts to tighten as I think about everything eating away at me.

"This was just two people, Hawk. We saved two people. It took the work of moving mountains and we lost a good agent in the process, but that's it." I squeeze my eyes shut and hunch lower in my chair, trying to angle myself away from the operators focused on the surveillance feeds. "We were promised everyone in Moose Lake. *Piping Pan*, I made a deal with the freakin' devil that I'm probably going to regret a hundred times over but there are still so many out there—"

"Phoenix, stop," my brother scolds me. "Stop trying to put the weight of the world on your shoulders, okay? None of this is your fault. Not Thane's death, not Rosalyn's attitude, not the fate of everyone still missing. You've done good, Fifi. Stop judging yourself so harshly."

I take a shaky breath. "I wish you were here. I feel useless at the moment. I could use a hug."

"I know." He sighs. "I'm sending you an air hug right now. Smell that spicy taco? That's my breath in your ear."

I laugh a little despite myself.

"Have you tried haggis over there yet?" he asks.

"Still too scared."

"What do you mean? Food stuffed in a sheep's stomach doesn't sound super tasty to you?"

"Not really." I pinch the bridge of my nose with my thumb and forefinger. "I miss you, dog-breath."

"Aww, I miss you too, ya wee whelp."

"That was a terrible attempt at a Scottish accent."

"Well, I guess you'll have to give me some pointers when you get back. Speaking of which, any idea when that'll be?"

"I don't know. Soon, I hope. How are things at home?"

"Oh, fine," he says with dramatic flair. "I already told you the fill-in agent is the offspring of a troll and kelpie, right?"

Oh, Hawk. I certainly don't look forward to meeting whatever replacement they sent to help him manage the Moose Lake Field Office. "Yes, you did, and I still don't know how to picture that in my head."

"Big lazy fart plus random bursts of violent aggression. It makes complete sense."

"Keep telling yourself that." I pull the ponytail holder off my hair and start finger combing the tangled strands. That, along with the pain meds and talking with my brother, helps to ease my headache. "Anything else interesting?"

"Charlie stopped by and agreed with me about Mr. Fill-in." Hawk always refers to the agent that way so I don't actually know the guy's name yet. "He also not so politely reminded me that you had better bring his books back home in mint condition."

"Sure thing. And . . . what about you?"

"I'm golden. My lucky charm is still kicking." Meaning, the pendant with my blood continues to function.

"Good," I say and lean back in the chair with my head against the wall. "That's real good."

"Young lady, you sound tired," he says in a mock condescending tone. "Go get some sleep."

"Is that an order?" I say and close my eyes, ready to conk out right there.

"Most assuredly. Go on."

I force myself into an upright sitting position. "All right, all right. I'm going."

"Hey, Phoenix, before you go . . ."

"Yeah?"

"You're a freakin' hero and I'm proud of you. You remember that, and promise me you'll remind yourself of that every day until you get home and then I can remind you myself."

I roll my lips together, blink fast, and say hoarsely, "I promise."

4

I'm in the middle of brushing my teeth in one of the community bathrooms in the Vaults when Tawnee finds me. Despite the early hour and my own disarrayed appearance, she's energetic, groomed, and sharply dressed in a black outfit with a Spartan pin—an upside down V insignia—on her chest.

"We're about to start the process," she says and sets a cup of coffee on the edge of the sink in front of me. "Genna's asking for you, so finish up quick and meet me in the medical suite."

I spit out the toothpaste in my mouth so I can speak.

"She's asking for me? Why?"

"Jefferson told her who you are and she wants a familiar face from her past present if we're going to do this. Hurry up."

She flies out of the room, her huge carrot curls bouncing around her shoulders before she disappears. I hastily finish brushing my teeth, finger comb my hair into a ponytail, throw on a pair of green cargo pants and a black long-sleeved shirt, and rush out of the barracks with the coffee in hand.

Genna wants a familiar face from her past? I didn't realize she knows me or would remember. I certainly don't remember her. She *is* a few years older than me so her memory might be better, sure, but I'm still surprised she'd know who I am. I wonder what Jefferson told her about me.

I reach the medical suite and Dr. Lyall meets me at the door with a porcelain teacup in his hairy hand.

"Good morning, Junior Agent," he says and clears his throat with a bit of a growl. "Come, take a walk with me before Spartan McDonnell requests your presence."

"She sort of already did," I say, trying not to be rude but also stressing I ought to be going.

He doesn't listen but places his hand on my shoulder and guides me down a hallway away from the medical suite.

"I have been notified that Miss Barnes is about to give her official statement regarding her abduction and her accounting of the last fourteen years," he says quietly and leans in to talk more privately. We pause halfway along the empty hallway and hold our beverages between us. "As these things go, we find it best that female agents and doctors handle this sensitive conversation as it tends to make the victims feel safer and more willing to talk about their experiences."

"Tawnee said she asked for me personally."

"Yes, indeed," he says and sips at his tea. "Having someone from her past undoubtedly makes her feel she will be talking to someone she can trust. However, I realize you are unexperienced with such a dialogue, correct?"

I nod and worry my lower lip. "I don't want to screw this up but she wants to talk to me, so . . ."

"Spartan McDonnell and Nurse Stewart will be with you to help. Her father and I will also be observing from a safe distance." He leans in close and puts his hand on my shoulder again. "Just let her talk. Be open. Don't make any statements that appear as if you are questioning her story or casting judgment on what she's been through. However, they will ask her a few questions to discern her level of attachment to Dasc. She may react in an aggressive manner but remember this—we don't know everything she's been through. We want to help her, not isolate her."

"Okay. I got it." I think. I may be a little more nervous now.

He offers me a sharp smile and we return to the medical suite together. Tawnee is waiting inside and glances at her wristwatch before spotting us.

She quirks an eyebrow at me. "I told you to be quick."

"Yes, ma'am."

Dr. Lyall waves the Spartan off. "I was offering some advice before she goes in considering the situation.

"Right. Well, let's get to it. This way, Phoenix."

We walk past the rows of beds and enter a door I hadn't noticed before at the very end. We enter a low-lying hallway and quickly take a right into what appears to be a private medical room slash lounge. There's a hospital bed but there's also a circle of poofy chairs and sofa on the other side of the room. Everything, from the chairs to the rug to the paint on the walls, is made up of bright cheerful colors. I imagine it's supposed to help someone staying in here feel more upbeat or something.

Jefferson sits on the couch beside his daughter. He's clean shaven and wearing an official IMS jacket—the first time I've ever seen him in one or beardless for that matter. Genna's changed into clothes almost identical to mine, except she's in a t-shirt that shows off her toned arms. Jefferson's got an arm slung around her shoulders and she leans into him. Seeing them side by side like this, I pay attention to the details and notice the similarities. They have the same color eyes and same nose. Heck, Genna has even mastered the Jefferson scowl that she uses on Nurse Stewart who's sitting across from them in a silly purple chair.

Dr. Lyall waits at the door and gestures to Jefferson to follow him. Jefferson sighs and plants a kiss on the top of his daughter's head before rising to his feet and leaving with the doctor. They shut the door behind them as they go, leaving us women to chitchat. I'm terrible at this stuff. I really shouldn't be here. Tawnee walks forward and I follow in her wake.

"We were never properly introduced," she says and stretches out her hand to Genna who looks at it uncertainly before shaking it. "I'm Spartan Tawnee McDonnell. I'm the leader of the team that's been searching for you." She gestures to me next. "And this is—"

"Phoenix," Genna answers for her and rises to shake my hand. Her grip is strong. "Phoenix Mason. I remember you."

"You do?"

"My mother used to babysit you and your brother while your parents were out chasing monsters. We played together as kids."

I smile sheepishly and raise my shoulders. "I'm sorry, I don't remember. I hardly remember anything from back then."

A clever looking smile appears on her face and her dark eyes glitter. I don't know what it's supposed to mean so I clear my throat and move to take a seat on the farthest end of the couch while Genna sits on the other side. She continues to watch me and that smile doesn't fade.

"You don't seem very comfortable," she comments.

"I'm not," I admit. "I'm not good at this sort of thing. My brother is the one who knows what to say."

"Hawk."

"Yeah. Hawk, my twin."

Tawnee sets a small device on a coffee table between all of us. "Genna, this is going to record your statement. It's to document everything for evidence in our investigation. Is that okay with you?"

"It's fine," she says and leans forward with her forearms resting on her thighs. "You don't have to treat me like I'm fine china. I'm willing to talk. It wasn't necessary for the girl squad to gather either, you know."

"We only want to make this setting as comfortable for you as possible," Nurse Stewart interjects using a tone one might for a small child.

Genna gives her a withering look. "Putting me in one of the furthest rooms from the exit with three separate security lockdowns in place between me and there does't exactly make me feel *comfortable*. It makes me feel like I'm being held as a hostage."

I blink. She knows all that?

"That's for your safety," the nurse insists.

"Don't talk to me about safety," she snaps.

Wow, this isn't getting off to a great start.

"Nurse Stewart," Tawnee says in a very calm, commanding tone, "if you'd kindly leave the room, we can take it from here."

Her very round face turns red. "But you need a *licensed*—"

"Now." Tawnee's voice leaves no room for argument.

Sputtering indignantly, Nurse Stewart rises from her chair and trudges out of the room. Once she's gone there's a long moment of silence that stretches between the three of us. I guess this is a little peculiar, having only a couple of field agents do this sort of thing. I have a feeling a doctor or psychiatrist is usually required. What if we don't know the right kind of questions to ask?

"I'm sorry," Tawnee says eventually after Genna's been given time to cool off. I keep my eye on her hoping she doesn't suddenly snap like Rosalyn. "We aren't trying to offend you, Genna. Clearly, we prepared for someone of a different disposition than you. It seems like your circumstances are unique."

"I wouldn't say that," she says quietly. "I'm not unique in my circumstances. There are hundreds, thousands of others like me out there. I'm just the only one that's wound up here."

"You mean other people Dasc has taken," I say.

She nods but doesn't display any outward signs of anxiety like wringing her hands or biting her lip or tapping her feet. She's stoic.

"I guess I should start at the beginning if you're going to understand any of it," she says before turning to me. "But first, I want to know how you took down Dasc. I need to hear it."

I glance at Tawnee for some kind of confirmation that I'm okay to spill these secrets considering what happened last time. She nods, so I say, "He went back to Moose Lake in October of last year and started turning people in town. My brother and I . . . well, we sort of got sent out there because we got in trouble. We screwed up our first assignment and—that's not really important, is it?" I clear my throat. "Anyway, that's when we met Jefferson and, after Dasc tried to have a patsy take the fall and a shapeshifter tried to kill us, he gathered up the wolves and captured us. My mother had left behind a gun with wolfsbane bullets and I emptied the entire clip into his chest to free the werewolves under his control including my brother. He's in custody now."

She listens attentively and a frown draws on her face. "What happened to the Masons? I mean, your parents?"

I appreciate the swirls in the rug under my feet as I hang my head and take a deep breath. "He killed them around the same time you were taken. And Hawk was turned."

"But . . ." She contemplates me for a long moment. "Your brother didn't go missing?"

"We were saved and taken to Underground. So, he's a werewolf and I'm . . ." I take a mechanical pencil from the coffee table the nurse left behind and crush it into bits in my hand. "Special."

"Blessed," she murmurs and holds her chin in her hand. "So a dragon saved you."

"Yup."

"I guess that makes sense," she says as if she's talking to herself now and not us. "A lot of people have been hunting him for a long time. Someone would have come for him eventually."

"Well, that's my story," I say and shrug uncertainly.

"Thank you." She runs her fingers through her chin-length hair before clasping her hands together before her. "Then I guess I better tell my story."

When Genna starts to talk, it's like Tawnee fades from the room. It's just me and Genna as she talks about when she was first bitten. Her father had been out investigating with my parents when a black wolf and his entourage broke into their house, attacked and bit her mother, and then bit her too before Jefferson showed up with my father to save them. But they were already too late.

"My mother was like you," Genna says quietly. "Gifted with magic. The werewolf disease wasn't compatible with her blood. I watched my mother die right in front of me."

I roll my lips and study the rug again, twisting my hands together. Both our mothers had died trying to protect us. I suddenly recall Jefferson's expression when I had survived being bitten by a werewolf. He was shocked, surprised, and so very sad. He never told me what had happened to his wife, only that she was killed. I had no idea she had been like me, except only one of us survived the encounter.

"That branded me," Genna continues softly. "I held on to that moment. I remembered it whenever I had moments of doubt or confusion in the future. I reminded myself how she died, that Dasc killed my mother."

"What happened after that?" I ask quietly.

It was another week after Genna was turned until Jefferson ran off to help my parents and left Genna with a family friend. While her father was away, a compulsion came over her.

"I ran and couldn't stop running. I didn't want to go but I couldn't stop myself."

"Dasc was influencing you," I say.

"I didn't know that at the time. I didn't figure out until six months later, but yes."

"Where did you run to?"

"Canada."

Which was where she met a lot of other kids. She and a boy named James were "discovered and saved" in the woods by Dasc himself under the pretense of being some Good Samaritan werewolf. He frightened them with stories that if they went home they would turn on their families and hurt the ones they loved. He convinced them that he was the only one that could help them control the beast inside.

"But he was the one actually causing the compulsions," I say.

She nods and shows the first signs of anxiety. She clenches her hands together and her arms shake with the force of squeezing her fingers. "We didn't know any better for a long time. We were kids. He used that compulsion on us all the time. But I knew. I knew when he left that it would fade away, that I would be me again. I put it together. James and I tried to convince the others but they wouldn't listen. Obviously, that's what Dasc wanted all along. People that would be loyal to him even when he wasn't around putting it into their heads directly."

A sour taste forms in my mouth as Genna describes her childhood. Dasc had taken a lot of children and raised them in an all werewolf community with others he had kidnapped as children but were now adults. Everyone was loyal, everyone obedient. They were never mistreated or abused but always lied to. Genna tried to tell the other kids the truth about how werewolves were treated—she knew because of her father, an IMS agent—but they believed Dasc's lies that the world hated them, that the only people they could trust were other werewolves. Even their own families wouldn't want them back.

"And eventually all the other kids believed the lie," Genna says. "Everyone except James and me. We had promised each other we would make it home no matter what, and we intended to keep that promise."

She tugs out a slip of threadbare fabric she's been hiding in her shoe. She doesn't pass it over as if she doesn't trust anyone to hold it, but shows it to me cupped in the palm of her hand. It's hard to make out the faded letters, but it's obviously an address. The more I squint at it, the more I realize what I'm looking at.

"That's the address for the cabin," I murmur.

"Home."

"What is this?" I ask and manage to trail a finger across the first line before Genna snatches it back.

"It's the tag from the shoes I ran off in. My dad wrote my address on it so I could always find my way home if I ever got lost." Her eyelids flicker and a single tear rolls down her cheek. It's the most vulnerable I've seen her yet. She stares at the faded little tag like it has the answers of the universe on it. "I ripped it out before they took my shoes and I hid it from the people that raised me. Dasc never knew. He could never know."

Genna and James did everything they could to prove they were loyal servants after they witnessed another one of their friends try to flee and suffer the consequences. Kelsey, one of the youngest in their generation of kidnapped victims, tried to run home only to discover his family had been murdered by a gang of vampires.

"Vampires?" I ask. From what I learned a month ago about Dasc's control of the vampire populace, I find the incident strange. Genna stares at me. "You mean, vampires acting under Dasc's order."

"Dasc likes to send in other monsters to do his dirty work and cover up his own doings," she says darkly. "Then points the finger at them. Our friend blamed the vampires and became dedicated to the werewolf cause. We didn't know the truth until much later."

I run both hands over the top of my head as I recall the night Dasc nearly killed Hawk, Jefferson, and me. He tried to have the shapeshifter finish Jefferson off. There's not a doubt in my mind that Dasc would have pinned the blame on the shapeshifter when he laid the news of Jefferson's death at Genna's feet. It's a clever tactic. I guess he didn't care to do the same for me. He tried to force my own brother to kill me—but then I didn't have anyone else that cared about me in order to con them into avenging my death against some random monster.

"We knew we had to be smart about our escape," Genna explains. "If we just ran, our families would be killed. So we played his game, pretended to be the good little soldiers he wanted us to be."

"Soldiers for what?" I ask.

"To fight the war he always said was coming. He's been preparing for centuries. At least, that's what he told us," Genna says and tucks the little tag back into her shoe for safe keeping. "He didn't know when the fight would come again but knew it would eventually. So he needed soldiers loyal to the very end, ones capable of unusual combat and stealth."

I lean across the couch and brace a hand on the back cushions. "Wait, he said the fight would come *again*? So, this war's happened before?"

She tilts her head to the side. "He hasn't elaborated to the IMS, has he? Kept his information close to the chest as usual."

"Yeah, that's about right. He likes to be ominous and has only said that a war is coming. We've figured out there's a 'she' on the opposing side and there are lamia involved, but that's it."

"Figures." She rolls her eyes and leans back into the sofa. "I'm sure he's got some plan for revealing it bit by bit, dragging you along and helping his plans at the same time."

"But you know?"

"I know. I've seen it start with my own eyes." She crosses her arms over her chest and her brow falls into shadow with the tilt of her head. "The lamia are the forward guard, the warning that the big bad is waking up and about to make an appearance. I thought they were going to be stealthy about their movements, and they have to a point, but their attack yesterday and earlier in Moose Lake changes things."

Tawnee and I share a look. Well, this sounds ominous and terrible.

"And who is the big bad, Genna?" I ask. "Who's leading the fight?"

"The one who started all the legendary wars before. The history books said the dragons killed her in the last war over five hundred years ago but Dasc says she feigned her death, went into hiding, and has been regaining her strength and building her forces ever since."

"We need a name," Tawnee interrupts.

Genna glares in her direction. "Echidna. The mother of monsters."

I don't know whether to laugh, get angry, or believe this ridiculous statement. Well, Genna is certainly right about what the history books say. The last great war that ever befell the legendary community ended with the death of Echidna at the hands of Draco and the other majestics.

Then I think of the leviathan attack. I think of the lamia that have almost killed me on several occasions. Creatures that are supposed to be extinct but are alive and killing.

Could this be true?

"Why would Dasc hide this?" I ask.

Genna laughs. "I doubt you even believe *me*. Why would anyone believe Dasc if he blamed all his bad behavior on a monster recorded as being dead five hundred years ago? Yeah, that'd go over well. My guess? He never would have told you. He's only out for himself, and that means biding his time until he's free again."

"You sound pretty sure that's going to happen," I say and wait for a reaction like Rosalyn's.

"I think Dasc will do whatever it takes to get what he wants. And what he wants, he usually gets. Speaking of which . . ."

For the next hour she explains all she knows about Dasc's tactics, how he trained his forces, and what little she knows of his plans. As I had suspected before, she confirms that Dasc sent her to Scotland to find the bean nighe and meet up with another one of his werewolf cells. Unfortunately, he had the common sense to leave the groups of his werewolf captives separate without knowledge of each other. That way if one of them turned—like Genna—they wouldn't be able to reveal the location of everyone, just those they knew.

"Rosalyn came with me, obviously," she says. "As I'm sure you've noticed, she's clung to Dasc's teachings as if they're gospel. I think Dasc might have suspected I had other intentions in finding the bean nighe and sent Rosalyn to make sure I did what I was told."

"And what were your other intentions?" I ask.

"I wanted to know how to kill Dasc," she says matter-of-factly. "Otherwise the rest of the werewolves are never going to be free. The cycle has to end and the only way it does is with his death."

Tawnee speaks up. "And did you? Find the bean nighe, that is."

She shakes her head, angry again. "I tracked it all the way to the castle but it must have slipped away when the lamia arrived."

That news aside, Genna plows ahead with what she knows about the people missing from Moose Lake and the few other cells she's come into contact with. From what she tells us, it's clear Dasc has werewolves stationed and raised all over the world preparing for the inevitable conflict with Echidna. Eventually we move out of the medical ward and into one of the conference rooms used for planning missions. We're quickly joined by Jefferson and a few technicians who find us what we need. We spread maps of Scotland, the United States, and Canada across the central table and Genna points out secret bases or locations Dasc uses to communicate with other groups of subservient monsters like the vampires.

She taps a pen on La Crosse and I say, "Well, we definitely know about that one."

"You do?" She holds a pen in her mouth as she makes another note on Canada in red marker with an experienced hand using a compass and protractor. The more I discover about Genna, the more impressive she becomes, like being able to locate a hidden werewolf base in Canada using her own recollections from landmarks and distances running in the woods, then translating that into math and being able to mark its precise location on a map.

"We had a run in with the vampires," Jefferson interjects. "Dasc led us to that location so we could stop a war from breaking out." He shrugs and taps the end of a pencil on the table.

She removes the pen from her mouth to write some calculations on a notepad. "And Dasc just told you where it was."

I look to Jefferson and he shakes his head ever so slightly while his daughter is distracted by her equation. I hold my tongue, still unsure of what we can and cannot tell Genna. Do we let her know that Dasc has been talking to me and only me? How about the life debt I owe him? Would that make her suspicious of my own motivations for some reason? Or would that bring out a Rosalyn type reaction? *Pixies*, sometimes this feels like trying to walk on broken glass around a sleeping hydra.

"He was trying to protect the werewolves in Minnesota," Jefferson says. "So, yeah. He did."

"That's . . . unusual." She shakes her head and keeps pointing out locations and jotting notes about each.

The rest of us let her have space and do her thing,

nodding as she explains things to us. She's kept a remarkable amount of information in her head about the number of werewolves at each location, secret phrases or codes used to get in, traps or methods of keeping the location safe, the amount and kind of weapons, which places will be the worst to get into, and which ones have Whispers stationed there.

"I've heard that before," I murmur.

"A Whisper is a leader or guardian trusted with carrying out Dasc's orders in his stead," she explains. "The ones that 'carry out his will,'" she says with added air quotes.

So that's what the vampires were talking about when we first met them in La Crosse. They thought I was Dasc's Whisper carrying out his orders.

Tawnee stands at the edge of the table with her arms crossed. "He sent you to find the bean nighe. Does that mean *you* are a Whisper, Genna?"

The pen drops from Genna's hand and rolls across the map before it stops over Canada. A heavy silence falls over the room as her hands clench and her eyes bore into the map of Scotland. Her shoulders tense and rise.

Oh, no. That did it. We've just triggered the Rosalyn response, haven't we? Said the wrong phrase and she's about to lash out, become something other than what she's been showing us for the last several hours.

Instead, she raises her head, runs a hand over her mouth, and clears her throat.

"Yes," she says quietly in such a way she sounds ashamed of the truth. "Yes, I am. It was the only way I thought Dasc would tell me where all the cells are, but even that wasn't enough."

She sniffs once, clears her throat again, and continues to pour over the maps but much more subdued. What on earth just happened? What horror did she revisit in her head connected to being a Whisper? Granted, I can imagine becoming one of Dasc's most trusted subjects can't come easy. What horrible things did Genna do to earn his favor?

She quietly marks the last of the locations she knows of and the other agents in the room snap photos of the maps, take notes, plug information into computers, and make phone calls. She sets her pen down and looks haunted, arms wrapped around herself, head hanging, and eyes distant. Jefferson puts a hand on her shoulder but this time she doesn't lean into him like she usually does. She remains frozen for a long while before she puts a hand on top of his and remains that way.

Tawnee pulls me off to the side while the techs continue to plug things into their databases. They ask only a few short questions to clarify particular notes or details which Genna answers in short, clipped sentences. I'm led to the doorway and we halt outside the room.

"I contacted our director and we're going to be sending teams to the places she mapped here in Scotland," Tawnee says in an undertone, our heads bowed together to talk in conspiratorial tones. "He also got in touch with your Director Knox and you have orders to return with Genna, Jefferson, and Rosalyn to Underground. Genna's been a huge help but they want to sort out some things over there."

"What's that supposed to mean?" I ask in the same tone, not wanting to be overhead by the people in the room behind us.

"It's time to go home," she says and offers me a warm

smile before clapping me on the shoulder. "You're American citizens. You need to head back to your jurisdiction. Jefferson deserves time to reconnect with his daughter. And Director Knox hopes that reuniting Rosalyn with her family might do her some good, break that bond she has with Dasc."

The plan sounds great and I sure hope it works for Rosalyn, but I seriously have my doubts.

"Besides," she continues. "I hear you need to go train for the trials coming up."

I give a single laugh and rub the back of my neck with both hands. "I swear, I'd completely forgotten with everything that's happened."

"You'll do great. I'm sad we redheads can't stick together but that's life for you."

"How soon are we supposed to leave?" I ask.

She glances at her watch and flips her hair over her shoulder. "You should start packing up immediately to catch the next flight out. I already made the necessary arrangements to send you off."

It seems strange knowing I'll be going home. Not only me, but Jefferson's daughter. We did it. We really did it.

"I'll let the others know," I say.

"Before you do," she says and lowers her tone even more, slinging an arm around my shoulders so our heads are near bent together. "Director Knox also had some orders specifically for you."

"He did?"

She glances towards the room and whispers, "He's concerned about Genna. Despite all the information she's given us, there's still a chance there's more to her than she lets on. He said Dasc has played the innocent bystander before. There's no reason to think he hasn't taught his soldiers the same."

I frown. I don't like the sound of where this is going. "So, what exactly are my orders?"

"Keep an eye on her. You're in the perfect position to do so without raising suspicion. If you see any red flags, you report to the director immediately."

"Jefferson isn't going to like that," I say, not to mention that *I* am not going to like this.

"That's the second half of your orders," she says. "Jefferson isn't to know."

5

I feel like I've got a bomb strapped to my chest with the weight of my orders, and every time Jefferson talks to me or looks my way, I swear it's going to go off. He even asks if I'm okay at one point. Oh, yeah. I'm fine.

I'm such a liar.

Sinclair and Ross drive us to London so we don't miss our nonstop flight to Minneapolis and walk us into the terminal to see us off. I give them both hugs and before I know it, we're waving farewell and heading through the terminal with our charges. Genna sticks close to her father, her eyes watching everyone around us with suspicion as if every single person, including an elderly man with a walker and a three-year-old running past, is the enemy. We follow behind Tawnee who's got sky marshal credentials in her pocket and keeps a hand on Rosalyn who looks like she wants to kill us. Her wrists are cuffed but those are hidden under a hoodie thrown over them to make her look more casual, like a teenager being dragged home instead of a criminal.

Tawnee gets us around security and we board our flight to go back home. We ride in first class, more to keep Rosalyn separated from the rest of the passengers for their safety than anything else, and after a seriously long flight, we land at the Minneapolis-Saint Paul International Airport. My internal clock is all screwed up so when we land and it's still afternoon and light out, my head hurts.

I spot a group of agents waiting for us in nondescript clothing under a sign one of them is holding.

Funny-looking ginger, grouchy old man, and friends.

I laugh. At the sound, the sign lowers to reveal the person holding it is my brother. I jog forward with my carry-on bag bouncing side to side and my brother does the same, shoving his sign off on an agent and running towards me. We meet part way laughing so hard we probably look deranged to any normal people watching, and share a bone-breaking hug.

"I missed your ugly mug," I say and hear his back crack as I hold on tight enough to lift him off his feet.

He groans as I set him back on the floor. "Thanks, I don't have to see that chiropractor anymore."

"Happy to help."

He shrugs away and gives me a big goofy grin. "How was your flight?"

"Long. And so weird. Nine hours and it's still only 3:00 in the afternoon."

"Great Scott!" he shouts and grabs my shoulders with exaggerated excitement. "You've discovered time travel!"

One of the agents waiting for us laughs at Hawk's outburst as they walk over to greet the rest of our party. Jefferson and Genna come up behind us along with Tawnee and Rosalyn. Before any sort of introductions are made, the agents urge us to keep moving so we can get to Underground as soon as possible. We pick up our pace but Hawk latches onto Genna and can't seem to take his eyes off her. I'm sure he wants a good look at Jefferson's daughter since we've been hearing about her since we got to Moose Lake.

We don't have to wait for additional luggage, so we move quickly out of the airport to the two black SUVs waiting for us. I take a deep breath once we're outside and survey the snow, the sounds of the Twin Cities, the smell of Minnesota air. Home.

It takes us twenty minutes to drive through the Cities and reach our destination at the power park. Our driver badges his way past the guards and we pile out in front of the cement bunker on the back of the lot. Genna, as she always seems to be doing, watches everything and everyone closely. Rosalyn does the same and I've got that bad feeling in the pit of my stomach again. Together we march inside and take one of the big black lifts into Underground.

I'm actually surprised Director Knox wanted us all to head straight to Underground. For months he's been directing werewolves, even trusted IMS agents, out of the hidden city to keep them away from Dasc's influence who's being held in the penitent cells. Now he's letting two werewolves with suspect loyalties in? What if they find out this is where Dasc is being held? I keep my eyes on Genna's back, the director's orders at the very forefront of my mind. His orders didn't say if I could tell my brother or not. I'm dying to tell him. I hate carrying secrets on my own.

We reach the bottom of the long chute, the roar of the river diminishing beneath the incredibly thick concrete that houses Underground. Bernie, the faun guard, salutes us as we enter and comes over to shake my hand.

"Welcome home, Phoenix," he says, his deer-like ears standing straightforward as a sign of happiness.

"Thanks, Bernie. It's good to be back."

He stays behind as we move into the market that's lively at this time of the afternoon. I fight a yawn and battle jet lag to keep up with the group moving towards IMS Division Headquarters in the heart of the city. Jefferson points out things of interest to his daughter while Rosalyn scoffs behind them. Tawnee waves at Old Man Two the centaur and he waves back. It dawns on me that Old Man Two is from Scotland so it's possible he knows her. Otherwise, I doubt he would ever wave at a stranger. Then he waves at me, too. I wave in return, surprised.

"Wow, he didn't frown at you or anything," Hawk comments.

We reach the reception area of headquarters and I can't help but get a twinge of anxiety every time I come here. It's a force of habit from all the times I've been in trouble. But not today. Today Director Knox is here to meet us with a smile and shakes my hand personally.

"Junior Agent Mason," he says. "Welcome back."

"Thank you, sir."

He looks over my shoulder and I move aside to let him pass. Jefferson introduces his daughter and the director shakes her hand as well. The way she holds herself—straight-backed and poised—she looks more like an agent than a rescued victim.

"We've been analyzing the information you gave us," he says. "The Edinburgh Division already found one of the hideouts you marked and identified two werewolves found there as missing persons from London."

"How are they being treated?" she asks and a muscle in her jaw tenses.

"They're going to be reunited with their families shortly. You've begun a great thing, Ms. Barnes. The IMS is in your debt."

She doesn't respond except for a single nod. He directs Tawnee to escort Rosalyn to another wing of headquarters to speak with a counselor and arrange a meeting with her brother. Once they're gone, the other agents return to whatever they had been doing before they came to fetch us. The rest of us follow the director to his office. We walk along the hallway on the second floor with one wall a giant glass pane overlooking the strange stone courtyard in the middle of headquarters.

Genna pauses at the window and stares at the arch of black stone in the middle covered in golden dragon script. Jefferson puts a hand on her arm and she very slowly moves away from the window to continue with the rest of us to the director's office.

Once we're inside and take up all the available seats, Director Knox debriefs us on what's going to happen next. He explains that the IMS will be approaching each of the locations Genna revealed in attempts to locate what missing persons they can to return them home. Those with reactions like Rosalyn will be held for treatment and will work with family members and counselors alike to try to revert any brainwashing they have suffered. Genna's expression doesn't waiver from neutral interest but out of the corner of my eye I spot her clenching the bottom edge of her seat, which is out of the director's line of sight.

"I'm sure you're tired from your flight," he says. "I've made accommodations available here in Underground so you can adjust before you make the final stretch home. Masons, it's your old apartment so I'm sure you know where to go."

"Yes, sir," my brother and I say in unison.

"Phoenix, if you'd be so kind as to finish up a bit of paperwork regarding your report of Scotland in records before you leave. Hawk, please escort the Barneses to where they can spend the night."

He gestures to the door dismissing us. We rise and move out in silence. I'm the last one out of the room and when I glance back, the director gives a solemn nod before I close the door. I tell Hawk and the others to go on without me and they agree—no one likes doing paperwork.

Taking the hallway in the opposite direction, I round the corner, go down a flight of stairs, start along another hallway that leads directly to the records office, and then pause when something catches my eye through the open door on my left. I rock back on my heels and swivel my head to find Draco in the courtyard framed beneath the stone arch. The air around him courses with tendrils of blue lightning that pulse like a heartbeat as they slowly stretch outwards from him to the arch. The golden letters on the black, glossy stone glow steadily brighter until suddenly there's a faint pop and the light and lightning vanishes.

Draco lifts his gaze and his eyes shimmer with their own brilliant light for a moment until he's a normal man again in an all-black suit, clean shaven, short brown hair, average build—nothing too over the top to suggest what lies beneath is a powerhouse of energy.

And he's staring straight at me.

I swallow.

I haven't seen him since before the vampire attack in Duluth and Moose Lake. That was before I knew about Scholar, helped hide that clever dragon's existence, had been warned not to trust Draco, used a power I didn't know I even possessed to stop a pair of lamia, and more recently found myself somewhat protected from another lamia with that same power. Everything's changed.

I had been nervous around him before but now there's also a twinge of trepidation.

He keeps staring like he wants something but doesn't speak so I decide to continue on to records in order to escape that gaze.

"Junior Agent Mason," he calls and I grimace out of sight before turning around and walking into the courtyard.

I've never been in this part of headquarters before. In fact, as far as I know, hardly anyone ever comes in here. Draco is probably the first person I can recall standing directly in the shadow of the black arch. I gaze up at it from this new angle. There's a faint hum in the stone that becomes louder the closer I get to it. I quickly look away again.

Draco clasps his hands together behind his back and waits for me to meet him under the arch. I keep a respectful—and cautious—distance apart once I reach him. The last time we were closer than this, he was shouting in my face because I made a life debt with Dasc in order to secure the safe return of Genna and the other missing people.

"I'm glad to see you've returned safely," he says in a soft-spoken manner that isn't usual for him. It puts me more on edge. "You performed admirably during your mission in Scotland."

"Thank you, sir."

"I need you to keep doing so."

I fight the frown trying to work its way onto my face.

"Of course, sir."

"I wanted to make it clear that your latest orders do not stem from Director Knox but from me." He takes a step forward to close that careful distance I put between us. His features are cold and very clearly unhappy. "I do not trust this Genevieve Barnes, even less so Rosalyn Graham. Any puppet of Dasc's is dangerous and a potential liability. The director's decision to bring them here without the proper precautions was a mistake, one I would have corrected if I had been advised of the details."

His eyes flash. Woe to the person who failed to pass along the details to Draco.

"With all due respect, sir, Genna has been extremely cooperative and helpful so far."

"And that is precisely why I do not trust her. One uses a stick, one uses a carrot. Both are trying to achieve the same end."

"And what's that?"

"I thought you were clever," he says sharply. "Surely you know what they are after."

Well, he's certainly touchy when he gets in a mood. What's that old saying? Never cross a dragon.

"You're saying Genna gave up the locations of all those hideouts and werewolf cells in order to help free Dasc. How does that work?"

He takes another step closer and angles his head towards me. I stop breathing.

"These ghosts of yesteryear you have been trying to recover are not the children they once were," he whispers, hot dragon breath blowing in my face. "They have been trained to hunt, to kill, to deceive. The woman you are praising is not the innocent daughter Jefferson Barnes lost fourteen years ago. She is a weapon. And if you do not keep a subtle eye on her, I will take more proactive means to keep this agency safe and Dasc secure."

He steps past me and I release the breath I had been holding.

"These orders are closed book," he continues as he circles around behind me to face the arch. "You do not tell anyone and that includes your brother. People like Genevieve make extra sure not to slip up when they know someone is watching. If you suspect anything, you report directly to me. Are we clear?"

A hard lump forms in my throat and I find it difficult to swallow around it to say in a small voice, "Crystal clear."

"Then I will expect regular updates. Best to hurry along before she starts to suspect something is afoot."

"Yes, sir," I murmur and head in the direction of the records office.

"Where are you going, Mason?" he asks behind me.

I turn around and point in the direction I'm heading but he raises an eyebrow in response.

"No one actually needed me in records, did they?"

"No."

"Right." Just a ruse to throw off any suspicion where I was when Draco wanted to talk to me personally. Of course. I duck my head, walk quickly in the opposite direction of records, and hurry into a nearby bathroom. I check the short, human-size, and extra-large stalls for anyone in here before splashing my face with cool water. I work on my breathing exercises again since I'm getting so worked up.

Another secret. Another burden. Why do I keep getting them like I'm some kind of collector? Hawk and I are at a good place. We shared all our secrets, formed one of our own with Scholar and the blood pendant. The very last thing I want to do is lie again. If Jefferson ever finds out that I'm spying on his daughter behind his back to prove Draco's paranoia true, he'll hate me. Hawk will be just as angry—I'll be playing up on the legendary community's fear and distrust of werewolves.

Why on earth did Draco have to put me in this position?

Having taken too much time as it is, I dry my face with some paper towels and make my way out of headquarters. I take a detour into the market, convincing myself that I don't need to worry because Genna's not going to do anything suspicious. She's going to be the same brave soul she's been presenting herself as, the lost and found daughter, the warrior, the protector of the other lost werewolves.

I stop at the nymph vendor and buy a big bag of smoked paprika popcorn. I glance around for my friends, Celina the faun or Doocan the giant or Witty, but they're nowhere to be found. Huh. Maybe they're at the movie theater or something. With a sigh, I realize I've procrastinated long enough and wind my way between the shoppers, restaurants, elves and fauns rushing by, to the living quarters of Underground. I pass the cement giant housing, the centaur and faun fields, and eventually reach the Roman marble apartments. I stand on the front steps and my eyes travel up the two stories to the balcony that Hawk and I used to stay up late on watching the lights dim in time with the sun outside and the fire sprites dart around in the dark when they could shine the brightest.

Everything's different now, isn't it?

When I clomp up the stairs with my bag of popcorn, I find Hawk walking through the living room with a pile of blankets. He pauses and his eyes zoom in on the bag in my hand.

"Popcorn?" he asks and dons a big smile.

"Umm, yeah. Some food to share, you know . . ." I can't seem to find a normal rhythm of talking and thinking anymore. It feels like up is down and down is up. Having Genna thought of like a criminal mastermind—the girl I've been trying to find since we captured Dasc—has left me questioning everything I'm doing.

"Hey, everything okay with your report or whatever?" he asks and his smile fades.

I try to wipe the confusion and dismay off my face, pass it off as jet lag or something, and set the bag of popcorn on the coffee table to buy me time to come up with a convenient lie.

"Yeah, the clerk was just a crab. I guess I didn't file my report the right way through the server or whatever." I wave a hand dismissively and walk past him to stand out on the balcony. Two seconds into this thing and I already hate it. I hate lying and it's always the worst when it's to my brother.

"You okay?" he asks.

"Yeah, I'm just tired," I say, which is mostly the truth. "I'd usually be trying to sleep by this time. I need to adjust, that's all."

"Well, I figured we could let Genna have your old room and Jefferson can take mine." He nods his head toward the bedrooms and I spot Genna and Jefferson talking quietly sitting side by side on Hawk's old bed. "I'm setting you a spot on the couch here."

I watch him over my shoulder as he spreads out a couple of blankets and a pillow on the couch for me. "How thoughtful."

"That means I can have some of that popcorn, right?" He gives me another grin.

"Yup. Have at it. Take as much as you want." I return to watching the street below and the fields nearby where a group of fauns are tending to their indoor garden.

Hawk walks over with bag in hand chewing loudly. He offers it to me but I shake my head.

"Sooooo you buy popcorn and then don't even want it?" he asks, shoving another fistful of it into his mouth.

"I lost my appetite."

"Between the market and here?"

I shrug, so he shrugs and keeps eating. Eventually he starts to pester me about my trip and how Scotland was and if I brought any souvenirs back. I distract him, and myself, with a collection of photos I took with my phone. I wish I had more to show him but there's a decent number of landscape shots when I thought to take them, a few of members of our team, and one of us all together in the Vaults' dining hall before we headed out. Seeing Thane makes my inner darkness return.

"You seem different," he says quietly and I look up from the group photo to find him watching me closely.

"Do I?" I mutter and page through the last photos I managed to take of the castle in Edinburgh.

"So. What's new?" He raps his fingers on the railing and leans forward on his forearms.

I join him there leaning backwards against the railing so I can keep an eye on the door to where Genna and Jefferson are having their private discussion.

"She's not what I imagined," I whisper.

He matches my tone. "Yeah, you can say that again. She's certainly not a traumatized little girl. More like a mysterious, toned enigma . . ."

He studies the doorway leading to Genna and his lips slowly pucker as he narrows his eyes. I cock an eyebrow and nudge him sharply with my elbow. He scowls at me and returns to watching the street.

"What was that for?" he grumbles.

"You like her, don't you?" I whisper.

"What? She's a nice person."

"No, no. You *like* her. Like the way you liked that actress in—what was it called . . ." I snap my fingers as I try to think of the name of the movie he dragged me to because he thought the lead actress was hot.

"Pssh." He makes a face and shrugs his shoulders. "I don't know what you're talking about."

"*The Matrix*!" I say as it comes to me. "You thought she was *so cool* and *so awesome* and you went and found every other movie she had ever been in—"

"Oh, shut up," he says and shoves me away but I bounce right back.

"You do, don't you?" I prop my chin in my hands, bracing my elbows on the railing so my face is right next to his. "You can tell me. You certainly told me enough to make me want to puke when it was what's-her-face—"

He glares at me and eventually gives a non-committal shrug.

"You realize that's a really terrible can of pixies to open, right?" I continue to whisper. "One, she's Jefferson's daughter. Two, you know nothing about her. Three, she's Jefferson's daughter."

"Yeah, I get it. I just think she's—"

"*So cool* and *so awesome*?"

"I hate you."

"I love you, too."

He sighs, heaving his shoulders dramatically. We fall silent and the humor in both of us fades into somber reflection. He runs a hand through his hair before tucking in next to me, bracing his forearms on the railing once again.

"I just think that after everything she's been through— being ripped away from her family, fighting Dasc's compulsion, being raised by a psychopath—she still managed to make it home in one piece and hand over information to save hundreds of others. I'd say she's pretty darn impressive."

My gaze drops. "Yeah. I guess she is."

He bumps me with his shoulder. "And so are you. Did you keep your promise?"

"What?"

"You completely forgot already, didn't you?"

I suddenly recall the last conversation I had with my brother over the phone in Scotland. He told me I was a hero—what a false belief. I close my eyes as it hits me and I nod. "No, of course not. I told myself I was a winner in the mirror this morning."

"Liar."

"Yeah, that's true," I mutter and rub my face with my hands, feeling sleep crawl over me again.

"That time difference getting to you?" he asks and finishes off the rest of the popcorn even though it had been a big bag. He wads it up and makes a long jump shot at the trashcan on the other side of the room. It hits the wall and tumbles in. "Try and get some shut eye."

"Yeah. What about you? Where are you sleeping?"

"Oh, I'll form a cocoon and hang from the ceiling tonight."

"In reality . . ."

"Honest truth." He presses a hand to his heart and winks.

He doesn't elaborate and I'm not going to ask. I don't bother changing since all of my clothes are dirty anyway, but I freshen up in the bathroom before laying on the couch. The clock on the wall tells me its 4:30 p.m. Meh, whatever. I'll adjust my sleep later. I stare blankly at the ceiling until sleep takes me.

My dreams are chaotic as usual. Dasc hardly shows up for once but is instead replaced by Draco flitting in and out of focus, offering me a gun and telling me to do what's necessary. I chase someone through the woods, then over the hills of Scotland. Always running. Sometimes I can't tell if I'm running after someone or running away. Maybe it's both.

I wake to a loud crack. I blink several times, bringing the coffee table and balcony into focus, and try to separate my dreams from reality. Was that crack in my head? Or real?

I push myself into a sitting position and swivel around to see Hawk hanging in a hammock strung between two marble pillars near the door. His head peeks out like a bat from under its wing to see what the noise is, too. Huh, I guess he wasn't lying after all.

Another crack and this time frantic hushed voices.

Sleep slips out of my mind and I'm quickly on my feet, drawing my mother's gun from the top of my rucksack propped against the foot of the couch. Moving silently on my tippy toes, I make for the partway open door to Genna's room. Faint light comes in through the window to drape the room in soft grays and deep, undisturbed shadows. My heart is racing up into my throat as I clear through the door and come to a quick stop, lowering my gun and hiding it behind my thigh.

Genna is tucked into a corner of the room in a fighting stance as Jefferson stands a few feet away trying to calm her. She's got the small nightstand grasped in her hands and holds it up like a bat. My eyes dart around the room trying to figure out what's going on when I hear another crack outside the apartment. Genna swivels towards the sound and Jefferson holds both hands out towards her in a placating gesture.

Hawk sneaks into the room behind me and murmurs, "Stupid centaur got his hoof caught in a pot outside and is trying to get it off."

Piping Pan, what an idiot.

"Genna, it's okay," Jefferson says gently. "We're not under attack. You can put that down."

Genna growls under her breath and relaxes her grip on the nightstand until it clatters to the floor. Her breathing is shaky and she flexes her hands before starting to pace. When she spots Hawk and me, she averts her eyes.

"I'm sorry," she says roughly. "I didn't—I didn't realize. I just heard the sound and—"

"It's all right. I've got you." Jefferson motions with open arms and she steps into his embrace, closing her eyes and gripping him tight as if he might disappear. "I've got you, baby girl."

Hawk and I take that as our cue to backtrack out of the room. He closes the door most of the way behind us and then we stand together near the couch, uncertain what to say or do.

She sounded so ashamed of her reaction, her gut instinct to defend herself from a surprising sound in the night. Even after all her explanations and stories, I can't truly imagine everything she's been through.

This is the monster Draco is afraid of?

I'm not ready to wake up the following morning. I'm nowhere near adjusted to the time zone change yet but Hawk drags me off the couch and gets me going. We move quietly so as not to wake up Genna or Jefferson but quickly discover Genna is already awake and doing push-ups in her room. Well, she's certainly dedicated to her craft. I purse my lips and tiptoe into the bathroom to change.

As Hawk and I are about to exit the apartment, Genna emerges from her room dressed in exercise clothes same as us. Actually, she's dressed in my spare running shorts and tank top. How the heck did she even snag my clothes? She's leaner than me and has more of a straight-cut body shape so my clothes are a little loose on her.

"Where are you going?" she asks.

"To the track," Hawk says. "We need to stay in prime shape for the trials."

"Trials?"

"Our agent exams basically."

She nods and lifts a foot to adjust the tongue of her worn shoe. "Mind if I join you? Exercising helps me focus."

My brother and I share a look. I shrug and he bobs his head.

"Yeah, sure," he answers for us.

"Leave a note or something," I add and point to Jefferson's door. "If you're gone when he wakes up he's going to freak out."

"Yeah," she says quietly and grabs a notepad from her room to leave a message at her father's bedside before slipping away with us.

The light in Underground begins to brighten and we trot down the long lane of apartment buildings past Japanese grottos, fields, sprite pools, the electricity generation cavern, and arrive at the great stone pillars that mark the entrance of the stadium. Red and blue banners with golden letters pronouncing the victors of previous aetherball tournaments hang from the walls between the three different entrances. The one we take on the right has a banner for the fire sprites as the previous winners of the midsummer games.

We walk through a long alley bordered by stands on either side and greet a pack of elves dancing their way out carrying a boombox. Genna watches them curiously for a long time, walking backwards a ways, before we reach the ground floor of the stadium. A black and red racetrack encircles a span of turf in the center littered of exercise equipment, goalie posts, and fire sprite perches set up high on long metal poles. A slew of fire sprites sit up there in little splashes of oil and flicker between various shades of flames to illuminate the stadium. It gives the place an almost dreamlike quality as the light strobes blue to red to yellow and back again.

"Cool," Genna says, smiling up at the sprites.

Hawk and I do a few warm up stretches and Genna does the same.

"So, are we running in a pack?" Hawk asks. "Or is this a competition?"

"Oh, it's definitely on." I grin and get in place at the starting line. "Distance?"

He does the same on my left. "Five-miler sound good?"

"Sure."

We both turn to ask Genna her preference to include her but she's already at the starting position on my right, eyes forward and ready to rumble. We shrug to each other and Hawk gives the countdown before we take off. It certainly is a competition and we race each other round and round the track. Genna keeps pace easily but doesn't pull ahead. She keeps in line with Hawk and me.

Even though I'm in tip-top shape, Genna and Hawk's werewolf genes really start to show. Since their bodies repair faster, they can handle the stress of intense runs a lot better than I can. I do the five miles easy as you please but it's obvious the other two don't have the same amount of aches I do at the end of it. That's why I need to keep pushing myself. I always want to be able to keep up with my brother.

Hawk looks like he's about to win when Genna bursts into a sprint and beats him to the finish line. Irritated, I come in last. Freakin' werewolves. Genna's got a huge grin on her face and when Hawk goes to give her a high-five, she looks startled for a moment before she passively slaps her hand to his. The more I watch her, the more I notice these little ticks, her uncertain reactions to what other people deem normal social interaction.

Someone claps at our finish and Jefferson makes his way down the stands with a cup of coffee held in the crook of his elbow. He beams at his daughter with tears in his eyes, every inch the proud father. I wonder if this is the first thing he's ever been able to see his daughter compete in.

"Well done," he says. "That's my girl."

Her smile vanishes and that haunted expression returns again. Jefferson looks horrified.

"I'm sorry," he says. "Did I say something wrong?"

She shakes her head and focuses on stretching her arms. "Dasc used to say that to me all the time, that's all."

The divide between us rears up again with the little things we will never truly understand about Genna's stolen life. All the things we take for granted mean something entirely different to her. Even such a simple phrase as "that's my girl" can be the knife ripping open a fresh wound.

Jefferson stands aside as we lapse into an awkward silence while we stretch out our calves and hamstrings. Genna keeps her eyes downcast. As a group we return to the apartment and take turns using the shower. None of us seem able to shake the dour mood that's settled in so Jefferson suggests treating us to breakfast. We each shrug and follow his lead out the door.

We take a table at Old Man Two's between a group of agents and fauns when a surprise guest arrives to join us.

"May I join you?" Tawnee asks. Her curly hair looks wilder than usual and she's got shadows under her eyes.

I push out the chair next to me and she takes it with a soft "thank you." She surveys our little group and stretches out a hand towards Hawk across from her.

"The other ginger," she says with a smile and shakes his hand. "Happy to make your acquaintance. We never really had time to talk the other day."

They exchange some pleasantries before the conversation is interrupted by the arrival of our breakfast—eggs, cheese, and muffins with a side of blueberries. While we eat, Tawnee fills us in on the latest news. Rosalyn is currently speaking with a counselor and her brother is being escorted from Moose Lake to meet her in a controlled environment. Tawnee also heard from Edinburgh Division that they're putting together teams to approach the other locations Genna laid out.

"So, I'll be heading out later today," she says. "I'm sure they can use all the help they can get, especially considering what's going on in Europe right now."

I pause with my fork en route to my mouth. "What's going on in Europe?"

"I take it you haven't heard then?" she asks. We shake our heads. "Faunus, one of the major faun colonies in Greece, was attacked yesterday. They lost a lot of people. And then there was some kind of attack on Paris Division Headquarters. I don't know details of either of the attacks yet but I heard a rumor that a lamia was spotted at Faunus."

"Piping Pan," Hawk mutters and I nod in agreement.

Sounds like everything is getting worse—the beginning of a war, perhaps? The one Dasc keeps warning will begin and which Genna pointed to Echidna as the leader? Genna sits silent and brooding next to Jefferson. He puts a hand on top of hers but she hardly seems to notice.

We finish our breakfast and after conversing some more, I learn that a number of fauns have left Underground to go help friends and family in Faunus. That must be why I haven't seen Celina. I have no doubt that she would have been running to the nearest transport the second she heard the news. It's possible Doocan went with her. Those two have an odd sort of bond and I hardly ever see one without the other.

I'm lost in my thoughts about wars and missing friends when a lanky agent comes over requesting Genna and Jefferson's presence in the director's office and mine in "records." Unfortunately, Hawk isn't summoned anywhere so he sits dejected at the table as the three of us move away to headquarters. We walk the colonnade beneath the trees and Genna watches the water sprites playing in the fountains at regular intervals along the path. Despite the hardcore attitude she's had about some things, the innocent playfulness of the sprites she's seen today seems to enthrall her.

We reach headquarters and the secretary has both Barneses have a seat while I pass through in the general direction of the records office. When I pass the doorway that leads to the courtyard, I sigh when I find Draco waiting there for me again.

"You know, everyone's going to think I'm illiterate or something if you keep calling me to records," I say.

"While Miss Barnes is in the vicinity, I intend to keep your time conversing with Dasc a secret," he says and gestures for me to follow him.

Oh, so this is really a Dasc visit. I thought they'd moved him by now since they're allowing werewolves free range in Underground again. I anticipate he'll lead me out of headquarters and to the penitent cells but instead we march along the hallways, other agents moving quickly to the side to let us pass, and enter what appears to be a janitor's closet except it seems exceptionally clean and bare of most things a janitor would need. There's only a broom leaning against the wall and a few bottles of cleaner as if someone was told to make this spot look inconspicuous and then got distracted halfway through.

Draco runs a hand down the center of the back wall. A line of dragon script glows upon his touch with a sizzling sound and the wall splits in two, opening to a stairwell leading into darkness. When Draco gestures for me to go first, a lump forms in my throat. Yeah, this doesn't seem shady or suspicious at all. Scholar's warning echoes in my head again. Don't trust Draco. But what am I supposed to do? Tell him no thank you and walk away?

I take a deep breath and proceed cautiously down the steps. The second I hit the third step, the stone beneath my feet pulses blue and light spreads out like a ripple across the stairs and up the walls until the whole place has a faint shimmering light coming off it.

"Cool," I breathe and keep moving. The long set of stairs starts to zig-zag back and forth between landings until at last I reach the bottom.

It's a black wall like the one above. I shuffle out of the way so Draco can do whatever he did upstairs but he gestures for me to lead the way again.

"Go on," he says and looks at me in such a way that I feel this is a test.

I face the wall and place my hand in the middle, trailing my fingers across its glossy surface like he had before. The same golden dragon script appears and fades away as the wall opens for me. I walk through and blink against the bright lights reflecting off the white walls. There's no mistaking where we are. We're in the penitent cells. This must be Draco's secret backdoor. Why he needs one, I have no idea.

He passes by me with a ghost of a smile and takes the lead. I roll my eyes. Dragons.

This is a section of the cells I've never been to. Some of the doors are extremely large, probably to fit the bigger monsters that roam the world. Not only are the doors bigger but back here I can hear muffled screams, crying, and voices shouting to be set free. The air is heavy as if I can feel the weight of the faun magic being exerted on the prisoners, forcing them to relive their victims' last moments of fear and pain as their own. I falter following Draco and stop to listen to the horrible sounds.

The majestic dragon pauses, his hands held loosely at his sides yet imposing in his black suit in the middle of the pristine white hallway.

"You have never been allowed this far down," Draco says. "To where the truth of spilled blood is heard echoing in the halls. To where the devils find the essence of the fear they have inflicted and once savored. They sing their sorrows trapped within these walls. Every last monster and murderer and traitor compose their symphonies here. All but one."

He doesn't need to elaborate anymore in his creepy way for me to know who he's talking about.

"Dasc," I say.

"Come."

I follow behind the swish of his long suit coat to a door further along the hall. There's a gargoyle sentry posted outside holding a bio-mech gun in its hand. It doesn't move an inch from its stony pose as Draco and I approach. Draco presses his hand to the wall next to the magically shielded door and a small window reveals itself. Inside, Dasc sits cross-legged on the floor against a padded wall in his usual white penitent garb. His eyes are closed, head tilted back, and for a brief second a smile crosses his face. His calm demeanor in the face of what sets the others screeching terrifies me more than the sounds around me.

What kind of monster is he truly?

His eyes open and he finds me at the door. I quickly pull away and back up a few paces so he can't see me anymore. My heart thunders in my chest. Draco doesn't move but his eyes follow me, testing me again.

"Why show me this?" I ask, needing to know why I've been dragged here just to see Dasc savoring what destroys others.

"I want you to know the totality of the monster we are trying to unravel," he says. "Nothing quite conveys the truth like seeing it for one's self. This is the thing that raised Genevieve Barnes and Rosalyn Graham. Do not under-estimate what he is capable of."

"If you're so worried about him, then why are you letting werewolves back into Underground?" I counter. "I thought Director Knox had been trying to keep them out of Dasc's range of influence."

"We have been performing tests to determine his reach," Draco says calmly. "And continuing a ban against werewolves would only serve to make it obvious this city houses Dasc's presence. The werewolves have been allowed to return as a smoke screen to our enemies. Even so, Dasc and his werewolves are not to be trifled with. I do not take this matter lightly."

"Fine. I get it," I snap.

"I do not think you do." He clasps his hands behind his back and for a brief second his eyes narrow into blue reptilian slits—the eyes of his true form. "I assume you heard of the assault on Faunus and the facility in Paris." I nod. "They are two seemingly unrelated incidents, but at each location there were sightings of wolves during the attacks. The werewolves were involved somehow and Dasc is the key to figuring out why."

The werewolves are attacking? "But he's been locked up here this whole time. How could he know?"

"Trust me. He knows."

Paranoid old dragon.

"So what now?" I ask. "Are we . . . are we interrogating him here?"

"Not unless you want to feel the effects of a penitent cell." His gaze cuts through me and I try not to appear overly anxious when I shake my head.

Draco gives instructions to the gargoyle and it escorts me through the hallways to the conference room with the big black table to wait until Dasc has been secured in an interrogation room. I exhale sharply once I'm alone and pace around the table, too anxious to take a seat. If only Dasc had picked someone else to be his go-to person. It's put me in an awfully difficult position and kept me under the eye of Draco which is *not* where I want to be.

The door cracks open and I look up. Witty rolls into the room in his wheelchair cautiously as if afraid he's intruding. Always the cautious one. But then he gives me a smile and a small measure of the tension eases out of my shoulders.

"Hey, it's good to see you," I say and walk over to give him a hug.

"Glad you made it back in one piece," he says and pats me on the back before pulling away.

We've been friends for a long time, so even though I haven't seen him in a while I can see the changes in him. His black hair's grown out a bit and there are white strands around his temples. He's good at internalizing stress so I'm not too surprised. His clothes are wrinkled as though he slept in them and there's something different in his expression I can't quite put my finger on.

"You look like you've aged about fifty years," I say, which earns me a chuckle.

"Same to you. How was Scotland?"

"Wet. Trying. Beautiful."

"Heh. Sounds poetic."

I give a dramatic bow. "I'm a poet and I didn't even know it."

"Heh. Yeah." He coughs into his hand. "You must be training for the trials and all that now, I guess."

I bite my lower lip and make a conscious effort not to glance at Witty's defunct legs in his wheelchair. I've never seen him as handicapped—he's an absolute genius after all—but a majority of the trials involve physical tests. His disability disqualifies him from the get-go as a field agent. It's not fair to him. It's not his fault a hydra ruined his chances of running into the fight with the rest of us.

"Umm, I—yeah." Oh, yeah. Super smooth. I'm an idiot, but I don't know what to say.

"It's okay," he says and tries to appear unconcerned but the effect is ruined as he clenches onto the wheels of his chair and inches them back and forth incessantly to the point they start to squeak. "I can still take the boards and get a position here easy. I mean, I'm already working tech in the armory and cells, obviously, and that's . . . yeah. It's great. It's fine. Really."

I open and close my mouth a few times as I run through different things I could say in my head until I settle on, "For what it's worth, I know you'll be brilliant in whatever you end up doing."

A muscle twitches in his jaw. "Yeah. Thanks."

Before things can get anymore awkward than they already are, the door swings open to Draco standing in the hallway.

"It's time," he says.

"What's the plan?" I ask. It feels strange doing this with just Draco and Witty here. I'm used to Director Knox being involved and Jefferson being my guide, my rock.

"You'll be asking questions to determine his interest in Faunus and the Paris Division without directly stating the involvement of werewolves."

"Is that all?"

"Bring up Genna. I want to witness his reaction."

I run my tongue over my teeth, mulling over how to approach that subject, and follow Draco out the door. Witty rolls along behind us. We pause in front of a sealed door where Major Lynch, the penitent cell warden, waits with an enhanced bio-mech gun held casually in his hands.

"Earpiece?" I ask Draco as he starts to walk away towards the observation room.

He smirks. "Do you need one?"

It only takes me a second to think it over. "No. I guess not."

He slips away and Witty gives me a thumbs up before disappearing in the room after the dragon. Major Lynch nods respectfully to me and I do the same to him before the barrier drops on the door.

Dasc sits patiently in his chair, hands chained together and resting on the tabletop. His eyes follow me as I move across the room and take the seat opposite him. He's not smiling like he usually does when I talk with him which I had come to think of as his way to taunt me. Now he's even more eerie without it.

"So. Back at last," he says. "How was Scotland?"

"Adventurous," I reply dryly and mimic his pose with my hands held loosely on top of the table. "So, since I've answered your first question, how about you tell what you know about Faunus?"

He tilts his head to the side and quirks an eyebrow. "That's a rather different change of pace. What do I know about it?" I nod once in confirmation. "It's the largest faun community left in the world and is said to have the most marvelous wine."

"That's it?"

"If you want something more specific, you'll have to clarify," he says innocently. "My turn. Did you find the bean nighe?"

"Really? You don't care at all if we found Genna or not."

He clicks his tongue and shakes his head. "Phoenix, if you hadn't found her, you would still be in Scotland. The bean nighe."

I scowl. "No. It was gone by the time we got to the castle."

"Pity."

"Yeah, it's a real tragedy. So you've never been to Faunus or had any interest in the city?"

He raps his fingers on the table and I have the urge to slam my fist on them. "You seem rather attached to Faunus. I take it something's happened and my name came up?"

"Answer the question, Lycaon."

With an exaggerated sigh, he leans back in his chair. "My, you are intolerable today. I visited Faunus not long before I returned to Moose Lake. I needed to consult with an old acquaintance about an investment in France."

My blood pounds in my ears. "Paris."

He drops his cocky attitude and straightens. "Something *has* happened."

It can't be a coincidence. Dasc most likely *is* connected to the attacks but since he's been here for the last four months, it's probably because someone was trying to find him by retracing his footsteps. Could it be his werewolves searching for their lost leader? That thought gives me an ache in my chest. All those people being bent and twisted to become so loyal to the man who stole them from their homes. It's disgusting.

Dasc snaps his fingers in my face. "Phoenix? Something on your mind?"

"What was your investment in Paris?" I ask.

"No, no. I answered your question last." He waggles his finger at me like I'm a naughty child. "You know how this works."

"*Fine.*"

"How is Genevieve doing? And don't just give me the most general answer you can come up with. I want details."

"I thought you didn't care."

"I never said that." He angles his head so he can peer at me through his eyebrows. "Details, Phoenix."

Well, Draco wanted me to bring up Genna to see Dasc's reaction. I remove my hands from the table, lean back in my chair, and cross my arms over my chest so I can better resist the urge to strangle Dasc.

"Physically, she's fantastic. Beat me in a run this morning. Mentally, by most outward appearances she seems like she's hardly been affected by being your lackey and captive for the majority of her life." I clench my jaw as I think of what happened last night. "But I've noticed the small things that set her apart. I've seen the way she looks at innocent things around her and is astounded that something *can* be innocent. She's constantly on alert, sees everything around her as a threat, and always thinks she's about to be under attack."

My hands shake as I continue. "You stripped away her childhood. You killed her mother and took her from her father. Now, even though she's been a victim in all this, she's being treated with suspicion because of what you turned her into. You ruined her life."

"I just took a page out of the dragon handbook."

After everything, that's what he gives me? My voice is strained as I try not to yell at him when I say, "Excuse me?"

"Look at the comparison, Phoenix. Really look between what I did and your own upbringing." He starts talking faster like he needs to get this all out in one go. "With a lack of parents, the child is removed from their own circumstances and brought to a community that raises them. Loyalty and affection is instilled in that child. They love the people that raised them, saved them from a lonely, destitute life. Then they are trained to fight, to know that the things outside their community are the enemy and they must defend their own kindred at all costs. And they do. They fight and die for that cause. Loyalty like that can't be bought or taught. It can only be nurtured from childhood, turning you into the absolute weapon you are today. You think I'm a monster for what I did? Why don't you take a closer look at—"

The door slams open and Draco sweeps in like a dark wind in his black suit. His dragon slit eyes are ablaze and he waves a hand over Draco's shackles. They spring open under his command and he lifts Dasc from his chair with one hand, yanking him effortlessly through the door.

"What are you doing?" I shout at the dragon's back and launch out of my seat.

"This meeting's over," Draco snarls, the angriest I've ever seen him. The air around him shimmers with heat and I take a step back, remembering his nickname as the Firestorm of Europe. He can literally set everything around him on fire.

Dasc starts laughing as he's dragged down the hall towards his cell. Two gargoyles appear out of nowhere to flank them. I stay where I am watching in disbelief as Witty comes out of the observation room and rolls to a stop beside me.

"Think about it!" Dasc shouts over his shoulder. "Who's the bigger fool? Genna and my wolves? Or you and the rest of the Blessed?"

7

A faint ringing fills my ears and I'm dizzy.

The comparisons are too similar and too true. Then Draco's furious interruption only expounded on Dasc's theory. Have the Blessed, myself included, been so easily manipulated like Dasc's werewolf communities? Have we been so blinded in our faithful devotion to the cause of the IMS that we've failed to see the truth in our past?

The first question Dasc ever asked me in the interrogations was how long it took Draco to appear after my parents were murdered.

A chill crawls up my spine.

Draco had a perfect and compelling response—he received a message that my parents had searched for Lycaon in the system and had come as fast as he could.

Or did he?

Dasc isn't the only one not to trust Draco. Scholar, a

dragon herself, has warned me about him and the intentions of the majestics. What more does she know but was unwilling to share at the time?

Another thought pops into my head, something Charlie had mentioned ages ago when we were talking about the Blessed. He said no Blessed has family and that Hawk and I are the rare exception. We're all loners with superpowers. Loners taken in and raised by the legendary community so places like Underground, the Vaults, and Dreamland are considered home.

So how do the dragons decide who becomes Blessed? Why only choose the loners, the drifters, the ones without familial attachments?

Dasc's rantings hit too close to home and open my eyes to a truth I don't want to consider.

"Phoenix?"

I blink. Witty grasps my hand and stares up at me with wide eyes from his wheelchair.

"I need to get out of here," I mutter and pull my hand out of his to navigate the hallways to the main exit of the penitent cells, electing not to use Draco's stupid hidden entrance. I don't care if I'm supposed to wait for his royal majesty to come back—I don't want to be anywhere near Draco right now.

Witty keeps pace with me, his arms pumping the wheels of his chair in even strokes. We reach the exit and the magical barrier drops to allow us through the massive doors. The usual centaur, unicorn, and gargoyles guard the foyer on the other side. I don't spare any of them a passing glance but keep moving, bursting through the next door and taking a hasty left.

"Phoenix, where are you going?" Witty pants behind me.

The cement walls of Underground surround me but instead of giving me that calming sense of being home, I suddenly feel trapped. I never had any choice in becoming what I am, did I? When Hawk and I were raised here, our only real expectation was to grow up to be IMS agents, to fight the good fight. But that was always Draco's plan, wasn't it? Take the orphans and turn them into weapons. I've been learning how to fight since I was a kid. I was so proud to be special.

"I need some air," I say and hurry past the market.

"Maybe you should—"

"*Witty,*" I snap and wheel about on him. "Leave me alone, okay?"

He finally lets his wheelchair roll to a halt and I continue on to the chutes. I ride one of the platforms to the top with a couple of agents and rush out the door up top. I can feel the agents' eyes on me as they split off to SUVs parked in the lot but they don't try to stop me. I keep walking, then walk some more, and walk a bit further on trails through a wooded area until I reach the Stone Arch Bridge. A cold wind cuts through my clothes since I'm not wearing a jacket. I hug my arms to myself and don't turn back.

I keep my head bowed as a few pedestrians and joggers pass me on the bridge over the Mississippi River. Eventually I stop, face northwest, and watch the St. Anthony waterfall tumble and foam.

The wind is strong over the open expanse above the water and it whips my hair about into a tangled mess. My face numbs and I run the back of my hand under my nose multiple times.

This mess has hit me hard in my core. I'm beginning to question everything I was ever taught when I was growing up in Underground. I remember agents would come up to me when we went on strolls for class around the city. They would say they needed every talented Blessed out in the field, that we were the backbone of the IMS to keep the monsters at bay. It's been drilled into my head that I'm needed. I always felt I got my powers in order to protect my brother, but in reality all I was ever meant to be was a destructive weapon wielded at the will of a majestic dragon.

"Hey."

I startle as Hawk walks up behind me. Figures he'd come find me. He passes over my winter jacket and I quickly throw it on to shelter in its thick padding.

"What are you doing out here?" I ask.

"Witty came and got me," he says and leans against the railing of the bridge. "Said you were upset."

"Understatement," I grumble and keep my eyes on the waterfall.

He tucks his hands into his pockets and crosses one ankle over the other. "You want to talk about it?"

I let out a sharp breath. "I just realized the difference between arrogance and wisdom, that's all."

"Umm, what?"

"Scholar said—never mind. You weren't paying attention when she said that. You were busy picking out that." I point to his chest where the coin pendant rests beneath his clothes.

"What exactly are we talking about?" he asks.

I shuffle forward to the railing until our shoulders are touching. He turns about so we're both facing the waterfall and tuck our heads in close to each other to make our conversation more private.

We have a long talk out on the bridge as the sun climbs higher in the sky and oblivious civilians pass by behind us. I tell my brother about Dasc, his comparison between the werewolves and the Blessed, about Scholar's warnings, her words about the organization we work for, about the suspicions I still carry about our parents' deaths, and the confusion I feel. When I finish, Hawk is quiet for a long time. The river surges beneath our feet and I watch the water without really seeing.

"First off, come here," Hawk says and gestures with both hands for me to turn towards him. I do and he gives me a bear hug. I tuck my chin into his shoulder savoring the comfort of my brother's embrace. "Now, I'm going to say a few things and you're probably going to argue with me, but just hear me out, okay?"

"Okay," I mumble into the fabric of his jacket.

"Dasc is manipulating you again."

I pull away from him with a frown. "But if you honestly—"

"What did I just say?" He raises both eyebrows critically. I roll my eyes and gesture with one hand for him to continue. "Thank you. And *if I honestly* think about what he said, I can see how twisted in the head he is. Phoenix, he tried to mimic something the dragons do because it works, but he's screwed up a few key ingredients. First off, he's the one murdering the families to secure his soldiers for the future or whatever. The dragons come in after the fact to give people like us a home. There's a difference between filling a need and murdering a bunch of people to create a need. Do you see what I'm getting at here?"

"Yeah," I grumble, "but what if the dragons *are* creating the need?"

"If that were true, don't you think someone would have figured that out by now? That dragons are going around killing people and taking their kids? Phoenix, Dasc *admitted* to killing our parents. Draco didn't do that."

"Draco still could have waited for the right moment to swoop in."

Hawk sighs and tucks his hands into his pockets. "Look, you can play the conspiracy theorist all day, but the fact of the matter is Draco saved us. Dasc killed our parents and Genna's mother. Which one do you think we should trust?"

"Okay, then what about Scholar's warnings, huh?"

"We shouldn't speculate until we can talk to her again and ask her ourselves," he says. "Maybe she meant to stay away from his cooking, who knows?"

I roll my eyes. "What are the chances we're going to see her again?"

"I have a feeling she'll be back. Besides, we'll probably need a refill soon." He pats his sternum where the pendant rests. "So I'm sure she'll pop up."

"Do you . . . do you feel like you need a refill?" I ask.

He gives me a sharp look. "Don't try and change the subject. I'm fine."

"Fine."

"And, as I was saying, given the right words you can twist anything to look like something else. You can say that the new headphones I got you for Christmas were a clever tactic to make you love me more because I gave you a gift to encourage greater feelings of affection."

I narrow my eyes. "Pixies, you *are* sinister. Your clever plan worked."

He gives an extremely over the top evil laugh you might hear in a children's cartoon and rubs his hands together. "Yes, it's all coming together. Soon now, I will have you in my evil twin clutches. Hey, can I borrow your .45?"

"What? No."

He gasps. "What? You mean you don't feel like you *owe* it to me because I gave you those headphones?" He wiggles his eyebrows at me and I slug him lightly in the shoulder.

"Yeah, I see your point."

"We always have choices," he says. "And after what happened to Mom and Dad, would you really want to do anything else with your life? Become a physical therapist? Dentist? Lawyer maybe?"

"No," I say quietly. "I guess not."

"Good, because I still want to be an agent despite all this and it'd be awfully lonely without my sister sticking around for the ride."

My shoulders droop and I hang my head. "I'm sorry," I grumble. "I overreacted. I'm not good at applying cool logic."

"Well, I'll always be here to be the cool logic machine." He grins and throws an arm around my shoulders to steer me towards Underground. "We should do something fun tonight. We haven't celebrated your victorious return yet. Movie night?"

"Sounds like a plan."

We walk step in step back to the city hidden beneath the

Mississippi River. Hawk talks to fill in the silence and take my mind off everything else. He tells me more about the grumpy fill-in agent in Moose Lake and various pranks Hawk played on him, like swapping out his orange juice for water mixed with cheese powder and taping a harmonica to the grill of his car. I'm cracking up by the time we reach the apartment.

Hawk is part way through a joke about a centaur bartender when we hear a crash on the other side of the door and shouting. Hawk rams his shoulder into the door and we break through together to find Genna standing in the middle of the living room, the coffee table overturned at her feet, glass shards from a broken dish scattered across the floor, and Jefferson shell-shocked in the kitchen. We all freeze, eyes flickering between each other as Genna pants where she stands, a menacing grimace on her face.

Words escape me but Hawk manages to recover from the surprise fast enough to crack a joke. "Uh, house cleaning?"

Which is apparently the wrong thing to say. Genna immediately stalks out to the balcony and Jefferson glares at us before stomping after his daughter. Hawk makes to follow but I grab his arm to keep him in place.

"Should we go?" I whisper.

"What?" He looks at me like I'm crazy. "She's been attacking our stuff. I want to know what's going on."

He stares at my hand until I let go reluctantly. We sneak towards the balcony to witness the conversation going on between Jefferson and Genna.

"There's nothing I can do," Jefferson says. "I'm sorry but I'm just a field agent."

"I didn't go through hell and manage to escape only for them not to believe me," she growls. "They're all fools."

Hawk dares to interrupt. "What happened?"

Both Barneses pin him with their matching dark eyes.

"They don't believe me," Genna says. "They don't believe that Echidna is back. Apparently I'm not to be trusted until I prove myself. I've already been *branded*." She holds up her hand to show a probation ring on her finger before letting her arm fall limp to her side. "As if giving me the serum wasn't enough, now I must *contain myself*."

My eyes are drawn to Hawk but I quickly look away. A spike of fear goes through me at the mere thought of Hawk having to undergo the same—both the serum and a probation ring to track his transformations. Poison and shackles.

"They want to keep her here, too," Jefferson adds quietly. "They won't let me take her home yet."

"Why?" Hawk and I ask in unison.

"Dasc, basically. Worried about his influence and what she might do once granted more freedom."

Well, that sounds like it came straight out of the mouth of Draco. You know, I get being cautious, but refusing to allow Genna to finally go home and be free? That's unacceptable.

I rip off my jacket, toss it onto the couch, and march for the door. "I'll be back."

"Where are you going?" Jefferson calls.

"To make this right."

It doesn't take me long to reach headquarters. I pause briefly to tell the secretary I need to see Director Knox. I'm told he's currently busy and I can't see him. When I ask to see Draco, I'm told he's also unavailable. Great.

"Thanks," I say with false pleasantness. "I'll make my way to records then."

She looks confused but doesn't say anything as I march off into the building. I'm not sure what I'm doing but I'm going to make it work somehow. Following the familiar path through headquarters and avoiding eye contact with the agents I pass, I end up in front of the door to the stone courtyard and the strange black arch. I hesitate in the doorway, wondering vaguely if I'll get in trouble being here, before stepping quietly into the vacant courtyard. There's no sign of Draco but this has been his favorite haunt lately.

I glance over my shoulder and up at the windows on the second floor but don't find anyone watching me. Inching forward with a foreboding feeling that I shouldn't be here, I approach one end of the black stone arch and gaze at the golden dragon script etched into its glossy surface. As before, I sense a hum from the stone and the pulse of power. I stretch out a hand. My fingers hover an inch away. A strange force lingers a hairsbreadth away, different air, different earth, different sky. What is this thing? What does it—

"You aren't supposed to be in here."

I gasp and steal my hand away from the arch before its pulse draws me in. Director Knox stands in the doorway with his hands clasped behind his back. He's in his usual pristine suit, every bit the suave professional. Although I would expect a scowl, he doesn't seem nearly as annoyed with me as he used to before I stopped Dasc in Moose Lake. He must have warmed up to me at last.

"I'm sorry," I say and step further away from the arch. "I was looking for Draco. Or you, actually, sir."

"Yes, I suspected you might find your way here." He moves into the courtyard, eyes glued to the arch. "I already spoke to Draco about the incident with Dasc."

"Oh. Well, that's not why I'm here."

His gaze drops to me and he rolls his shoulders. "Genna."

"Genna." I close the distance across the courtyard. "You have to let her go home."

"I *have* to?"

"I would respectfully request that she be allowed to go home."

"Junior Agent Mason, you of all people should understand why we can't allow that," he says.

"I, of all people, know the importance of family and home," I reply more sharply than I mean to. I roll my lips and clear my throat. "Sir, she hasn't seen her home in over fourteen years. She needs this. If you hold home away from her now, you'll never build any trust with her. You'll only make Dasc's ramblings sound legitimate. We aren't supposed to be her enemy. Please."

"And Rosalyn?" he says. "What would you have us do about her?"

"She clearly needs time to sort things out. I'm sure having her brother here will help."

He taps his foot and purses his lips. This indecision is uncharacteristic for him. I wait breathless, hoping that my plea has made a difference.

"You realize your orders haven't changed," he says.

"I do."

"Her probation ring stays on and I expect frequent reports from you."

"Does that mean—"

"Yes," he sighs. "Draco isn't going to like it, but you're right. If we treat people like the enemy, we tend to make enemies."

I stand there with my mouth agape. "Well . . . great. I—I didn't realize—"

"It'd be so easy?" A smile touches his lips. "Let's just say you weren't the only one with reservations. I only needed to have my own thoughts confirmed by a reasonable, outside voice."

"I don't know about *reasonable*, sir."

He laughs, a deep rumbling sound. I don't know if I've ever heard it before.

"I'll make the necessary arrangements," he says. "And Mason?"

"Yes?"

"Keep sharp. I expect you back in May for the trials."

I crack a grin. "Yes, sir."

There's a spring in my step as I hustle out of the building, glad I don't bump into Draco on my way out, and hurry to the apartment. Hawk's on the balcony keeping any eye out for me so I wave once I'm in range. I take the steps two at a time and open the door with a grand sweeping entrance.

Genna and Jefferson look up from where they're sitting on the couch. Someone's swept up the glass shards since I left and rightened the coffee table.

"Pack your bags," I announce to the room. "We're all going home."

"Seriously?" Hawk asks.

"Yup! Director Knox changed his mind."

Genna rises from her spot on the couch. "You convinced him? How?"

"I . . ." My smile fades a bit. "I, uhh . . . well, ever since I helped take down Dasc, he values my opinion. And to be honest, he didn't think it was fair either."

"But he's the director," Genna presses on. "If he didn't think it was fair, why did he order that I stay here in the first place?"

Jefferson takes his daughter's hand. "The majestic dragons are technically the leaders of the IMS. One could easily override an order from the director. Let's not look a gift horse in the mouth, okay? If Phoenix managed to get us a ride home, let's take it before anyone changes their mind."

She nods but doesn't look anywhere near done prying into this. It's not easy to pull the wool over her eyes. She's too sharp like her father.

It doesn't take any of us long to get ready to leave. We've hardly even unpacked the bags we've been using. Before we know it, we're taking the long chutes up to the surface and to an SUV waiting for us in the parking lot of the power park. I take the wheel and Hawk sits shotgun so the father-daughter pair can sit and talk in the row behind us. We move out of Minneapolis and into the quiet countryside as Jefferson points out things to Genna. Now that we're almost there, I feel terribly anxious to get home to Moose Lake.

It's overcast when we finally take the off ramp, drive through Moose Lake on the main drag, and reach Soldier Road.

"We're home," Jefferson says and I catch Genna's achingly desperate expression in the rearview mirror.

We rumble down the driveway and come to a stop in front of the small, weathered cabin. The roof has been patched recently—a day project at the hands of Hawk apparently—and the barn looms over it like a mama bear next to its shaggy cub. It probably doesn't look like much to a stranger but to me it's home. I step out of the SUV into a muddy puddle and haul my bag over my shoulder.

Genna exits slowly with wide eyes fixated on the cabin. "I never thought I'd see this place again."

Her father is at her side in an instant and they move as a pair into the cabin. Hawk and I remain a few steps behind to let them have their moment as we carry in the bags. The way Genna looks at the cabin—like it's a mansion—does some good for the ache in my chest. It makes me feel like I've done something right. I suffered Dasc and vampires and lamia to make this moment happen. I'm smiling without realizing it and Hawk nudges me with his elbow.

"Good work, Fifi," he whispers before setting the bags on the floor in the kitchen.

There's no sign of Mr. Fill-in Agent except for a note left behind that says *I'm gone and not coming back. Good riddance.* With that out of the way, the buzz of excitement infects us all and carries us through rearranging the living spaces to accommodate Genna's return home. We agree Genna will take Hawk's bed and he'll move his things into the loft of the barn. Jefferson and I will stay where we are. While Genna stops in the bathroom and I tug out some spare clothes for her, Jefferson comes over to lay a hand on my shoulder.

"Phoenix, can I ask you a favor?" he whispers.

I set the clothes aside to give him my full attention. "Yeah, sure. Name it."

"Stick close to Genna when you can. I think your . . . *influence* will help her."

Meaning, my anti-werewolf-crazy blood will keep any instinctual crap from getting in the way of her recovery. I can handle that. In fact, it gives me an excuse to stay closer to her in order to follow through on my orders. That thought sours in my head and I grimace without meaning to.

"What?" Jefferson asks sharply. "Is there a problem with that?"

"No, no, sorry," I say and try to amend what he thought my expression meant. Pixies, this is going to be a bigger headache than I thought, isn't it? "I was thinking of something else. I would be more than happy to help however I can. Seriously."

His scowl fades but doesn't go away entirely. "Thanks."

He claps me twice on the back before moving off. I set out the clothes on the lower bunk and return to the kitchen to find Hawk shuffling through the fridge.

"So, uh, Mr. Fill-in ate most of the food," he announces.

I poke him in the ribs. "Liar."

"So, someone ate most of the food," he revises. "Any requests? I'll go hit up the grocery store."

"I'll come with," I volunteer. I'm getting a vibe from Genna and Jefferson that they want to have a chat in their old home together privately. Genna's sitting on top of the table and twisting a bit of string between her fingers, head bowed. Jefferson stands next to her like a bodyguard.

We put together a list and say a quick goodbye before escaping to the SUV. I put the vehicle into gear and we pull away.

"Hey, so who was this Agent Fill-in?" I ask. "I thought I was finally going to meet him."

"Well, actually, you already have, and he probably fled as soon as he heard we were coming back," he says casually and shrugs. "It was Cobb."

I hit the brakes hard at the end of the driveway and we lurch against our seat belts.

"*Cobb?*"

"Cobb."

"*The* Cobb?

He shrugs again and holds up his hands. "Do we know a different one?"

"The one that left us high and dry at Werevine Pharmaceutical? The one that got suspended and blamed us for it? The one I'm sure that's been gunning for us?"

"Yes!"

I slug him in the shoulder and he winces. "Why didn't you ever tell me he was the fill-in agent?"

"Because I knew you'd freak out! Geez, you psycho!" He rubs at his shoulder and shoots me daggers. "I knew that if *you* knew I was stuck with Cobb, you'd be worrying about that and not focusing one hundred percent on finding Genna and the others in Scotland. I knew you were already worrying enough about me because of—well, because of my issues. I didn't want to add to that."

I lean back in my seat and stare at my brother. Pixies, I can imagine Cobb must have given Hawk a hard time. That guy knows how to hold a grudge. Why on earth would the

IMS assign Cobb to work with one of us when Director Knox knows he hates us? And Hawk put up with it, made me think it was just some random, lazy agent that he was having fun pulling pranks on this whole time. He must have been miserable.

"What?" Hawk asks and I realize I've been staring at him overlong.

I face the windshield again and roll my palms on the steering wheel. "Nothing."

It's a quiet trip to the local grocery store with nothing but the oldies station playing between us. When I shift the SUV into park, we remain seated for a moment as we unbuckle.

"Did you really swap out his orange juice for cheese water?" I ask.

Hawk's smile returns in full force. "You bet I did. I also dipped his cigarettes in that stuff you put on a toothache. His mouth went numb. You should have seen him trying to chew me out when his lips wouldn't work."

I laugh harder than I have in a long time as we exit the SUV and walk across the parking lot into the store. It's not terribly busy inside and we take our time browsing the cereal boxes, swapping inappropriate jokes in the fruit section, and riding on the cart down empty isles. It feels good to goof off just for the heck of it. Life is normal again if only for a little while.

"We are *not* getting that," I tell Hawk as he holds out a jar of pickled pigs' feet he found on a shelf.

He wiggles the jar at me. "Aww, look at those itty bitty toes! Doesn't that stir your appetite?"

"It's stirring something all right." I mime throwing up

into the cart. A woman near the end of the aisle abruptly changes direction and walks away.

Hawk puts the jar back and we giggle all the way to the frozen food section. We stick our heads in one of the freezers together to pick out a container of ice cream, fight over Rocky Road and Moose Tracks, and end up pulling out both. When we close the fogged glass door, we both startle at a woman standing there with the pigs' feet jar held in her hands.

"Sure you won't change your mind?" she says. "They're quite sumptuous if you have the heart to try them."

The pint of ice cream slips from my hands and hits the floor with a loud thud.

There's no mistaking that face. The sharp contours of the cheekbones, the tightly pursed lips, the dark hair pulled into a bun at the nape of her neck, the intelligent eyes looking at me critically, her stick thin frame hidden beneath a tan trench coat.

"Scholar?"

"Obviously."

8

Scholar had said she would come back for me. I didn't expect it would be at the grocery store with her holding a jar of pickled pigs' feet. What a strange dragon.

She sets the jar in our cart and brushes past Hawk, whispering something in his ear before pattering down the aisle in small heeled boots. I move to follow but my brother grabs my arm and keeps me in place.

"What did she say to you?" I whisper.

"We're supposed to finish shopping then meet her outside," he says under his breath. "We can't talk here."

"Why not?"

He rolls his eyes. "We're in the middle of a grocery store, Fifi. It's not exactly private. And there's that." He inclines his head towards a surveillance camera on the ceiling overlooking the aisle.

"Okay. Fine. But this ice cream's going to melt."

Taking both pints, my brother tosses them into the freezer. We make a hasty exit through the checkout line, Hawk not chatting up the cashier for once, and stuff the groceries into our SUV. As soon as we put the cart away, we hop into the vehicle and wait in our seats, watching the lot around us with eagle eyes. Somehow, despite being alert, Scholar still manages to slip past us and slides into the second row of seats.

"My, isn't this nostalgic," she quips. "Phoenix, if you would kindly take us out of the city."

"We aren't heading to your house are we?" I ask.

"Don't be foolish, dear. We both know that house is being monitored."

I bob my head to the side. That's true. Even though it's not supposed to be readily known, I discovered there's at least one IMS agent watching Scholar's mansion at all times. Scholar said it before and it's only become more apparent—everyone wants to find her. The worst part is I still don't know why.

Scholar directs me towards the interstate but instead of getting on, we cross over and drive through the parking lot of the state park. She guides me to a road heading in the opposite direction of the camper parking, away from where I had my showdown with Dasc last October on the shores of the lake.

"Yes, this should do nicely," Scholar says once we reach the end of the dirt road.

I throw the vehicle into park and swivel about in my seat to talk to her but she's already moving out the door. Hawk and I swiftly unbuckle and trail her into the woods. Where on earth are we going? I look to my brother but he shrugs.

Scholar stops in the middle of a well-worn deer trail. "A moment, if you'd please."

She extends her hands palm out to either side and turns into a statue that way with her back towards us. For a second I think she's about to shift into her dragon form but she remains human in appearance as a faint hum fills my ears and a pulse races over my skin. The air wavers all around us and a few birds fly off at the odd disturbance. We wait a good thirty seconds before Scholar lowers her hands and the strange feeling disappears.

She spins about on her toes in the soft ground and there's a feline quality to the movement. The same way she moves as a dragon—lithe and fluid.

"We are alone," she announces. "Straight to business then. I see you are both alive and well despite your own efforts."

Hawk smirks but I glower at the human-looking dragon in front of me.

"You've been keeping tabs on us?" I ask.

"Clearly. Your brother has been flirting with death by instigating an old fool while you have been dancing around Whispers and lamia." She clucks her tongue. "It's truly a wonder you two have survived for as long as you have."

"Wow, that's pretty creepy," Hawk says. "Exactly how close have you been watching us?"

She cocks her head in his direction. "The harmonica on the car was my favorite."

He swallows and then mutters to me, "Remind me to close the shade on the bathroom window."

"I also know that you—" Her focus shifts to me. "—were the only one to withstand the onslaught of the leviathan scream. Your abilities are becoming more powerful."

"Powerful *enough*, do you think?" I ask and don't even question how she knows about that bit. I'm quickly learning not to underestimate what she's capable of.

"Only one way to find out." She whips a syringe out of the pocket of her trench coat and spins it between her fingers.

Scholar has me take a seat on a fallen log as she takes a blood sample from my arm. Once she's done, she beckons Hawk closer and motions with an outstretched hand to pass over the pendant. He tugs it out from under his clothes and places it in her palm. We look on silently as she pops it open with the press of her finger and adds a few drops of fresh blood from the syringe before closing it up and returning it to my brother.

"Now then," she says and rises, brushing off her trench coat. "I haven't returned solely for the purpose of collecting your blood. As I understand it, both of you will be participating in the trials very soon to become full-fledged agents."

"We head to Underground in May," Hawk says.

"Then I hope you understand the danger both of you are in."

My brother and I exchange a glance, questioning if either of us knows what she's talking about but we're both as confused as I feel. Scholar shakes her head and crosses her arms over her chest, rapping her fingers on her biceps.

"Each prospective agent not only undergoes the rigors of the trials but must pass the evaluation stage. You are tested psychologically, physically, and a full examination is conducted of your blood."

Of course. Figures.

"Not only will they discover Hawk does not have

evidence of the serum in his system, but there is a great chance they will discover your capabilities, Phoenix." She pauses a moment to let that sink in. "It is a rare occurrence, but some junior agents have gone through these examinations only to disappear shortly after."

"You're joking," I say, unable to stop myself.

"I have witnessed it myself."

"Back before you were being hunted?" I ask and narrow my eyes. What do we *really* know about Scholar other than the fact Jefferson trusts her? "Why exactly is everyone after you, Scholar? What did you do?"

"Secrets are secrets for a reason," she growls. "Meaning you don't tell everyone you know what they are."

"How are we supposed to trust you if we don't know a thing about you?" I argue. I'm sick of playing games and being lied to. I get enough of it from Dasc.

She pulls back her shoulders. "You do not have to trust me and I do not have to prove myself to you."

"Then maybe I should just call Draco right now and tell him where you are."

Hawk grabs my arm. "Phoenix, can I talk to you for a second?" He drags me backwards and I stumble along until we're fifteen feet away from Scholar who promptly becomes very interested in a chickadee on a branch above her head.

"*What?*" I hiss and yank my arm out of my brother's grip.

"What's gotten into you?" he whispers. "Scholar is helping us. She's helping *me*. She's kept our secrets. Why are you trying to make her angry?"

"Aren't you the least bit curious why she's afraid of being found by the IMS?"

"Of course I am, but I'm not about to go aggravate a dragon." He grabs my shoulder roughly. "Give her the benefit of the doubt for the time being, okay? Jefferson trusts her. He must have his reasons. And you're still upset about Draco and Dasc."

"That's not what this is about."

"Yeah, whatever. Chill out. It sounded like she was about to help us get through the trials. You want that, don't you?"

I scowl at him but eventually nod.

"Good." He pats me on the back and we return to Scholar together.

"Family meeting adjourned?" she asks.

Hawk keeps a hand on my shoulder and I take that as a sign he's taking control. Fine. He can do what he wants.

"What do you know about the evaluations?" Hawk asks. "What can we do to pass them without suspicion?"

"A small bit of deception may be necessary in order for Phoenix to pass, but the answer is quite simple and utterly difficult for you, my dear." For once, her expression loses that sharp edge and if I didn't know any better, I'd say she looks apologetic for what she's about to say next. "You'll need to take the serum."

The statement hits both of us hard. The air leaves my lungs and Hawk's whole body tenses beside me. No. Not this. Not this for my brother. I may not know what the serum feels like but I know what it does to my brother. I've seen the fear in his eyes whenever he's been asked to take it. I've witnessed the lengths he's willing to go in order to avoid it. I heard the desperation in his voice when he confessed he either needed a cure or there was no fight left in him if he had to take the serum again.

"There has to be another way." I step closer to Scholar, willing her to understand, ready to beg if I have to. "There has to."

"I'm afraid there is not," she says. "The only consolation I can give you is that he does not have to take it indefinitely. He needs it in his system only long enough for its presence to be detected when they take a blood sample."

I lay a hand on Hawk's back as he hunches over and braces his hands on his knees.

"They only take the one sample?" I ask. "That's it? So, he only needs to take it once?"

"Yes, but the effect of the serum lingers for days. He will be in duress until the effects wear off."

He hasn't taken it since we were children and has never shared the true extent of his pain. I don't know how strongly it will affect him when it comes time for him to take it again. From his current reaction, I suspect he's thinking the same thing.

He slowly straightens but keeps his eyes averted.

"Maybe there's another way," I say. "I could cure him. Right now."

"A worthy goal but I think we both know you are not yet up to the task," Scholar says. "You might also find some difficulty in explaining how Hawk is no longer infected. The obvious choice remains clear. The serum must be taken."

Hawk swallows audibly and I keep my focus on the prickly yellow grass beneath my feet as I stave off a bout of guilt. I should be able to do more. Will I ever be enough?

"You also tend to expend all your energy in frightful bursts," she continues. "Your magic is a surge but you must learn to focus it into a guided force with pinpoint accuracy."

"I don't have a clue what you're talking about," I say.

"Let me put it in words you will understand then."

"Please do."

"You have absolutely no control."

"What?" I protest. "I have *some* control."

"If you were a fire sprite trying to light a candle, you would have burned down the whole of Moose Lake by now."

"She has a point," Hawk says rather unhelpfully. I shoot daggers at him but he shrugs. "Every time you've tried using your gift, you completely burn yourself out. There's got to be a better way of doing it."

"There isn't another way *to* do it," I argue.

Scholar clicks her tongue and starts to circle around me like examining a poor, sad unicorn gone to seed.

"We will have to work on that attitude *and* posture," she says. "Or else you will not make it through the trials at all. So, when I am able to elude those hunting me and return here, I would like to train you."

"Train me?"

She completes her circle and takes my hand in hers, flips it palm up to inspect something I can't see, then lets go again to peer into my face.

"When I call," she says, "I expect you to answer and meet me here to work on your abilities. After all, raw talent alone is worthless. Just as you are training your mind and body for the mental and physical exertions of the trials, you must also be honing the magic in your blood."

That sounds difficult—and exciting. I've never been trained by a dragon before.

"But we must be mindful," she continues and narrows

her eyes. "There are more than IMS agents and your run of the mill monsters searching for me."

"Epsilon." The lamia that got away.

"She is still out there biding her time in the dark. But she is not my only concern. It did not pass me by that Genna has at last returned home."

"You're suspicious of her, too? Pixies, everyone keeps looking at her like a villain." I'm about to say more before I catch myself. I'm not supposed to tell anyone about Draco's orders to keep an eye on Genna. And I don't know Scholar, not really. What is her interest in all of this? Why help us?

"Hey," Hawk says and interrupts my thoughts. "*I* don't look at her like she's a villain."

I roll my eyes. "No, you just *look* at her."

Scholar clears her throat. "I merely have my reservations. Dasc is loath to give up any resources at his disposal. If he guided you to Genna, then he must believe he can use her in some manner even if she does not want to be his instrument. But that is enough talk. If you are gone too long the Barneses will inevitably become suspicious."

She starts to walk away so I follow after.

"Wait!" I call. "I still have so many questions. Why did you warn me against Draco? What do you know about the Blessed?"

"All in due course," she says without pausing.

"What about Echidna?"

Scholar immediately comes to a halt and twists about to pin me with a terrifying and furious gaze where I stand tangled in the brush behind her.

"What did you say?" she asks hardly above a whisper.

"Echidna." I wrestle my way through some branches

and thorny bushes to get closer to her. "Genna said that's who is leading the other side of Dasc's war. She and the rest of the kidnapped werewolves were trained as soldiers to fight Echidna and her monsters. The lamia are supposedly the forward guard."

Scholar closes her eyes and tilts her face towards the sky. The presence and strength she always carries herself with melts away and she becomes a lonely woman beneath a bare forest, lost and afraid. But the vulnerability lasts for only a few seconds before she rolls her shoulders and transforms in front of me, her clothes and body meshing and changing shape until she stands on all fours in her dragon form. Her long tail curls around her vibrant green body and the spikes along her back bristle.

"Meet me here tomorrow at noon," she says with a reptilian snarl. "We have work to do."

Without any explanation, she barrels into the woods at full speed, branches snapping in her wake. I stay where I am and watch her disappear. Scholar wouldn't have reacted that strongly if the whole Echidna thing was a lie, would she? Could it be true that the mother of monsters, the biggest bad to put all other bads to shame, is back from the grave?

"We should get going," Hawk says.

"Yeah." I turn around and we follow the deer trail to where the SUV is parked. I sit shotgun this time as Hawk takes the wheel. Neither of us speaks. News of Hawk having to take the serum again is still weighing on both our minds. Not only do we have to worry about Genna, Echidna, and actually passing the trials like everyone else, but being discovered for what we are and what we've done. We both have secrets buried out in the woods. Literally.

No. No time to think about that—about the terrible things we did to hide what Hawk did to Ashley's dog. A shiver runs through me.

"Do you think we can do this?" I ask. "Do you *want* to do this?"

The rumble of the SUV is the only reply I get.

We return to the cabin in short order and haul in the groceries to find no one's home. A spike of anxiety hits me. Maybe we shouldn't have left Genna alone with Jefferson. I mean, she sure seems to love her father but after all the warnings I've been getting from dragons to look out for her, I can't help but worry.

Leaving the groceries behind, I hurry to the barn. If they left, the Green Monster would be gone. If it's still here, then . . . then I don't know what to think. Hawk follows in my wake and we find the door to the barn ajar. Odd. I nod silently to it and Hawk motions for me to tread carefully as he himself takes cautious steps forward to minimize the sound. I lead the way and lean slowly in through the open door.

The Green Monster is right where it always is. The tarp is thrown off to the side, though, and the hood is propped open. The clink of metal catches my attention so I lean in farther.

What I see makes me stop my advance and retreat into the shadow of the door to watch. Jefferson is showing Genna his arrangement of tools and carries over a tin of oil to the Green Monster. They're both smiling and carefree in the midst of a quiet conversation I don't want to interrupt, yet can't help but listen to. Hawk nudges me in the back so I shuffle further out so he can see what I see.

"Yeah, and you used to drop my wrenches under the car all the time," Jefferson says and laughs. It isn't the sort he's used with me and Hawk. No, this comes from deep down, a sound I didn't even know he could make. Genna is changing everything about him and delving into the rich joy he buried somewhere far beneath.

"We'd find them eventually," Genna says with a grin and leans in under the open hood to watch her father add fresh oil. "Hey, remember that old bike you got me for my birthday?"

Jefferson's voice is muffled from where he hunches over. "Yeah, the pink one with the tassels. You used to pretend it was a unicorn you were riding into battle and nearly ran over the neighbor's cat."

"I almost forgot." She grins and flips a wrench end over end in her hand. "Mom got so mad."

A subtle shift sweeps over the pair of them and they fall silent. Jefferson clears his throat and caps the tin of oil before stowing it along the wall next to his rows of tools.

"I miss her," he says as he wipes off his hands with a dirty rag.

I step quietly out of the doorway and Hawk slides over with me, both of us leaning against the outside wall of the barn. We really shouldn't be eavesdropping but I want to know. Jefferson has never spoken of his wife except in mere passing to explain his relentless hunt for Dasc. That monster not only took his daughter away but murdered his wife. I'm still close enough to the door so I peek inside.

"I never really understood at the time that she was Blessed," Genna says. She closes the hood of the Green Monster and takes a seat on top. If Hawk or I tried something like that, Jefferson would chew us out. "She used to make the flowers dance."

"Yeah, she, uh . . ." Jefferson takes a shaky breath and scratches at his temple, giving himself a moment to collect himself. "Your mother had a special talent for botany. No one around town could figure out how she always won the vegetable competition at the county fair. She made the most beautiful gardens."

"There aren't any gardens here anymore," Genna says so quietly I almost don't catch her words.

"A lot of things fell apart after—after everything that happened. I couldn't . . ." The pain in his voice makes me start to tear up. I remember the state Jefferson was in when we first got here, and that was after years of him being by himself without hope of ever finding his daughter again. The fridge was full of alcohol, he hardly slept, and he certainly kept himself secluded.

"You look so much like your mother," Jefferson says. "I'm glad you didn't get your looks from me. You're beautiful, Genna. Inside and out. You're beautiful."

I can't see Genna's expression from my spot but she gets off the hood of the 442 and walks over to wrap her father in a hug. He cups the back of her head like one might a small child and holds her close.

"I've got you, baby girl," he says and a spike goes through my heart.

We shouldn't be intruding on this. These aren't our memories to share. I jerk my head towards the cabin and Hawk and I quietly make our exit. We take our time putting the groceries away and busying ourselves making supper for the four of us, which really just entails throwing a couple of pizzas into the oven. Eventually Jefferson and Genna come in to eat. We take our pizza slices on paper plates and pile into Jefferson's room to sit around his old tube TV to watch *The Princess Bride.* We laugh together and lounge around but Genna is focused intently on the movie as if she's never seen a movie before in her life. Come to think of it, maybe she hasn't since she was a little girl.

When the credits roll, we clean up our mess and split off to get ready for bed. It's a little early for sleeping but we're all still tired from the time change coming back to the States. I grow nervous when Hawk heads out to the barn to sleep on the spare cot and I'm left alone with Genna in the room I usually share with my brother. Jefferson lingers in the kitchen as if afraid Genna will disappear again if he doesn't stick close. In time, he turns off the light, wishes us goodnight, and heads into his own room.

While I climb into the top bunk, Genna stretches on the floor in an old pair of sweatpants of mine and a blue t-shirt. She continues to do that in the dark for some time as I stare up at the ceiling, unsure if I'm supposed to start a conversation or something since we're both still awake and in the same room. I'll have to ask Hawk for pointers on awkward encounters in the morning.

But Genna doesn't talk and neither do I. Eventually I start to nod off when movement nearby startles me awake again.

Genna stands on her tip toes with a hand braced on the edge of my mattress only a foot from my face. Her dark eyes glitter like the glossy finish of Draco's black stone arch—powerful and menacing. Although dark, with the light of the floodlight outside that Hawk forgot to turn off, it's obvious she's furious about something.

She leans in closer until I can feel her breath on my face. Everything about her puts me on edge and I prop myself up, in the same motion sliding a hand under my pillow for my mother's gun. Draco's and Scholar's warnings thunder in my head.

My gun's not there.

Genna draws up her other hand to point the barrel of my .45 at my chest.

"We're going to have a chat," she growls.

9

I consider shouting for Jefferson. Dang it, things had been going so well up until this point. Genna had been proving Draco wrong every moment she laughed with us, shared heartfelt memories and experiences with her father, and gave up all the secret locations for the werewolves.

"What are you doing?" I keep my voice quiet. I don't want to spook her and end up getting shot.

"How long have you been working for Dasc?"

I blink. "Excuse me?"

"Don't play coy. The IMS never would have sent a *junior* agent with a team to find me and the others." Despite the situation we're currently in, she appears rather calm accusing me and keeping a gun leveled at my chest. "There had to be something unique about you, something only you could do. The IMS couldn't have followed the clues and avoided the traps I left behind without inside knowledge.

Dasc led you to me. And the only reason you would be there on the hunt is because he wanted you to be."

"Genna, you don't understand." I judge the distance between the gun and the reach of my arm. I'm in an awkward position but I might be able to take the gun away in a surprise motion if I try.

"Everything Dasc does, he does for a reason." She draws away from the mattress and out of my reach as if she knows exactly what I might try to do. "He wouldn't lead you to me and hand me over into IMS custody for no reason. He wants me here and he wants you here, but I'm never going to play his games again. I'm home. And I'll do anything I have to in order to keep my father safe, including stopping you."

Oh, boy. "Listen to me, please." I slowly push myself up into a sitting position, careful not to make any sudden movements, and hold my hands out to the sides to show I don't mean to make a move—not that I have a lot of options at this point. "I don't work for Dasc. I'd kill that smug piece of hydra dung if I could. Pixies, I almost *did* kill him."

She doesn't lower the gun. "Yet he's still alive."

"Yeah, I miscalculated the amount of wolfsbane bullets I needed to plug him with," I say dryly. "He killed my parents. He cursed my brother. Why would I ever help him?"

"The IMS seems to have the same opinion about me," Genna growls. "I have no reason to help him but they think I've got a hidden agenda. I'm just returning the favor. You need to *convince* me, Phoenix."

"Or what? You'll shoot me?" I really don't like having a gun aimed at me. It's even more of an insult considering it's *my* gun.

"I'll do what I have to," she says and I don't doubt her for a second. "Not all of the choices given to us are easy like the fairy tale world you live in. Sometimes there are nothing but bad choices. Choosing the lesser of two evils doesn't make me an evil person."

"I never said it did."

"*Convince me* you're not working for him." She gestures with the barrel of the gun for emphasis—as if she really needs to make herself more plain.

I know everyone's been telling me that Genna shouldn't find out about Dasc's and my little arrangement but I don't think they ever anticipated this scenario happening.

"You want the truth? Fine." I lean over the edge of the mattress towards her. "Dasc healed, miracles be damned. He survived our encounter and when the IMS tried to interrogate him, he wouldn't say a word. We had him. Jefferson finally had a way to find you and everyone else who's been taken, but Dasc was silent. Then I got a call telling me to head down straight away only to find Dasc had changed his mind. He'd talk. Oh, yeah. Big surprise. Great news. But he'd only talk to me."

I scoot closer and Genna backs up a pace, unrelenting. I need her to understand the nightmare this has been for me.

"That cocky schweinhund tried to have my brother kill me," I say and jab my thumb at my chest. "He ripped away my family, but I owed it to Jefferson to try and find you. So, I went and talked to him. First thing he does is rub the death of my parents in my face." I'm beginning to breathe hard trying to keep my anger in check and not shout. "He brought me there to torment me because I beat him. Then he *still* didn't want to cooperate straight away. We had to deal with vampires and lamia before I finally made a deal to find you. I made—"

Crap. I've said too much. The pact I made with Dasc isn't common knowledge and shouldn't be considering how easily it could be used against me.

"Made what?" Genna asks.

"I . . ."

"Made *what?* What bargain could you have possibly made?"

My shoulders droop as I feel the weight of it upon me. My palms get sweaty the way they always do when I think too long and hard about Dasc. Even with Genna pointing a gun at me, I hadn't starting sweating until now.

I heave a sigh and hold her gaze. "I didn't know what I was doing. I didn't know until the moment I did it."

"What are you talking about?"

"A life debt." Draco's going to kill me for letting this slip. "I promised Dasc a life debt in order to secure your safe return and as many others as we could get."

For the first time, the barrel of the gun drops an inch but not enough to make me comfortable.

"You did that for me?" Genna asks quietly. "For someone you couldn't even remember? Someone you didn't know?"

"Yes."

"Why?"

"Because Jefferson means a great deal to me, and you mean the world to him."

That hangs between us for a solid fifteen seconds before Genna asks, "But why you? Why did Dasc single you out to be his confidant?"

"I've been wondering that since this all started."

The gun lowers until Genna holds it loosely at her side. The tight knot in my chest starts to loosen but she still has the weapon in her hand and can draw it up again at any moment if she wants.

"Were you really going to shoot me?" I ask.

"To protect my father? Of course."

Oh, that's super comforting. I guess offing me is practically a non-issue because *obviously* she would have killed me without a second thought if I was Dasc's puppet and putting Jefferson in danger.

Genna swivels the gun around in her hand and holds it out handle first to me. "All those times you disappeared in Underground, you were going to talk to him weren't you?"

"Yes." One out of two anyway, but there's no way I'm going to tell her about Draco's orders to keep an eye on her—with good reason I've discovered. I take my gun and pull back the slide to pop the bullet out of the chamber. *Pixies*, she really was going to shoot me.

Without another word, Genna slips into the lower bunk. I lean over the edge of my mattress to make sure she's not readying a knife to dig into my back or something, but she pulls up the covers and rolls onto her side to face the wall. She doesn't even bother to offer an apology. That's part of her character though, isn't it? She clearly doesn't have a problem with making a tough, merciless decision and if she's willing to go the distance, why apologize for it?

Genna may seem like a loose cannon but it doesn't slip by me that she waited until now to confront me. Every other time we've been together, we've been in secure IMS facilities with other people close by, not counting Jefferson and Hawk. If she had her doubts from the beginning, she hid them well enough that I never even suspected she would draw a gun on me. She waited until we were out in the countryside, alone at night, after having discovered where my weapon was in order to subdue me.

She's not crazy. She's lethal.

I don't try to sleep. It's a little hard to when there's the threat of your bunkmate trying to kill you in the middle of the night. For a while I consider her hatred of Dasc and how she's convinced me of that hatred. She's willing to kill me if I threaten her family by mere association with Dasc. But as the hours drag on and I remain seated in my bed with my back to the wall, I realize how much I gave away in that gunpoint confessional. She knows I owe a life debt to Dasc, she knows Dasc is being kept somewhere in Underground, and she knows I'm valuable to Dasc in some way. None of these things I would have ever mentioned if not trying to convince her that I'm not the bad guy. Had it all been about protecting her father? Or had I been played for a complete and utter fool?

Just like Dasc when he took on the guise of a friendly teacher at the high school. You draw more pixies with sugar, right? Genna is every bit his protégé. His Whisper.

Sometime in the early hours of the morning I fall asleep with my mother's gun in my hand. I wake with a jolt when I slip from my sitting position and my head hits the mattress. Pale sunlight illuminates the brown grass outside and the weatherworn boards of the barn beyond. I rub the sleep from my eyes, quickly check that my gun is still in my hand, and lean over the mattress to find Genna isn't in bed anymore.

My feet hit the floor with a thud. I switch to threat mode in an instant and make a sharp, clean exit out of my bedroom with my gun up at chest height into the kitchen.

Genna hovers around the stovetop making scrambled eggs while Jefferson sits at the table reading a newspaper. He's so absorbed by what he's reading that he doesn't immediately see me walk into the room with my gun drawn. Genna garners my attention as her eyes flick from my face to my gun and back again, before jumping to her father.

At that moment Jefferson puts his newspaper aside and notices me. I quickly ease up my stance and hide the gun behind my thigh, turning my body at an angle so he shouldn't be able to notice it.

He's all smiles. "Morning! Genna's offered to make breakfast for everyone. I hope you're hungry."

I've never seen him so happy before. He's usually a grouch and even more so the morning. He's never greeted me with a "hey, how are you" or peppy "good morning" since I moved here. Even the wrinkles on his face are less pronounced, not so sharp and severe. His eyes aren't such squinty pinpricks and he's put more effort into his hair.

Pixies, telling him what happened last night might break him.

"I like to do things myself," Genna says. "It feels good to have control back. To be home."

If it's even possible, Jefferson's smile grows brighter with the light of knowing his only family had returned. That pure joy on his face burns deep in my chest.

"I'm going to be taking time off for a while," he announces and beams at his daughter. Genna walks over to give him a one-armed hug. A picturesque loving family. "I've assured Director Knox that you and Hawk can manage business affairs. I'll still be here if you need me but my focus needs to be on my family."

I struggle past the lump in my throat to say, "Of course."

"Great. Thank you, Phoenix. For everything."

No, don't do that. Don't thank me for how great everything is, because everything is *not* great. I fumble for words in my head and end up standing there silent and unmoving. Jefferson's smile begins to fade as he notices there's something wrong so I clear my throat and nod, hoping that's an acceptable response.

I'm saved by Hawk coming through the front door and drawing everyone's attention. Genna returns to the stovetop and Jefferson gives my brother just as friendly a greeting. Hawk smiles and claps him on the shoulder before his eyes land on me, quickly narrow, and latch onto the hand I'm hiding behind my leg. When he looks like he's about to make a commotion or point out the fact I've got my gun out, I shake my head an infinitesimal amount.

"I should go change," I say and slide backwards into my bedroom.

I shut the door behind me and instantly go for my cell phone to send Hawk a quick text.

Stay cool. I'll meet you in the barn to explain.

In my haste I don't bother caring what I change into. I'm so distracted I put my shirt on inside out and have to redress before I march into the kitchen again. Hawk's already vanished. Genna has finished cooking the eggs and offers me a plate she's scooped a portion onto. Yeah right, like I'm going to take any food offered by her at this point.

"I'll eat later, thanks," I say and make for the door.

"Phoenix, she went to all that trouble to make you breakfast," Jefferson scolds from his spot at the table. "The least you can do is take a plate."

Oh, you've got to be kidding me. "*Pixies*, you sound like Fredrick the faun and his stupid no-thank-you bites."

"Phoenix Mason you are going to eat that plate of eggs she made for you!" The amount of anger in his voice is shocking, especially for something so ridiculous as refusing to eat a plate of breakfast.

Genna speaks up on my behalf. What a surprise. "Dad, it's okay."

The rage monster in Jefferson dies away at the soft words from his daughter and he returns to his newspaper. I'm suddenly glad I didn't bring up last night—if he reacts that badly about breakfast, there's no telling what he would have done if I accused his daughter of threatening me with a gun. He probably would have said I deserved it or something.

Not wanting to make the situation worse, I take the hot plate of eggs from Genna, give her a keen glare, and take it with me out to the barn. Hawk is waiting on the bottom step of the stairs and launches to his feet when I enter.

"What on earth is going on?" he demands.

I wave him on and we move up the steps to take seats in front of the two computers. I toss the plate onto the desk and a few bits of scrambled eggs roll away to soak into the keyboard.

"Well, Genna drew my gun on me last night," I say and fight the hot flush burning up my neck and cheeks.

"*What?* And you're just mentioning this now?"

"Don't snap at me, Hawk, okay?" I lean forward to perch

my elbows on my thighs and massage my temples with my fingertips. "I swear this gets more and more complicated every day."

He sucks in a loud, forceful breath, a clear sign he's doing his best to remain calm. "Okay," he says. "Tell me what happened."

To the best of my memory, I relay the events of last night and all the things we both said. When I finish, Hawk clenches his jaw and leans back in his swivel chair to stare up at the ceiling.

"Well, that's . . . I mean, yay! She hates Dasc but . . . *piping Pan*, she's got issues."

"Not without reason," I grumble.

"So, what are we going to do about it?"

"That's the question, isn't it?"

He cocks an eyebrow at me. "You ought to tell someone."

"I just did."

"Besides me."

He swivels about and scoots his chair towards me to lay his hands on my shoulders so I'm forced to look at him. "Look, I get that you want to protect Jefferson by protecting Genna, but *she drew a gun on you*. I gotta look out for my twin. If you don't say something, I will. This isn't like you're selling her out, Fifi. She's terrified of Dasc. I get it. I really do. But you can't leave this lie."

When I don't give an immediate response, he shakes me back and forth in my chair making the wheels beneath me squeak.

"Okay. I'll make a call," I say. "But not right now in case Jefferson stampedes in here. I'll call on my way out to the park."

"As long as you do." He pats me on top of the head like I'm a dog so I shove his chair, except I push a little too hard and he almost tips over. "Woah, woah! Over eager, missy."

I crack a laugh and turn to log into my computer.

Hawk scoots over again to tap me on the arm. "But since we're on the topic of touchy subjects, I've got a new one for you. Hurry up and log in."

"Great, now what?" I connect to the IMS servers and Hawk has me check the news feeds. The top story is about the attack on Faunus and the seemingly unrelated one in Paris. There were several deaths at each attack and others wounded.

"Keep reading," Hawk says over my shoulder and points to a specific sentence.

"'*Evidence suggests a splinter werewolf group was behind both attacks.*' Yeah, Draco mentioned that and had me question Dasc about it. Draco thought his brainwashed followers might be behind it." I shake my head. "All those people . . ."

"Do we say anything?" Hawk asks and musses his hair until it's in complete disarray. "To Genna or Jefferson, I mean. I don't want to trigger a fit or something with Genna."

"If she needs to know about it, I'm sure someone from headquarters will give her a call," I mutter and finish reading the article. "They don't say anything about why they think those two places were attacked."

"They're still investigating. I'm sure someone will figure something out." He puffs out his cheeks and blows out an exasperated breath. "I'm more worried about how this will affect people like me in general. Werewolves don't have a lot of fans to begin with. This is going to make everything worse."

Hawk's eyes are downcast and dark shadows linger in the creases beneath his eyebrows. I know how sore a subject this is. Hawk had the werewolf disease thrust upon him and he's lived with the stigma ever since. And he's right. Once word spreads that werewolves are connected to the attacks, things could get ugly fast.

I distract myself from that unpleasant thought by paging through my e-mail. There's one from Director Knox letting me know they are going to suspend talks with Dasc for the time being until they are able to sort out information and people recovered from the sites Genna revealed. They've been conducting raids since we laid the groundwork. Hawk and I compare the list of persons identified from the raids against our list of local missing persons.

"That's seven out of twenty-one," Hawk says and crosses out seven names from the list taped to the wall. "We're finally doing it. We're bringing them home. Maybe this wall can stop being so depressing."

"Yeah." Maybe. Considering how both Genna and Rosalyn have turned out, finding these missing people comes with a lot of strings attached. "There are standby orders attached to this e-mail. They want to assess everyone's condition before we notify any local families."

"That almost doesn't seem fair. These people have waited long enough, don't you think?"

I don't respond.

He makes a few more notes on the list of missing persons before returning to his computer to fill out some reports.

"So, what's been going on, Captain?" I ask. "How's Moose Lake?"

He shrugs. "Pretty typical. It's awesome not having to do schoolwork on top of everything else, so there's that."

After the battle with the lamia, Melody had confronted the high school principal and revealed us to be "agents working on an undercover sting." The best part was that we had a valid excuse to finally quit school. I'm certainly glad that's over with. Hawk fills me in on what little else has been going on including a boy trying to bring his werewolf brother into kindergarten for show and tell.

"Yeah, so now the teachers think he's got an overactive imagination and warned his mom that he might be taking books too seriously," he says.

I join in his laughter. It's hilarious how willing ignorant people are to continue being ignorant. The IMS doesn't need to concoct cover stories half the time—people simply don't want to believe there's more out there. They come up with perfectly reasonable excuses and tell themselves that their reality is the only reality.

If only that could be true for everything.

Hawk slaps me on the knee. "We should do some probation rounds. Come on, twinsie."

I get to my feet but hesitate by the computer, gripping the back of my chair with both hands and kneading the leather. "Hey, are we sure we're okay leaving Genna alone with Jefferson?"

"Jefferson can handle himself," he says. "And it sure seems he's the last person she would ever try to hurt. Also, Scholar probably has cameras hidden in the fridge or something and is bound to let us know if there's a problem."

He shrugs on his jacket and mutters, "Creepy how much she knew about my pranks."

We trot down the stairs together but I let Hawk inform Jefferson on his own that we're heading out for a bit. I don't want to thrust myself into the middle of that atmosphere again so soon. I still can't believe how viciously Jefferson responded when I refused breakfast. Speaking of, my stomach rumbles as if it heard my thoughts. I left the plate of eggs at the computer. If they aren't poisoned, I'm sure Hawk will eat them up later.

Hawk jogs outside and jingles the keys in his hand. "Would you like the honor?"

"Sure," I say and catch the keys in my outstretched hand.

"Don't crash."

"Har-har." I roll my eyes and slide into the driver's seat. "You and Jefferson have to let that go, man."

"Just watch out for semis."

I glare at him, turn the ignition, and then accelerate fast. Before he manages to get his seat belt on, I slam on the brakes to check him. He lurches forward in his seat and throws out a hand to brace himself on the dash. I crack a smile as he glowers at me and fumbles to get himself buckled in.

After stopping for coffee and food at Java Jitters, we work our way through town to visit all the werewolves currently at home to check their probation rings and ask them the standard questions about how they're doing, if they've had any odd urges or chunks of missing time. As Hawk said before, everything is fine. There hasn't been trouble in Moose Lake for the last month while I've been away except for the occasional hiccup.

At each place, we also check the logs the werewolves keep of their serum injections. A weight settles in my lungs as I look at page after page of neatly written or typed text with dates and times and dosages. Every single person hovers around us when we do this, anxious to make sure their logs are in order and that they're taking the serum exactly how they're supposed to so they don't go full on wolf by accident.

I think of the log book Hawk keeps at the cabin. It's full of the same kind of notes with little scratch outs as if he misspelled a date or something and needed to correct it. It's not immaculate because that would be too suspicious if his log is inspected. No one's log is perfect—except for Mrs. Ferguson's perhaps, who has a trite of OCD—and it's important that Hawk looks like he lives and breathes that log book.

Because if someone looked too closely, they might find out every word is a lie.

I've got a lump in my throat as we leave Mrs. Ferguson's house. We're both quiet when we grab a bite to eat at a small pizza restaurant as noon draws near. We won't be able to meet with Scholar for long. After school gets out, we'll need to check on all the kids and teens. At least Moose Lake has been doing well enough lately that we'll be able to end the probation tours soon. I won't have to be such a blatant liar right to their faces then. That cheers me up only slightly.

We eventually finish our meal and I drive us a short ways before stopping at the gas station.

"Hey, could you go grab some snacks for me?" I ask my brother.

He raises an eyebrow. "We just ate."

"You know how I get when I overexert my abilities. If I'm going to train with Scholar, then we should be prepared."

"You can't get them yourself?"

"This gas station makes me nervous ever since I had someone tail me from it and try to hit me with a semi."

He rolls his eyes and throws open his door. "Fine, but I'm going to get stuff I like and you'll live to regret my choices."

As soon as he shuts the door and walks across the lot, I pull out my cell phone and dial the direct number for Director Knox. A woman briefly comes on to confirm my identity before I talk to the director. And to think, less than a year ago he almost canned me from the IMS. Now we're having private conversations on his direct line.

"Junior Agent Mason," he says when he picks up. "Hearing radius status?"

"All clear but I don't have long." I keep an eye on Hawk through the windows of the store as he browses the aisles. "Sir, I know I'm supposed to report directly to Draco but I wasn't given the proper channels to go through."

"Indeed. For the time being, you can continue to contact me directly and I'll pass along your updates to Draco personally so no one is left out of the loop." He says the last bit dryly. I take it he's irritated that Draco attempted to cut him out. "But remember we need to keep this closed book. If word got out that we're investigating one of the rescued werewolf captives, it would destabilize an already delicate situation."

"Yes, sir."

"What do you have for me, Mason?"

"There was . . . an incident last night." I worry my lip and watch Hawk pile an armful of chips and snacks onto the counter before chatting up the pretty blonde clerk. I'm running out of time and need to make a snap decision. Tell the whole truth and let Genna suffer the consequences? Or try to protect her? If she had pulled a gun on my brother, I know exactly what I would be telling the director. But no, it had been me and I had been willing to live with that.

"Go on," the director prods when I take too long debating with myself.

"We had a confrontation, Genna and me. No one was hurt but she—well, she threatened me with my own gun when she thought I was working for Dasc."

There's a beat of silence and I can picture the director scowling in his office as he takes this bit of news in.

"So, she is a threat," he says.

I wince. I knew this was going to happen. What did I expect?

"Sir, she was trying to protect her father. There's no doubt in my mind that she would do anything to protect her family. Like I said, no one was hurt and she returned my gun once I convinced her of my own loyalties." As the clerk inside the store starts to bag up Hawk's snacks, I say in a rush, "I think she was only acting in the way she was taught by Dasc. It's how she was trained to respond to a threat. Swiftly and firmly."

"Which is a problem. If she thinks that is the way to handle a situation, then she would be better off returning to Underground under close supervision."

"I think that would do more harm than good," I argue—more like plead. "Director, please. Just give us more time. If that's how she was raised, then let us show her a better way. Making her feel like a prisoner is only going to associate the IMS with Dasc's methods. We need to be better."

Hawk strolls out of the store swinging a bag in each hand. Pixies.

"I'm out of time," I say. "What do you want me to do?"

"I understand your position, Mason. I'll give you a couple days. If the situation hasn't improved, I'm going to have her transported to Underground. Do you think you can handle her if things get out of control?"

Can I? That's a loaded question, but what other choice do I have?

"You can count on me, sir."

I end the call a second before Hawk hops into the passenger seat and shoves the bags into the footwell.

"Who were you talking to?" he asks and eyes the phone in my hand.

I turn on the ignition to give myself a moment to sort my thoughts and contemplate what on earth I'm going to do about Genna before answering.

"I called in what Genna did like you wanted," I say. "And?"

I force a smile. "Everything's going to be fine."

10

We enter the state park and jostle about on the dirt road to where we spoke with Scholar the other day. Once we reach the end of the road, I throw the vehicle into park and turn off the ignition. Even though it had been sunny earlier, clouds have rolled in along with a gray hue and bitter wind. We step out into a biting sprinkle of rain that chases a pair of hikers to their vehicle. I guess spring hasn't decided to really make a show in Minnesota yet and winter still clings desperately to the bare trees and brown grass.

I hug my rain jacket to myself and flip up the hood, wishing I had worn my mother's old bomber jacket instead.

"Soooooo . . ." Hawk turns around on the spot. "Are we supposed to meet her out in the woods you think?"

I shrug. "I guess. She didn't exactly specify."

We stand a moment longer next to the SUV before Hawk leads the way on the path we had taken before into the trees. While the wind is less in the middle of the forest, it still sways the trees, rattles the dead leaves, and keeps up a constant tumultuous sound that makes it impossible to hear if there is anyone else nearby moving through the underbrush like we are. You know, it would be great if Scholar got a cell phone one of these days so we could just call her instead of picking through the wilderness looking for her.

I look down at my feet to move carefully over a fallen log and end up running into Hawk from behind as he comes to a sudden halt. He reaches back and grabs the sleeve of my jacket to keep me from moving while in the same instant he digs into his pants pocket where I know he keeps his bio-mech gun.

Beyond him about thirty feet ahead I see what's frightened him. A woman stands with her face obscured by her jacket hood but long dark tendrils of hair fall out and are caught in a manic dance by the wind. Her bare hands flex like eagle talons with black claws on the ends of her fingertips ready to grasp at helpless prey.

I know those claws, that hair, that hunched stance of a predator.

"Epsilon," I breathe and grab my brother's shoulder.

We have to get out of here. We have to run. There's no telling what kind of blood she has in her system so there's no telling how to fight her. How did she find us? What if she's been here the whole time but hiding? I thought Scholar had scared her off. And where's Scholar for that matter?

Hawk draws his bio-mech gun and fires without hesitation. Branches snap and the grass bends beneath the pulse-like beam from the gun. Epsilon lunges into a roll out of the way, easily avoiding the blast. I'm in the middle of whipping my .45 out of the holster at the small of my back when the lamia stretches her hand towards us and a shockwave blasts through the air, taking down trees, blowing a swath through the soil, and scattering chunks of grass everywhere before it hits us.

My legs catch on the log behind me and I'm sent spinning head over heels. Hawk's body thumps against mine before I land face first in the cold dirt. Groaning, I push myself up and hunt for the .45 that was knocked from my hand. My brother drags his legs off my back and rolls to his feet at the same time I lurch forward for my gun on the ground an arm's length away.

Another wave hits us and sends us in different directions this time. The force of it passes through me like a giant punching me in the chest and I crush a prickly bush in my fall. Its sharp little twigs jab at me from every angle and I'm pretty sure I'm bleeding somewhere.

I know this powerful force we're up against. I've faced it before. This is the deadly power that Scholar wields. And somehow Epsilon has gotten a taste of the dragon's blood.

What's happened to Scholar?

The faint reverb of the bio-mech gun firing reaches me through the roar of the wind. I struggle upright again to find Hawk drawing a bead on Epsilon as she ducks in and out between the trees. He lets off a series of pulses while I get my feet under me and search for my gun again. A stray shockwave rocks a tree in front of me and its roots creak as it teeters ominously in my direction. Crap. The tree starts to fall and I run out of the way at a crouch beneath the hail of bark and branches. The ground beneath my feet shakes when its trunk smashes into the ground where I had been moments before.

"Cover me!" I shout to my brother as I spot the glint of metal and pearl of my gun. It's not going to be of much use but hopefully it'll slow Epsilon enough so we can reach the SUV where there's a store of blades. The only way we're making it out of here is if we can chop her head off.

Hawk lets off pulse after pulse as he stands, then takes a knee, rolls out of the way of a shockwave, and springs to his feet again. My hands close around the cold grip of my mother's old .45. Dirt flies as I lift it off the ground and lean into a solid stance to fire two shots in Epsilon's direction. Unfortunately, she twirls to hide behind the wide branches of a spruce tree to avoid my fire. The sounds of my gun compared to the bio-mech gun are laughably extreme in volume.

"Leapfrog!" I shout at Hawk.

He nods and takes off in the direction of the SUV. I let off a few more rounds before Hawk is in position and starts shooting the bio-mech to provide cover as I hurry behind him. We do this several times, one of us laying down cover fire as the other backs up a secure distance to lay cover for the other. It works and I can see the SUV between the trees when, as Hawk makes his run, a shockwave hits him in the middle of his back and he's sent sprawling into the underbrush.

"Hawk!"

I fire off two more rounds to keep Epsilon at bay before the slide locks back on my .45. It's empty. Shockwaves blast through the bare foliage and I duck behind a nearby tree to shield myself, feeling the force of it pass through the soles of my feet as the ground shakes.

"Get to the SUV!" Hawk shouts, his voice muffled as he tries to roll over on the ground to bring up his bio-mech gun.

As he lets off several blasts, I sprint for the vehicle. Another wave passes forcefully through the ground and I almost lose my balance, having to reach out to a nearby birch to steady myself.

Then a horrible sound fills my ears and stops my heart. Hawk screams. It's not the sound of panic or fear but of absolute pain.

Something deep inside my chest rears its ugly head and I wheel around baring my teeth. Heat catches on my skin and the light rain collecting on my jacket steams.

Epsilon stands over Hawk prone on the ground, both hands stretched out towards him. The air wavers before her palms at the force of the concussive power she lets off in a steady stream into his chest. His screams tear me apart as Scholar's power under the lamia's control tears at him.

I forgo the SUV and race through the brush towards my brother. I don't need a blade to kill Epsilon. I'll rip her head clean off her neck. I'm heading at her full steam and closing the distance quickly as I snap branches out of my way when she finally takes notice. Keeping one hand focused on Hawk, she raises her other one to direct her waves at me.

Hawk's cries reverberate in my skull.

"I'LL KILL YOU!" I scream at the lamia and when the shockwave comes to knock me back, I literally punch right through it. Fist raised, I let out a crazed roar and keep going. The next wave makes my feet trip over themselves but I manage to stay upright and throw up both my hands as if I can physically stop the next shockwave.

I don't expect it to actually work.

The wave dissipates and the steady stream she's pushing into Hawk's chest weakens.

I'm burning up but I let the animal inside me take control and kill the power in Epsilon's veins. I stopped her before. I'll do it again. Permanently. Keeping my hands up and palms out, I push through the shockwaves as I take one step at a time until I'm almost on her. Hawk gasps for air on the ground.

When I throw a punch at her jaw, she twirls past my attack and strikes low, sweeping my feet out from under me. I hit the ground hard. She moves for Hawk once more but I roll across the uneven ground, come up between my brother and her, and send my fist driving into the ground.

If she thought her shockwaves were bad, I bet she wasn't expecting this. The ground fissures before me in a crackling swath of exploding soil with Epsilon caught right in the middle of it. She tumbles into the widening split of earth and disappears beneath the haze of soil and grass drifting through the air. I rise shakily to my feet, panting hard, and wait for her next move.

The forest grows still without the sound of birds or insects which I'm sure we've driven off. The only sound is the faint patter of rain droplets on the leaves and our jackets. Everything settles and Epsilon slowly rises from the broken pit I made. A shimmering bubble of light surrounds her and I realize she's thrown up a barrier to protect herself. Lamia's don't protect themselves. They attack. She's afraid. Good. She *should* be afraid of me.

I remain where I am in a protective stance before my brother. He shuffles behind me, groaning as he moves.

"Hawk, stay down," I say without taking my eyes off Epsilon. I don't have a clue how badly he's hurt but I'm sure moving around isn't going to do him any good.

Just like that barrier isn't going to do Epsilon any good.

I stretch out a hand and guide that powerful instinct deep in my bones. I stopped the lamia before. I stopped the shockwaves. Now I'm going to rip that barrier away and end this for good to protect my brother.

The shimmering light doesn't want to cow under the power that's in my blood though. I burn up and know I'm already close to the edge of my limits, but if I don't get through that barrier Epsilon will kill us. So I fight to keep that power going, feeling the heat surging through my arm and setting my heart and head on fire. I taste blood in my mouth as it dribbles from my nose. I'm pushing myself so hard I can feel every muscle in my body tense like a rubber band about to snap. I remember the last time I took it this far. I went under for two days.

The light of the barrier begins to fade.

Epsilon waves a hand and the barrier disappears as if she knows it's a pointless gesture anyway. I let go of the power burning through me and I collapse to my knees as it all comes rushing back in. Darkness clouds my vision.

Now I've done it. I'm vulnerable and the lamia knows it. She takes two steps forward ready to end me when a pulse pushes past my shoulder from behind, blowing my hair about with it, and hits Epsilon in the chest. She stumbles backwards with a grunt. Now would be an excellent time for me to swoop in and rip her head clean from her shoulders but my tank's empty. I can only kneel there in the wet soil panting as she regains her feet.

Hawk fires again but this time she's ready. A barrier springs up to absorb the pulse. My brother crawls up on all fours and slumps on the ground beside me, using my shoulder to support himself as he raises the bio-mech gun again as our last defense. Neither of us can move much and I've got no secret weapons left.

This is it.

As Epsilon hides behind her shield, my brother and I share one last look. Neither sad nor scared. Resolved. If this is the way we go out, then we go out together.

The shield lowers and a small, well-aimed shockwave is all it takes to knock the bio-mech gun out of Hawk's hand. It tumbles away into the grass out of reach.

Epsilon's shadow falls over us and I find my hand in Hawk's.

Then the unexpected happens. The lamia's claws shift into normal human fingernails, her long dark hair recedes until it's several inches shorter, and she draws back her hood.

"What?" Hawk breathes beside me, voicing the disbelief I feel.

It's not Epsilon staring us down. It's not any lamia.

She reaches out towards me and I take her offered hand. When she pulls me to my feet, I find I have enough strength to throw the full weight of my body behind a right hook into her jaw.

"SCHOLAR, I'M GOING TO KILL YOU!" I shout.

The dragon in human form stumbles to the side from the blow and I collapse to the ground again where Hawk catches me clumsily in his arms. However, unlike us, Scholar recovers quickly and works her jaw.

"I did deserve that, I suppose," she says.

"You think?" Hawk snaps.

"We do not have time for half measures," the dragon responds rather calmly considering. "I have been watching you both long enough to know that Phoenix's true abilities do not shine more brightly than when her brother's life is in mortal peril. I created a disguise I knew would fool you both and forced you both to a point where only raw instinctual power is left at your disposal. I must say, you certainly did not disappoint, my dear."

I pick up a loose rock nearby and chuck it in her general direction before laying on the forest floor. Hawk does the same beside me, gripping his chest and wheezing.

"We thought we were going to die," I say between pants. I can hardly catch my breath. "You let us think we were going to die."

"Nothing draws out the most deeply imbedded parts of ourselves like life or death scenarios. This is only the first step." Scholar's talking like we only started our preliminary math homework and this is all very necessary.

"How on earth do we know you're really Scholar?" I wave a hand weakly in her direction. "You just morphed your appearance."

"You know very well I am no shapeshifter as they cannot replicate another person's powers as I demonstrated."

"Yeah, you *demonstrated* them all right," I growl.

"And lamia cannot control more than one power at a time, such as my abilities and a shapeshifter's, so obviously I cannot be a lamia either. It is me. You know we dragons are more than capable of changing our appearance.”

“Doesn’t matter,” I say and close my eyes, letting the sprinkle of rain cool my burning face. “I don’t care who you are. You don’t do that to my brother and walk away.”

“This was not some random assault for vengeance or any of the petty things humans fight each other over. This was an experiment.”

“Yeah,” Hawk wheezes. “That totally makes this hurt less.”

I reach out blindly and pat Hawk’s shoulder. His fingers wrap around my hand in turn and give me a gentle squeeze to let me know he’s all right even though his breathing is coming in painful rasps. *Piping Pan*, I’m going to wring Scholar’s neck as soon as my strength returns.

“Some rest and you will both be fine,” Scholar says, which only fuels my desire to punch her. “Hawk, you will heal fast enough with what is in your blood. Phoenix, some food and a nap and I am sure you will be back on your feet.”

“I hate you,” Hawk and I say in unison.

“Just because someone *can* heal,” Hawk says, “Doesn’t give you the right to try and explode their internal organs.”

“Hmm,” is her short, unapologetic reply—sort of like Genna’s response after she held a gun on me. What charmers.

I open my eyes and struggle into a sitting position. Hawk follows suit and we lean on each other to stay upright since I’m pretty sure I’d probably tip right over if my shoulder wasn’t propped up against his.

Scholar stands over us with her arms crossed. As random a thought as it is, I realize this is the first time I’ve ever seen her with her hair down. It's usually up in a tight bun at the nape of her neck. With it loose, the dark waves make her look years younger. Granted, I'm sure she can look however she wants to, but her sharp, angular facial features really compliment her personality.

"Shall I explain how the benefits will far outweigh your discomfort?" she says.

"Discomfort?" Hawk grumbles. "Understatement."

She ignores his comment. "I think we can all agree that the most potent of Phoenix's abilities only rise to the surface when you are in mortal peril." She gestures to Hawk and he glares at her. "Under normal circumstances, she only produces a sort of calming ambience. While somewhat effective as a local deterrent, if our end goal is to abolish the werewolf disease, we will never achieve that end through ordinary measures."

I'm not a fan of being referred to as if I'm not even here. She makes this sound like a far away problem happening to a hospital patient with no say in the matter. I don't like it at all. My head hangs and I don't have the energy to lift it. I could really use a pick me up but our snacks are in the SUV.

"Magic is like any other talent or muscle. If you do not use it on a frequent basis, your ability to wield it will deteriorate."

"So you're saying I ought to be in life-threatening situations more often?" I mutter.

"I am saying you need to be able to control it when you are not in one," she counters. "The core response you bury under a self-sacrificing psychosis comes out like a punch and takes everything out of you. Look at you."

I manage the strength to angle my head and glare. "Yeah, *thanks*. I feel fantastic."

"If you can manage the trigger, control the power and focus, you can hone that power into something you can summon at any moment. It will not take over you—you will take over it. That is what this experiment was all about. Hitting that trigger. Your magic is so deeply entwined with your emotions that the only way to force it out is to push you to the breaking point."

I put my face in my hands and take several deep breaths. My head is pounding and I don't have any patience for this crap.

"If you're going to ramble on," I say, "can we at least do it after I've had a moment to rest and eat something?"

"We should not linger here long at any rate." Scholar glances at a watch on her wrist. "I am sure our little drama has caused enough noise."

I don't have the energy to yell at her for being such a prickly piece of flaming hydra dung. She doesn't seem to care how angry we both are anyway. She hoists me up by my armpits and carries me in her arms to the SUV. I feel like a giant baby being strapped into my car seat. She brings Hawk next—at least he manages to walk with her assistance—and we sit side by side in the second row of seats with the bag of snacks between us. We sit and devour the chips and gummies Hawk picked out while Scholar collects our fallen weapons from the woods. When she returns, she steals the car keys from me. She ignores my protests and takes the wheel, driving us at full speed out of the park and down one backroad then another in a confusing array of turns. She must be trying to make sure no one's following us.

I lose focus, hardly able to concern myself with where on earth she's taking us, and fall unconscious briefly. When

I come to, we've stopped in another woodsy area scattered with pine trees and evergreens near a narrow bubbling creek. Hawk is already out of his seat and comes around to open my door before sitting in the footwell, his back pressed against my legs. It's quiet here, wherever we are, but it's the sort of natural quiet before the bugs come awake in the spring and only a few birds call to each other off in the distance. The rain continues with a pleasant pitter patter to give the silence some depth. It's peaceful and the perfect setting for me to take another nap.

Except I don't get time to sleep off the stress and exertion from Scholar's stupid attack. The dragon comes through the trees in her human form with her hair in its usual bun to make her face look as sharp as it always had been when she was pretending to be a librarian. She appears oddly normal in her rain jacket, worn jeans, and hiking boots. But all psychopaths look normal until they deign to reveal the twisted workings beneath.

"Where are we?" I ask when she stops a few feet from where Hawk and I sit.

"Somewhere private."

"That's not an answer."

She clasps her hands behind her back and holds herself with impeccable posture. "I forgot you do not care for subtlety and subterfuge. Always so direct."

"Yeah, well, when you spit out answers like that, you tend to sound like Dasc. That and the fact you almost killed Hawk a short while ago, it's hard to trust you, particularly your vague answers."

Her sharp eyes glint in the gloomy light. "I said before, secrets are—"

"Secrets for a reason. I got that. Thanks." I stop to catch my breath. I can't believe how winded I am. "We kept your secret, Scholar. We told the IMS we only came across you because the selkies led us there when hunting the lamia. They were happy to take the blame, and the rest of us—for whatever reason—decided keeping you hidden was better than telling the truth. We *trusted* you. Why can't you return the favor?"

Scholar clenches her jaw and her chest heaves like she's fighting to hold in an angry shout or some very violent emotions.

Always the clever peacekeeper, Hawk joins in. "Look, we all want the same thing, right? A cure for the werewolf disease. We're on the same side. Maybe we could help more if you'd share what your plans are for Phoenix. Help us understand what needs to be done. Mutual cooperation would go a long way for all of us."

How he manages to be so calm, I have no idea. He clutches a hand to his chest but other than that, he's good at hiding his pain. At least he's stopped wheezing. The thought of him being hurt continues to boil my blood, though.

"As wise as your words are," Scholar says, "I must continue to take precautions. Trust can be a cruel thing when it is abused."

I roll my eyes. "What's that supposed to mean?"

Her gaze cuts through me and I recoil in my seat. "It means I have lived hundreds of your life spans and felt the cruel barbs of trust and loyalty used against me. We have mutual goals, yes, and I will assist however I can, but the only being on this miserable planet I trust completely is myself. You can rest assured that I will never compromise your secrets but I ask that you respect mine as well." She gives her shoulders a quick roll. "And you should stop being so snappish with a sense of entitlement. I do not owe you anything, Phoenix, and you do not owe me anything either."

I swallow and avert my gaze to the surrounding trees. "That sounds like a pretty dark way to view the world."

"And since when has the world been anything but?"

"Politics and morals aside," Hawk interrupts and talks with his hands. "What's the plan?"

Scholar starts to pace as we sit in the open door of the SUV. "This experiment was more than just bringing out your power in full strength." She nods to me. "It revealed something even more extraordinary."

I try to remain patient as she holds off on cutting straight to the chase. "And what was that?"

"You stopped me." Scholar swivels on the balls of her feet to face us. "Not the werewolf disease, not the same twisted energy that keeps the lamia alive, *me*. Pure, natural magic. What's inside you is effective not only against monsters. If my theory is correct, you have some kind of control over *all* magic. A gatekeeper as it were."

I don't know if it's just me or being so completely drained that I can hardly stay awake, but this isn't making sense.

"Come again?"

"You shuttered my shockwaves. You began to break my barrier. When the lamia attacked my home and you travelled with that teleporter—"

"Charlie, yeah."

"You did not experience the same pain as everyone else. Your abilities could signify a paramount shift in the very reality of our world." Scholar starts gesturing animatedly with a feverish excitement. An image of a mad scientist brewing chaos in a lab comes to mind. "This is only the beginning. If you can learn to harness your power . . ."

The reality of what she's saying starts to sink in. Me? Some kind of all-powerful being? I've only ever wanted to save my brother, but I guess that includes threats of any kind—monsters and magic wielders alike.

"She'll be hunted," Hawk says quietly. "The monsters will want to kill her and I doubt anyone with a little something extra in their veins is going to like it much either."

"I am afraid what you say is true," Scholar says and resumes her astute posture again. "But the more control she has over it, the better her chances of not being discovered."

So I could train with Scholar, face that dark swirling energy inside of me, become a weapon for good or ill. I want to control it. I don't want it to be some slumbering recluse that only comes out when Hawk's in immediate danger. It'll take discipline, no small amount of time I'm sure, and teaching I can probably only get from Scholar.

I blow out a heavy breath. "And if I'm strong enough, cure the werewolf disease for good?"

"There is not a doubt in my mind."

"Okay, then I have conditions."

"Of course."

"You don't ever touch my brother again."

She cocks her head. "Naturally."

"I want to hear you say it."

"I will not harm your brother again. Any other terms?"

I look to my brother but he shrugs.

"No," I say. "I guess not."

"Good. Then here are my terms for teaching you. My whereabouts are to remain unknown. Our training sessions are to remain unknown. I fear that includes not telling dear old Jefferson Barnes as his judgment is clouded by his daughter at present."

"No argument here," I mutter and Hawk gives me a sharp look. "Okay. I agree to your terms."

Scholar steps forward to extend her hand and I take it weakly.

"Then we begin tomorrow."

11

I nap stretched out in the second row of the SUV while Hawk keeps watch in the driver's seat. Expending that much power and energy exhausted me. When I finally wake, I don't rouse immediately. Light glimmers against my closed eyelids and the steady plink of rain drums on the roof of the vehicle.

Scholar's words tumble endlessly in my mind. *This is only the beginning. If you can learn to harness your power . . .*

What deadly power flows in my veins? What creature am I to have stopped a dragon's magic?

All my life I've been told that magic fights other magic. What's in my blood should combat the magic around me, not control it, not be this gatekeeper Scholar seems to think I am. I had imagined that my ability was like purified destruction—something able to wipe out the magical disease in my brother's blood without hurting him and halt the twisted life force that kept the lamia alive. But now—now I'm not sure what I am.

I prop myself up on my elbows to read the time on the dash. It's almost four o'clock.

"Hey, sleeping beauty," Hawk says and gives an impressive yawn.

I rub the sleep from my eyes. "Sounds like you could've used some beauty sleep yourself."

"Nah, I'm okay."

"Are you?"

My eyes linger on the hand he has pressed against the underside of his ribs as if trying to suppress pain in his chest. That slumbering beast inside me growls at his obvious discomfort. He notices my line of sight and quickly drops his hand. I raise my eyebrows and he rolls his eyes.

"Seriously, I'm fine," he says.

"Did she break your ribs?"

"That's not—I was just working out some trapped gas, that's all. I wasn't tending to my poor broken bones."

It's my turn to roll my eyes. "Trust me, Hawk. If you were working out gas, I would know it. Everyone in a five block radius would know it."

He glares at me for only a moment before he gives a half-hearted shrug and says, "Eh, that's true."

"I'm going to rip her arms out of her sockets for doing that to you," I growl. The echo of Hawk's screams still rings in my ears. How *dare* she.

He slings an arm around the headrest of his seat and shifts about to face me. "Woah, woah, hold on there, terminator. Scholar had a solid point to make and I'll be fine."

"And what point was that, exactly?"

"That I'm your trigger. I'm your weak spot," he says quietly.

I blink and turn away, watching the rain run in rivulets down the side window. "That's not true. You bring out the best in me, magic or otherwise."

"Sure, you threw out some crazy powerful mojo back there, but then you also collapsed shortly after. I make you vulnerable."

"Can we . . . . can we not do this?" I say without facing him, not daring to. That slumbering beast inside me cracks an eye open but I keep it locked up. That raw power I wield frightens me but what scares me even more is what I'm willing to do for my brother—more like what *wouldn't* I do for him? What wouldn't I destroy? Who wouldn't I stop? But he's my family. My only family.

"My point is that you need Scholar's training," he continues. "You seemed reluctant about it but you shouldn't be. This will be good."

Becoming an all-powerful gatekeeper that'll make every magic wielder in the world want my head on a platter. Yeah. That'll be great.

"We should do the rest of our probation rounds," I say.

My mind needs to be focused on something else for a while. I clamber into the front passenger seat and rip open another bag of potato chips as Hawk starts up the SUV and takes us to town.

We're both subdued as we go house to house to check on the werewolf students that got out of school almost an hour ago. Many of them seem happy to talk and gossip with Hawk despite the reason we're here. They give me their polite hellos as well but I had never been the popular sort like my brother. He puts them at ease and has them cracking smiles within no time while we scan their probation rings and check their log books. But when we get to Matt Jones's house, a subtle shift comes over Hawk and the smile he gives Matt as he opens the door is almost feral.

"Matt," he says tersely.

Moose Lake's all-star athlete and perpetual ladies' man takes a step back from my brother's frightening smile, all his brawn and looks like a costume hiding a little, terrified boy underneath. I take no pity on him—none at all. He and his stupid friends were the reason Hawk ran off a month ago in the woods where he came across Duke's scent while in full-out hunting mode as a werewolf—the reason Duke is now dead.

I haven't forgotten and neither has Hawk.

Matt scans the yard and road behind us before gesturing for us to come in. He says nothing, cowed beneath the gleam in Hawk's eye, and holds out his hand with the probation ring like an obedient dog.

"Hmm, that's not good," Hawk says under his breath as he browses through the readings. His eyebrows knit together in a frown and Matt shifts uncomfortably on his feet, sweat glistening on his flat forehead. "That's not good at all."

"What is it?" I ask and lean over his shoulder, worried about what he's found.

I see nothing off about the flat line and the swells indicating when he took the serum to counteract the werewolf disease.

Hawk gestures at the screen. "This means I can't arrest

him, dang it. I've still got to put up with coming here on a regular basis."

I bite my lip to keep from barking out a laugh.

Matt relaxes for a moment before his face turns bright red and the muscles under the sleeves of his shirt ripple as they flex. He's obviously furious but if he wants to start a fight, he can be my guest. Hawk would win that battle any day.

Hawk holds out his hand impatiently. "Log?"

Practically spitting and near blue in the face, Matt whips out his log book and chucks it at Hawk. My brother catches it lightly with an expression of utter boredom and flips through the pages. He eventually gives a short bob of his head letting us know everything seems to be in order and passes the log back. Our job done, we head out of the house.

"Wow," I say as we climb into the SUV and I slide into the passenger's seat. I still feel completely sapped of energy so I have no qualm about letting my brother drive. "Matt didn't say a single word the entire time we were there."

"That's probably because the last time I was here—you were in Scotland—I sort of threatened him." Hawk gives me a mischievous smile and starts the vehicle.

Well, that sounds bad. "You *threatened* him?"

He shrugs and we pull out of the driveway. "I said if he ever spoke a word to me again, I'd rip out his tongue and throw him in an IMS internment camp in Siberia where they string up violent werewolves, but he'd never be able to plead his innocence because, you know, he wouldn't be able to talk without his tongue."

I stare at my brother—my calm, unassuming brother—

and wonder at the trove of violence and clever lies hiding beneath.

"That was pretty dark," I say.

"Yeah, well . . . at least he shut up after that. I considered having someone show up on his front doorstep and talk with a Russian accent to really freak him out but I didn't."

"*Pixies*, Hawk. I thought you were the one who said we need to earn their trust, not barge in with IMS authority and threats."

"He deserved it," he snarls.

A glint of steel enters his eyes and I leave it lie. Although, it does make me wonder what else he did around here while Jefferson and I were gone.

I clear my throat. "Where to next?"

"Only one place left." He swallows and rolls his grip on the steering wheel. "The Nelsons' house."

Ashley.

The only friend I really had in this town apart from Jefferson. I haven't seen her in over a month, not since that day Jefferson and I arrested Jason when he tried to abscond from probation and take Ashley with him. She had been so angry then. There's no telling what kind of reception I'll get from her.

And that's without her knowing we're behind her beloved dog's disappearance.

I fight the nervous energy rising in my chest, my fingers shaking from the drain of fighting Scholar earlier and the expectation of the confrontation to inevitably come. We don't speak as we take the backroads to her house and rumble up the bumpy gravel driveway. Hawk brings us to a stop alongside her rusty Buick.

"Do you want to wait here?" Hawk asks with his hands paused on the door handle and latch of his seat belt, waiting for an answer.

I gulp down my pride and fear. "No, I'll go with."

He nods and we get out together in sync. The house and surrounding yard and forest are quiet except for the distant calls of songbirds. I dodge around a muddy puddle in the driveway and march up the front porch steps alongside my brother. Hawk pushes the doorbell and we wait a good long minute before the door opens.

Ashley's in a drab long-sleeved shirt with the ends of the sleeves stretched down over her hands—no vibrant fandom shirt for her today which is so out of character. In fact, there's hardly anything about her that seems familiar apart from the ponytail. Ripped jeans, a dour expression with no life in it, shadows under her eyes, and the fabric of her shirt clings to muscles that hadn't existed before.

"Oh, it's you," she says, those once jubilant eyes pinning me with disgust. "I guess you're finally back from whatever hole you've been hiding in."

"I wasn't hiding in a hole," I growl.

Hawk puts a hand on my elbow to rein me in. "We're here for the usual checkup."

Those sharp eyes swivel on him. "You ever going to tell me where Jason is?"

Probably in some werewolf containment facility waiting for a cure since he can't possibly take the serum considering his reaction to it. My face burns thinking about it.

"I'm sorry, Ashley—" Hawk starts to say but he's quickly cut off.

"Save it," she snaps and thrusts her hand out to display

her probation ring. "Do what you have to then get off my porch."

Every word drips with venom, rips with cruel barbs of white-hot anger.

"What happened to you?" I ask, unable to stop the question from slipping out in my shock and surprise.

Hawk is hardly able to read her probation ring before she rips her hand away and stalks through the doorway to stand nose to nose with me.

"You have some nerve showing up here and looking down at me like you're so *perfect*," she snarls. Flecks of spit hit my face and I flinch. "Jason is gone because of you. He needed your help, not handcuffs! Not confinement! Not being thrown into a black hole without any word to his friends or family."

She shoves me hard in the chest and, given the state I'm currently in, I stumble a few steps backwards. I have no words to counter. My mouth hangs agape as she rages on.

"My dog is missing and I'm pretty sure is—is *dead* at this point." She chokes on the word and tears run over her cheeks. "I have to deal with this—" She waves the probation ring in my face, "—and, not that you care, but my dad's gotten worse. Yeah. He's in the hospital right now because his heart—he's—"

She heaves a ragged breath and spins away from us, a hand covering her mouth and her shoulders shaking.

I don't know what to do. I tenuously stretch out a hand before recoiling it as she wheels about to shout in my face.

"Everything went to crap the second you came here!"

Shell-shocked, I struggle for the words to make this right. "Ashley, I—"

"I was your friend! I trusted you!" Her hands are balled into fists at her sides, a muscle in her neck straining as she yells at me, her entire small frame shaking in her anger. "You couldn't even do your job right and now I'm some kind of freak!"

I feel the prick behind my eyes but fight it. I will not cry. I will not weep for the friendship crumbling into dust at my feet, for the ache in my chest knowing that she's right about everything.

"I'm so sorry," I say past the bands of pain constricting my chest and squeezing my lungs. "I never meant for any of this to happen."

"It's too little too late." She storms into her house and hurls her log book at my head. I barely catch it inches away from breaking my nose.

"Ashley," Hawk sharply remands her.

"I don't give a crap!" she shouts. "You can both go to hell."

The door slams in our faces so hard that the windows of the house shake.

A deep silence follows as even the nearby birds have stopped their calls. I realize I'm shaking and when I turn to my brother, he's as pale as a vampire, his lips thin and white.

Every word from Ashley rang with horrible truths neither of us wanted to be reminded of, each one hitting much too close to home. We *hadn't* been fast enough to stop her from getting bitten. We *did* arrest Jason and lock him up.

We killed Duke.

"She deserves to know the truth," Hawk says and moves for the door.

I'm in motion before he can take two steps and wrench him away from the handle.

"*No.*"

His eyes cut through me. "Then we're no better than the people that hid the truth from us about what happened to our parents. You don't hide something like that."

It feels like a slap in the face but I don't renege my grip. "You can't."

"It's my secret. I have every right to—"

"It's *our* secret."

"And whose fault is that?"

I blink at the anger in his face—directed at *me*. "What's that supposed to mean?"

He steps backwards and I let him go. He shrugs out his arm and his cold eyes turn away as he makes for the porch steps. "Nothing. Forget I said anything."

Shoulders hunched and hands thrust in his pockets, he stalks to the SUV. I let out a shuddering breath. Having Ashley rip me to pieces hurt like crazy. Having Hawk angry at me for what happened with Duke hurts even more.

With trembling fingers I open Ashley's log book and run through the dates and numbers. I can hardly focus on what I'm supposed to be doing. Reading the same bit over and over again until it finally sinks in, I give her log the okay and mark my initials on the last completed page. Ever so quietly, I open the front door and leave the log on a little table in the entryway next to Ashley's keychain before making my way out.

I slide into the front passenger seat and Hawk immediately reverses down the driveway without a word.

It's an uncomfortable silence all the way to the cabin as the rain peters out.

We reach the cabin's driveway sheltered by towering pines by the time I gather my courage to ask, "Do we need to talk?"

"No, we're good." His response is a little too fast, too sharp.

"Are you sure?"

"I said we're good."

He's in a rush to exit the vehicle so I take my time and mutter, "Yeah, right."

Hawk vanishes into the barn a second before the door to the cabin opens and Genna walks out to meet me at the side of the SUV. I subtly shift my stance to feel the reassuring weight of my mother's .45 pressed against the small of my back—before I remember it's empty and would be of absolutely no use if Genna decided to attack me. I could still threaten her with it, though. *She* doesn't know it's empty.

Pixies, why did it have to come to this? I immediately assume Genna is a threat to my safety and my brother.

Genna's eyes rove over my defensive stance before she stops a good ten feet away and leaves her hands loose at her sides. I realize she's wearing my *Go Fire Sprites!* sweatshirt and I fight the urge to shout at her to give it back.

"Can I talk to you?" she asks.

In a bitter mood, I just shrug. I don't want to get into this at the moment.

"I wanted to . . ." She clears her throat and bites the inside of her cheek as she obviously struggles for the right words. "I wanted to apologize for last night. When I held a gun on you."

"You don't have to elaborate," I say rather coldly. "I know what you're talking about."

"Good." She says it in a replication of my tone. "Well, my father said I should apologize. So, I'm sorry. It was wrong of me."

From the tone of her voice, it's obvious apologizing wasn't of her own volition. What a shocker. Although I'm surprised she told Jefferson, and even more so that he made her apologize. I figured he would have taken his daughter's side regardless of the right or wrong of it.

"Um . . . thanks," I say, unsure what more she wants from me.

"So, we're good?"

Hawk's words ring in my head, the bite to them clear. *I said we're good.*

"Yeah," I say quietly. "Sure. I guess so."

"And, Phoenix, I—" She takes a deep breath and a small, polite smile adorns her face. It changes everything about her. That mask of stone melts away at her attempt to show an expression of warmth and appreciation. The edges around her eyes crinkle and dimples form. The chilly air toys with the wavy strands of her black hair and for a single moment she seems normal. Free. Happy. "I never said thank you for reuniting me with my father. So . . . thank you."

My response comes automatically. "You're welcome."

Her gaze slips past me to something over my shoulder. "I'm not going to attack her."

I spin about to find Hawk lingering in the shadow of the

doorway to the barn watching our little encounter. Having been caught, he strides forward with his hands in his pockets and a casual swagger to his step that he saves for when he's trying to be intimidating or impressive. He stops in the space between me and Genna, a human barrier to any sort of confrontation that might occur.

Even though I'm sure he's still mad at me, his first thought is to protect me.

"You can't blame me for being cautious given what you did last night," he says.

"I'd think you foolish if you weren't," she says, the ghost of a smile on her face. "And I prefer it when you're forward. I've had enough of scheming liars to last a lifetime."

"I'll be sure to keep that in mind."

Pixies, is he flirting? I can't honestly tell with his back to me. It sounds like he's smiling though.

"Well, since we're on an honest streak," she says, "can I ask why you're both covered in dirt?"

I survey my jacket and pants. We had brushed ourselves off earlier but remnants of our fight with Scholar have stained the legs of my pants and there are faint smudges on the front of my jacket. Crap. I forgot how observant Genna is.

Hawk doesn't even flinch when he says, "Had a scuffle in the woods. It's good exercise."

"Interesting. Care to elaborate?"

"Not really."

Well, at least he's being honest.

"I don't know about you two but I'm starving," I say, an innocent change in subject. My stomach rumbles for emphasis. Despite all of the snacks I plowed my way through, I'm still worn out from battling Scholar and a full meal sounds mighty fine indeed.

Genna's eyes cut to me. "We haven't made supper yet. Dad was thinking of ordering in."

"No, no, you don't want that," Hawk says. "We just went shopping. I can cook."

I snort. "Can you?"

My brother shoots me a dirty look. "I guess we'll find out together. Shall we?"

He gestures with one arm for her to lead the way and inclines his head. Genna retreats into the cabin with Hawk close on her heels. I fall into step behind them and find Jefferson pouring over an old photo album at the table. He looks up when we enter and his eyes pass right over the dirt smudges on me and Hawk and go straight to his daughter like a magnet finding its attraction.

"We're making dinner," Hawk announces and goes to the cupboard where he starts suggesting meals to Genna. She stands over his shoulder as though extremely interested in the noodles, flour, and box mixes he points out.

Sensing I'm not needed for this discussion, I sneak into the bedroom and change into a fresh pair of clothes before dumping my stained ones in the hamper. My limbs are leaden with the drain of magical power today and the terrible night before so I slump onto Genna's bed. I'll just take a quick moment to myself. I'm not a great cook anyway. They don't need my help.

So tired. I'll take a quick rest, that's all. I lie down and fall asleep the second my head hits the pillow.

I'm shaken awake by a rough hand on my shoulder sometime later and I jerk away from the touch, instantly reaching for the gun under my pillow before remembering I'm not in my own bed.

Jefferson bends over me and withdraws his hand. "Food's ready."

Blinking the fog of sleep away, I smell something delicious wafting in from the next room. I roll up into a sitting position with a groan and cup my face with both hands, elbows braced on my knees. A strange sound reaches me in my defunct state—laughter. *Genna* laughing.

"Are you okay?" Jefferson asks, drawing me out of my meandering thoughts. "You looked like the living dead when you came back. That, and all the dried mud didn't help."

So he did notice—noticed and didn't bother to care with Genna in the room. Something ugly rears its head in my chest and makes me want to shove past Jefferson and storm out of the cabin. But that's stupid. I'm being stupid. I have no right to be irritated with Jefferson for being more concerned about his daughter who just came back after fourteen years. He knows I can take care of myself and I didn't make a deal out of it when I returned to the cabin. Besides, I don't have time to be irritated about something so meaningless when I've got Ashley and werewolves and dragons to be concerned about.

Instead I ask, "Jefferson, what happened to Jason?"

"Hmm?"

"Jason. The boy that went off the serum and slipped his probation ring. We arrested him at Ashley's place." The boy we've forgotten and left behind.

Jefferson straightens and crosses his arms over his chest. "I'm not sure. We'll have to ask for an update on him. But after supper. Come on, you clearly need to eat something."

He offers me a hand and I gladly take it so he can haul me to my feet. We enter the kitchen where Hawk is entertaining Genna at the table by making the cracked shell of an egg talk with a scruffy French accent. She laughs at the absurdity of it. At least she appreciates Hawk's and my kind of humor.

The table has been pulled out from the wall so we can all sit around it and is set with Jefferson's worn ceramic dishes on placemats of old newspaper. Pots of steaming mashed potatoes, gravy, and corn crowd the center along with a basket of freshly baked rolls.

For a long moment I gape at the scene and bountiful feast before me as Jefferson takes a seat. It's straight out of a movie—a family gathering around to share a home cooked meal. I've never been in the middle of such a seemingly simple affair, never been a part of a family group. It's always just been me and Hawk sharing meals by our lonesome as friends came and went in Underground. Celina would join us, sure, and Doocan nearly as often, but it was never quite like this.

And we are a family—Jefferson, Genna, Hawk, and me. All of us. Even as dysfunctional as we are—family.

"You going to stare at it or are you going to help eat it?" Jefferson asks gruffly.

I move around the table and take the last spot between Jefferson and Hawk.

"You guys made all this?" I ask and take the offered soda Hawk passes me.

"No, a couple of fauns breezed in here," Hawk says and rolls his eyes. "Well, dig in."

Genna snaps out a hand and grabs Hawk's wrist when

he moves to serve himself. We all pause and stare. She quickly relinquishes her grip when she realizes the attention in the room has zeroed in on her.

"We're supposed to . . ." She looks to her father as if seeking someone to back her up but when he's as clueless as the rest of us, she swallows and averts her eyes. "Never mind."

"What is it?" Jefferson asks as he reaches towards her across the table but she draws her hands into her lap.

She keeps her eyes on her plate. "It's nothing."

"You can tell me anything."

I bite my lower lip and try to pretend as if I'm not a part of this conversation but it's a little hard when you're sitting at the smallest table possible a few feet from each other.

She swallows again. "We always—the alpha always ate first."

There's that elephant in the room again, blowing a trumpet and dancing naked on the tabletop. Genna's captivity, her upbringing by Dasc, the random odd social skills that make it plain she wasn't raised like the rest of us. A hush falls over our little family of werewolves, an old crank, and a strange Blessed. Genna's so focused on her dinner plate I'm surprised it doesn't burst into flames.

Breaking the looming cloud of awkwardness, Hawk sets a forearm on the tabletop and leans towards her. "And what makes you think I'm not alpha material?"

He wiggles his eyebrows at her and those cold gray eyes cut to him. For a second I fear she's snapped and is about to attack when the corners of her lips twitch. I ease out the breath I had been holding and in an instant four pairs of hands reach for the food. We help ourselves noisily to cover up the interruption that Dasc's wayward teachings caused and dig into the delicious food with a vengeance. Nothing but the clink of silverware fills the cabin for a while and when that ends, before another wave of awkward can take over, Hawk launches into a story about when he challenged a centaur to a race—since Genna might like such a tale given her interest in races.

I lean back in my chair and become a near silent observer—joining the others in laughter every so often—and absorb this moment of comfortable happiness.

But as always, that dark voice creeps into my thoughts from the back of my mind. I recall Scholar's warning about Genna, about Dasc, about revealing my capabilities.

And I wonder how long any of this will last.

12

The storm clouds have moved on by the next morning leaving a heavy swath of humidity in their wake, but at least it's clear blue skies as I drive to the park alone. Moisture glistens off the new buds and gnarled bark of the trees that line the road.

Hawk insisted that he come but after what happened last time, even though Scholar promised never to harm my brother again, my faith in her promise is dwarfed by my concern for my brother. Granted, despite our happy gathering last night, I'm not sure how much safer he is staying behind to work on the obstacle course in our woods with Genna—more like keep her and Jefferson distracted as I head off alone on the false pretense of going shopping. We're really going to need to work on our excuses if I'm going to train with Scholar frequently or we're going to run out of them fast.

I expect to meet Scholar in the park itself but as soon as I cross the bridge she steps out of the trees with the agile swiftness I only associate with her. I slam on the brakes and pull off onto the shoulder. The SUV doesn't even come to a full stop before she opens the door and slips into the second row of seats. Right. She doesn't like the front seat if she can help it.

"Continue on this road, dear," she says by way of greeting.

"Hello to you too," I grumble and accelerate back onto the road.

"I have always found the perpetual use of pleasantries such a dull bore and quite utterly useless," she says. I glance at her in the rearview mirror. She sits perched like a queen with rigid poise. "Words are not needed to acknowledge the fact that we are aware of each other's presence once the first introduction is established, unless the purpose of it is to make one aware."

I fight the roll of my eyes. "And it's polite."

"There is a difference between sounding a parrot and intending politeness."

"What?"

"Focus on the road, dear."

I do as she says and wait for instructions like every other time I've driven with her as my backseat navigator. As usual, I'm kept in the dark up until the second I need to know where to turn. Where we're heading isn't far. Scholar has me take a left and follow a narrow road into the trees, then a right onto a dead end street and eventually stop in front of a sprawling two-story house with cedar beams bracing the front entrance.

"Wow, nice digs," I say. "Is this where you live now?"

"Temporarily. The occupants are currently away on vacation to Mexico for the next month."

A nasty feeling twists my stomach. "So you're squatting here? This is someone's home."

"Yes, but unfortunately my own home was disturbed and is no longer of use to me."

I don't meet her gaze in the rearview mirror. Yeah, that's my fault. In a desperate bid to save Hawk from the clutches of the lamia, I inadvertently guided them right to Scholar's doorstep. Revealed to the enemy and watched daily by the IMS, she can never go back there. It was such a nice mansion too.

Scholar eases out of the SUV and walks quickly but silently to the front porch. She doesn't wait for me to catch up before unlocking the front door—somehow producing a key for this house belonging to strangers—and disappears inside. Worrying my lower lip, and glancing around to make sure there's no one in the vicinity to watch me commit a crime, I exit the SUV and follow after the dragon.

I pause in the entryway that opens up to the second floor and gaze at the dark wood floors, the fancy stairs and railing before me, the expensive looking paintings on the wall of various types of candy, and the pristine cleanliness of the place. I can see the kitchen, living room, and parlor from where I stand. The whole place is airy and open and screams of wealth. Not a single pair of shoes, jacket, photo, or painting is out of place. Feeling rather guilty in my dirty shoes, I tug them off and set them in the allocated rock-lined shoe tray before padding in my socks after Scholar into the living room directly ahead.

We weave around the leather-upholstered furniture and halt on either side of a glass coffee table in the center. I drag my feet through the plush carpet and stare at the collection of jewelry spread in a meticulous pattern on the table. Scholar gestures one-handed to them and I realize the pieces aren't your ordinary pearls and necklaces. Dragon script is carved into the silver, bronze, and gold pendants that are shaped like animals or dragons mid-flight. These are Scholar's handcrafted heirlooms. She must have grabbed them before she fled her mansion.

"What's all this for?" I ask.

"Your first test. Take a seat."

I sit cross-legged on the soft carpet before the table and rest my elbows on the cold glass top. Scholar mimics my posture on the opposite side with a much more regal air than I'll ever be able to manage.

"As I said before, you lack control over your abilities and are therefore unable to unlock them to their fullest potential," she begins. "Such lack of control is easily remedied through discipline and practice. The test before you has a simple objective." She waves a hand over her trinkets. "Each is purely ordinary except for one I have laced with magic. The test is to figure out which one has power contained within it. You may not touch them or throw out your cloud of energy to make it react. You must locate it on your senses alone."

"I've never done anything like that before," I say and glower at the tricky bits of metal on display. "I don't know how."

"That is why this is a lesson, Phoenix," she says and raises her eyebrows at me. "Now listen closely. The easiest way to take control of your ability is to give it a physical manifestation. Abstract thoughts can easily be redirected or skewed or changed. When a physical element is added to the task, it gives one's mind an anchor. That is why stretching out a hand to direct my shockwaves is the best way to deploy them. You have to give yourself guidance."

"Okay. That makes sense. I think."

She rolls her shoulders. "Picture it this way. When you attempted to stop me from attacking your brother—"

"Don't remind me," I grumble.

"—it was as if you were casting a wide fishing net. You threw everything you had in all directions in order to catch my power and bend it to your will. The energy used for such a task is monumental to the point that if you stretch that net too far, the lines will snap, and you will collapse in on yourself."

"Yeah, I know what that feels like."

"Then you will understand that if you can focus that energy into a single line of rope and throw it directly at your intended target, the power consumed would be only a small fraction of your net. You would no longer be a 'one-trick pony' as they say. Such a charming phrase. You use less, you can do more. Do you understand?"

"I think so." If I focus my power into that single rope, I won't need as much energy to do what I want to do. I won't collapse the next time I try to stop something or someone from hurting my brother. "What do I have to do?"

"Magic fights magic. You should be able to feel other magic if you're looking for it. Imagine threads that tie everything together. Reach out to find them. You are a weaver at your loom. The world is your tapestry. You can shape it however you see fit. You just need to be able to envision it."

Right. A giant loom.

"What does a loom look like again?"

Her eyes morph into dragon slits even though the rest of her stays the same uptight human. "Is there another analogy you would prefer?"

"Never mind. Thread's good. I can do thread."

"Then, if you would." She sweeps a hand over the trinkets again for emphasis.

I inhaled deeply and let out the breath slow as I hover a hand over the trinkets on the table.

"Remember, do not touch," Scholar says. "Your sense of touch can fool you. Search for the tug and pull."

I nod as if I understand but I really have no idea what I'm doing. I've never been able to sense magic before. There's no Blessed I know of that can. Then again, I'm not like every other Blessed, am I? Unique to the point of being more than dangerous—becoming revolutionary.

My hand sweeps slowly over the trinkets and I wait for something magical to happen, to have that moment the hero in the story unlocks their powers and finally gets ahold of them. That's what happens in all the superhero movies, right? The moment of awakening, the secret training with their very zen master—like the stoic dragon sitting across from me—and then all the pieces fall together as they realize the true meaning for their life.

Except I don't get that moment of clarity. I feel nothing except for the chill in this abandoned house. And I most certainly am not finding any stupid strings on some mystical loom of destiny. Shape the world how I see fit—

what a joke. I can hardly patch my own life together without blasting holes through the middle of it. Like ruining my friendship with Ashley. Like burying myself under six feet of secrets. Like covering up Duke's death and having to live with that guilt day after day—

"You're getting off track, dear." Scholar remains stoic as I jerk my head up.

"What? How did you—"

"You were starting to scowl before looking more depressed than a faun whose garden has been trampled by a troll in search of mushrooms."

"That's . . . oddly specific."

She blinks slowly as if my comments are forcing her to consciously remain placid. "And also true, is it not?"

I roll my head around my shoulders. "I'm fine."

Okay. Game time. I can do this.

My hand pantomimes washing a car in agonizingly slow circles as I hunt for that tug. Threads of magic. Right.

Nothing. Absolutely nothing tugs or pulls or whatever the crap Scholar thinks I'm going to find. But maybe I do need another analogy, another way to picture the scene and find what I'm looking for. To put a face or a thing to an abstract idea of power and energy.

Maybe finding other magic is like feeling the beat in a techno song? Seeing a friend's face in a crowd?

Recognizing smells in a kitchen?

Smells like mashed potatoes and gravy and rolls fresh from the oven, mingling with the sounds of Hawk and Genna laughing.

Smells like blood and sweat and fear, the sounds of a lamia's hiss in the background and Charlie's wheezing breath as he dies next me with his blood being drained, knowing my brother would be next.

Smells like wet earth from thunderstorms, the drum of rain, the shock of fear as a monster enters our house, my parents murdered, and Hawk—oh, Hawk—

My hand jerks to a halt. I feel the heat on my skin pressing out in all directions from my body. A hot, smothering net searching and seeking and hunting.

Find the tug.

Find the tug.

Where's the stupid *tug*?

A pendant shaped like a bird a few inches to the left suddenly pops and I flinch. The metal burns brightly for a split second like a spark before it lies harmless and plain again amongst its kin.

"You were not supposed to make it react," Scholar says dully. "You were only supposed to find it."

"Well, I found it."

"You cast a net wide enough to cover the room. Of course you found it."

My temper bubbles to the surface and I curl my hands into fists on the tabletop. "Look, I don't know what I'm doing. There's no tug. There's no freakin' mystical loom. I don't *feel* anything."

"On the contrary, I think you may feel too much."

"Yeah, that's called frustration with a big dose of anger."

"That is not what I mean," she says and the hard tone of her voice makes me shut up. "You wear your heart on your sleeve. Whatever you feel, you put all of your being into it, whether that be guilt or anger or love or sadness. You have no mastery of subtlety or precision. You need to be an arrow threading a needle, not a nuclear bomb destroying a country."

"Enough with the analogies," I snap. "I get it."

"I do not think you do." Those dragon slit eyes taunt me. "I can *feel* that explosion when it goes off. If you do not learn to rein in your emotions and power, if you have an episode like that in the vicinity of Draco, he will know. And then you will disappear."

"You know, you're always threatening that," I say and try to ignore how badly my cheeks are burning. "Why don't you explain that to me? Why warn me about Draco? What do you honestly think he would do to me?"

"How about I make a bargain with you?" She scoops the trinkets towards herself using her forearms and hands. "If you can find the tug and tell me where it is without setting it off, I will share a secret."

"Just one?"

"Yes, for there are many."

"And if I pass the stage after that?"

"Then I may be inclined to share another."

I let out a humorless laugh and shake my head. "That sounds an awful lot like my current bargain with Dasc."

The floor beneath me trembles and Scholar's eyes glint.

"Do not compare me to him," she says deathly quiet—a warning that if I do so again she will act out and the trembling in the floor will be the nicest thing she does.

The rumbling in the house peters out and Scholar calmly rearranges the trinkets, the bird in flight gone from the ensemble, and spreads them across the glass coffee table.

"Try again."

I offer her my very best glare before holding out my

hand palm down once again, praying for a tug to make this training session end.

A nearby clock ticks out the painful seconds, then minutes, then hour or more—I lose track of time—as my hand hovers and I try to find the needle in the haystack. Scholar doesn't lose her patience but has me start over again and again when my frustration gets the better of me and I push out the energy in my veins.

"I want you to try something new this time," Scholar says as she resets the board so to speak and the trinkets are shuffled around. "Tell me, what is your fondest memory of magic?"

Well, at the moment my brain is completely blank what with anger and frustration chewing away at me. There's little room left for normal thought and happy memories.

I shrug. "I don't know."

"What do you think of when you think of magic?"

"I don't know."

"Yes, you do."

"I don't know!" I shout and throw up my hands. "Magic, it was—it was just there."

"Just where?"

"Underground." I feel a tug deep in my chest as I think of it. Of the fauns and their beautiful gardens. Of the air thick with the aroma of Old Man Two's restaurant. Of the air sprites playing across the high cement ceilings. Of the fire sprites creating fireworks in the stadium when they're in a particularly good mood. Of movies late at night next to a faun and giant. Of dancing elves, irritable unicorns, ever watchful gargoyles, stoic centaurs. Warmth and light and comfort and— "Home."

That tug grows deeper in my chest, filling me up and hollowing me out.

"Try again."

I stretch my fingers out over the pendants.

Home. The word reverberates in my head. Home.

I follow that tug, that pull of the familiar weight of the air in Underground, the smell, the sounds, the life that permeated those hidden walls. Hawk and me. My family.

Home.

I point to a pendant of a dragon curled up in a circle, its tail wrapped around the curved rim of its body. Scholar gives me a sharp smile and a nod of approval.

"You have chosen . . . wisely."

Using the tip of her pointer finger, she pushes the pendant towards me and I cup it in my palm. The burnished silver is cool against my skin, no larger than a nickel.

"You can keep that," she says. "If you ever get lost or are in peril, I'll be able to find you."

That doesn't sound as comforting as it's probably meant to be, because I don't particularly like the idea of being followed. But considering how my IMS training out in the field has started—with a werewolf uprising, attempted vampire take over, and death matches with lamia—a little insurance of a helpful dragon waiting in the wings can't hurt. I throw the thin chain over my head and tuck the pendant under my shirt to keep it hidden like Hawk's.

"Thank you."

"Oh, such manners. But I believe I also owe you something else. A secret."

"I thought we didn't owe each other anything. Your words."

The corners of her mouth tilt upward. "I am glad something sunk in at least." She sighs and bows her shoulders inwards. "I want you to trust me, Phoenix, and to understand. Knowledge is power and the greatest weapon you will ever wield. It is how I have managed to stay alive as long as I have."

"I guess I understand why you spent so much time as a librarian then."

That earns me a chuckle. "Infinity is trapped between worn pages written by a billion souls crying out to be heard in a universe where they are but sand slipping through time's fingers."

I feel like everything that comes out of this dragon's mouth is incredibly poetic and deep, yet so roundabout and frustrating at the same time.

"So, what's the secret?" I ask to prod her back in the right direction before she becomes even more philosophical about libraries and books.

"If you are to understand, then I must lay the foundation and firstly tell you that everything you think you know about the majestics is wrong. What clever lies have been spun to keep the dedicated followers in the IMS and legendary community ignorant have become historical truths—except for those that have lived long enough to know otherwise."

"Someone like you?"

Her expression sours and she suddenly looks much older, as if the weight of a thousand years or more is pressing through the human mask she wears.

"Someone exactly like me," she murmurs, her voice sad and broken. This isn't the Scholar I know, not the tougher than nails and who-gives-a-crap fighter that took on a couple of lamia, who defies majestics and monsters alike. I wonder what she's thinking of in her impossibly lengthy past to make her seem so fragile.

Then the shadow of that loss and hurting vanishes and she straightens where she sits, hands clasped politely in her lap.

"First off, there are not six majestic class dragons in the world as you have been led to believe. There are seven."

My brow crinkles in my confusion. "Seven? Who's the seventh?"

"Echidna. The mother of monsters."

13

Echidna.

Every history book, every story I've ever been told has made it clear there are, and have only ever been, six majestic class dragons. Dragons that wield the power to transform the earth, command the skies, undo the world.

But Echidna—she has always been a monster in the tales, a two-tailed creature of alabaster and bone with the burning red eyes of the devil. Always the cautionary tale of what lurks in the darkest corners and haunts dreams and devours children. She's also the core of the majestic dragon mythos and their triumphant victory over evil.

If what Scholar says is true, then every story ever told to me was a lie.

Echidna wasn't just some spawn of foul magic the majestics destroyed. She was *one* of them.

"But—she—w-what?" I sputter, unable to come up with anything coherent.

"Truly consider all you have been told, Phoenix. The power Echidna commanded, how she withstood the majestics for so long, the havoc she caused on the world. Do you really think there is such a creature capable of those feats without being a majestic herself?"

No. In the end, I guess Scholar's truth makes more sense than the lies I've been fed my whole life. Lies that the entire legendary community believes.

"Why?" I rasp, feeling that familiar sensation of the walls closing in and crumbling around me, just like when Dasc compared the Blessed to his pack of werewolves. "Why the deception?"

"Faith in the majestics tends to border between fear and awe at their power. If the world knew that one of them had created every single monster that walks the earth, how do you think that balance would tip?"

"If they're so powerful, why would they even care what people thought of them?"

"Because subservient followers are so much easier to control, and fear, while effective for subjugation, is also the catalyst for rebellion and upheaval." She twists her hands in her lap and exhales sharply. "So, as the victors, the majestics are the ones who wrote history, who cleansed any records of what Echidna was with fire. Many a library burned in those days."

Darkness passes over her face and the house shudders under her obvious rage at anyone purposefully destroying a library.

"Such a waste," she snarls.

"But you know the truth."

"Yes."

"How?"

"Because I was there."

I stare at Scholar, so unassuming in her bland clothes and unassuming appearance of a tired librarian. Underneath that disguise lingers a dragon's soul and the form of a terrene. I've questioned it before, how she's lived so long when her kind have one of the shortest lifespans of the dragon classes. She said she didn't fit into any categorization, that she was unique.

And to have been alive when the majestics took down Echidna . . .

"What are you?" I whisper.

The room pulses with a wave of her power and I feel it push through me and shake the house. She closes her eyes briefly and looks like she could very well be mediating in her cross-legged pose.

"That is a secret for another time," she says and stands. "It's time for you to go."

"But—"

"I will be in touch again so we can continue your training. In the meantime, practice on your own. Locate something of magic at your residence by using the technique you used today."

She starts to scoop up her trinkets and it's clear we're done. I rise to my feet and pad silently to the door.

"Oh, and Phoenix?" she calls.

I pause in the middle of tugging my shoes on. "Yeah?"

"Be careful who you trust, and when you tell your brother of what was said here today—as I am sure you will—be mindful of who else may be listening."

Creepy. A shiver goes down my spine and I finish putting on my shoes before trekking outside. It's still sunny out but after what I learned inside, the warmth on my skin feels false as if that too is a lie. I get in the SUV and sit in the driver's seat trying to draw my thoughts back to normal things, like regulating werewolves and training for the trials. But I keep dwelling on Scholar's words as if they are the tug I've been looking for.

Because subservient followers are so much easier to control.

What was it Dasc challenged me to consider? Who was the bigger fool—me or Genna? One blindingly following the majestics and the other under the tutelage of a psycho werewolf.

I'm beginning to think I lost that battle.

I start up the SUV and head towards Moose Lake. I'm nearly at the cabin when I suddenly remember that my excuse for leaving today was shopping. It'll be suspicious if I come home after hours of being gone with nothing to show for it. Grumbling to myself and a headache quickly coming on, I turn around in a random driveway and head into town again. I make for the Shop-More and walk in a daze through the racks of cheap shirts and jeans. I grab a few things at random as I mull over the fact that there are seven majestics and—according to Genna—the biggest bad of them all has returned from the grave to wage war.

I blink and realize I'm holding toddler clothes with stars and rainbows on them. What am I doing? I dump them on a nearby rack and turn around until I find the woman's department. I try to focus on getting Genna some clothes since she has basically nothing, but I can't stop thinking about dragons and lies and burning libraries.

If the stories are true about Lycaon, Dasc's alter ego, then he was turned into a werewolf by Echidna—a majestic dragon. Apart from that making Dasc impossibly old, he would also know the truth about Echidna, wouldn't he? How could he not? There's no way I'd be able to ask him, though, not without Draco knowing about it.

I drape the bundle of clothes over my forearm and hurry through checkout. When I make it back to the field office, I find Hawk and Genna sparring through the open doors of the barn. Jefferson leans against the side of the Green Monster watching them, his fingers clenching the fabric of his plaid shirt as though he's worried Genna's going to get hurt. I halt in the doorway with a plastic bag hanging from either hand and watch the flurry of limbs in a vicious dance of equally matched skill. Despite the fact Genna gets a solid hit to Hawk's jaw, my brother smiles like an idiot throughout the match.

Deciding I don't want to intrude or make myself known, I backtrack to the cabin and set the two bags of clothes on Genna's lower bunk. Since the others are distracted, I decide to practice on what Scholar taught me as a way to keep myself distracted. I stand in the middle of the bedroom and close my eyes. I think of Underground and every bit of magic infused there, and wait to feel that tug of home from somewhere in the room.

I'm not sure how long I stand there as my thoughts drift from home to majestic dragons and Dasc. Apparently it's too long because when I open my eyes, I find Genna standing in the doorway watching me.

I jump and press a hand to my heart. "*Pixies*, I didn't hear you come in."

"Yeah, I know," she says and crosses her arms over her chest. "What are you doing?"

"Appreciating solitude. Or so I thought, anyway." I gesture to the bags on the lower bunk to divert her attention. "Those are for you by the way."

Her eyes slide from me to the bags and back again. "Why?"

My shoulders hitch. "Because you don't have a lot of clothes?"

"What's the catch?"

"There is none. Although, I would like my sweatshirt back. I'm pretty partial to it."

She cocks her head and I'm immediately reminded of Dasc. "Who's money did you use to buy all that?"

"Mine."

"I don't understand."

"Yeah, me neither."

She pushes off from the doorframe and moves to inspect the bags. It's nothing fancy, just a selection of plain t-shirts, a tank top or two, some underthings, and two pairs of jeans. Genna lifts each item, flips it front and back as if checking for hidden tracking devices or something, and then folds them neatly into three stacks. She keeps her back turned so I can't see her expression.

"I hope it all fits," I say to fill in the awkward silence. "If not, let me know and I can return what you don't like. I sort of estimated size-wise since you've been wearing my stuff. Nothing with logos or anything because—well, I figured simpler was better. I guess I should have had you tag along but . . . I didn't know if you'd want that. I guess I don't really know you well enough to ask if you'd be comfortable—sorry,

I'm rambling. I do that when I don't know what to say. Or do. Or—I'm going to shut up now. Please say something."

She holds herself rigid without turning around as she says, "I'm not used to receiving gifts without strings attached. I'm not used to kindness being nothing more than kindness."

I swallow. Although I did want to get Genna some clothes, my first thought had been having a solid cover for lying about where I was today. I guess my kindness wasn't for the sake of being kind—and that thought feels heavy in my chest.

Genna isn't meant to be the villain, but so far I haven't given her a lot of opportunities to be anything else, what with Draco's suspicions being crammed down my throat.

"A lot of things are different than I'd thought they'd be," she continues in a softer voice. "What I'd been told they'd be."

"What do you mean?"

She takes a seat on the edge of the mattress to face me, bracing both hands behind her. "We—me and the others that were taken—were taught to fear ever returning to our families. A tactic to keep us loyal, sure, but to keep us . . . on edge about the prospect of ever getting home to the point most of us just stopped trying."

Curiosity gnaws at me and I tuck my hands into my back pockets, teetering back and forth on my feet before asking, "What did they tell you would happen to make you so afraid?"

"They said we would be hated for what we are. We would be shunned as werewolves." She gives a small shrug. "I thought it true for the first two days after you found me. Then we came here. Things aren't what I'd feared."

"Well, the world's not perfect," I say and allow myself to be honest. "There are some people that will treat you like something nasty stuck to the bottom of their shoe, but it's not all bad and the serum made things better."

"I appreciate your honesty. Yours and your brother's." Her gaze drifts to the toes of my shoes. "I've spent enough of my life around two-faced liars and sweet-talking snakes. It's been difficult realizing that I don't have to be a part of that anymore."

I worry my lower lip and try to think like my brother for an appropriate way to respond. Instead, I sort of word vomit. "I'm not the easiest person to get along with. I didn't have a lot of friends at school and I got in trouble and then I—well, I sort of pushed away some new friends recently and—the point is, I'm going to try. I'd like to be your friend, Genna."

Her dark eyes soften with a smile. "I appreciate that."

"Well, great. That's great."

"What do normal friends do?"

"Uh, they . . . they watch movies together, swap bad jokes, give each other gifts on their birthdays, confide in each other, that sort of thing. No strings attached."

"I like the sound of that." She bundles a pair of jeans, a black t-shirt, and underthings from the selection of new clothes and hoists them into her arms. "Well, I'm going to go take a shower."

I shuffle out of her way and she passes me with a friendly smile. Just when I think I'm going to be alone again to practice and sort out my thoughts, Hawk sneaks into the room, his sweat soaked shirt thrown like a towel over his shoulder and his bare chest covered in marked red spots. Genna sure wasn't pulling her punches.

"Does this look like the beach?" I grouse. "This is Minnesota. Put a shirt on."

He rolls his eyes and doesn't move from his spot leaning against the doorframe. His eyes drift to the bathroom where a faucet gurgles as the showerhead turns on. Hawk inches into the room and shuts the door behind him. The smell of his sweat fills the small space and I resist the urge to thrust open the window.

"Where's Jefferson?" I ask.

"Making a run to get pizza as a reward."

"A reward for what?"

He shrugs. "Genna being here. There really is no reason apart from wanting to do everything in his power to make his daughter happy."

"Well, pizza would do that for me."

He doesn't smile at my joke but steps closer and lowers his voice. "So, how'd it go?"

I consider that very loaded question for a long moment. "There's a lot I need to tell you and we need to be extra careful when we talk about it."

"Oh?"

"Hawk, what she told me . . ." I shake my head.

Hawk balls up his shirt and makes a rim shot into the laundry basket before coming closer.

"About you?" he prods.

"No. Look, we should go somewhere *away* if we want to chat."

"Okay . . ."

"Trust me."

I get up and lead the way out. He grabs a hand towel and dries himself off quick before throwing on a random shirt and following me into the SUV. I shut and lock the doors to be safe. He raises his eyebrows. I'm sure I seem pretty paranoid but after what Scholar told me, I figure every precaution is a good precaution.

Once we're alone in the seclusion of the SUV, I explain the test Scholar had me perform and the knowledge she shared when I succeeded. Hawk stares out the windshield at the cabin with his arms crossed and his eyebrows slowly drawing together as I talk.

When I finish, he takes a full minute before saying, "But that's . . . that's hard to swallow."

"I know."

"*Seven* majestics? One the ultimate evil? A giant conspiracy to hide it all? And what the heck is Scholar really? No terrene class dragon lives that long."

"I don't know but I'm going to find out. I'll practice and pass her tests and get more out of her."

He leans his head back against the seat. "This is so crazy."

"Yeah, and we've got to keep our lips sealed on this. No one else knows. Not anyone. And we keep it that way."

He blows out a long breath. "Man, I hate keeping stuff from Jefferson. We used to be Team Thunderstruck. Now look at us."

"I know." I fiddle with the bottom of my shirt. It's not just Jefferson I'm hiding stuff from. "I don't like it any more than you do."

We become absorbed in our own thoughts and sit in silence. Never in all my time growing up in Underground could I have imagined ending up where I am now— consorting with a hidden dragon, interrogating an alpha monster, keeping secrets from Hawk. I always thought the world would be cut and dry between good and evil, right and wrong. After talking with Scholar and meeting Genna, the world is more gray than I ever realized and I feel like every decision I make is going to tip me into darkness.

"So what now?" Hawk asks.

"First things first." I sit up and crack my back. "You're going to take a shower."

He laughs under his breath and gives me a quick salute before exiting the SUV. While he vanishes into the cabin, I make for the barn and trudge up the stairs to the loft. I log into my account on the computer to check my messages and the IMS feeds. There are more progress reports from Faunus and the Paris Division. They are still collecting evidence and many of those wounded are recovering. There's no more mention of werewolf splinter cells, just a little message at the end saying the investigation is ongoing and all areas designated mythical in the region should be on high alert.

I find a message from Celina in my inbox. She did indeed travel to Faunus along with Doocan the giant to aid her people. She's doing well but some relatives of hers are not. She lost a cousin in the attack and her words are much more subdued than usual. I hate feeling so far away and unable to do anything. I reply to her e-mail with as much encouragement and support as I can muster but I know my words are inadequate at expressing how I feel.

A new message pops up with an alert on my screen from Director Knox. Nervous, I open it to find a short message updating me on the Dasc situation. The interrogations are still on hold for the moment but they have experienced a "not so unexpected turn of events" regarding the werewolves recently rescued from the main Canadian camp Genna revealed. He doesn't elaborate but says they may need my services soon and he wants a new update on our "other project" via phone. I guess he doesn't even want to mention spying on Genna in an e-mail.

"Phoenix?"

I quickly close the e-mail as I hear Jefferson stomp up the stairs. The message center disappears a second before he emerges on the landing.

"Yeah?" I ask and get to my feet.

He waves me over and turns around. "Pizza's here."

"Coming."

I hurry after him. I'm starving.

When we reach the cabin, Genna and Hawk are already helping themselves around the kitchen table and distributing cans of soda to the four places at the table. Another family meal. This looks like it might become a regular thing—not that I would mind.

Genna's wet hair hangs in wavy curtains around her face and she wears the new clothes I got her which seem to fit just fine. Hawk is fresh from a shower himself, thank goodness. Jefferson and I move in to grab ourselves some slices and then everyone takes up the seats we had the night before. For a short while there's nothing but the sound of chewing before I notice Jefferson's eyes lingering on Genna's clothes.

"Are those new?" he asks.

Genna points at me with a piece of pizza. "Courtesy of Phoenix."

His beady eyes widen as they shift to me. "You bought my daughter clothes?"

My face burns under his intense stare. "Yeah."

"That was very thoughtful of you. Thank you." He beams at me as if I just saved the universe from destruction and got him concert tickets to see his favorite band. Guilt chews on my insides and my enthusiasm for the food dies.

The silence fills in again until Jefferson clears his throat and asks, "So, how are you two handling your responsibilities? Everything okay?"

"Yeah, the city's fine," Hawk says. "I was thinking of organizing a game soon. We haven't had one in over a month thanks to Mr. Cranky-pants-fill-in-agent." His eyes dart to me. "People have been asking for the games to make a comeback."

Jefferson's easy going demeanor instantly changes and he's that old crank we first met again. "I don't think that's a good idea."

"Why?" Hawk and I ask in unison, our pizza momentarily forgotten.

When his attention narrows in on his daughter before he blinks away that intensity and stares at his plate, the answer is clear enough. He's worried about Genna.

She gets the message as well and frowns. "What games?"

Before Hawk can even open his mouth, Jefferson says, "It's nothing."

Unwilling to back down—just like her father—Genna leans across the table towards my brother and asks even louder, "What games?"

Oh, boy. The line's been drawn.

"Uhhhh . . ." His eyes flicker between Genna's reptile smile and Jefferson's death scowl. I quickly cram a piece of pizza in my mouth before anyone can ask for my opinion.

Hawk finally caves. "The games we used to host for the werewolves to help with the instincts and let them out in a healthy way."

Genna blinks. Jefferson's scowl only deepens.

"You hosted werewolf games?" she says and a terrifying glint of competition enters her eyes. "What kind of games?"

There's a storm brewing on my right and Hawk deliberately avoids looking at it, all of his attention focused on Genna as he says, "Capture the flag, soccer, blackout, races—the six-legged race was hilarious, by the way—a few other odds and ends, depending on how creative we got."

"And everyone got to run around as wolves? You're allowed to do that?"

"Well, it was all done under supervision, of course."

She props her chin in her hand. "Huh. That sounds like fun actually."

Jefferson clears his throat. "It's really not necessary."

"Isn't it?" she counters. "Werewolf instincts are like an itch that needs scratching. If we don't let it out now and then it'll drive us mad. I think this is a great idea. People like me learn how to control that part of their life in a way that doesn't get them in trouble. I think that's very necessary."

I'm used to family drama but only when it's between me and Hawk. I think I severely underestimated how awkward it is looking in on someone else's familial battles. It's clear there are some strong wills duking it out from Genna's icy stare to her father's taken aback surprise.

"There shouldn't be any instincts with the serum," Jefferson says.

"Dad, have you ever been a werewolf?" She raises an

eyebrow and a muscle in Jefferson's jaw twitches. "A game would be good. I've been wanting to stretch my four legs."

He gives an odd jerk of his head as if he relents but does so unwillingly. I turn my head so Jefferson can't see and mouth "is that true?" to my brother. He's never mentioned such an itch before or feeling a need to transform. Hawk gives a noncommittal shrug and keeps eating.

"We need to be careful about revealing your presence here," Jefferson says and clasps his hands together on top of the table. "Family members and friends who have people missing are going to have a lot of questions for you once they know who you are."

Oh, *pixies*. I bite my lower lip. "Yeah, about that. We have orders to keep a lid on the people we've recovered for the time being. They don't want us telling the families yet."

Those cold brutal eyes of Genna round on me. "What?"

I glance to Hawk for support but he's struggling to chew past a huge piece of food in his mouth. "Well, given the way Rosalyn reacted, they wanted to make sure everyone was . . . okay before having them reunite with their families."

"They *need* this." Although seemingly calm, there's a frosty edge to her tone. "They need to be shown their true families again, to be reminded of what it was like before Dasc took us away."

"I'm sorry, but those are our orders."

Jefferson reaches out towards his daughter but she recoils from him.

"Honey, they're just taking precautions," he says. "I'm sure it won't be forever."

"That's the same thing Dasc said when he told us we

couldn't go home." She rises, walks at a measured pace into the bedroom, and shuts the door behind her.

The once friendly and familial atmosphere disappears. A heavy, dour silence falls in her wake and the pizza lies untouched on our plates. Well, that could have gone better.

"You had to bring that up?" Jefferson growls.

It feels like a slap in the face. "Jefferson, I—"

"I think you two should probably get to your training, don't you think?" He scoops up the pizza box without another word and shoves the leftovers into the fridge without asking if we want more. He keeps his back to us and forcefully starts to clean some dishes to the point he almost breaks a plate.

Hawk jerks his head to the door and I follow after, the heat of Jefferson's anger burning my cheeks and turning my breath harsh. We slip out of the house and into the barn where I start to pace in the sparring area, hands planted on my waist and fingers digging into my sides.

"He just—I didn't mean to—I—" I sputter and gesture angrily towards the cabin.

"It's not your fault," Hawk says where he stands with his arms crossed.

"Everything I do just ticks him off!" I shout and pause in my pacing to throw a punch into a nearby training dummy. The head painted on a wood beam explodes in a hail of splinters that ping against the wall of the barn. Hawk doesn't say a word as I stand there panting and flexing my hand, the scratches and abrasions across my knuckles stinging. "Ever since Genna came back, I can't do anything right. If I so much as look at her funny, Jefferson rips my head off."

"I know," he says quietly. His calmness works on my nerves and I force myself to even out my breathing.

"I didn't mean to make her upset."

"I know that, too."

"I get *why* she's upset, but it's not like I can do anything about it. We have orders."

He nods and steps closer. "We all have to be patient."

"I hate being patient."

"Oh, that I definitely know." He stops in front of me. "If I give you a hug, will that help you calm down or will you punch me?"

I glare at him. "Don't try to hug me."

He backs away slowly with hands raised. "Okay, how about a sparring match? Would that help?"

I purse my lips. "I might break your bones by accident."

"I like my limbs too much to risk it then. A run? Obstacle course? I think you need to work this off."

"Oh, you know me so well."

"Or maybe some meditation while we sit in a circle and hum?"

I roll my eyes. "Obstacle course sounds good to me."

"Great. Let's go."

"Our exercise clothes are back in the bedroom."

He shrugs and starts walking backwards out of the barn with a smirk. "We need some practice running around in street clothes. We won't always be in our tights and tanks. I'll race you there."

True to his word, he turns on his heel and sprints outside. I chase after him past the homemade gun range, along the wooden fence, through some lingering puddles, and into the woods on the far side of the cabin. Hawk outstrips me on the narrow trail through the brush to the obstacle course we and Jefferson set up to help us train and prepare for the trials. It's composed of an assortment of old barrels, wooden beams, felled trees, rope nets, and old barbed wire duct-taped into a grid.

Hawk immediately starts to scrabble up a fallen thirty foot log that's propped up at a forty-five degree angle against an enormous oak.

I pause at the bottom. "Didn't you just do all this with Genna earlier?"

"Yeah. So?" He tosses me a grin over his shoulder and hurries the rest of the way.

With a sigh, I hunker into a crouch to grasp the rough tree bark with my bare hands and test my balance and footing as I move up the log on all fours. Any time I slide, my palms scrape against the bark but I've built up some calluses after having done this course a hundred times over.

When I reach the very top—which is a considerable height—I choose my footing carefully as I lower myself onto my butt, turn around at the end of the log, and grasp the thick rope tied around the upper trunk of the oak. I ease myself carefully into position until my feet are against the side of the oak, then rappel at a slow pace so as not to burn my hands on the rope. Down, down, down I go until my feet touch solid ground again.

I race to catch up with Hawk who has already reached the barbed wire grid and is crawling along beneath.

I lose myself in the physical challenges, focusing on the exact placement of my hands and feet, the angle of my body, my treacherous surroundings, and forget about everything else. We pass through the barbed wire, to a wall we have to climb over, to parallel lines of tires to jump through, to a series of barrels we roll between as practice for quickly moving in and out of cover, a series of balance beams, more climbing, and then a sprint to the finish.

Hawk, as usual, beats me to the end and we both take a moment to catch our breath. My clothes are filthy and cling to my sweaty skin but the cool air is refreshing and fills up my lungs with the breath of spring. The woods are beginning to come alive as summer slowly makes its way towards us but at least the bugs haven't arrived in force yet. I've never been out here in the full heat of summer. I wonder what it'll be like in the woods then.

Our moment of rest is abruptly ended by Jefferson yelling at the top of his lungs.

"GENNA!"

Without a moment's hesitation, we fly back to the cabin, our feet pounding the muddy ground, and find Jefferson grasping at his hair in the middle of the driveway.

He whirls about on us and the momentary look of relief is replaced by anguish.

"What's happened?" Hawk asks.

"She's gone," he rasps. "Genna's gone."

14

Our trio flies into a whirlwind of motion as we race into the barn and I lead the charge up the stairs two at a time.

"She took the SUV," Jefferson says at the back of the pack. "I have no idea where she's going."

I slide into my chair and realize my computer is still on and logged in. My hands freeze over the keyboard. "This isn't how I left it."

"Who cares about the computer?" Jefferson thunders, clearly not in his right mind.

"Because if none of us used it, then that means Genna did."

Crap. I'm going to be in major trouble over this security breach. What on earth was Genna doing on here? I open the internet browser and check the history. There's a recent search that I certainly didn't do for "James Marshall + parents + Moose Lake" which leads to a newspaper archive with a story on James Marshall and a number of other kids missing from Moose Lake. From 1996.

"James," I breathe. "That James."

Hawk leans over my shoulder to see what I'm looking at. "What?"

"When Genna told her story, she said there was a boy named James kidnapped at the same time she was. Her best friend. She never said what happened to him and we haven't seen him on the list of werewolves rescued. She's looking for his parents."

Jefferson appears over my other shoulder. "The Marshalls? They moved out of the area."

"Where to?" Hawk asks.

"I don't know."

I check the history of the IMS servers next. "Genna figured that out too." I gesture to the recent search history for James' kidnapping profile. "They moved to Duluth."

"Move aside," Jefferson says.

I get out of the chair and he slides into it to immediately pull up the program that tracks the data from the probation rings. He brings up Genna's probation ring in particular and enters a password to access a secure portion of the site I didn't know even existed. A few more clicks and a map appears showing a green dot moving north along the interstate.

"There she is," he mutters to himself.

"Is that—there's a tracker on those rings?" I ask.

"A security measure, just in case. Only certain agents can trigger the GPS."

"Like you."

He doesn't respond but barrels out of the loft to the

Green Monster. Hawk's expression is grim as we follow after. My brother doesn't give me any argument as I take the front passenger seat and he slides into the back a second before Jefferson guns it. Jerked side to side from the force of acceleration and fast turns, I brace one hand on the door to steady myself. With the other, I reach into my pocket for my phone.

"Who are you calling?" Jefferson asks sharply. "The IMS? You can't—"

"*Relax.* I'm calling someone who can help us."

His narrowed eyes make it clear he doesn't trust me, even though he has no reason not to. I find the right contact and it rings a few times before the line is picked up.

"Long time, no returned books," Charlie says by way of greeting.

"Long time, *in a different country*."

"Yeah, yeah. To what do I owe this pleasure, Junior Agent Mason?"

"I need your help, Junior Agent Jaeger."

I can almost hear his smirk through the phone when he says, "You *need* my help?"

"Don't get so full of yourself. We've got a situation." After a sideways glance at Jefferson, who's staring stonily ahead, I give Charlie the quick, undetailed rundown of our spot of trouble.

"So you want me to intercept her?" he asks without room for judgment or questions, which I appreciate. I can count on Charlie being strictly about the job when it matters.

"I'm not sure how she'll react. That could be a very bad idea."

"You think she's dangerous?"

I gnaw on my lower lip and think of a way to put it that makes it sound better than the reality. "She's upset. Her father should be the one to talk to her and bring her back. We want to keep this low key."

"You mean, you don't want me to tell Melody."

"I mean we don't know what's going on and we don't want more trouble than is warranted."

He sighs. "Okay. So what *do* you want me to do?"

"Follow her. Stop her if she does try something but otherwise wait for us to get there. She should be entering Duluth in about ten minutes via the interstate in our standard issue SUV. I'll text you the address where we think she's heading."

"Roger that."

"Thanks, Charlie. I owe you."

"I think I owe you more than you owe me. I'll be in touch," he says and hangs up.

I text him the current address for the Marshalls before tucking the phone into my pocket and settling in to impatiently wait out the long drive to Duluth. No music is turned on so we have nothing but the roar of the 442's engine and our heavy silence for company.

This is my fault. I shouldn't have brought up the orders from the IMS and made Genna so upset. *Of course* it would make her upset. I should have known that. Now she's running off which is only going to get herself—and probably me—in trouble.

And the Marshalls. What on earth is she thinking? What is she going to tell them? And what happened to James? Considering her lack of information in that regard, I can only figure it's not good news.

At long last, Duluth stretches before us, a painting of buildings and streets over the rolling hills to the edge of Lake Superior and the harbor. The Marshalls live on the top of the hill near the mall. Jefferson guns it through town, flirting dangerously close with traffic moving much too slow for the pace he's setting. The sun glints off the hoods of the cars and I squint against the glare. When we finally pull off the interstate and start our ascent, I realize we're on the same road Charlie and I had our epic chase after a fleeing vampire. Well, epic until it ended in us being arrested. Good times.

We continue up the hill and follow the road that heads towards the county jail—another stop on my prior visit to Duluth. Yeah. Super fun.

Snow still clings to the ground in the deep shadows of ditches and around the corners of businesses that line the busy road. Spring hasn't fully set in and winter is fighting desperately to keep its clutches on Minnesota. Bitter and remorseless—sort of like Genna.

Jefferson takes a few turns into a woodsy suburban area and pulls in behind a black SUV where Charlie leans against the driver's door waiting for us. Jefferson kills the engine and we bail out of the Green Monster to greet him. Once out of the car, I realize there's another black SUV stopped directly ahead of Charlie's where Genna's head is visible above the headrest in the driver's seat.

"Glad you could make it," Charlie says and rolls his shoulders, working the pristine fabric of his designer jacket. "I followed her here when she suddenly stopped. I went to go check on her and—"

"I should go talk to her," Jefferson says, cutting him off,

and stalks towards the other SUV where his daughter is waiting.

Charlie looks taken aback and remains where he is with his hands in his pockets. The three of us hang back as Jefferson opens the driver's door and has a hushed yet fevered conversation with his daughter.

"You were saying?" I prod Charlie.

"Right. She said she knew who I worked for and that she was going to wait here on purpose until you showed up. Made it sound like her plan all along was for you guys to come find her here."

"What? Why?" Hawk asks.

Charlie shrugs. "I just got wrangled into this about a half-hour ago. I have no clue what's going on."

I bob my head to the side with a grimace. "Sorry. I needed someone to find her fast that I could trust."

His face softens a fraction and those pale green eyes lock onto me, slowly trailing over my clothes. "You gotten into mud wrestling lately? You're filthy."

I give him my best scowl. "Oh, shut up, mister I-look-handsome-at-every-hour-of-the-day."

His eyebrows rise and a smile spreads on his face. My cheeks grow hot.

"I mean, you're always so well-dressed and your hair is always perfect, and you—stop looking at me like that. I'm going to stop talking."

"Oh, by all means, please continue. I do enjoy praise."

Hawk clears his throat loudly. "I think Genna's getting out."

My brother shuffles around us as Genna indeed exits the vehicle to keep talking with her father. I remain where I am for a moment longer and self-consciously brush off my mud stained clothes. Charlie's smile remains as he pulls a red handkerchief out of his pocket and passes it over to me.

"You've got dirt on your face," he says.

I angrily lick the end of the handkerchief and scrub at my face. "Who the heck carries a handkerchief?"

"You're welcome. And you missed a spot." He taps a finger to a spot above my brow. "Right there."

I grumble a thank you before rubbing my skin raw and shove the piece of cloth at him before moving forward to see what's going on with Genna. Hawk stands a few feet apart from Jefferson and Genna arguing in the open door of the SUV.

"That doesn't matter!" Jefferson says. "You're just giving them reasons to haul you back there! I won't lose you again, Genna. I can't."

"And what does that say about the IMS if they make you that worried?" Genna argues.

"That's not the point. You should have come to me first."

Hawk cuts in. "Guys, you're making a scene."

Both of the Barneses wheel about on him, eyes glinting, but Hawk's right. A man has stopped at his mailbox down the road to watch the argument and at the house nearest us a little girl peers out between curtains. We avert our eyes and the fight sizzles out.

Feeling that someone needs to take control of the situation since Jefferson is clearly compromised, I speak up. "What's going on? Genna, why did you come out here?"

"Because it was the only way I could get you to come here," she says and plants her hands on her hips to make an imposing figure. I realize she's wearing Hawk's leather jacket which she must have snagged on her way out, and as the wind catches her short hair to wave it like streaks of black lightning about her stormy gray eyes, she looks every bit the powerful figure I see in the movies. She holds herself the same way Draco does—with self-assured confidence behind which is barely restrained power and she knows it.

"Why, exactly, did you want us to come here?" I ask.

"So you can see what your gag order really means." She points to a blue two-story house across the street. "The Marshalls live there. Their son has been missing for over fourteen years. You would deny them the truth of what happened to him? If it was you, and your brother was missing, how would you feel if the truth was kept from you? They deserve answers."

"And what happened to James? What are you planning on telling them?"

"The truth. That he died a hero. And that we made a promise to each other, that if either of us ever made it back home, we would tell the other's parents what happened to us." She swallows and her eyes narrow as if challenging me to question her motives.

I can't deny that if I were in the shoes of the Marshalls, I would want to know. They have a *right* to know. And the order was really only regarding those they rescued. This is different. Their son won't be coming home.

"We're already here," Hawk says quietly. "We might as well. Genna's right."

"Are we talking about James Marshall?" Charlie chimes in. Genna gives a single sharp nod. "And what if, after you tell the Marshalls, they pass along word that one of the kidnapped victims is dead? The rest of the families will demand answers or think their people are dead too. It'd stir up chaos."

And would also incite the families against the IMS and force them to release all of the people they had rescued—which I think was Genna's plan all along.

"Do they even know?" Hawk asks. "What James became?"

"They're red-flagged in the system," Charlie answers. "They don't know about the other side of the world. They believe it was a typical kidnapping and Agent Boyd was their FBI contact in the area once they moved to Duluth. I looked them up while I was waiting for you to show up."

"Then they probably won't even know that James' disappearance is related to the others in the area. There's no reason to think a panic would spread."

"Can we take that chance?" Charlie counters.

I'm torn between the two positions. In the end, word will get out sooner or later about the fate of Dasc's kidnapped victims. Wouldn't it be better for the Marshalls to know the truth before they hear something otherwise and have their hope wasted on thinking their son will come back?

"They deserve to know," I say quietly.

Charlie sighs. "I don't think it's our call to make."

"Then I'll take responsibility for it."

"You're a junior agent. If anyone gets in trouble, it'll probably be Agent Barnes."

"He's temporarily retired. Hawk and I have taken up the duties for the Moose Lake Field Office."

His eyebrows shoot up again. "You don't have a supervising agent?"

"They trust us. It'll be fine."

Jefferson adds, "I'd still take responsibility anyway. I think my daughter's right. The Marshalls ought to know. We'll chalk this all up as our idea in the first place so there's not a breach of her own probation."

I worry my lower lip and avoid Jefferson's gaze as he makes plain his intentions to break the rules. Charlie tenses beside me. We've broken the rules ourselves before, but that was to stop a vampire from fleeing after he hurt someone. This is different. And Genna's a werewolf. I recall Charlie has some sordid past involving werewolves that makes him rather touchy on the subject.

"Agent Barnes—" he begins, and I'm sure a sound argument is about to follow, but Jefferson wraps an arm around his daughter's shoulder and they ignore Charlie, walking step in step towards the Marshalls' home.

Charlie throws up his hands. "What is he thinking? Phoenix, you can't let them cover up a probation violation."

I put a hand on his chest to keep him back as he seems liable to march after them. I look to my brother and jerk my head in their direction. "Catch up to them, will you? I'll be there in a second."

Hawk nods and jogs ahead to reach them on the curb before they can walk up the sidewalk to the front door.

"Phoenix—"

"I'm not going to let it slide, okay?" I say quietly so the others can't hear. "Look, Charlie, you're not the only one concerned here. I'll be reporting this because that's my job, but I think Genna also has a point. The Marshalls would be finding out about their son soon enough anyway, and having someone who knew him personally explain it is probably the best way they're going to hear it."

A muscle twitches in his jaw and he glares off into the distance before looking me in the eye again. "Fine, but she and Agent Barnes aren't going in there by themselves."

"Hawk and I will—"

"You and your brother look like you've been rolling in the mud," he says. "I'm pretty sure your appearance is going to send the wrong message if you go in there. I'll go. This is my jurisdiction anyway."

His eyes flick to my hand still on his chest—which I've forgotten is here—and I quickly let it drop.

"Okay. Fine."

He heaves a sigh and squares his shoulders before muttering, "Melody's going to kill me later."

Before he can march off, I catch his arm. "Hey, leave a line open for me, will you? I need to hear what goes on in there."

"Why?"

Because I have orders from Draco and Director Knox to keep a close eye on Genna and report what she's up to. This, of course, I don't say, and fall on the lame excuse of, "For my peace of mind?"

He rolls his eyes. "Fine."

After calling me and then leaving his cell phone on in his pocket, he catches up to the others on the porch and has a quick conversation with Hawk which sends my brother back to wait with me by the SUVs as the Barneses and Charlie ring the doorbell. After some time of waiting, the door opens to a thin lady with a mess of curls piled on top of her head. Through the open call, I hear them identify themselves as FBI agents. Jefferson flashes his badge, and the woman lets them inside.

"Come on," I say to Hawk and pull him away to sit with me in the Green Monster. Once inside with the doors closed, I put the phone on speaker so we can both listen to the conversation going on inside the house.

"What's this about?" a woman's voice asks.

"Mrs. Marshall, we're sorry to arrive unannounced," Jefferson says. "Is your husband home?"

"He's in the kitchen on lunch break from work."

"I think it's best if we speak to both of you."

There's a general shuffling and we wait a few moments before I catch the subtle thud of footsteps.

"Mr. Marshall," Jefferson says, giving us some context. "Why don't you take a seat?"

"What's this about?" Mr. Marshall asks warily.

"We have news regarding your son."

"You do?" The expectation in Mrs. Marshall's voice breaks my heart. This is a mother hoping to hear the best, fearing the worst, and having lived with both expectations for over fourteen years. I can't even begin to imagine what this is like for her.

"I'm so sorry to bring you this news but . . . we received information that your son is dead."

It's difficult to keep listening for the minute that follows. There's a sharp intake of breath from someone on the other end of the line before despaired murmurs and shaking rasps that turn into sobs from both the mother and father. A tight knot forms in my chest and I subconsciously curl in on myself, tucking my hands in under my chin and biting my lip. The phone remains on the seat between me and Hawk in the back of the Green Monster voicing the echoes of grief from a family receiving confirmation of their worst fears.

Jefferson quickly introduces his daughter and Genna takes over the conversation.

"Your son James was not the only child kidnapped," she says gently. "If you'll let me, I'd like to tell you about him. We were friends and we promised each other that if one of us made it home, we would pass along a message to the other's family."

"Y-you . . . you knew him?" the father manages to say in broken syllables.

"Yes. I was taken at the same time."

"By who? What kind of—what monster—" It's all Mr. Marshall manages to get out before lapsing into raspy cries again.

I bring up my hands to press my fists against my mouth. I don't dare look at Hawk. Seeing the pain I'm feeling right now reflected in his eyes would send me over the edge into tears. This is awful.

"A man by the name of Dasc," Genna continues, keeping her voice steady and calm. "James and I were just two of many children he took."

"Please," Mrs. Marshall rasps. "*Please*, tell me what happened. Why? Why did this man take my son?"

As gently as she might, Genna briefly explains how Dasc rounded up children for some kind of zealot army. She doesn't mention a word about werewolves. To people who don't know the truth, spilling that secret would be like slapping them in the face when they've just learned their child is dead. So Genna spins a story of the truth leaving out the mystical elements. She says how Dasc was a radical hell-bent on making an army of loyal soldiers in order to wage his own personal war against the world, how their families were threatened to make them comply, how they did everything they could to keep their families and each other safe.

"James was my best friend," she says. "Through the dark days we kept each other strong. We promised each other that one day we would make it home."

"How did he die?" Mr. Marshall asks. He's regained some control over himself during Genna's explanation.

There's a long pause where the only sound is Mrs. Marshall sniffling.

"We thought we had a chance to escape while in Paris," she says. "But Dasc was too clever. He—he had James killed and I spent the rest of my time in a black hole before I was rescued."

I lower my hands to the collar of my jacket as I frown. The conclusion to Genna's story isn't fitting for me. She certainly wasn't in a black hole when we "rescued" her. She was running free in Scotland tracking down a bean nighe.

The father asks so quietly I almost don't hear him. "Did he suffer?"

"No," Genna answers in an equally somber tone. "It was quick. For what it's worth, although we were always held against our will, we were not abused. Dasc did his best to brainwash us to his cause but . . . James was strong. He never stopped trying to get back home. To get back to his family. And he wanted you to know, if he never did get the chance, that he loved you and never once stopped thinking about you, and he knew you loved him too."

"My little boy," Mrs. Marshall cries and bursts into violent sobs.

I take a shuddering breath and fight against the prick behind my eyes, the rawness in my throat. Hawk shuffles closer and holds out a hand to me. I take it with my own and we rest our entwined fingers on the seat between us.

I can't even imagine what my life would be like if Dasc had taken Hawk with him. Would I be the one sitting in Mrs. Marhsall's place getting the horrible news that my brother is dead? Or would he have turned out like Rosalyn? A broken, twisted soul compassionate to the monster that had enslaved him?

"Thank you." It's Mr. Marshall, sounding broken and small. "For telling us."

"I'm so sorry," Genna says. "The only comfort I can give you is that the man who took us is dead. Justice found him."

A lie. A blatant lie on top of the pile of misdirection and half-truths she had already given them.

There's an audible sigh and more sobs. Shuffling reverbs through the phone and after some murmured phrase I don't quite catch, Jefferson, Genna, and Charlie come out the front door. Hawk and I exit the car to meet them outside the SUVs. It's clear no one feels like talking, eyes downcast, brows drawn, mouths tight.

But I can't help myself. "Why did you tell them Dasc is dead?"

Everyone turns to me like I just laughed at a funeral. I pull my shoulders in and thrust my hands into my pockets.

"So they could move on," Genna replies evenly. "They deserve that. We all deserve that."

That logic I can't argue with. As long as the Marshalls

never discover the truth, that their son's kidnapper and murderer is still alive and well.

But this whole solemn affair has made me rethink my stance about keeping the rescued werewolves a secret. The Marshalls had clearly needed the truth about their son, even if it lacked the supernatural bits. They needed closure—just like the closure I had needed about my parents' deaths.

And when I talk to Director Knox next, I'll remind him of that too.

15

The silence of the empty bedroom surrounds me and pulses in my ears as I sit cross-legged on the floor with my eyes closed, searching for that familiar tug of magic. Hawk hid the pendant Scholar gave me somewhere in the room. He's currently distracting Genna with a challenge to beat him on the obstacle course with Jefferson looking on as I sit in the cabin alone practicing what Scholar taught me.

It's been a week since we visited the Marshalls. A week since I came home and received a message from Director Knox that a Whisper had escaped one of their raids and they made the decision to continue to keep the werewolves under lockdown so they could evaluate the potential threat. A week full of Genna glowering, Jefferson scowling in my direction, and Hawk trying to make nice with everyone. A week of no word from Scholar.

A frown pulls at my face and the angry, restless buzz of

thoughts disturbs my concentration. Despite that, I sense the thread in the room as if I discovered a familiar friend nearby through the force of their presence alone. I rise to my feet and move to the dresser, dig through a loose smattering of socks, and pull the pendant out of one rolled up in a ball near the back. I sling the thin chain over my head and admire the curled dragon detailed in pale silver before tucking it under my shirt.

A single week of practice is all it's taken for my senses to change as if someone had opened a lock on my brain and unleashed a power dormant inside me all this time. Once my eyes opened to that tug, it's something I can't turn off. Every time Genna or Hawk enter the house, I know it. I can *feel* them—a faint bitter presence that taps on my shoulder as if to say "hello, I'm here." And within the last day I realized the difference between Scholar's pendant and the magical disease swirling in their blood. While the magic of Scholar's pendant is pure energy like a spark in the dark, what lies in Genna and my brother's blood is like the acrid smell of smoke swelling above a hungry fire. A warning of danger, of lethality.

I do my best to ignore it.

I pull out my phone and check the time before opening a secure app that shows me the precise location of Genna's probation ring. The dot hovers close by in the woods surrounding the cabin. After Genna ran off to the Marshalls, Director Knox gave me the access codes to activate the GPS on her probation ring—after he chewed me out, of course. I let Genna slip right through my fingers. It was difficult enough convincing the director not to send a team of agents to secretly spy on us to make sure it doesn't happen again. That would only invite all sorts of trouble. So now I've been checking my app like clockwork ever since I got the new application. Jefferson doesn't know about it, neither does Hawk, and I plan to keep it that way.

A reminder buzzes on my phone that I had set earlier. A message pops up that just says, *brace yourself.*

Rosalyn has been making enough progress that the director is allowing her brother, Deputy Graham, to bring her home to Moose Lake. One more werewolf I need to keep a close eye on and one who's already made her opinion of me evident enough by jamming a stun gun into my neck. They should be arriving soon.

Tugging on my favorite *Go Fire Sprites!* sweatshirt that I finally got back from Genna, I walk outside. I make for the obstacle course but meet the others halfway across the gun range. Hawk and Genna are both breathing harder than normal and have spots of dirt on their clothes. That new tug of bitter magic greets me.

"Deputy Graham will be showing up soon," I say. "We should get going."

Genna nods grimly and the three of them move off for the cabin to get cleaned up. I hang around outside and pull out my pearl-handed .45 from where I have it hidden at the small of my back. After checking the slide and magazine, I return it to its holster and tug my sweatshirt over it.

While Jefferson comes out to start the SUV and turn it around, I amble to the plot of overturned earth alongside the cabin. There's a series of plastic boxes holding an array of flowers next to it ready to be planted. Jefferson, Genna, and I had gone to a greenhouse in town to get flowers the other day while Hawk went on some probation rounds by himself. I made the excuse of not wanting to encounter Ashley again for my reason to go with Genna. He didn't question it, considering Ashley's last reaction to me, even though the truth was I was sticking like glue to Genna. She had lit up like a fire sprite during the midsummer solstice as she moved excitedly from plant to plant. I couldn't see the appeal myself but her exuberance had been infectious. The weight of years being under the heel of Dasc had vanished.

Now, as she stalks out of the cabin in her black t-shirt and dark jacket to match her dark expression, that person excited by daisies is gone. This is the Whisper, the shadowy menace that haunts children's nightmares.

"Let's go," she says, her cold eyes passing over me briefly as she marches to the SUV and takes shotgun. Hawk raises an eyebrow, shrugs, and slides into the second row where I join him a second later.

We rumble along in uncomfortable silence. I know I'm certainly not looking forward to this visit but we need to make sure Rosalyn is able to settle in and knows the ground rules for living in Moose Lake. Genna insisted that her presence is absolutely necessary in order for Rosalyn to accept her new reality. Jefferson said it couldn't hurt—although I could count a number of ways it could—but I'm in no mood to argue. Arguing with Jefferson about his daughter is pointless anyway.

Jefferson takes us through town before heading east into a woodsy area, past tightly packed in houses overshadowed by enormous maple trees, before we stop in front of a quaint brick house with a single car garage. Spruce trees crowd around the sides of the short driveway and a weeping willow droops with new buds next to the front porch.

A squad car takes up the spot in front of the garage, *Carlton County Sheriff's Office* in golden letters across the side.

"Looks like they're here," I say to no one in particular.

No one responds and we walk in an uneasy group to the front door. Hawk rings the doorbell. A few seconds pass before Deputy Graham opens the door. He looks haggard with a five o'clock shadow, bags under his eyes, and a rumpled plaid shirt. He combs his fingers through his shaggy hair and heaves a sigh. My chest tightens at his obvious distress.

"Come in," he says and opens the door wide.

Hawk spearheads the way into a tight living room boxed in by a sofa, reclining chair, and television stand. He immediately moves for the reclining chair and inspects the lever on the side to lift the leg rest. I punch him lightly in the shoulder as I pass to the sofa. He scowls at me—me being the fun ruiner—but he leaves the leg rest alone. Jefferson sits next to me on the sofa but Genna stands in the middle of the room with her arms crossed. She doesn't give any normal human indicia like tapping her feet or fingers to express her anxiety or restlessness. No, she stands like a statue, imposing and grim.

"Where is she?" she demands none too kindly.

The deputy's expression hardens. I wouldn't be too happy if someone came into my home and started bossing me around either.

"Wait here," is all he says.

He disappears down a short hallway directly across from where I sit and I espy three doors that way. To my left is the opening to the kitchen and just past that is another room I can't quite see. I'm acutely aware of the exits, of the front door mere feet away and the backdoor through the far side of the kitchen. I feel the weight and shift of the .45 in its holster at the small of my back. My eyes scan the room for where the deputy may keep his guns and anything else that could be used as a weapon. Granted, with Rosalyn, I'm sure anything could be used as a weapon.

Since my last encounter involved her trying to stun me and take out my comrades, I'm not real keen on a repeat scenario.

The deputy's heavy footsteps announce his return and he steps aside once he reaches the living room to make way for his sister. Rosalyn wears the same sour expression as when I first met her. I'm starting to think her face is stuck that way with a sneering lilt to her mouth. And to think, she'd actually be quite beautiful if she ever decided to smile. Her long brown hair is rolled into a single spiral over her right shoulder. She's also wearing the same clothes from when we had our encounter in Scotland sans the rain jacket.

Rosalyn halts on the fringe of the living room and has a staring contest with Genna. Neither of the girls move a muscle for at least a minute but the rising tension is palpable.

Like two wolves sizing each other up.

"Roz," Genna finally says in a clipped fashion.

"Genevieve."

"Made yourself at home?"

"Enduring."

"Tried to kill anyone yet?"

Rosalyn's eyes narrow slightly. "Contemplating."

"Relatively okay otherwise?"

"Physically."

"Still sore about what's happened, I take it?"

"Obviously."

The single word responses are peculiar and Rosalyn seems irritated that she's giving them from the cross look on her face.

"Let's have a seat," Genna says and gestures to a small table in the kitchen.

Amazingly, Rosalyn obeys without a moment's hesitation and takes a seat at the table out of sight. When Genna moves to follow after her, she turns enough so I can see the sparkle in her eyes and the lingering smug smile. Well, she clearly seems to be enjoying herself for whatever reason.

As the two girls take seats at the table, the rest of us lean forward in our chairs to watch their interaction unfold. Deputy Graham lingers by the recliner for a moment before deciding to start a pot of coffee on the counter next to the kitchen table.

"Things have changed," Genna says. She's relaxed in her chair and completely at ease, one leg crossed over the other with her foot held loosely in the air under the table.

Rosalyn sits in complete opposite form—body rigid, arms tucked tightly to her sides, the muscles in her jaw clenched, and hands curled into fists.

"The mission is still the same," Rosalyn retorts, the most she's said yet in a single go.

"The mission has changed," Genna says more forcefully. "Our duty is to protect our own, and that includes saving them from Dasc's influence."

"Our duty is to the war."

Genna gives an exasperated sigh. "I thought they said you were getting better."

"I'm fine exactly the way I am."

"So you're fine not being alpha?" Genna quips and Rosalyn's face turns a deep shade of red within seconds.

Jealousy. Power. That's the struggle I'm sensing going on here. Genna said before that she was a Whisper, one of Dasc's followers trusted to carry out his will. I don't doubt that Rosalyn is jealous of Genna's status as such, especially considering how loyal she's been to Dasc throughout all this. Genna seems to be dangling that fact in front of Rosalyn's face as if daring her to do something about it, provoke a fight even. She's supposed to be helping Rosalyn adjust, not cause more conflict. We already have enough of that.

"You do realize that none of that matters here," Genna continues, her cocky demeanor subtly shifting into something more embracing. "There's no pack. There's just people and family. We're finally home."

Rosalyn's eye twitches. "I don't even know the meaning of the word."

"Yes, you do." Genna inclines her head in the deputy's direction. "You know who he is. You remember from before, I know you do. Your gentle giant. You said that about him before to me. Do you remember?"

The deputy freezes with one hand hovering over the handle of the coffee pot even though it's not ready to be poured.

"Well, I remember even if you don't," Genna says. "Everything I did was to return you to the people who truly love you, to a place where we aren't controlled and have things expected of us in return for our lives. We can be whatever we want here."

Rosalyn doesn't say anything which is unsettling. When we first met, she took every opportunity she could to slap sass in my face. It's unclear to me whether her silence is caused by Genna's words or apparent higher ranking status.

"Doesn't matter," Rosalyn eventually says and there's a collective slumping of shoulders in our room as she doesn't take the turn we're hoping for in this conversation. "We're still werewolves. We will *always* be werewolves."

"We're not bound by it anymore," Genna insists and slides a hand across the table, reaching towards her comrade in a gesture almost pleading. "Can't you feel it? The change with the serum? Dasc always said it would break us apart but it hasn't. It's helped clear my head. The weight in my blood has lifted."

"Mine's just as heavy as before," Rosalyn says. "The serum isn't some miracle from the heavens. You're living in a fantasy."

Or the more likely scenario is that my influence is creating this greater feeling of change in Genna. She's been hanging around me a lot whereas Rosalyn has not. I do my best not to give myself away by making any movement or change of expression at this line of conversation. I fight the urge to glance at my brother or Jefferson.

"Things will get better," Genna says.

"Will they? Have you spoken with any of the others?"

Crap. We're heading in a very bad direction here. If Rosalyn learns that the other werewolves are being held in lockdown, I'm afraid we're going to trigger a nasty reaction. I can vividly remember the shocks going through my body when Rosalyn learned I was the one that nearly killed Dasc. If she's still as dedicated to his cause as before, that little tidbit of information could really set us back. She could even lash out at Deputy Graham as he sets a cup of coffee in front of her. Although, she doesn't seem to even notice his presence in the room as if he's part of the wall. I can understand why he looks so disheveled if that's the attitude she's been giving him this whole time.

"Given the way you reacted when you were found," Genna says dryly, "they're feeling hesitant about letting the others return home just yet. So thanks for that."

It's true that Rosalyn's response is part of it, but Genna doesn't know the other half of the problem—of the rogue werewolf faction that attacked Faunus and the facility in Paris. There are too many volatile variables in play and the IMS is trying to get a hand on the situation however they can, even if that means keeping the werewolves from their families.

As much as my gut twists thinking about it, seeing Rosalyn here with Jared is only making me think that precaution is well deserved. It's clear Rosalyn isn't as far along with accepting her situation as we were led to believe.

In fact, I think I'm going to need to keep a closer eye on her than Genna.

Roslayn rocks back in her chair, lifting the front legs into the air. "Well, what about the war? Ignoring it isn't going to make it go away."

"I know that. I gave the IMS all the information I had. This is their battle now. We were forced into being soldiers. I don't want that life."

She scoffs and rolls her eyes. "You won't be able to hide in this town forever, Genevieve. Neither of us will."

A dark shadow crosses Genna's face and she clenches her jaw, the first sign she's made that any of Rosalyn's comments have gotten to her. Is she worried that her past is going to come back to haunt her? That she's not safe in Moose Lake? It suddenly dawns on me that Genna could be afraid of reprisal. She had told me before how Dasc would send monsters after the families of those that attempted to leave him. My eyes flick to Jefferson leaning forward on the edge of the couch beside me. If anyone did come after Genna for exposing a great number of Dasc's forces, they would be coming to kill her father for revenge. I'll have to keep closer tabs on him too.

"Things are different now," Genna says. "Dasc is sealed away. The wolves are free."

"Don't expect the others to believe that," Rosalyn says and turns away as if she's done talking.

"And you?" Genna asks. "What about you?"

"I'm not going to be reaching out if that's what you're worried about. I won't be looking to call down the wrath of the pack for something *you* did."

"I'm trying to *save* us."

"Keep telling yourself that."

Well, this is blowing up in our faces in spectacular fashion. Maybe bringing Genna along wasn't such a great idea. She doesn't seem to have persuaded Rosalyn to take it easy one bit.

Genna rises from the table and nods to Deputy Graham before returning to the living room where the rest of us sit.

Surprisingly, Rosalyn follows and her attention settles on us three agents.

"Is there anything else you wanted?" she demands.

Wow, she's going to be a treat to work with.

Thankfully, Hawk decides to speak up for the rest of us. "We just wanted to check in and let you know what to expect around here, what the rules are."

"Such as?"

He explains that she and Genna both need to keep a low profile for the time being for everyone's sake, that he and I will be coming to check up on her daily to make sure she's adjusting and isn't having any problems and to ensure she's taking the serum. She stares flatly at him and when he's done talking, she flashes me a feral smile.

"I look forward to it," she says and whisks out of the room to where I assume her bedroom is.

There's an audible round of relieved sighs when Rosalyn's hostile presence leaves the room. Genna stands at the end of the hall with her arms crossed, eyes glued to where her former comrade has disappeared.

"What do you think?" Deputy Graham asks and kneads his knuckles into the top of his thighs as he waits expectantly for Genna to answer.

She takes a long moment to respond, giving us plenty of time to worry, before she says "She won't be causing trouble, even if she's not happy about it."

"Are you sure?"

Genna nods and turns away from the hall to face the rest of us. "Well enough."

"That's good, I guess."

Her expression softens as she tilts her head to look into Jared's face—he's at least half a foot taller than she is.

"I'm sorry," she says. "Our life wasn't easy. This change is going to be difficult for her, but I'll do everything I can to make sure she figures herself out."

"Thank you." The words come out mingled with relief. It's strange how afraid he seems. A giant trying to wrangle a firecracker of a little sister but from the look on his face you'd think he's been tasked with putting a bridle on a hydra.

I rise from the couch. "If you need anything or there's a situation, call immediately."

"Of course." He nods, his eyes vacant as he combs a hand through his hair. "Our parents will be coming up soon. I think that'll help her."

"Let's hope so," Genna says gently.

The others rise and we walk out together to the SUV. It's an odd shift moving from the inside of that depressing and tension-high atmosphere to the sunny spring day outside. The clouds have moved off and warmth radiates on the side of my body where sunlight hits me. I pause for a moment to soak it in and Genna does the same with the passenger door held open in her grip.

Then I feel it, that bitter tendril of magic tapping on my shoulder to tell me there's another werewolf nearby apart from the two immediately beside me and the two inside the house. It's become increasingly easier to make out the sensation of the presence of magic, diseased or otherwise. I scan the area around us but there's no one in sight.

"What is it?" Hawk asks from inside the SUV.

The presence fades away into the distance. It was probably just another local werewolf out for a walk. All that talk inside about revenge is making me overanxious. I certainly hope none of Dasc's werewolves out there are seeking some kind of comeuppance for Genna or Rosalyn.

I slide into the SUV next to my brother but Genna takes a moment longer to get into the front. Her dark gaze sweeps the driveway and street beyond, a frown on her face. At last satisfied—or possibly disappointed—she gets in, buckles her seat belt, and Jefferson takes us to the cabin. On the ride I can't help but linger over Genna's words to Rosalyn and Deputy Graham. Everything she's done, whether it be pointing a gun in my face or running to the Marshalls, has been to protect her family and save the werewolves. I can't fault her for that. And perhaps it's time I gave her a little more credit for her efforts.

When we reach home, Jefferson and Genna split off to the barn while Hawk and I change into our exercise clothes. For the rest of the day, my brother and I train hard in preparation for the upcoming trials. The days may be growing longer but time is getting shorter for us to be prepared for the tests that will decide if we become full-fledged agents or not and where we'll be posted if we do pass. The number of days slipping away between then and now feeds the slithering beast of anxiety in the back of my mind. We're drawing closer to having our blood tested, to Hawk temporarily taking the serum, and our futures being decided. Not like it's a huge deal or anything. It's only our entire lives and everything we've been through and all our training boiling down to a month of tests.

We give the obstacle course several goes, mastering our balance, adaptability, and endurance. Then it's a bout of sparring in the barn. We spend time with each of the various weapons from our small armory. Next we race on the backroads and trails before we return and run the obstacle course some more. It's nearing supper by the time we walk back to the barn sweaty and covered in dirt.

Humming catches my ear and as we round the corner of the cabin, we find Genna planting her flowers in the bed of soil she broke earlier. Jefferson works on patching a rusted watering can with duct tape a few feet away. He keeps halting his work to gaze lovingly at his daughter as she hums an unfamiliar song. Hawk and I continue to the barn so as not to interrupt their little gardening party.

Once we get inside and take the stairs to the loft, Hawk says offhand, "She has a nice voice."

"Yeah, she does," I reply and pick up the book I had left next to my computer earlier. "Better than my singing voice for sure."

"Oh, definitely."

I make to slug him in the shoulder but he dodges and moves around to the other computer. For the next half hour we pour over books with lengthy descriptions of monsters and their strengths and weaknesses. We'll need to be able to identify each one on a moment's notice during the trials. I've already read this book a hundred times so I have difficulty concentrating on the text that's all but burned into my retinas at this point. An insistent pull in the back of my thoughts eventually makes me slam the book closed. Hawk twitches at the sudden sound.

"Come on," I say and set the book aside.

He removes his crossed feet from where he had them propped up on the desk. "Where are we going?"

"To get a little bonding time."

He raises an eyebrow but follows after as I descend the steps and make my way over to the garden around the backside of the cabin where Genna still hums while Jefferson churns the dirt with a smile.

"Umm . . ." I clear my throat, suddenly anxious. "Hi."

Both Barneses look up from their work.

"Yes?" Jefferson says gruffly.

"Do you want some help?"

They blink in unison before exchanging a look that's a conversation all its own. Thankfully, instead of appearing peeved by my request, they smile and Jefferson waves me over.

"You can give me a hand with the trellis we're going to set up." He stands and dusts himself off.

I follow him to a stack of gardening supplies by the cabin wall while Hawk bends down to scoop dirt so Genna can plant a potful of lilies. Jefferson and I haul over a rather large wooden trellis and as a team we plant something called clematis which is supposedly going to give us some very pretty purple flowers when it blooms. Genna directs us as she lays out the plans for the rest of the flower bed and then we move over to the gun range where we churn up two more beds to border the ends of the range. We sit and crouch in comfortable silence as we plant potatoes, peas, raspberry bushes, green beans, tomatoes, cucumbers, rhubarb, and spinach. The food we grow will make a nice compliment to the venison and eggs we always eat here.

As I crouch in the dirt with a smile and the setting sun on my back, I wonder if Hawk and I will even be around to enjoy the harvest from these gardens. We'll be heading to Underground for the trials in May. Then after we've completed the trials there's no telling where we'll end up. There's a good chance we won't be coming back to Moose Lake. A pit forms in my stomach. This place has really been growing on me—the place itself and the people here. It won't be easy saying goodbye.

I sit back on my heels and laugh as Hawk tries to teach Genna a rowdy song with questionable lyrics as Jefferson looks on with a scowl, the tomato plants in his hands all but forgotten.

At least there are no goodbyes today.

16

"**Y**ou seem to be in better spirits," Scholar says as I pour over the trinkets spread on the tabletop between us. We've set up in the kitchen this time of the home of the unsuspecting family currently vacationing in Mexico. I hover my hand over the pristine granite tabletop at the eat-in counter and dangle my legs on the high stool as Scholar stands straight-backed across from me.

"I guess that's because I am for the moment," I say.

It's been two weeks of nothing but smooth sailing since Rosalyn came home to live with her brother in town. I've been pleasantly surprised that nothing horrific has happened. It's a miracle, to be honest. I thought Rosalyn for sure was going to be the final ingredient for the city exploding but I was wrong. Just as Genna said, Rosalyn hasn't been a problem. Each day we've checked up on her she's been a little more cooperative and less hostile. Jared doesn't look like he's ready to pull his hair out or fall into a mess of tears anymore. In fact, he actually smiled the other day and was I sure glad to see it.

Then there's Genna, a hard-working ray of sunshine. She's been training alongside Hawk and me, and not just the obstacle course. She joins us on runs, practices sparring, frequently wins the obstacle course, and gobbles up all the knowledge we have on monsters. But the place she is clearly the happiest is working in her gardens. They've begun to bloom and have transformed the patched up, duct tape riddled field office into a beautiful landscape. She's worked tirelessly to expand the gardens, do upkeep, weed, water, and nurture in every way possible. There's always the sound of joyful humming coming from somewhere around the cabin these days.

"Things are going well, I take it?" Scholar asks.

"For once."

"You are making excellent progress, by the way." She nods to the trinkets before me. She's got me working on a test where I try to make only one trinket glow at a time. They apparently react when they come in contact with outside magic and give off a faint blue light. It's made a visual for me of how I cast out my magic in a net. So, now I'm being forced to throw out a single line to each trinket in turn, trying to make only one glow in a single moment without affecting the others. It's proving difficult and I've only managed it once so far in our hour long session. At least I've gotten the part about sensing magic down. I feel the ebb and flow of magic around Scholar and the pinpricks in each pendant with ease.

"I don't feel like I'm making great bounds or anything,"

I say under my breath and try to concentrate on holding myself in and just let a single tendril of my own power touch a pendant squarely in the middle shaped like a gryphon.

"You underestimate your abilities, and without relation to others' training experiences I suspect you would not know the full extent of my admiration for your progress."

"What now?" A swath of pendants begin to glow around the tiny gryphon.

"Focus, dear."

I draw in my power again but it's hard to keep myself contained. I've been walking around with my magic like a web around me constantly. Trying to change that and rein myself in is proving extremely difficult.

"If it comforts you, I have never had a student grasp the concepts and practical application of these methods as fast as you have." She tilts her head to the side and adds as an afterthought, "Save one."

"Oh?" The other trinkets dim somewhat and I feel like I'm about to pop a vein in my forehead from narrowing in on that metal gryphon that I swear is taunting me. I can't help but feel pleased and distracted by Scholar's compliment, though. A sense of pride fills me up. To be her quickest study, when she's sure to have had countless students given her apparently long life, is gratifying.

"You're getting consumed by your thoughts," Scholar scolds as the trinkets begin to glow more brightly. "You must learn to control yourself even under distraction."

"Right. I'm trying."

"This ability will become essential in your very near future, I assure you."

"How so?" I mutter as I try to talk and focus at the same time.

"This is going to be your sleight of hand in order to pass the blood testing at the trials."

The entire mass of trinkets glow as I completely lose my concentration. "What?"

Scholar scowls and points at her collection glowing bright blue. "That is decidedly what we do *not* want to happen."

"But how is this going to help me pass the testing?"

"We will focus on that later. For now, indulge me."

I heave a sigh, roll my shoulders, and try again.

The task itself makes me realize that I've got pressure built up inside me and the more I try to hold it in, the more constricted I feel. When I let it out as—for lack of a better word—an aura around me, the pressure lessens so I don't notice it. It's like if I don't let it out, the power inside me would rip me apart from the inside. I've felt the start of it as sweat beads on my forehead and I finally manage to make only the gryphon glow like a beacon in the darkness of the other cold, unaffected trinkets and babbles. Holding it all in and reaching out that thin strand like a thread looping through the eye of a needle, the eye being the metal gryphon, my ribs start to ache and burn and pressure forms in my head like extreme congestion to the point of pain.

When Scholar finally nods, I let myself go with a great exhale and release the tension throughout my body. The mass of pendants, rings, and pins instantly begin to glow.

"Well done," the dragon congratulates me.

I run the back of my hand over my forehead. "Thanks. Can you explain something to me, though?"

"I will do my best."

"If I have that much power in me to the point it hurts keeping it all in, why does it take so much out of me when I try to use that power? Shouldn't it be like an endless supply?"

"I believe it has to do with overextending yourself without a true point of focus. Even a majestic dragon may overexert themselves with such an act. Remember our fishing net and fishing line analogy." She taps a finger on the counter top. "When you have mastered this, your ability may appear greatly magnified when you focus on a single target instead of throwing it about in every which direction."

That sounds reassuring. All I have to do is master this then.

"Do you think I'll be strong *enough*?" I ask and sit back on the stool, consciously stopping myself from biting my lip so as not to appear overly anxious. I know Scholar understands my true question.

"I certainly hope so," she says quietly.

I finger the dragon pendant around my neck, Scholar's gift and emergency token if in danger. Scholar takes her time scooping up the trinkets into a bag, making it clear our session is done for the day. She passes over three tokens and presses them into my palm—a wolf, a bird of prey, and the gryphon.

"For practice in secret on your own," she says and then wraps her thin arm around my shoulders in an oddly comforting gesture to guide me off the stool. "Come."

She leads me to the living room and has me take a seat on the couch as she transforms in the open space between the kitchen and entry way. She walks into the room in her dragon form and lays stretched out on the floor. Her scaly hide of green and blue reflects the overhead lights but there's no sunshine to truly illuminate her scales since all of the blinds in the house have been drawn to keep out prying eyes. I can only imagine the panic if a neighbor spotted a dragon lounging next door.

"Tell me what you know of the majestics," Scholar says.

I guess it's story time again. "Umm, like everything?"

"Let's start small. Who are the majestics?"

"Well, there's Draco, obviously. He's sort of been the leader of the majestics, and people call him the Firestorm of Europe. Then there's Ryūjin, the Ocean King." I start to tally them off on my fingers. "Then there's Jangwa, the African Behemoth. Eris, the Trickster. Caelum, Master of the Skies, and Terra, the Worldly Queen. Only Draco, Ryūjin and Jangwa have been seen recently. The others vanished and fell off the map."

"Complete with their self-proclaimed titles, bravo." She claps her forepaws. "But you're forgetting one already."

I swallow. "Echidna, the Mother of Monsters."

"Well done." She arches her neck and a shiver passes down her spine, shaking the row of deadly spikes along her back. "Now then. I hope you are a keen student of history, and know the tale of the last war." I nod. "So you learned how a strange monster rose out of a black void and immersed itself in a magical font of pure energy, turning it into the beast history knows as Echidna. And what would such a beast want except more power? Thus began the near endless cycle of war raged between the majestics and Echidna and her brood of devils. It was during that dark time that the clever Terra, alongside Draco, created the first Blessed to help them fight their war."

She waves a forepaw in the air and sashays her head back and forth as she says, "There were many heroic deeds, the majestics were benevolent gods, and so on and so forth as history has been stuffed with the fluff of heaping propaganda and praise. In the end, they all made sacrifices to end Echidna for good. Terra was poisoned, Draco nearly killed, Caelum's wings broken, and the legendary forces decimated. The remaining monsters fled into hiding where they would bide their time until a new uprising could begin."

The way she explains it with obvious puffery makes it clear that this version of events is not the truth.

"So what really happened?"

Her jewel-like slit eyes catch the overhead lights and flicker with sparks. "Sacrifices were made, but there was more betrayal involved to the ruin of all. For you see, the Blessed were not some divine creation gifted by the sudden and unexplained genius of Terra and Draco. The Blessed were certainly granted their abilities to combat the tide of monsters but they were made from observing Echidna's own methods."

The air leaves the room and my head swims as the entire world tilts.

"Excuse me?" I say breathlessly.

"Echidna had always been mad. Born that way, I suppose. She was different from the others and nurtured a seed of darkness in her soul. The magic in her veins was twisted. The nature of how and why have never been explained. She simply was. And in her madness, as her magic changed and darkened the things around her, the other majestics saw her as a threat to the world and to themselves. Such rejection and hostility only intensified that darkness. She was alone and her loneliness bred desperation."

The familiarity of the story reminds me of something Jefferson once said. Werewolves don't like to be alone so they create packs, like Dasc did. I know exactly where Scholar is going with this story.

"So she created monsters," I say.

Scholar nods. "Through her blood she made the alphas of each of the many species of monsters that roam the world today. She had grown a cult around herself, men and beasts that worshipped her powers—and not all of it was destruction. In fact, she had some of the most powerful healing magic ever encountered that remains unmatched even to this day. But that healing came at a cost. Her followers drank her blood and the darkness inside them became unleashed in exchange for the cure to their ills."

I think of Dasc and the clip of wolfsbane bullets I plugged into his chest. Witty said it with awe before—he has healing abilities unheard of. The alpha of his kind.

"Dasc drank her blood?"

"Indeed. It is as grotesque and gruesome as it sounds. That single act transformed him into the first of the werewolves and an everlasting blight upon the world. The same act created the lamia, and from them the vampires are descended. Every other foul demon with diseased magic came from her blood. That is why even though your original ability focused on your brother's curse, it also affected the lamia. The disease in their veins is the same even if it transformed them differently. Why do you think all monsters are so notoriously difficult to kill? Because they came from Echidna's twisted healing powers."

All those monsters were originally humans or beasts that drank a majestic dragon's blood . . . My knees wobble even though I'm sitting and I set my elbows on my thighs to brace my head in my hands.

"The leviathans? Hydra? What about them?" I ask, disbelief gnawing at me.

"Born of Echidna. It's best not to ask how that occurred, but she laid many eggs which can lie dormant for centuries. That is why we still face their threat today, even if some fools thought they were extinct."

Echidna had always been some ghost story for people like me, something far away and untouchable. Now Echidna and the threat of what she is feels very real and daunting.

"So, the Blessed . . . you said they were created after observing Echidna. Does that mean—did I drink Draco's blood?"

"No, but in the past others did," Scholar says. "The magic in a majestic's blood is so powerful that it killed many humans outright at the attempt, and those that did survive were called Magus. They were so immensely powerful that the majestics were fearful of creating too many of their kind, afraid they may create more of the very monsters they were trying to fight. Overtime they learned how to pass on a seed of magic without any consumption, which produced a much more efficient practice and ended with far better results."

Thank goodness for that. I can't imagine if I had been forced to drink blood as a child. A part of me is still afraid I had and don't remember. Maybe that's why I'm so different from all the other Blessed I know. It makes me feel unclean, violated . . . a monster.

"Are you sure?" I ask quietly. The thought of it weighs upon me so much that I have to voice my fear and receive a concrete answer.

"I am quite certain that your abilities manifested only from the touch of a dragon, not the blood of one."

The weight in my lungs settles but I still feel weak, like every part of me is wrong. The world continues to tilt on its side. How can no one else know about this?

"And Echidna herself?" I ask, needing to know more. "What happened to her? Genna said she's come back but the majestics killed her, didn't they?"

"They certainly thought so." Scholar lets loose a breath that rattles her spikes and makes the webbed fringe around her face tremble. "All of their plans had previously failed. Every time they thought they had stopped Echidna or mortally wounded her, she went into hiding and recovered only to strike again. Terra was the one who finally decided that the one who might know how best to stop a monster was another monster."

"She allied with the monsters?" I ask, aghast.

Scholar's eyes narrow. "Not that she would have called it such. It was a necessary evil to transgress with one of the alphas in order to learn the secret to ending Echidna forever. Would you have not done the same? Have you not done so already?"

Her words feel like a punch to the gut. "My situation with Dasc is different."

"Is it really?" She props her long thin muzzle on the joint of her foreleg with a judicious air. "Pray, tell me how that is so."

I swallow and clamp my mouth shut, unable to make a

satisfactory reply, and she resumes her previous sprawled pose on the floor. The fringe around her face and neck smooths out until it lays flat with her scaly skin.

"So, in the face of adversity, Terra sought out the werewolves with Eris who helped her slip past their defenses to meet with Dasc directly. After some clever negotiations, Terra discovered that Dasc had reasons of his own for wanting Echidna dead and agreed to help."

"But why would he?" I ask. "I thought he was one of Echidna's followers."

"For a time he was, until Echidna had his family murdered out of jealousy and to ensure his sole attention."

"I didn't know," I say quietly. I know the pain of losing family in such a brutal way. I might have even felt sorry for him if he hadn't been the one to inflict that pain on me and mine. But while my circumstances led me towards justice, he chose revenge it seems.

"It is not something he will ever discuss, I can assure you, and woe to those who think it wise to bring up the subject." She looks down her long muzzle at me in clear warning that I should never bring the subject up with him during my interrogations. Not that I was planning on it. That would make it pretty obvious that I learned the story from someone which would lead to Scholar.

"Regardless of his animosities towards Echidna, simple revenge was not enough for him. He knew the majestics wanted him dead for his own foul deeds so he planned a contingency for when the war was over. It was not discovered by the others until later that Terra had struck an accord with Dasc and solidified a life debt to him in order to secure his aid."

"*What?* A majestic struck a deal?" I'm left reeling and clamp a hand to my forehead. A majestic dragon—one of the most powerful beings on the planet—struck a life debt with Dasc? The same kind I myself made with him, the threat of it still hanging over my head.

"She knew the cost," Scholar says solemnly. "And she paid it in the end."

"But—but what *happened?*"

"Terra and Eris returned to the majestics with the news that the werewolves would give them the opportunity to end the wars forever. They did not speak of Terra's deal." She raps her claws on the carpet, each one producing a dull thud. The dragon stares off for a moment lost in her own thoughts before she continues.

"Dasc did as he promised. He was still a prized follower of Echidna and was allowed entrance to her inner fortifications. Jangwa and Caelum set a ruse to lure her most destructive protectors away along the coast with the last legion of their forces. At the same moment, Dasc had some of his wolf pack lead Draco and a contingent of dragons past the traps she had constructed in her fortress deep inside a volcanic island. Ryūjin created yet another distraction along the shores while Terra snuck in through the lava tunnels using her abilities.

"The plan worked. The majestics infiltrated her defenses and when the battle commenced, it brought the entire mountain down around them. Draco took the brunt of Echidna's attacks and was nearly overcome if not for Dasc in that moment biting Echidna. Even though she had created him, his own disease had twisted into something else and weakened her."

The werewolf disease was able to weaken a majestic? Just how powerful is the disease? I know what it does to the Blessed—it kills, maims, and changes their lives forever. But to think it could have such an effect on a majestic with magic a thousand times more powerful than any Blessed. The serum, the sole "cure" out there, only manages to tame it with frequent doses so it must be from something equally as powerful. Before that, the werewolves were hunted and wiped out under the order of the IMS—which operates under the orders of Draco. He knew the danger it posed not only to the world but to the majestics themselves. I can understand his intense hunt to find Dasc a little more.

"In the ensuing chaos," Scholar continues, "most of the lamia and many of the dragons were killed, Draco nearly died as well, and the mountain was razed by Terra's power. Echidna was buried and destroyed during that battle or so they thought."

"But not according to Dasc," I cut in. "And Genna."

"Indeed." Her fringe droops when she lowers her head as if in shame.

The way Scholar speaks of Echidna's power . . . we don't stand a chance if the mother of monsters rises again. The majestics could barely defeat her with all of them working together. Now several of the majestics haven't been seen for centuries and no one knows where they disappeared to. We would need all of them if another war was to begin.

"What about the majestics? What happened to them?" I ask.

"At the end of the battle, Caleum's wings were broken while giving defense against the monsters. Ryūjin and Jangwa went back to their own territories. Draco wanted to kill Dasc as punishment for his crimes but, as you will recall, Terra owed Dasc a life debt."

I swallow and vividly remember when Draco chewed me out for unknowingly making the same bargain with Dasc. "I can't imagine that ended well."

"No. No, it did not. Compelled by the life debt, Terra battled Draco and secured Dasc's escape from the wreckage of the mountain. However, in the chaos Draco's mate was bitten by one of Dasc's followers in their own desperation to free themselves and their master. The disease drove his mate to madness and in the end . . . she took her own life to end her suffering."

A heavy foreboding silence fills the space between us. Draco's obsession with hunting Dasc and the werewolves becomes perfectly clear. It's why he's been so aggressive towards Genna and the other werewolves, why he has me keeping a keen eye on them. Honestly, I'm surprised he hasn't outright killed them all.

"Draco swore vengeance," Scholar says softly. "Against Dasc and against Terra for her hand in his escape. His terrible wrath was unrelenting to the point he wanted them not only to die but to suffer. He tricked Terra into a meeting to resolve their differences and bring peace between them. He even invited Dasc, who wisely refused and sent a Whisper in his stead. However, Draco made a low, unworthy promise to the Whisper that he would spare Dasc's life if the Whisper bit Terra. At the meeting, Draco trapped Terra and she was bitten by the Whisper. Of course, Draco didn't keep his promise. He killed the Whisper immediately after and continued his hunt for Dasc over the centuries—until now."

"No wonder you've been warning me about Draco," I mutter. I can understand doing everything you can to stop your enemies, but such backstabbing—it's so underhanded and cruel. "But what about Terra? Did she survive?"

The scaly skin around Scholar's eyes tightens. "She did and managed to escape with the help of her friend Eris. But Terra was cursed from that day forward. She and Eris went separately into hiding to escape Draco's wrath."

The very same Draco that I've been having private meetings with, that I've been spying on Genna for. He's been a symbol of power and guidance for the IMS since its inception. To learn what he did to Terra out of his own twisted grief is unthinkable.

"And you?" I ask. "You're hiding from him and the IMS, aren't you?" Inspiration hits me. "Do you know where Terra is? You're one of her brood, right? You must know. She could help us—her and Eris both, and all of the majestics."

Scholar stretches her neck to her full height, and pins me beneath those poison green slit eyes. I feel that pulse of power wash over me again which seems to happen when she's upset.

"A story for next time. I fear our session must come to an end." She raises her tail and flicks the end in the direction of the clock on the wall. I've been here for almost two hours. "The rest shall be explained in due course."

"But—"

"I will call upon you again when I am ready."

A clear dismissal. I push off from the couch and make sure I have my little collection of trinkets secured in a bag Scholar gives me for practice later. I've got a lot on my mind and plenty to think about in the meantime. The green dragon murmurs a farewell about being careful before I trudge out the door. When I get into the SUV, I sit in the driver's seat and stare out the window at the surrounding trees. I'm not sure how long I sit there as I mull over majestics and betrayal and how on earth I'm going to be able to ever face Draco again with a neutral expression. My head is swimming and my skin feels uncomfortably tight from all that practice of holding in my wellspring of magic.

Eventually I shift into gear and do my best to focus on the road before me on the way to the cabin.

Everything I had been taught about the majestics and Echidna has been wrong. And there was certainly never any mention of werewolves being involved in taking out Echidna. Nothing about Draco's madness over the loss of his mate. Nothing of him betraying Terra in the end. For all the world knows—and as much as I knew before Scholar opened my eyes to the truth—was that some of the majestics faded into the background to lead reclusive lives or perform work for the IMS in the shadows. A ruse, and one perpetuated by Draco no doubt in order to uphold the near saintlike persona of the majestics. Even their class name is meant to inspire awe and trust.

The question Dasc posed to me surfaces once again, brutal and looming.

Who are the bigger fools? The Blessed or the werewolves?

I'm still tasting the sour answer to that question as I pull into the driveway at the cabin. The door to the barn opens seconds after I exit the SUV and Hawk waves me over. I try to shake the hunch in my shoulders and the morbid look on my face. It's like stepping into a different reality, one in which everyone else is crazy and I'm the only sane person left.

"We just got word," my brother says as I walk over to him.

I can't possibly think of anything apart from majestic dragons right now. "Word of what?"

"Another attack." He holds the door open wide for me with a stalwart expression as if he's trying to put up a strong front even though he's obviously upset.

"Where?" I ask, the cloud quickly lifting at his distress.

"Scotland. The Vaults were attacked."

The news stations are unsure what to call the explosion in the lower levels of the Castle of Edinburgh. It happened somewhere deep underground that rocked the castle, and crews are still determining the extent of damage and persons injured or dead. There are images of smoke curling into the sky, first responders combing the area, and police setting up a perimeter. It's a mess.

The IMS feeds paint a completely different picture from the innocent onlookers above. There was a coordinated attacked on the Vaults not four hours ago. The charges detonated were aimed at exits to effectively block off the headquarters for an extended period until they were able to get a pack of earth sprites to safely clear out the rubble. All IMS efforts are currently focused on securing the area, making sure the Vaults are not exposed to the general public, and that the assailants are apprehended.

The last line of the most current feed suggests a possible connection between the Paris and Faunus attacks.

Genna studies the article over my shoulder, one hand cupped under her chin as she surveys the details. There was no point keeping the suspected werewolf attacks from her any longer. Hawk and Jefferson look on from the sidelines, Jefferson hovering behind his daughter while Hawk leans all the way back in the other swivel chair.

"What do you think?" I ask. "Any ideas?"

Her frown deepens. "Maybe. Maybe not. Nothing springs to mind as being definite and that worries me more."

"Why?"

"Because of the seemingly senseless pattern of the attacks. If I could figure out what's going on, we might actually be able to stop another attack. But with the way these are going—"

"The randomness makes them more effective," Jefferson says gruffly. "Because we can't anticipate where they'll attack next."

"Yeah, but who are they?" I ask pointedly in Genna's direction. She *is* a Whisper after all. You think she'd have some idea who these renegade werewolves are.

"I don't know," she says and I believe her.

"At least we know Dasc isn't giving the orders," Hawk says.

Genna shakes her head. "Not necessarily."

The three of us snap our heads in her direction.

"What?" Jefferson says.

She cross her arms over her chest. "You guys honestly thought Dasc wouldn't have contingencies in place if he was ever captured? He left orders with his Whispers to be carried out in his stead if he ever *did* find himself incapacitated."

"Orders like what?" I ask, suspicious yet again. We've been building a rapport over the last several weeks but she certainly kept this little bit of information to herself.

"Like free him for starters. Obviously," she says.

"Oh, right. *Obviously*," I say, unable to rein in my flare of temper. "And you didn't think to mention this earlier?"

"*Phoenix*," Jefferson cuts across me severely.

Genna doesn't seem the least bit fazed though, as usual. "If I had told the IMS that I had orders to free Dasc if I had the chance, do you really think they would have ever let me go home?"

"No." And for good reason. I know it certainly throws my previous perceptions out the window and makes me reevaluate her motives. Although, I must admit, Genna has been proving herself day after day to be exactly as she appears to be—a lost girl striving to rebuild a normal life at the home she had been stolen away from.

"I never intended to follow through on such orders," she continues. "He can rot for the rest of his miserable immortal life for all I care, but the other Whispers had the same orders. These attacks may be somehow related. Maybe they're attacking places they think he's being held."

"Faunus?" I say. "Why attack there? He clearly wouldn't be held there."

"Like I said, nothing jumps out at me as being definite," Genna says. "I'm guessing as much as you."

I face my computer again to avoid her stare and Jefferson's dagger eyes. "I'm going to see if I can find anything out from my friends in Scotland."

While I type up an e-mail to Tawnee, Hawk rises from his own chair and starts to pace on the other side of the computer desk. Jefferson takes up the spot he vacated and Genna continues to hover in the background, moving over to inspect the list of missing persons on our wall.

I send my Spartan friend a quick message asking if she's okay and what she knows about the attack since she would have undoubtedly been in the area. I'm in the middle of reading the latest message from Director Knox saying they may need another conference with Dasc soon when Hawk grabs the top of my computer monitor with both hands to get my attention.

"I think the rest of the werewolves should know," he says.

"Know what?"

"You know exactly what I mean. With this latest attack, the IMS is going to be extra cautious with all of the werewolves even if they weren't even remotely involved. They might tighten up restrictions, have us be more vigilant about probation. The others should know."

I heave a sigh and prop my chin in my hand, my elbow braced on the desktop. "You want to hold a meeting?"

"Or host a game. Drop the bad news but let them have one last hurrah before an order comes saying they can't even transform or something. People have been asking for one for a while. Plus, we can put them on alert in case—" His eyes dart to Genna for a moment. "In case any other strange werewolves come sniffing."

"That's not a bad idea," Jefferson says. "If they know of danger ahead of time, we might be able to stop it head on if it comes to that."

Genna instantly appears over my shoulder again. "I'm up for a game. It'd be good for Roz, too."

"Well then, that settles it," Hawk says.

I'm surprised Jefferson isn't arguing against this plan despite how aggressively he did before. The thought of werewolves coming to hunt Genna for treachery must have changed his mind. And Hawk does have a valid point. I'd be surprised if the IMS *didn't* up restrictions on the movement of werewolves.

Phone calls are made and texts sent out via our private network to the werewolves under our care and protection. Rosalyn even replies with a text that says "Great. As long as I get to hit something."

While Hawk spreads the rest of the message and makes plans with farmer Wick to use his expansive property to host capture the flag, I head into the cabin to hide away Scholar's bag of trinkets under a loose floorboard. I carefully put the board back in place and shuffle the laundry basket and my gym bag over it. I change into my exercise clothes and use what free time I have to work on the obstacle course, go through a quick bout of sparring, and set out for a jog. My brother and Genna join me for the last leg of training and we run as a group on a five mile circuit along the backroads and bike trail before returning to the cabin.

I lose myself in my thoughts while I perform the exercises by muscle memory. My mind is full of majestic dragons, rampaging werewolves, and a slumbering evil waking. I'll need to fill Hawk in on everything when we get a moment to ourselves—if I can do Scholar's story justice. Speaking of which, how does she even know all of this? It sounded like everything that happened became hush-hush and even libraries were burned to the ground to cover up the truth about Echidna, not to mention what Draco did. Does anyone else know?

"Hey, you okay?" my brother asks after we clean up and get ready to meet everyone at Wick's place. "You seem distracted."

Genna shuffles past the doorway to our bedroom, making it patently clear that we are not alone and I'm not free to talk about what's on my mind at the moment.

"Just a lot going on," I say offhand but give him a significant look when Genna's not in view to let him know there is definitely more going on.

He makes a subtle "ah-ha!" face as his eyebrows go up and his mouth forms a small circle before he finishes zipping up his jacket.

"Well, we should get going," he announces and strides out into the kitchen where Jefferson and Genna are waiting. "We'll want to get there ahead of the crowds."

"Right," Jefferson grumbles and leads the way out.

We pile into the SUV and for once Genna elects to sit in the backseat next to Hawk so she can bombard him with questions about what to expect, what the other werewolves are like, what's considered acceptable behavior, and so on and so forth. I sit up front next to Jefferson for the first time in what seems like years, even though it's hardly even been a month.

An awkward silence falls between us with Hawk and Genna's chat a swell of white noise in the background. I guess we've fallen into an uneasy sort of truce. I've made him angry more than a few times in regards to Genna but he never would have found his daughter without me. And yet, even over so short a time, has he forgotten I made a life debt to Dasc for him? That we scoured Scotland together for a long, terrible month? Not to mention the tricks and turns I've navigated just to get his daughter home and keep her there?

After everything, I'm as distant from Jefferson now as the day I first met him. Aren't friendships supposed to move forward, not backward?

We reach Mr. Wick's farm and pile out to enjoy the beautiful spring day that feels like a laughable contrast to the dark thoughts swirling in my head. Mr. Wick himself comes out to greet us and warns us of the muddy areas brought on by the rain and thunderstorms. When Jefferson introduces Genna, his small eyes go wide. The farmer shakes Genna's hand and passes on his friendliest congratulations of returning home. I have a feeling his sentiments, and less welcoming ones, are going to be shared shortly by a lot of people prompted by Genna and Rosalyn's appearances here today. The lost have finally returned home. Two of them anyway, and questions about the others still missing will undoubtedly rise. It's inevitable. Our trip to the greenhouse together didn't go unnoticed and a few people have already asked Hawk obtusely who Genna is.

I hope we don't create an angry mob when they find out those rescued are being held.

The four of us and Mr. Wick go scout the field of play deep in the woods. The area is indeed muddy and there are pools of standing water in the low dips between trees and the rolling hills. The werewolves are used to getting dirty though. It won't be a problem.

As we walk back to the SUV to get the jerseys and flags, I fight the urge to look in the direction where Hawk had run off before and our secret remains buried. It's best not to draw any attention that way.

The werewolves start to show up in droves, many of them having carpooled, and immediately set out to determine who will be on what team. From the handful of senior citizens, to the working adults, to the teenagers still in school, to the small kids, there's a bond of community here. Every single one shares a secret from the rest of town and the rest of the world—they harbor something dark inside them that sets them apart. They each know the pain of the transformation. They know the value in keeping their secrets.

The surge of bitter power around me is almost staggering now that I know to look for it.

Rosalyn and Deputy Graham show up in his squad car and park near the front of the long driveway. They walk step in step, Jared towering over his lithe sister, and both seem eager to get to the game. Even Rosalyn is smiling— although somehow it makes her appear more mischievous and threatening.

"Is everyone here?" the deputy asks when he reaches us.

"Everyone who could make it," Hawk answers. "We should get this show on the road."

Jared turns to his sister. "Are you ready?"

"*I'm* ready. I don't know if *they* are." She gestures to the woods where the last stragglers are hurrying to the field.

Genna's lips twitch into a smile. "I don't think anyone can possibly prepare themselves for you, Roz."

"Sass is so unbecoming on you," Rosalyn says haughtily and walks down the trail with a confident bounce in her step. "It clearly suits me better."

Together we bring up the end of the line and meet up

with the others that have congregated in the forest. The waiting crowd is bathed sporadically in patches of sunlight, others falling into shadow beneath the trees. Hawk steps up on the plastic box holding the jerseys and uses it like a stage to get a good height over his audience. Eyes draw to him and he smiles as he spreads his arms wide to get their attention.

"I want to thank everyone who showed up today," he says clearly but not to the point of shouting. We've got a good hundred people here. It's the largest crowd we've ever gathered. "As we said in our invitation, there is some news that you should all be aware of."

Hawk begins to explain in a rather simplistic fashion the attacks that have occurred over in Europe. While he talks, I scan everyone's faces. Trepidation is the most common expression I can make out, amongst confusion, and even some anger.

"What does this mean for us?" a voice calls out from the crowd. I'm pretty sure it's Ashley. When she had arrived earlier, she didn't even look in my direction as if I didn't exist.

"I'll be honest with you. It probably means there may be more restrictions put in place to ensure everyone's safety," Hawk says and a ripple of murmuring passes through the crowd. The resentment is obvious and it suddenly occurs to me that there are a heck of a lot more werewolves than agents here. "But as I said, we don't know why these attacks have happened and it's important we remain on our guard. If you see any suspicious activity or other werewolves you don't know in the area, please contact us immediately. Your safety is our priority."

There's a general sound of agreement and all eyes are glued to Hawk, waiting for him to tell them what to do next. I've never been more thankful for his near alpha-like status with the werewolves in Moose Lake.

At this point Hawk turns partway to gesture to Genna and Rosalyn standing a few steps behind him. They don't move or react when the force of the crowd's attention falls on them.

"As I'm sure some of you have realized, we have two new additions to the field today. I'd like you all to welcome home Genevieve Barnes and Rosalyn Graham."

Gasps follow, excited whispers, and someone starts up a round of applause which quickly escalates along with whistles and celebratory whoops. I guess a lot of people know who they are. Granted, the kidnappings in the area are pretty famous considering the number of them.

"I would ask that you please respect their boundaries and privacy," he says rather sternly. Jefferson and Deputy Graham nod their approval beside me. "They are here today to get to know the Moose Lake community and be with their families. We ask that you give them the same courtesy you would give your own families. Now, let the game begin!"

Despite Hawk's warning, there's almost immediately a flood of people wanting to talk to Genna and Rosalyn and find out if their disappearances were connected to the other ones in town. Jefferson and Deputy Graham put up a stern wall between the questioners and their prey, both men drawing on their training to subdue the crowd and their protective instincts to forcibly make others back down. It's not exactly the friendliest of scenes and I lurk with Genna and Rosalyn behind their screen of family protectors.

Although both girls hold themselves steady in the face of such eagerness, desperation, and curiosity, they tense and share cryptic looks with each other.

Hawk eventually manages to draw the attention of the crowd to himself again and I help him distribute jerseys. The team captains are chosen—Hawk and Mr. Wick—before the teams are divided into two groups. While Hawk picks Genna for his team, Rosalyn instantly announces she must be on the opposing team and glares at Mr. Wick until he hesitantly chooses her. The devilish smile she gives Genna makes me nervous but Genna only grins in return just as sinister. Well, that doesn't turn my palms sweaty or anything. Maybe bringing them out here wasn't a good idea.

It takes a long time to sort the teams. Matt and Adam Glass join Wick's team while my humble snitch, Peter, is chosen by Hawk. Ashley pointedly marches over to Wick until he picks her for his team as well. Most of the people who came want to play but there are several that excuse themselves or setup to watch from the sidelines. One of the poor mothers has her hands full trying to round up a gang of three young children who all decided they should pop into wolf cubs. Deputy Graham and their grandfather go chasing after them with Jefferson on their heels.

I do my best to keep order as the teams and spectators chat and everyone becomes more playful by the second—almost like a pack of puppies finally realizing they're free to do what they want. In the midst of coordinating where the spectators can sit without impeding the game, I hear Rosalyn and Genna giving Deputy Graham a right scare after he comes back huffing from chasing the unruly werewolf pups.

"I suppose maiming isn't allowed in the rules?" Roslayn asks in such a serious manner that I stop what I'm doing to stare. I'm not the only one.

"Don't worry," Genna says in the same matter-of-fact voice. "I won't maim you."

"Can I claw her eyes out?" Rosalyn continues with a stony face. "What exactly are the terms of combat here?"

Deputy Graham looks close to pulling his hair out and glances uneasily at the people around him. "This isn't combat, this is a game."

She waves a hand dismissively. "We used to do war games all the time."

"These aren't—no, you're not attacking anyone. Your team captures the flag. You can tag people."

"Can I body slam them? Does that count as tagging?"

"E-excuse me?"

"What about hamstringing? Is that allowed?"

"Good Lord—"

Genna pats the deputy on the arm with a pitying look. "I've got this." She faces Rosalyn and counts off on her fingers. "No bodily injury, attempts of bodily injury, or reckless endangerment. Touch, no foul."

"Well, why didn't you guys say so in the first place?" Rosalyn says loudly. She throws up her hands and storms away shouting, "What fun is that?"

A hush falls around those closest to Rosalyn who heard her outburst and everyone makes sure to give her a wide berth as she paces furiously. Rosalyn turns on my snitch Peter nearby, who looks small in his superhero t-shirt, and shouts angrily at him, "The weak will never survive!"

Warm laughter from Genna breaks the brittle tension

and she starts to stretch. Hawk moves off to coordinate the rest of his team. The second he steps away, Ben Ferguson fills in the spot he vacated next to Genna. I smell trouble a mile away as he tries to start up a conversation. Genna continues her stretches, occasionally throwing him glances but it's clear she's not interested in what he has to say. Her eyes instead dart frequently to where Rosalyn is stretching twenty feet away and to Hawk moving between his teammates passing out red jerseys.

It takes more than that to dissuade Ben, though, once he's set on a prospective future girlfriend. I know from experience. Thankfully, Charlie's false pretense as my boyfriend managed to kill that prospect dead. At least I didn't have to endure any rumors for long at school considering I left for Scotland soon afterward.

Once Hawk passes a jersey to Genna, she makes a quick exit from Ben and moves to help her teammates who are starting to shift across the field put on their own jerseys. Ben clutches onto his but doesn't join the rest of the players immediately. Instead he comes to talk to me.

"Hey, Phoenix," he says with a smile. "Long time no see. You haven't come around with Hawk on the probation rounds so much."

"Yeah, I've been busy with other stuff," I say. "Sorry I haven't swung by. How've you been?"

"I'm good. I'll be graduating at the end of the school year so I can't complain." He brushes his shaggy hair out of his eyes. "How about you? You still with Charlie? Things going okay?"

Piping Pan, he's still on that, isn't he? I thought Genna's presence had distracted him from me. Unwilling to offer him any hope that I might possibly be available, I say, "Oh, I'm great. Charlie's great. We're fantastic. Thanks for asking." I offer him a smile I hope looks sincere and he nods his head in acceptance of my little lie. Thank goodness for that.

"That's good," he says. "Yeah, real good."

Wow, and here I thought I'm the awkward one. I point to the field. "You better get out there if you want to play, Ben."

"Right. Of course." He salutes me as he jogs backwards and then turns about to join the others, most of which have shifted into their wolf forms.

A rumbling whisper and low throaty growls pass through the players and spectators at something I missed when Ben had me distracted. The wolves part for a moment so I can see what's garnered their attention.

Hawk kneels to help pull a red jersey over the furry head of an all-black wolf.

I freeze, every muscle feeling the sudden shock of adrenaline and deep seated fear as I stare at the spitting image of Dasc in his wolf form. There are no other all black wolves in Moose Lake and its presence in the middle of people held captive under the previous black wolf's sway causes an uneasy feeling amongst everyone gathered.

From the red jersey, it's obvious the black wolf is not Rosalyn. No, this is Genna's transformation in all its glory.

A Whisper.

It hits me more strongly than any other time since I've known her.

Genna is dangerous. Genna was one of Dasc's right-hand warriors.

She seems unfazed by the uneasy growling and whispers spreading out around her. She shakes herself out, her large ears slapping back and forth on her neck, and a shiver passes all the way down her body to her tail. She's not at big as Dasc in his own form but the resemblance is uncanny.

Hawk finally shifts beside her and pulls his jersey on by himself. Genna tugs at the bottom seam to pull it all the way on for him, an oddly friendly gesture. Maybe it just seems odd because of what she looks like to me right now. Genna certainly has been on good terms with Hawk since she first arrived. I shouldn't be surprised.

Tearing my eyes from her, I scan the crowd for Rosalyn wondering if she'll be the same. She stands out from the crowd by her unusual coloring and anxious pacing in the center of the field. She's nearly all silver with the faintest darkening along her spine and a large blast of black fur on her muzzle as if someone blew soot in her face.

I clear my throat and clap my hands to get everyone's attention. The wolves turn to face me and with Genna's black form in the crowd, I'm reminded of that fateful night when Dasc tried to kill me. I swallow.

"I want a nice clean game!" I shout to be heard by everyone. "No one goes outside the perimeter—that's the fence to the north, the line of spruce trees to the west and east, and the spectator line here. If you get tagged, you go to your opponent's jail until one of your teammates successfully makes it to you without being touched to get you out. The first team with three flag captures wins. Team's ready?" Hawk and Mr. Wick bark in answer. "Okay, then . . . GO!"

The wolves race around each other in a flurry. Deputy

Graham, Mrs. Ferguson, two other volunteers, and I spread out across the field to make sure no one goes out of bounds or gets too aggressive. There's a chorus of growls, barks, and a few howls as the frenzied energy grows with the spirit of the game.

It's obvious who the key players are within a minute of the game starting. Hawk, Genna, and Ben make separate charges into enemy territory to split the defenders to successfully rescue two of their teammates already captured in their over eager attempts to get the blue flag. While distracted, another group of red jerseys rush the flag only to be thwarted by Rosalyn, a silver blur between her teammates. Her tongue hangs out and she looks very much like she's smiling when she's not snarling viciously. Her brother warns her out a few times to tone it down.

As the game progresses and each team scores a point, I notice the difference in how Genna and Rosalyn move as opposed to everyone else on the field. There's a very smooth fluidity to their movements. There's nothing clunky or off about their slides, dodges, twists, and sprints. Even Hawk can't compare with their abilities. It's clear they've fully embraced their wolf half and trained extensively in that capacity.

Soldiers. That's what they are. Trained from a young age to be Dasc's fighters and leaders in the resurgence of an old war. Dasc knew Echidna would come back someday, somehow, and he's certainly made a good showing of getting ready for the conflict. The other werewolves on the field are sorely outmatched. Despite Ben trying to make an impressive showing for Genna whenever he can, her own skill outstrips his by a laughable margin. Not once is

Genna—or Rosalyn—sent to the jail. Not once do they let an opposing werewolf slip by them. The only ones that seem a challenge for them are each other and they certainly take plenty of runs at one another.

I'm so engrossed by their plays that I don't notice the howling in the distance until several others pause where they stand on the field, panting and tilting their heads to better catch the mournful sound. It sounds like it's coming from the north end of the field. I start to walk that way when Mrs. Ferguson comes running up to me, her curly hair flopping on her head.

"What is it?" I ask.

She points towards the direction of the howling. "You better come. Quickly."

Well, that's a surefire way to get me moving fast—cryptic, urgent warnings. Mrs. Ferguson turns about and sprints through the trees. I'm hot on her heels and Deputy Graham crashes along behind me. The game comes to an abrupt halt and the growls of play dwindle until only the lone howling remains.

Mrs. Ferguson takes us deeper and deeper into the woods until I realize we're well past the perimeter set for the game. We're heading towards Ashley's house. A lump forms in my throat as we keep running through the brush and trees on narrow game trails. I don't really recognize these woods but I know we're heading in the right direction. Dread fills me.

Please let us not be going where I think we are.

At last we slow and come to an abrupt halt as we enter a small clearing between the trees where Jefferson stands over the howling wolf. The dark coloring and splotch of white on the muzzle tells me it's none other than Ashley. Before her lies upturned earth and what is unmistakably clumps of light fur. As she raises her head for another long, heartbroken howl, I see a shredded collar held between her paws as if she had been trying to grasp it without hands. A dull dog tag is attached. I can't possibly read the name from this distance but I know exactly whose name is on it.

Duke.

18

My shaky legs feel like they're made of pudding as I try to walk closer to inspect the scene before me. There's a caged animal trying to escape out of my chest and I'm afraid if I don't contain it, if I don't sate its desperation, I'm going to either run away in a panic or blurt out the truth. I need to know everything they've found, what they think happened, if there's any evidence left behind to suggest that Hawk was the one behind Duke's death.

A treacherous coward, that's what I am. That's what I feel deep in my bones that makes me so horribly ashamed. I hid this from Ashley. I buried our secret. And yet . . . I would do it all over again if it meant keeping my brother safe. That's why I don't run or let the truth spill from my lips. My brother's safety is in immediate danger. The secret must remain hidden. No one can know Hawk killed Duke and that he hasn't been taking the serum. I can only imagine what Draco would do if he knew, let alone the IMS.

So, swallowing my disgust at myself, I step to Ashley's side and inspect the evidence.

Two months have passed since Duke's death so I expect to see signs of liquefaction, parts of the poor dog's skeleton unearthed. What I don't expect is the severe lack of any of this. In fact, it looks like what remains of the dog has been lying on top of the ground instead of having been buried beneath. I should know—I buried him. But the upturned earth I noticed earlier is actually the result of some animal clawing at the ground as it fed on the remains. From the looks of it, I'd guess a predator like a bear or cougar, or maybe some scavengers like coyotes came across it. All that's left of Duke are a few broken bits of bone and clumps of fur. And of course, his collar.

All of the evidence is gone. All the tell-tale factors that someone buried him and that he suffered werewolf bites are nowhere to be seen. A shudder ripples down my spine as I suppress my inward sigh of relief. I *am* a monster, aren't I?

"I'm so sorry," I say quietly.

Ashley growls and bares her teeth at me before snatching the dog collar up in her jaws and taking off. A reddish wolf darts after her along with an onyx one—Hawk and Genna. I can't let them face her alone. For all I know, Hawk will feel compelled to spill our darkest secret. I can't let him.

"I got it," I say to no one in particular and race through the trees after them.

Sprinting after werewolves is about as difficult as it sounds. By the time I get going there's not a shadow of them on the ground and I'm forced to pause and listen, trying to find out where they went. Nothing. Not a peep nor a song from a bird. I guess the werewolves scared off any wildlife in the area. So where would Ashley go? Home. It's the only place I can think of and the most logical. The Nelsons' property abuts Wick's farm. I mark the sun's dwindling position and adjust my path accordingly to head in the right direction.

It's a long trudge through prickly brushes, tall grass, hidden tree roots, and standing water. By the time I finally emerge from the woods and find myself in the shadow of the Nelsons' house, my shoes are soaked and sweat has gathered on my forehead. At least I know I've come to the right place. I can hear Ashley's sobs from out here. My gut twists and I walk through the backdoor that's ajar.

I run into Genna first who's hanging around in the hallway as her human self. Her bright red jersey is at odds with her dark clothes and the current situation. The second I step foot in the house, she whips her head around. When she spots me, she jerks her chin in the direction of the stairs. I move past her to where Hawk stands at the base of the steps and Ashley sits on the third one up, arms wrapped around herself and Duke's collar clutched in her hand. Her curtain of blonde hair hides her face from us as her body wracks with sobs. We appear to be the only ones in the house. There's no sign of her parents but I know her father's been in the hospital. I suppose that's where her mother will be as well.

I pause a few feet away out of sight from Ashley but Hawk spots me. I hold his gaze and shake my head ever so slowly. His face hardens and I can see the resolve there. He's going to tell Ashley the truth if he hasn't already. I take a step forward and he goes rigid, squaring up his shoulders as if ready to fight me on it.

No, I mouth. *Don't. Don't be stupid.*

He shakes his head. I'm losing this fight, and if he tells Ashley that he killed Duke, then I'm going to lose him too. I take another step and blink away the moisture building in my eyes in my panic and desperation.

Please, I mouth. *Please.*

Hawk looks angry, furious even. He kneels on the floor at the bottom of the steps and grasps the railing with one hand so he can lean forward.

"Ashley?" he says gently.

She sucks in a long shaky breath, sobs some more, then forces out, "Duke's dead. He's dead and some animal tore him apart. It's all my fault!"

Hawk looks so pained as he says, "No, it's not."

"Yes, it is!" she shouts. "I should have made sure he was always locked inside when I wasn't here. I *knew* this would happen. With all the werewolves howling around, of course he was going to run off!" She's cut off by another violent round of sobs and pieces of me start to break off and wither at her pain.

We did this.

I nearly jump out of my skin when Genna touches the side of my arm with a box of tissue and points at my former friend falling apart on the stairs. My shaking fingers grip the box and I push it through the slots of the railing onto the step beside Ashley. Hawk glares at me a moment before ripping out a tissue and putting it into Ashley's hand. She mutters something unintelligible and wipes at her face before blowing her nose.

"I hoped that—" She fights back a sob and her whole body quakes. "Maybe he was just—I mean, my dad's already—"

She breaks down again and is unable to speak. Hawk places a hand on top of hers.

"I'm sorry," he says. "I'm so, so sorry, Ash. But it's not your fault."

Don't. Don't say it. Please.

His eyes dart to me as I'm on the verge of tears as well. I might start crying but I'll also be hauling him off in half a second if he lets slip the secret. Maybe I should try beating him to the punch and come up with some other lie. But he could always call me out. It wouldn't work. He has to be the one to agree to keep up our false pretenses.

My brother's shoulders hunch inward and he says so softly that I almost don't hear, "It's not anyone's fault. He must have walked right into a bear or something. Heck, maybe even an actual wolf. I'd do anything to bring Duke back, I really would. I know how much he meant to you."

Hysterical once again, Ashley throws herself into Hawk's arms and they almost teeter down the steps together before he manages to catch his balance. He holds Ashley in a tight hug, his chin over her shoulder and one hand cupping the back of her head as she continues to cry.

But his eyes are on me. Angry. Resentful.

Why? Is he truly so angry at me for wanting to keep what happened a secret? If I hadn't done what I did, if I hadn't forced him to keep his mouth shut, he would have vanished two months ago into the same black hole Jason did.

I shuffle backwards out of the room and my brother's line of sight. The echoes of Ashley's cries reach me as I stand outside the backdoor and plant my hands on my waist. It's an effort to not breakdown and let the guilt chew me up. My chest burns and I take quick shallow breaths as I bat it down. Genna lingers in the hallway but I can feel her eyes on me. Let her think my being upset is solely about Ashley's pain—which is a great cause of it but not the only thing.

After what feels like an hour, Genna ghosts to my side like a breath of wind. I don't even hear her come up behind me.

"We should head back," she says.

"I can't leave him alone," I say.

"Can't?"

I shift uncomfortably on my feet. "I don't want to."

"Why? He seems perfectly capable on his own."

Such pointed questions. "Is there a reason I have to go?"

"Rosalyn's bound to start gnawing on someone without adequate supervision," she says dryly.

True. I chew the inside of my cheek trying to think of a perfectly acceptable excuse when I'm saved by the growl of a car engine. We turn in sync and move to the front of the house to look out the windows. Mrs. Nelson gets out of her car, her frizzy hair askew and shadows under her eyes visible from even this distance. We back away and as I move to my brother, Genna vanishes in an instant, a mere shadow through the backdoor. I guess this isn't an encounter she wants to face.

When Mrs. Nelson comes through the front door and sees her daughter in tears, she has a panicked moment of misunderstanding and confusion before the story about Duke comes out. Then Hawk moves aside so Mrs. Nelson can take his spot in hugging her daughter. She gives a single nod in our direction and it's clear it's time to go. Hawk shrugs past me and leads the way out the backdoor.

It's a long, terse walk to Mr. Wick's field. Hawk doesn't acknowledge my presence even though I walk beside him and there's no trace of Genna. I trail behind my brother so I can check the app on my phone without him noticing to make sure she hasn't run off, but her tracking dot shows she's at the field. Rosalyn's dot is there as well—her probation ring data was added to my app once she arrived in town.

By the time we reach the field, it's obvious word has spread about what Ashley found in the woods. There's subdued murmuring and no one is inclined to finish up the game, apart perhaps from Rosalyn who's over eager to smash in skulls. The large pack transforms one by one and the jerseys are dumped into the box set out. The crowd slowly disperses until only Hawk, Jefferson, Genna, and I are left. Deputy Graham and Rosalyn are the last to go, Rosalyn grumbling about not finishing the game and declaring a winner which is apparently all she cares about.

The car ride to the cabin is about as uncomfortable as I expect and even more so. Hawk steals shotgun so I ride in the back with Genna. My brother sits with his eyes straight ahead and when we pull up in front of the cabin, he strides out to the obstacle course without a single look behind him. With a muttered excuse about dirty laundry I should take care of, I quickly escape to the privacy of my room and shut the door behind me.

Once alone, I sink to the floor with my back to the lower bunk and brace my forehead against my palms. I try to remember the instructions for controlling one's breathing that I used for calming myself, but it's difficult to breathe at all, much less manage it as a painful, iron-tight grip holds my lungs.

I feel awful. I've now repeatedly lied to and lost one of my few friends in Moose Lake, and my brother sure seems to hate me for the moment. I wish I could change what happened, I really do. I wish Duke was still alive and Ashley had remained her bright, bubbly self.

But if I had to lie to protect my brother, I would do it all over again. That determination calms me somewhat even if I do feel more twisted because of it. If it had been any other werewolf . . . but no. It had been Hawk. And I would do anything for my family, no matter the consequences.

This had been my choice and I'll have to find a way to live with that.

It takes a while but my breathing evens out and I stand by the window waiting for Hawk to come inside. Faint clinks of silverware and dishes sound from the kitchen as Genna and Jefferson move about but they don't disturb my silent vigil. It's near dusk by the time Hawk finally marches through the gun range and into view. I fly out of the bedroom, through the kitchen past Genna and Jefferson at the table, and out to meet my brother before he reaches the barn.

"Hawk," I say but he doesn't pause or acknowledge me. "Are we going to talk about this?"

He slams the door to the barn behind him making it clear there isn't going to be a conversation where we come to terms like we usually do. No, he's shutting me out. I've never seen him this upset with me before. A shuddering breath rips out of me and I return to the cabin with my head bowed.

"Is everything okay between you two?" Jefferson asks as I pass him. It's the most concern he's shown me in a while which actually makes me feel worse. I don't deserve it.

"I don't want to talk about it," I mutter and close the bedroom door behind me.

I skip supper and lay in the upper bunk without even bothering to change. After staring at the ceiling for an hour or two, I close my eyes and twist the dragon pendant between my fingers, feeling the sensation of its small seed of magic bound within. Genna doesn't bother me with any questions or small talk when she gets ready for bed and goes to sleep. It takes me several hours later to drift off myself.

The following day doesn't get any better. Hawk still won't talk to me or even remain in the same vicinity for very long. We need to talk at some point and work through this but for now I let him have his space. Jefferson and Genna clearly notice that *something* is up and frequently glance in our direction, but neither of them say anything about it. When the four of us gather to weed and water the gardens, Hawk and I stick to separate ends of the gun range at different gardens.

I'm so distracted and distraught by Hawk's anger and avoidance that trying to practice on Scholar's lesson proves nearly impossible. I hide away in the SUV for short bouts of time and lay the pendants across the seat beside me. No matter how hard I try, all of the pendants glow fiercely. There's no shutting off the surge of energy pouring off me in my desperation to fix what's wrong between me and my brother.

During one such secluded practice, my phone buzzes and I pick up a call from a pay phone in town. Scholar beckons me out for another meeting and I agree to meet her at our usual spot in an hour. I wrack my brain for some kind of excuse but all I come up with to tell Jefferson and Genna is that I need some air. Neither of them apparently find this suspicious in the least.

I bring my bag of trinkets along and trudge into the fancy house that Scholar has claimed as hers while the owners are away. She takes up her usual spot on the opposite side of the coffee table to lounge in her natural dragon form and I take mine. For a long moment she doesn't say anything and neither do I, but her eyes rove over me, sharp and calculating.

"You are greatly distressed," she says.

"Yeah, no kidding, Captain Obvious," I snap, the frustration that's been building in me for the last few days boiling over.

"Your friend discovered the remains of her pet." It's not a question. I don't ask how she knows. Scholar seems to have eyes everywhere. "And yet your brother was not satisfied with the fortunate outcome of his own secret not being discovered."

I clench my jaw and my hands tighten on my arms as I sit with them crossed. "Yeah. You could say that."

"It was necessary, Phoenix."

"What was?"

"The dog's discovery."

I blink and study the dragon across from me. "Did you . . . did you have something to do with it?"

"Ashley Nelson needed closure before she uncovered damning evidence. The game in the local vicinity was an excellent means of getting her to the area to locate—"

"You set out Duke's remains on purpose?" I shout and rise from my seat on the sofa. My hands clench into fists and a surge of power rolls off me.

Scholar draws her head back on her long neck. I'm ready to strangle her.

"Phoenix, if nothing had been done, Ashley would have been driven to continue searching."

"He was buried!" I yell and swing an arm wide towards the door in the direction of the woods where the worst happened. "No one was going to find him!"

"You are very wrong indeed," she says. "Your friend has been investigating the woods around her home for some time, convinced that her lost pet could be found nearby. She very nearly uncovered your shallow grave. I had to act."

I breathe harshly and pace on my side of the table. "You knew? How?"

"I like to keep an eye on things."

"Yeah, that was real specific. Do you spy on everyone in town?"

"Only those that pose a threat to your safety and secrets."

That makes me halt in my tracks. Scholar stares at me evenly and clasps her forefeet together properly on the floor, arching her neck to its full height.

"Very much in the same fashion as you would protect your brother, I will not see harm come to you. We are in this together, you and I."

"In what?"

She gives me a feral smile which quickly fades and she averts her eyes. "Perhaps it is best if we did not meet today. You are clearly not able to focus."

I heave a sigh and make an effort to settle by returning to my spot on the sofa. "I need to train. I need to be able to pass the trials."

"Phoenix, you should go mend things with your brother. We can continue tomorrow."

"Are you sure? We haven't done anything today. What were you going to teach me?"

Scholar gets to her feet and looks away. "It was nothing. I shall tell you another time when you are ready."

"Wait, tell me? Tell me what?"

"Go home, dear. Continue to practice and we shall meet here tomorrow at the same time."

She stalks away with an agitated flick of her tail and vanishes into the adjoining kitchen. I shrug, roll my eyes, and make my way out of the house. Well, that was pointless. I can't believe Scholar dug up Duke's body and purposefully left a scene like that. Duke could have stayed hidden forever . . . couldn't he? I guess there's no point in wondering about it now. He's been discovered and I can't change that.

I drive away fuming. Eventually I reach the driveway to the cabin and my heart leaps into my throat as Ashley steps out of the pine trees and stands in the middle of the road directly in front of me. I slam on the brakes, eliciting a loud squeal, and shudder to a stop a few feet from hitting her. She doesn't move an inch and provokes a menacing image in her torn jeans and black jacket. I throw the SUV into park and open the driver's door.

"Ashley, what on earth are you doing?" I shout. "I could have hit you!"

She remains planted where she is glaring at me. I take a couple hesitant steps forward.

"I spoke to Matt yesterday," she says and a chill crawls down my spine. "He remembered something about the night Duke went missing. He and a couple of his friends ran off from the game that night and Hawk followed them. Matt said Hawk shifted and ran into the woods like a wild animal. Then you showed up. And you both disappeared in the direction where I—where I found—"

She sucks in a sharp breath as my heart thunders in my chest. My palms are sweaty and I curl my fingers over them, hoping to hide the tell-tale indicator.

"Did something happen?" she asks quietly. Steel glints in her eyes and I know there's no way she's going to back down from this.

"I don't know what you're asking," I say and manage to keep the shake out of my voice.

"Did a wild animal actually kill my dog?"

"That's what it looks like."

Her lip curls. "I want you to look me in the eye and tell me the truth," she snarls. "Did you or Hawk kill Duke? Or did you know about it and not tell me?"

I fight the compulsion to swallow my guilt. I make every pretense of being a truthful, trustworthy human being when I tell the most painful of lies to my friend's face.

"No," I say.

Ashley shakes her head, eyes swimming with fresh tears, and runs into the woods. I don't chase after her. What can I possibly say? Everything that comes out of my mouth is a lie. No, there's nothing I can do for Ashley.

The hairs on the back of my neck stand on end as I realize I'm being watched. I look up and find Hawk partway down the driveway, close enough to have heard the conversation with his sharp hearing. He draws up his shoulders and promptly turns on his heel to walk away.

"Hawk!" I call after him but he keeps on walking.

I race around to the SUV and hop in. I pull up to the cabin just as he shuts himself in the barn. Genna and Jefferson look up from where they're working on the gardens. My face burns as I throw the vehicle into park, leap out of the driver's door, and run into the barn after my brother, making sure to shut and lock the door on my way in.

Hawk paces in the middle of the dirt floor amongst the training dummies. I halt on the edge on the sparring area next to Jefferson's 442.

"Hawk."

Without warning, he grabs the closest training dummy by its arms and rips the top of it off before flinging the broken pieces across the barn with an almighty roar. I watch in shock as he then proceeds to pick up the box of jerseys nearby and hurl that to, then an empty filing box, the nunchucks, a broom, a shovel, and everything else within reach that he can get his hands on. I don't dare say a word as he demolishes the sparring area. He stops short of dismantling Jefferson's work station or harming the precious car, but splinters and jerseys litter the floor in his wake. He doesn't stop until he's got blood dripping off one hand from where he hurt himself in his rage. My brother—my caring, compassionate brother—stands in the middle of the wreckage like a beast breathing hard.

"Why?" he growls and at last lifts his gaze to me. "Why are we above facing the same consequences as everyone else?"

"Hawk—"

"Ashley has been through enough!" he shouts. "This whole town has! We were meant to be the protectors. We've locked away other people who went off the rails. Why am I any different, Phoenix?"

"I had to protect you!" I shout back, hands clenched at my sides and throat straining.

"And what if I don't want you to?"

I take a step back. "You don't—you don't mean that. You're just angry."

"You're darn right I'm angry!"

"And what would be the point of telling Ashley the truth?" I demand, my own rage rising. "You've got your pendant. We fixed the problem. It won't happen again. I won't let it."

He lets out a deranged laugh and throws his arms wide. "Won't let it? Oh, that's right. Because you're a control freak in more ways than one."

His words sting and cut deeper than I'd like.

"Well, forgive me if I do what I have to in order to stop you from throwing yourself on your sword all the time. You always act like everything is your fault and you deserve the worst punishment there is but you don't! That *schweinhund* rotting away in Underground does!"

"You hold me up on some pedestal like I can do no wrong! Well, guess what? I can. I *have*. Ignoring what I am and what I'm capable of isn't going to change me."

That uncomfortable prick behind my eyes comes on strong and I fight those stupid tears with every fiber of my being. I take a moment to inhale deeply and drop my voice to a normal level. "I know exactly who you are, Hawk. What happened—that wasn't you. And I'll never stop fighting for you. You're my family. I'd do anything for you."

"I know," he says sharply and his glare cuts me into tiny pieces. He kicks a chunk of wood out of his way. "I can't be here right now."

He storms past me and I chase after.

"Where are you going?" I call as he throws open the door.

"I'm going for a drive."

Using his own set of keys, he gets into the SUV and guns it. A cloud of dust kicks up in his wake. I stand shaking and forlorn staring after him, a sob trying to claw its way out of my throat.

I become keenly aware of Genna and Jefferson's eyes on me so I move sideways and head into the trees with no clear purpose or direction in mind. I just need to get away. The shadows beneath the trees draw me in as one of their own and I move undeterred and silent beneath the hanging branches. My feet carry me along until I come to a giant oak set with thick, heavy boughs. Wanting to disappear entirely, I climb my way up onto the lower branches and take a seat against the trunk, my legs tucked up tight to my chest. I'm up high enough that anyone passing below won't see me. Not that anyone would be walking through Jefferson's woods.

I lean my head against the rough bark and watch the sway of the budding leaves overhead, wanting them to hypnotize me so I can forget about everything that's happened. It's all turned into a nightmare, hasn't it? The ghosts of my past have come back to haunt me and create a chasm between my brother and me—something I never thought was possible. I've been such a headstrong fool.

"Mind if I join you?"

I nearly startle out of the tree. Genna stands on the roots looking up at me. When I don't make an answer—trying to figure out how I didn't hear her approach—she grasps the lowest branches and begins to haul herself up. Her skilled hands bring her up quickly and within moments she sits on the heavy branch beside me, her legs dangling over the side and hands braced on either side.

"Are you okay?" she asks.

I worry my lower lip and blink fast. "No. I'm not."

"I understand what you're going through."

"Do you?" I mutter and look away to the dancing branches of the trees around us.

"You're trying to protect your brother the only way you know how even if he doesn't approve. I get that." She cracks her back and inclines her head in my direction. "I do have a question though."

I'm really not in the mood but say, "Oh?"

"How long has Hawk not been taking the serum? And when did your own abilities to suppress the werewolf curse develop?"

19

If Genna hadn't grabbed the side of my leg to keep me upright, I would have fallen out of the tree. Such as it is, I consider leaping and running to find my brother.

She knows.

"What?" I breathe. No other coherent words are able to form in my mind, just a single thought. Run. Run. Run.

"I figured it out. I was trained to observe." She says this as if she's talking about the weather and swings her legs.

"What are you—" I try to swallow my panic. "What are you going to do about it?"

She cocks her head. "What exactly do you think I would do? Tell the IMS? Tell the other werewolves? From what I've seen and heard, I know not taking the serum is a serious offense. Why would I want to inflict that sort of damage on the only friends I have?"

"But how did you know? Both parts of it. Hawk and

me." I realize that by asking as much, I've also confirmed what she's guessed. Crap.

"Oh, little things that most people apparently ignore," she says and swings her dangling legs some more. "Like the subtle change that happens when you're close by. At first I thought it was the serum doing it, making me feel less compelled, but then I realized the effect diminished when you left for your mysterious little escapes. Once I figured that out, I noticed how closely you tend to stick by your brother. I get he's your best friend and all, but I wondered if there was more to it. That's when I paid more attention to see if Hawk was taking the serum and it became obvious he wasn't. Hawk accidentally killed that girl's dog judging by his and your reaction. You lied to protect him. And you have a gift you want to keep hidden. "

Pixies, can anyone figure out Hawk's secret and mine so easily? We'll have to be more careful somehow.

"I've been warned against revealing what I can do," I say upon deciding the gig truly is up. "Until I'm powerful enough to actually cure the disease, anyway, not just temper it." I find a weight lifts from my chest when I'm able to speak about it freely. Secrets can become so infinitely heavy. Duke is proof enough of that.

"What would happen if people knew?" she asks.

Since I'm telling the truth anyway, there's no point in trying to hide it. "Well, your father said I'd be stuck in a lab and they'd bleed me out."

"Hmm." Genna switches her attention to the trees around us and stops swinging her legs. "I guess no place is ever as perfect as it's made out to be, including the IMS. There's always dark under the surface somewhere."

"That doesn't mean it's all bad. There's a lot of good, too. And one day, once I'm ready, I'll be able to reveal what I can do and help the werewolves. I know I can do this, Genna. Someday I'm going to cure the werewolf disease for good."

She studies me and moisture gathers in her eyes. I've never seen her come anywhere close to crying before, but she's nearly about to with a smile on her face.

"You really think you can?" she asks softly, as if speaking any louder would break such fragile words of hopeful desperation.

"Yes."

Her smile widens and the traces of darkness lingering in her brow disappear. "I could be normal. Dasc wouldn't be able to control me or any of the others ever again."

"That's the plan."

She laughs and the sound is bright and joyful as if she's been set free. She closes her eyes and tilts her head back. Dappled sunshine plays across her face and it's like I'm looking at a little girl playing with her best friend, free of any cares or worries. I know with absolute certainty then that Genna won't betray my secret or Hawk's. No, I can trust Genna as I should have from the start. Only now do I see it.

"I'm glad I found you, Genna," I say. "I realize I'm not the easiest person to get to know, and you aren't either, but I'd like to think we're friends."

"We *are* friends. At least in any sense that I know friends." She shrugs. "Loyalty is important to me and I don't think I've ever known a person more loyal in the ways it matters most. We get each other. We're both willing to do whatever it takes to protect our family. I respect what you did to protect Hawk, even if he doesn't see it himself. But he will."

"I'm not so sure of that," I mutter and tuck my legs in closer to my chest. It's not real reassuring to hear Genna approve of what I did considering she threatened me at gunpoint before to see if I was a threat to her father.

"Anyone that's watched you two know there's nothing that can shake you. He'll come around."

"Thanks for the vote of confidence."

Her smile continues to linger. "Things will only get better. I have to believe that. I'm home. I'm with my father. I have friends. The werewolves are being rescued. The IMS has to release them at some point and they'll be reunited with their families too."

I certainly hope that happens and everything goes smoothly, but I know things are never that simple.

"I've also been meaning to say I *am* sorry." She sounds truly remorseful for the first time. "When I first met you, I misread the situation. I should never have threatened you."

"Apology accepted," I say and feel I can breathe a little easier. "I understand why you did it, even if I didn't necessarily enjoy having a gun pointed in my face."

Genna bites her lip and holds back a laugh.

"Friends?" She extends her hand to me.

I nod and shake her offered hand. "Friends."

"We should get back before my father starts hunting for me," she says and hops easy as you please to the branch below, then does a neat backflip to the ground.

"Show-off," I call and hurry after her in a less ostentatious fashion.

We walk together to the cabin where Jefferson stands anxiously outside the barn. When he sees us, he visibly relaxes.

"Everything all right?" he asks.

"No," Genna answers. "But we'll get there."

Well, she's certainly running on a high of optimism today, isn't she? They move to the gardens and I follow. Hawk hasn't returned yet and I don't mean to sit around and languish while I wait for him. We can sort this out. We have to.

The three of us work on watering the various gardens before I excuse myself to take a break and work on Scholar's pendants in the privacy of the bedroom. It takes a while, but I manage to make only the middle trinket glow. I focus on each of them in turn and work up a sweat holding in my power and concentrating it into a single tether to each trinket. Genna's influence has helped to settle my nerves and consuming doubts. If Genna can get through what she went through growing up, then Hawk and I can get through this.

A rumble sounds in the distance and I hide away Scholar's trinkets before heading outside. Hawk pulls up in the SUV and lowers the passenger side window when he stops beside me.

He leans across from the driver's seat. "Can we talk?" He seems much calmer already and if he's ready to talk, then I certainly am.

"Of course," I say and hop into the passenger's seat.

"We should go somewhere private." He bobs his head in the direction of Genna and Jefferson for emphasis.

I nod and he pulls out. We sit in silence as he takes the backroads and heads in the direction of the state park. He stares out the windshield intently, something off about the way he holds himself. He seems . . . tense.

"Are you okay?" I ask. It's a dumb question. We just had a huge fight. Of course he's not okay. Neither am I.

"I'm fine." He doesn't look in my direction and keeps on driving past the state park. We head deeper into the country and thick trees.

"Where are we going?"

"We're almost there."

I stare at him. Where else would we possibly go? It's not like we have a lot of secret meeting spots and he doesn't know where Scholar and I have been meeting. Something doesn't feel right. A tickle itches at my mind and I can't put my finger on it.

My phone buzzes in my pocket and I jump.

"Who is it?" Hawk asks.

I look at the photo that pops up on the screen. "Genna."

"Just let it go to voicemail."

There's no reason why I should. Genna doesn't call me. If she's calling me now, then there must be a good reason. So, ignoring my brother, I pick up.

"Hello?"

"Phoenix, don't look surprised, don't act surprised. Your life depends on it." It's not Genna. It's *Hawk*. My brother. My brother that is currently sitting next to me. I do my best to keep looking straight ahead. "Pretend Genna just asked you to pick up ice cream or something from the store while you're out."

"What kind of ice cream?" I ask, the first question that manages to form.

"The person sitting next to you is *not me*. It's a

berserker." Piping Pan. Of all the shapeshifters it had to be a rage monster that managed to fool me. But of course it would be. Berserkers are better at their craft that regular shapeshifters. Now that Hawk points it out to me, I understand why my "brother" felt so off. I'm sensing the diseased magic in the berserker's blood that's eerily similar to the werewolf disease but isn't quite the same. If only I had noticed it *before* I got into the SUV. Stupid, stupid, stupid. I had been too eager to make amends with Hawk and too distracted to notice the trap. I glance at my "brother's" hand just to make doubly sure and don't see the cut on his hand he got during his fit in the barn.

"You have to clue us in to where you are somehow," Hawk says. "We'll come to you."

How? I don't even know where this berserker is taking me.

"No, the ice cream store isn't out past the state park. It's on the main drag. What you're thinking of is . . ." *Pixies*, I'm drawing a blank. I stall for time. "Come again?"

"Phoenix, we need—" A shot rings out in the background and I jump at the sudden explosive sound. I hear shouts through the phone.

"What's going on?" No one replies and the line clicks dead. "Hello? Hawk!"

I stiffen as I realize what I just did by exclaiming my brother's name in panic. I jerk about to face my brother's imposter who's pulled a bio-mech gun out of his pocket. The SUV coasts as he aims it at my chest. I snap out my hand and push the barrel away from me as it goes off. The force hits the passenger side window and blows out the glass in a hail of sharp fragments. I don't feel the stinging cuts as I wrestle with the berserker in the confines of the SUV. He's quickly expanding in his seat, the perfect imitation of my brother's face turning a bright, hideous red.

I don't think. I react. With one hand I yank the steering wheel hard to the right and with the other I smash the berserker's seat belt buckle. He has enough time to let out an ear-splitting shriek and clamp a red hand around my throat before we're thrown about as the SUV careens into the ditch. I manage to flip the deactivation switch for the driver seat airbag a second before we smash into the trunk of a tree. Without an airbag to stop him and no seat belt to hold him back, the berserker sails through the windshield. My own airbag hits me full force and I black out.

Consciousness comes in stirring waves as my vision fades in and out of focus. My head feels like it's got an axe buried in it and my chest screams in pain at the seat belt digging into me. I shove the deployed airbag out of my way and swipe at a trickle of blood running into the corner of my eye. Smoke rises from the front of the SUV but through its screen, I see the unmoving body of the berserker on the ground.

I give a sigh of relief too soon—he starts to push himself up on bloody hands. Another shadow moves through the smoke in front of me, a hulking shape of red. There are two berserkers here now.

Fumbling with the belt holding me captive in my seat, I rip the buckle apart.

The berserker standing in front of the SUV over his comrade raises a gun in his hand. Bullets shatter what remains of the glass and ricochet off the hood as he opens fire. I grasp the back of the driver's seat and haul myself bodily into the footwell behind the first row. I avoid most of the gunfire but one grazes the side of my leg before I can tuck out of sight. A groan escapes me and my fingers claw at the black box under the seat in front of my face. I wrench it open as bullets continue to destroy what's left of the SUV. The acrid smell of smoke fills my lungs and I cough against it as it tries to smother me. If the bullets don't get me, then this thing catching fire and blowing up just might.

I tug the emergency kit free and find it empty. The berserker must have cleared out the SUV before picking me up for this death trip. All I've got is my mother's .45 digging into the small of my back where I always have it holstered. I crawl over to the door and, while remaining prone in the vehicle, pull out the gun and push open the door at the same moment. Instead of rising up as they might expect, I hang out under the bottom of the door and pop a few rounds at their approaching feet. The berserker shrieks and the gunfire stops long enough for me to pull myself out of the SUV and hustle around to the rear for cover.

Wiping my hand across my forehead, I discover tiny shards of glass sticking out of my skin and my fingers come away covered in blood. I feel woozy and know I'm not in a good position. Without a bio-mech gun or a source of electricity which is their weakness, these berserkers are going to be a nightmare to take down even with my mother's gun. Outnumbered and with a good chance my current cover is going to blow up on me, I know I need to reach the woods only a few feet away and hope I can outrun them until help arrives. *If* help arrives. It sounded like Hawk was under attack when he was on the phone.

Wait. I've got another ace up my sleeve. I clutch onto

the dragon pendant around my neck and pour my magic into it.

"Help me," I say, unsure how Scholar's emergency beacon is supposed to work. She had said if I was ever in trouble the pendant would let her know. If ever she was going to show up and save the day, now would be the time. I can't believe I let a shapeshifter get one up on me again.

The tree cover is ten feet away but the shadow of the berserker falls between me and it. I'll be completely exposed. The crunch of glass on the opposite side of the SUV tells me the other berserker is attempting to flank me where I crouch at the bumper. I try to focus on their bitter energy, draw in my power and focus it just like Scholar's been teaching me. Energy surges through me in waves with my adrenaline and I can feel my tethers attach to them, reshape their power as I see fit. Two gasps respond to my attempt to quash their strength and rage.

The vehicle groans and my power snaps back in as I leap away before the second berserker flips the SUV over on end. The other berserker slips out of the way to avoid getting crushed and rushes for me. I draw up my gun and fire point blank into its chest twice. It stutters in its dash but isn't stopped. Before those monstrous hands can get a grip around my neck, I make a forward roll through the grass directly into the brush, get my feet under me, and start running. Their shrieks follow me into the woods and bullets whiz by my head.

I have no idea if there are houses nearby but I can't lead these berserkers to other people. Not for the sake of keeping them in the dark but to keep anyone else from getting hurt.

Think, Phoenix. There has to be something I can do.

Electricity is a berserker's true weakness but I've got nothing I can possibly use out here in the middle of the forest. I keep running. The effort of hurdling fallen logs and adjusting my feet on treacherous roots feels instinctual after all those runs through the obstacle course at the field office.

All I've got is me, my training, my useless .45, and my abilities. It's got to be enough.

I manage a glance over my shoulder to find the berserkers closing the distance. Despite all those sprints and endurance runs, I'm not going to be able to outrun them. I'll have to out fight them. Well, if I'm going to make a stand, better now than when I don't have any strength left.

Veering for a partially fallen tree on my left, I race up the slippery bark and launch myself up into the nearest tree. The berserkers swing around the tree to meet me head on as I leap down and catch a low branch. In my momentum I kick out, release my hold, and plant my feet solidly in the chest of the one still wearing my brother's face. The force of my launch drives him into the ground and I absorb the shock of the landing by rolling off, nearly getting tangled in a bush in the process. The other quickly comes upon me with its gun raised. I duck low and ram my fist into the underside of his arm past his elbow. Bones shatter and the gun in his hand clatters to the ground. In a fluid motion, I bring up my other fist into his chin and then kick the gun away.

Fast strikes. Every motion and dodge counts when fighting berserkers. If they manage to get their hands around me or land a solid hit, I'll be done for. I have to be faster than them, move like smoke, and not get caught.

The berserker groans and rocks backward from the

blow to his now split chin. Spinning up in a roundhouse kick, gathering my energy into the muscles of my leg, I hit him squarely in the chest to send him crashing through the underbrush. The moment I land and catch my footing, the other one is directly in front of my face, having returned to his feet while I dealt with his comrade. I try to slip away from his reaching hands but too late. Hawk's distorted face snarls as enormous fingers wrap around my bicep. I try to hold onto him and use my power to lessen his strength but I'm not fast enough. The berserker whips me about with the full weight of his body and lets me loose.

I fly like a Frisbee spinning end over end until I my shins snap against a tree trunk and I tumble into a pile of dead branches. The shock from hitting the tree and my rough landing steals my breath away and I can't move as my whole body goes rigid. My shins are in agony and more than one snapped branch digs into me. Bruised, broken, and breathless, I can't get up fast enough to fight the berserker charging me. I manage to shakily bring up my .45 which I've miraculously managed to hang onto and unload. The berserker halts and stumbles over his feet as the bullets penetrate his body. Dark blood seeps from his chest. He wheezes and comes to a stop before he gives a low growl and keeps coming for me, resilient.

Freaking monsters!

I scramble for something around me to use as a weapon and drag myself backwards using my arms, my legs now absolutely useless. I back into the remains of a broken tree with splintered spikes rising from its stump. The berserker lunges. I roll onto my side and with a pained cry, kick the sharpened end of the stump in its direction. Unable to stop itself mid-leap, the berserker falls sickeningly on the end of the stump, impaled through its shoulder. Despite the thick chunk of wood sticking out its back, the berserker still tries to move. I shuffle out of its reach into a tree trunk.

Stretching my hands towards the relentless menace, I let my power tether to the berserker and taste its bitter magic in my mouth.

"No more," I growl.

The red quickly begins to fade from the berserker's skin and the body deflates until it looks like my brother fell in the woods and got himself impaled. The mockery before me makes me sick. The berserker continues to twitch and tries to push himself off. *Piping Pan*, these things really don't give up, do they?

I'm about to have another go of shaping the bitter magic in its veins when a gust of wind rattles through the woods. My loose hair snaps about my face an instant before the berserker is sent flying through the air by the powerful pulse ripping apart the forest. In the settling rain of dirt and debris, Scholar appears like a ghost. One second she's there like a legend of old, light blazing in her eyes as she stops to make sure I'm okay. The next second, another pulse tears trees and earth asunder and she vanishes. The wake of her wrath continues the way I had come, where the two berserkers I'm sure are now regretting their life choices.

I struggle to my feet and brace myself against the birch behind me. Dreading what I'll see, I lift the hem of my jeans to inspect my shins. The length of them are abraded, bloody, and turning nasty shades of color already. There's no way I'm running anywhere in this state. Limping through the path of destruction, I grimace my way along until Scholar appears once again. Her loose hair fans out behind her and the burning fury in her face makes her look like a wraith.

"Took you long enough," I say and pant through the pain doubling in my legs. I wouldn't be surprised if I have fractures. "Thanks for saving my butt."

"Can you run?" she says. No use for pleasantries. Right. I forgot.

"I doubt it—but Hawk's in trouble. Just go. You have to get to him."

She stalks towards me as her skin transforms into a shade of shimmering green. "And leave you out here where another monster can finish you off? I do not think that is wise."

Her body morphs from strict librarian to vicious dragon in only a few heartbeats. Her lean body twists around before me and the sharp spikes on her spine glint in the pale light beneath the trees.

"Hop on," she commands.

I grimace as I inspect her back. "Pointy spikes hurt to sit on, Scholar."

"Climb up. You will be fine." She lies prone in the grass and slithers a long tongue at me like an impatient snake.

I tuck my .45 into its holster and grab hold of the largest spike right at the top of her shoulders. The instant I do, all the spikes below it fold and flatten along her back in the same fashion the frill around her face does. Oh. That certainly helps. Without the prospect of getting stabbed by her spikes, I do my best to scramble up her slick scales and settle in. I breathe through clenched teeth as my legs and bicep ache horribly.

"Better hold on tight," she says.

Then we're running. I barely avoid impaling myself on the spikes further up Scholar's neck as I rock with the motion of her legs stretching out to their full length and pushing away from the ground in great bounding strides. Once I get the rhythm of her pace, I cling to her hide and adjust as she leaps over fallen trees, skirts around treacherous footing, ducks under low branches, and circumvents any nearby houses.

Despite the pain throughout my body, despite racing to save my brother, a thrill goes through me and makes my heart pound even faster.

I'm riding a *dragon*.

Her long, greyhound-like limbs get us through the woods at a monumental speed. Our surroundings blur until she eventually slows and we emerge before a house I recognize. It's Scholar's "vacation home" as it were. Parked outside is a nondescript, dark sedan. I slide off Scholar's back and my legs turn to pudding, dropping me to the hard ground. Scholar shifts into her human form and scoops me into her arms in the same way she did when she had been the one to cause the harm.

I'm slid into the passenger's seat and Scholar leaps into the seat beside me. She guns the engine and we floor it down the road—though after riding a dragon, it seems rather dull. The weight of everything that's just happened finally starts to sink in. We're under attack *again*. We have to get to Hawk. I don't know if he's okay or not.

"Where's your brother?" Scholar asks.

"He called from Genna's phone and she had been at the cabin last. That's where he has to be. I hope." And what about Genna? And Jefferson?

We fly through town. Scholar expertly weaves through the traffic without care or stopping. More than one horn honks at us.

"Why?" I ask. "Where did those berserkers come from? Who sent them?"

"I think there are at least two legitimate answers to those questions," Scholar says calmly despite the situation. "The first is Epsilon. It wouldn't be the first time the lamia have waited in the shadows for the opportune moment to strike and lure their enemies into a trap."

"And the second?"

"My dear, I do believe you are clever enough to have figured it out."

I keep my eyes on the road blurring past us. "Dasc's werewolves."

"Precisely."

Just like Genna and Rosalyn feared might happen. Retaliation for Dasc's capture and Genna turning the tables. The berserkers would make sense considering Dasc has worked with shapeshifters before and Genna made mention he likes to have other monsters do his dirty work when it suits him.

If it is indeed the werewolves, then it's very possible Rosalyn and Deputy Graham are in danger too. I reach for my cell phone to give them a call but realize it's gone. I must have lost it during my struggle with the berserker in the SUV. I don't have any way to warn them.

"Scholar, you're probably going to say no, but do you have a cell phone on you?"

"Glove compartment."

"Really?" I open the box in front of me and pull out a

flip phone. "I thought you didn't believe in phones. They're too easy to track."

"I keep a burner phone in case of an emergency."

Well, I'm sure glad she had the sense to get one. I power it up and first give Hawk a ring but it goes straight to voicemail. I try Deputy Graham next but it goes to voicemail again. Dang it. I don't know if he and Rosalyn are in trouble or not—I *do* know something is wrong where Hawk is. There's too much ground to cover and not enough time.

"Scholar, I need to call this in," I say to give her forewarning. She's been running from the IMS and Draco for countless ages for her secrets. If I call in the IMS, she'll need to hide, but I need her.

"Do what you must," she says. "There is still time for me to slip away when proper."

Heaving a sigh, I dial the number for division head-quarters. I swear, this has got to be a record for the number of times a junior agent has called in a code black.

The same woman's voice answers that had taken my previous code black a few months ago. "ID number?"

"0919-32, Junior Agent Phoenix Mason. Code black."

"Patching you to the emergency response team leader."

Oh, how nice of them. The last time they sent me to Witty because they didn't believe me. Times have changed I guess.

A deep male voice comes on the line. "This is Spartan leader. Go."

I explain the situation in a rush, providing as many specifics as I can without including Scholar as promised. I tell of the two berserkers, the suspected situation at the field office, and the other people in play.

"Team is wheels up in two minutes. ETA to your location twenty minutes. Local agents in Duluth are being contacted to assist."

"Copy."

"Take precautionary measures and proceed to assist. However, if not tactically sound, pull back."

"Acknowledged."

"Spartan leader out."

The line clicks.

"Help is on the way?" Scholar asks.

"The best, but we've got to hold out for twenty minutes."

In response, Scholar puts more pressure on the gas pedal and we fly over the road towards the field office and a fight.

20

We round the bend onto Soldier Road and squeal across the blacktop. We're nearly there. Above the tree tops a plume of black smoke rises from the direction of the cabin. Oh, no.

When Scholar turns off the road we find a sheriff's squad parked at an odd angle partway down the driveway. The lights on top flash, the doors stand ajar, and there's no one inside. It's an eerie sight. Scholar slams on the brakes and my chest aches as the seat belt puts sharp pressure on my injuries.

"That can't be good." I unlatch my seat belt and step out of the car to draw up my mother's gun. Scholar follows suit and we cautiously approach the squad car. I limp to the open driver's door and find blood splattered on the upholstery. What happened? Where's Deputy Graham? Why was he here?

Now that I'm outside the confines of the car, I can smell the acrid stench of smoke, feel heat wash over my face, and hear the sound of fire crackling in the distance. I glance to Scholar and she nods. Together we walk the rest of the way to the field office, sticking to the cover of the trees alongside the driveway. I'm not moving fast enough and I know it. I would have run to the cabin if I could but my stupid legs are holding me back. I risk a glance down and notice there are flecks of blood on my socks and the top of my sneakers. Dark stains have soaked through where my shins were brutalized against that tree trunk. It's not a good omen. Freaking berserkers.

I keep an eye on the woods around us and listen for sounds of a fight. We need to move faster. My breath comes in wheezing rasps as the pain in my legs threatens to make me fall. Scholar notices and offers her arm but I shake my head fervently.

"Just keep going," I rasp.

Have the others managed to hold out? *Pixies*, if anything happens to my brother . . . The last things we said to each other were bitter and full of anger. I can't let those be our final words.

I shake my head. I can't think like that. I need to keep moving.

We finally clear the trees and the sight before my eyes breaks my heart. The cabin is consumed by an inferno and billows of smoke rise from its wreckage. My home. Please oh please let no one be in there. Over the roar of the fire and crackling of wood, voices draw us to the barn which looks almost as bad. Most of the roof has caved in and parts of it smoke. What on earth?

The door hangs at an odd angle. Scholar leads the way stealthily forward as I limp along behind her. Something must garner her attention because she suddenly bolts inside and the ground shakes as she makes her presence known. I hurry in after and hold onto the door frame to remain upright as I take in the battle.

The inside of the barn is a complete mess. Half of the loft has fallen to the floor below, tools and upturned earth are everywhere, the stairs have collapsed, and parts of the computers lay sparking or hanging from what's left of the loft. Scorch marks mar the floor, walls, and broken beams in dark spurts as if someone had set off a pack of fireworks or had a fire sprite over for dinner. The 442 has a coat of dust and is sprinkled with bits of floorboard but is, surprisingly, still in one piece. I'm amazed the entire place hasn't collapsed in on itself.

In the midst of the debris, I spot Rosalyn unmoving on the other side of the barn with Jared hunched over her protectively. Part of her shirt is badly singed on her side.

Scholar stands with her back to me and a hand outstretched towards a boy kneeling on a bare patch of dirt before her. Genna stands just past her, a gun in each hand—one trained on the boy, the other on Scholar. Jefferson stands over her shoulder with a shotgun aimed at the unassuming boy as well. And—to my everlasting relief—Hawk emerges from the rubble of the back end of the barn. He's dirty and a bit banged up but otherwise he looks all right. I sag with relief. My brother must sense my gaze because his eyes find mine. He nods once letting me know he's fine.

"It's okay!" Jefferson shouts at his daughter. "She's a friend."

At his word, Genna lowers the gun aimed at Scholar but keeps the other one trained on the boy. She's got burns on her as well and everyone in the room is breathing hard like they've just endured the fight of their life. I limp into room and sense something strange about the boy now at their mercy. There are equal parts pure magic and bitter disease flowing through his veins. My movement must catch his attention because he glances in my direction—long enough for me to see that his eyes have burning light brimming in the depths of his irises.

This is no ordinary boy. Apart from his creepy eyes, what I sense in him tells me everything I need to know. He's Blessed like me but tainted by the werewolf disease. I would have been like him—or dead—had the magic in my own blood not cleansed my body when I had been bitten. From the looks of the cabin, the barn, and the others, I'd guess his special power borders on the fiery.

"Why?" Genna growls. "Why did you do this, Rory?"

The boy snarls at her and clutches at his stomach in pain. "Sometimes you have to gnaw off the infected parts in order to survive. You're a traitor, *Whisper*."

"I take that as answer enough," Scholar says dryly. "It seems you have offended the rest of Dasc's obedient followers."

Genna's face pulls into a twisted frown. "They don't understand. None of them do."

"They have clearly been brainwashed."

The boy snaps his jaws in Scholar's direction like a rabid

dog. I wonder if this is the Whisper that Director Knox said had escaped. Is this what Genna would be like if she hadn't kept her faith in her family?

The boy's eyes pass over us with seething hatred. He looks so young and might have been handsome if not for his features twisting into something malevolent and cruel— a deadly smile of victory even though he's clearly trapped.

"The pack survives."

He peels back his arms he had been clutching to his chest which I thought was meant to staunch some wound, but instead he holds a collection of ball bearings in his hands. His eyes gleam, steam rises off his skin, and an intense light blossoms from his chest beneath his disheveled shirt.

"Get down!" Scholar shouts.

Three explosions happen simultaneously. First, an explosion erupts from deep within the boy and expands in a blooming ball of fire. Second, Genna fires the gun at the boy's chest. Third, a shockwave pulses from Scholar—it throws me to the ground along with everyone else and pushes the force of the explosion away from Genna's direction. The barn is chaos and fire and terrible sound. More of the loft collapses along with part of the roof in a thunderous crash.

It all happens in mere seconds. Tucking in on myself until the immediate threat passes, I blink and cough the cloud of dust away. Scholar is the first one up, shoving a heavy beam off her shoulders and rising to her feet. She scans the room and pauses on me. I nod and wave towards the others. I didn't have anything fall on me so I don't need her help.

The world spins as I get up. Hawk follows suit on the other side of the barn. Thank my lucky stars, he's okay. Genna emerges from the debris next. One side of her face is red and her clothes are singed but she doesn't give pause for her injuries. Instead, she lunges for where Jefferson fell beside her. She rips away burning splinters of wood and pieces of shingles with heedless, single-minded focus. Scholar helps as well until Jefferson is uncovered in the wreckage. I limp forward, dreading what I'll see but knowing I need to help somehow.

"DAD!" Genna screams.

Jefferson isn't moving. I find I can't breathe and teeter where I stand lightheaded. Blood seeps from two ragged holes in his chest. The boy had become a living claymore mine. The ball bearings he had held in his hand acted like lethal projectiles when he exploded.

"He needs proper medical attention," Scholar says calmly despite the horrific situation before us. "Here, help me."

She wrenches off her own outer sweater and presses it to Jefferson's bleeding chest. The world narrows to the blood seeping between her fingers and Genna's horrified expression as she too places her hands on her father's chest, trying to trap his life force inside his body.

He'll bleed to death—just like my parents.

Everything sounds muted against my traumatized ears, but over the muffled echoes and ringing, I hear the sound of rotors drawing ever closer until they too are deafening. I glance through the hole in the ceiling and see the shadow of an IMS Osprey aircraft sweeping overhead to land in the clearing before the barn.

I stare at Scholar. "You have to go."

Her eyes glisten and harden as she looks upon her dying friend, my mentor, Genna's only family. But there's nothing more she can do here. She doesn't have healing powers.

Scholar rises to her feet as blood not her own drips from her hands. Genna hardly seems to notice her absence except to spread her hands out more to soak up Jefferson's blood. The dragon blinks a few times as if fighting through a haze before turning about and sprinting through a hole in the back of the barn to escape into the woods.

Seconds later a team surges through the front of the building in black armor, matte helmets, and dark masks covering the bottom half of their faces. Each wields an automatic weapon with the subtle sleek differences in design that mark them as bio-mech guns at their core. Twinges of magical power tap me on the shoulder, letting me know that half of their number are Blessed. The code black team has arrived.

"Hands where I can see them!" a male shouts who entered first. "Identify yourselves!"

"Phoenix Mason," I say quickly and spout off my ID number feeling numb. "I called in the code black. The threat's been neutralized but we have an agent down. He needs a doctor immediately."

The Spartan team spreads out in a supremely efficient manner to secure the perimeter while their team medic works to stabilize Jefferson for transport to the hospital. Each of the team members report to their squad leader that the area is clear and they've uncovered the body of the boy. Their words pass me by like white noise. Jefferson is dying. He's dying and there's nothing I can do about it.

The team takes up sentry positions and a couple of stretchers are brought in. They carry Jefferson and Rosalyn into the Osprey to transport them immediately to the nearest hospital. They're already making contact with the local IMS physician that had replaced Dr. Rosewell after she went missing. Genna, Hawk, Deputy Graham, and I clamber into the conspicuous aircraft after them. This all happens within the span of a minute if not less. The Spartans are nothing but efficient. The Spartan medic, pilot, and sharpshooter accompany us while the rest of their team stays behind as a rearguard to clean up the area. I can only hope Scholar has covered her tracks and gotten away to safety. She had taken a great risk by coming along to help. I owe her, probably more than I know.

The flight to the hospital is short but not fast enough. We touch down on the helicopter pad that is barely large enough to accommodate the Osprey with its elongated body and twin propeller engines that rotate into vertical position. Our resident physician, Dr. Thorne, waits along with a contingent of medical staff. The second the bay door opens, he and the rest hurry in to hoist Jefferson onto a gurney. They rush away with Genna fast on their heels while the Spartan medic and a couple of nurses get Rosalyn onto her own gurney before lifting me onto another. I want to argue about staying with Jefferson—I need to know what's happening—but they refuse my pleas and wheel me away into another section of the ER. Hawk keeps pace with us after he assures them he can walk on his own.

There's a flurry of activity as the nurses draw a curtain around me. Hawk waits just beyond with the Spartan medic while a doctor I don't know comes in to assist. They have to cut away the bottom half of my jeans to get to the worst damage. My legs look horrible and feel even worse. It's a miracle I had been walking around on them to be honest. The skin around my shins is swollen and has turned nasty shades of dark purple, green, and red. Blood drips from the abrasions along the front of my legs and stains my clothes.

The next fifteen minutes are a painful blur of cleaning the wounds on my legs and various other abrasions located all over my body from the car crash, explosion, and tangling with a pair of berserkers. Bits of glass are plucked from my face along with nasty splinters in my side. My legs are soaked in ice to control the swelling, bandages are wrapped on, and I'm given some drugs for the pain. Dr. Thorne comes in momentarily to make sure that everything with my blood on it is burned—for everyone's safety since I'm Blessed. My body aches horribly but that pales in comparison to the agony over Jefferson.

I'm swapped into a hospital gown and crowned with a gray blanket before being wheeled out of the ER to get some x-rays taken to make sure I don't have any broken bones. I sit uncomfortably in a large dark room and hold still as their machine takes its pictures. A nurse with intricately braided hair and a vague smile helps me into a wheelchair as Dr. Thorne gives me the optimistic news that I only have small hairline fractures in both legs. It'll take weeks to fully heal and I probably won't be quite recovered by the time the trials start. That seems so trivial at the moment, though.

At my request, the nurse pushes me around in the wheelchair in search of my brother and someone who can tell me how Jefferson is doing. We roll along until we find Hawk waiting out by the nurse's station in front of the surgical wing. He's got bandages wrapped around his arms and small ones holding together cuts along the top of his hairline. Genna, on the other hand, despite the obvious burns on her face from the explosion and blood dripping to the floor from somewhere on her person, won't let anyone near her. She paces frantically, breathing hard and grasping at her hair or clutching the back of her neck. Her overwhelming anxiety is difficult to watch.

"Genna, you have to let someone check you over," Hawk says as I roll to a stop ten feet away.

"I can't leave. My father's in there. I can't lose him again, Hawk. I can't lose him twice. I can't do that." Her frantic muttering falls away as Hawk continues to try to persuade her to let the doctors help her. The nurse that brought me here joins in, and after promising that she can be treated on the spot, Genna finally agrees to stay still long enough for the nurse and Dr. Thorne to take a look at her.

Hawk finally walks over to me and stops a few feet short. Something ugly sits between us—the fight neither of us wants to talk about but now's not the time to discuss it. Our mentor, and in some ways surrogate father, is in surgery at the far end of the hall behind the closed double doors leading to the surgical ward. I need Hawk right now, and I can see in his eyes that he needs me too. He bows his head and moves around to the back of my wheelchair to guide me to a row of chairs opposite where Genna is getting patched up in the nurse's station. He maneuvers me about so I'm in line with the chairs and then takes the seat next to me, bracing his elbows on his thighs and clasping his hands together.

"What have we gotten ourselves into?" he murmurs.

I gnaw on my smarting lip and fiddle with the edge of white gauze wrapped around my hand. I know what he means. We had always imagined working for the IMS would be a grand adventure. We were supposed to be white knights flying in on gryphons and stopping the enemy in broad strokes of white and black morality. But reality is messy. It's painful and dirty. The lines we thought we'd never cross, we've scratched out. The monsters have the faces of friends and our friends have become monsters. There's no great glory. There's no happily-ever-after ending. There's only one ugly fight after another. Being an agent isn't being a hero riding in to save the day. It's being a lightning rod in a thunderstorm and hoping beyond hope that the inevitable will never happen. But it has today. Jefferson is proof enough of that.

21

I sit alone in the waiting room, restricted to my wheelchair, and face the enormous window that overlooks the parking lot and row of houses beyond. The light is fading behind the trees and the streetlights cast a warm glow over the eerie shadows that move as a wind sways the leaves and power lines. I keep my magic tethers out as a precaution in case any shapeshifter tries to attack again. Scholar's pendant rests beneath the collar of my hospital gown, yet another defense if needed but one that I don't dare call upon.

Genna has stubbornly refused to move from the entrance of the surgical ward and taken up residence on the row of chairs next to it. Hawk is off coordinating with the Spartan team and numerous other agents that have currently swarmed the area. He had been glad I was okay but wasn't in a talking mood. He's still angry about the Duke and Ashley situation.

We both gave our statements to the Spartan leader so he could better assess the situation. Having to remove Scholar from the narrative ended up making me look like some kind of superhero—taking on two berserkers by myself, finding a nearby car, and then racing to the field office to save everyone. The Spartan looked impressed if not entirely convinced. I don't think anyone's really going to buy our story.

The second we were done, Hawk went with them to secure the other werewolves in town and left me behind. The general hustle and bustle of agents has left the hospital for some temporary command post I don't know where. I stayed with Genna's wrathful anxiety for as long as I could before I couldn't stand it anymore and wound up here. Deputy Graham paces the hallways at regular intervals with a few bandages taped to his face as he walks to and from his sister's room, who is resting and not in the best of shape.

Jefferson's still in surgery. How much could there possibly be to fix? Were vital organs hit? Did he lose too much blood?

Then that other nagging question continues to surface. Could I have done something more to save him?

I swallow past my dry tongue and watch the wind pull the leaves back and forth as if dancing with the trees. I can't even remember the last time I danced. It used to be my happy place but my heart's been bleeding out and there's nothing left of it to dedicate to something so innocent and carefree.

Mindlessly staring and going over the same hopeless thoughts over and over again, I'm so lost in myself that I almost don't hear someone enter. I don't take the energy to wheel myself about to see who it is. If they need to talk, I'm sure they'll make themselves known. Whoever it is, I feel that familiar twang of uncorrupted magic. A Blessed then. Most likely one of the Spartan team. A faint woodsy cologne reaches me as a shadow falls beside my wheelchair.

"Confined away from the flurry, I see."

I look up to find Charlie studying me. His hands are tucked into his—as always—fashionably tailored black jacket. He's wearing dark cargo pants though, a change of pace for him, and tactical boots that are dusty with recent outside use. He offers me a faint smile and nudges me in the shoulder with his elbow. I'm glad he's here.

"How are you?" he asks.

I swallow my urge to snap. I want something to pummel and have ever since Jefferson was injured, but I can't take any of it out on Charlie. He came here to help after all. He doesn't deserve any of my anger and frustration.

"Hurting," I say. "Feeling useless."

He bobs his head to the side as if to say "that's true" and moves around to sit on the armrest of a cushioned chair facing me. He props one foot up on the seat and leans forward on his forearms.

"Yeah, sitting it out in the hospital isn't ideal," he says. His gaze wanders the room and catches on a couple of nurses that walk by behind us and exit the waiting room until it's just us.

"Have you heard anything?" I ask and dread what sort of answer I'll receive.

"Agent Barnes is still in surgery but a doctor came out a minute ago to say he's been stabilized and should be coming out soon. I figured I should come tell you so you stop agonizing over it."

Oh, thank goodness. My chest heaves and I sort of puddle in my wheelchair, letting my strained muscles relax out of their rigid state at such good news. "Thanks."

His eyes rake the many bandages on my head where shards of glass were removed. "I hear this is the second time you've crashed a car."

No one will ever let me live that down, will they? I shrug. "Yeah well, this time I meant to."

He cocks on eyebrow. "You meant to?"

"I had a berserker in the driver's seat," I say. "And not a lot of options after he got his hand around my throat. So, I grabbed the wheel, undid his seat belt, and rammed us into a tree."

He laughs softly and his smile helps ease my pain a little.

"You've got guts," he says.

"Thankfully they're still inside me for the time being."

He laughs some more and that heavy weight across my shoulders lifts the tiniest amount. After another moment, silence drifts between us and he focuses on picking something under his thumbnail. I watch as he avoids making eye contact and grows fidgety. Am I the one making him uncomfortable? Or is it just the situation of trying to make small talk with someone in a somber setting? Or does he have more bad news yet to deliver?

"I should go," he says at last and stands, dusting off his flawlessly clean jacket. "I'm not great company. Anyway, you probably want to be alone."

He starts to walk away and I blurt out, "Don't go."

My throat tightens and there's an uncomfortable prick

behind my eyes as I feel desperate and terrified at the thought of sitting here all by myself, waiting for people to return. This place makes me feel it more than ever. Charlie's last words strike a chord in me and I realize something I've been blind to but in truth have known all along.

"I don't want to be alone," I whisper. My other words remain locked away but bounce around inside my skull. I'm terrified Jefferson's going to go the same way as my parents. I'm afraid I'm going to lose Hawk forever whether it be by his own choice or not. Everything I've done, even if it was in the course of saving the people I love, has been to fulfill this selfish inner desire and ward off the most horrifying fear. I don't want to be alone.

Charlie dips his head and returns to the chair he had been perched on before. He clears his throat and temples his fingers together, elbows braced on the armrests.

"I did warn you I'm terrible company, though."

"That's not true."

"I can't hold a conversation," he says. "Unless you want a long, tedious discussion about books. That's about all I've got material for."

"Speaking of books . . ." I wince at the thought of the destruction of the field office. "I think the ones Hawk and I borrowed are toast. I'll buy you new ones. I promise. I'm so sorry—"

He gives me a crooked smile. "There are always more books, Phoenix. Don't worry about it."

"Really?"

"I can't exactly blame you, can I?"

"Depends on if you're that kind of person."

He rolls his eyes. "I'm not that petty."

"That's good."

Our conversation dies out again and he looks anxious. Not a people person I take it. That's fine. I get that. He speaks my language—or doesn't speak, in this case.

"I also enjoy comfortable silence," I say quietly, which provokes more laughter on his part.

"Well, I don't know about *comfortable*—"

"Having a friend nearby is enough."

His lips twitch upward and he pulls over another chair so he can use it as a footrest.

"Comfortable silence it is then," he says and rests his head against the back of the chair. He crosses his arms over his chest and closes his eyes. "Does that include napping?"

"Sure."

"Snoring?"

"Then it's not exactly *silence* anymore."

He snorts and scoots lower into his chair until he's completely spread out between the two seats. "Wake me if you need me."

I watch him as he settles in to nap true to his word. His chest rises and falls in a steady rhythm and my eyes glue to the movement as I drift off in my own thoughts again. There is something greatly comforting about having someone else nearby that I know and can rely on. I wonder if that part of me that can control magic in others isn't because I'm trying to save Hawk, but because I'm trying to reach out and make a connection.

And although I'm sure Charlie has other things he ought to be doing, he chose to stay here when I needed a friend the most. For that, I'm eternally grateful.

"Thank you," I whisper.

"You're welcome," he murmurs and promptly falls asleep.

The bright lights of the waiting room feel like burning beacons as darkness falls beyond the window. Charlie's steady breathing, the thrum of the air vents, and the occasional footsteps of a passing nurse are the only sounds. I start to imagine monsters staring at me through those windows. I'm an easy target where I sit. My fears are subdued a little when I see one of the members of the Spartan team lounging around the front of the hospital doors acting as a lookout. I continue to feel anxious though and eventually shake Charlie awake.

He cracks one eye open and I realize he wasn't really asleep at all. "Yes?"

"Could you find my gun?" I ask quietly. "I think they gave my stuff to Hawk but I don't know what he did with them."

Charlie gives the room and windows a sweeping gaze as he sits up and stretches his arms to the ceiling. It's obvious he's checking for danger at my request to be armed. Once he's apparently satisfied the coast is clear he gives me a knowing look.

"Security blanket?" he says.

I glower at him. "I guess."

He pats a long pocket on the side of his cargo pants. "Not judging. Got mine right here." He stands and gives my shoulder a friendly squeeze as he yawns. "I'll be right back."

Smoothing the back of his hair and running his fingers through the front, self-consciously making sure he's presentable, he strolls out of the waiting room and into the hall. A clock on the wall ticks out the long painful minutes.

I wonder how Jefferson is doing? Surely he must be out of surgery by now. Driving myself mad with the thought of sitting here by myself for however long it takes Charlie to return, I wheel over to the open door—discovering my arms are also in a great deal of pain—and wait for a nurse to pass by.

"Excuse me," I call to the first one that comes near. She stops and after a quick chat, I find out Jefferson is indeed out of surgery but in the intensive care unit as he stabilizes. He lost a lot of blood and nearly died on the operating table. I clutch a hand to my throat and rub at my sternum. I hate hearing how people I love have suffered and knowing there is nothing I could do about it. She informs me they are not allowing friends in yet but will let me know when they do. I thank the nurse and she moves along after making sure I don't need anything myself.

I wheel to the surgical ward but Genna has vanished. Another lady at the nurse's station directs me to the ICU and at last I see her standing guard at the door to the unit. She's not alone. Rosalyn talks to her in whispers in her hospital gown, an IV bag hanging from a metal post that she uses like a walker.

I get close enough to catch Rosalyn say, "You knew this was going to happen. So what are you going to do about it?"

My wheelchair makes a subtle squeak and both girls swivel in my direction. When they see it's me, Rosalyn sweeps away with her IV stand in tow. Genna crosses her arms over her chest and watches her go, a scowl on her face. Well, that gives me an ominous feeling. At the end of the hallway, the deputy finds his sister and they walk off with arms slung over each other's shoulders.

"How's he doing?" I ask.

"They hope he'll wake tomorrow morning once the anesthesia wears off and he's rested," Genna says tersely. "He may have permanent damage. They don't know for sure."

My stomach drops out of me. Permanent damage. I swallow and ask, "And you?"

"I want to rip everyone to pieces," she snarls and makes no mention of her own injuries. I doubt she can even feel them in her current fury. I can't say that I blame her. I've been in the same position before.

"Do you want some company?"

She pauses in her pacing. Her shoulders drop for only a temporary moment of weakness before she says, "No. I'm fine here. You should get some rest."

"So should you."

"I'll heal. Faster than you at any rate." That's true. "I can't sleep anyway."

I know the feeling. "If you change your mind, I'll be around."

She nods and resumes pacing, probably already forgetting I made an offer. I really don't think she should be left alone at a time like this. I know I certainly don't want to be but I don't necessarily want to stay here either. Genna's posture and attitude is making it clear she truly is ready to rip someone to pieces. As I wheel back the way I came, I realize she isn't alone. One of the Spartan members is hanging about and nearly hidden in the nurse's station. She inclines her head slightly in my direction as I pass.

I notice a few other IMS agents scattered through the hospital. It looks like we have quite the guard posted here.

It's only fair given that one of our own is struggling for his life. My throat becomes raw thinking about it and I keep my gaze downcast.

"Hey, there you are!" Charlie rounds the corner and gives me a big, hearty wave. In his other hand is a black duffle bag. He strolls up looking cross. "You said get your gun and come back. I come back and you're gone!"

"I went to check on Genna and Jefferson." I point to the bag. "That's a little big for just my gun."

"Yeah, well . . ." He doesn't say anymore on the matter but doesn't sound real happy about it, whatever it is. "I'll pass your gun over once we're not in the middle of a hospital hallway."

"Good idea."

"More good news. I brought friends."

As if waiting for him to announce their presence, my brother and Agent Melody Boyd round the corner. Hawk's changed into clothes that are clearly not his and hefts a few shopping bags in each hand. Melody sets her own two duffle bags on the floor and immediately bends down to give me a hug. Her blonde curls tickle my face and my back aches from the embrace but it's not unwelcome. I didn't realize how much I've been in need of a hug.

She draws away and looks seriously concerned as her eyes sweep over me. "Is there anything I can get you? Anything you need?"

Always the helpful people person. There's plenty I need but not much she can give me. I shake my head.

"Well, we've set up in a few temporary rooms the hospital has offered for our use," she says. "Come on then."

She leads the way to a wing of ordinary hospital rooms.

Charlie takes up the duty of pushing me along so I don't have to wheel myself. The ICU isn't too far away and I catch sight of Genna gazing in the direction of her father's room. Surely they would let her in if she asked. Maybe she can. Maybe she's afraid to.

We pass a room where Rosalyn rests and Deputy Graham sits in a chair at her side with his feet propped on the edge of the mattress. They look relaxed and content in each other's company. It's a nice switch from the first time I saw them together. At least one thing has been mended instead of broken.

Our little group of four continues on to a room with two beds and a white curtain that hangs down the center to give some privacy between them.

"This is for the ladies," Melody announces and sets her bags on the bed closest to the window overlooking the road that connects to the parking lot. "Hawk, you and Charlie are across the hall."

The boys leave us to dump most of their stuff in the other room but quickly return. I don't fail to notice that Charlie keeps glancing around and stands near the doorway casually while Melody tends to stick closer to the window. They're acting as guards. I guess whatever is going on outside the hospital isn't looking good.

I stare morosely at the hospital bed, thinking of that one time Hawk, Charlie, and I stayed in Underground's medical ward for three days. Even in those days of recovering from some awful injuries, the future prospects seemed brighter than they do now.

"Your brother helped me pick up some clothes for you," Melody says and reveals what's in the shopping bags. There are numerous shirts, a pair of jeans, some generic underthings, a toothbrush, toothpaste, deodorant, and a hairbrush. Right. Because all of our things went up in a fireball. I roll my lips together and page through the items Melody so kindly got me.

"Thank you," I say quietly. "You didn't have to."

"Nonsense. We stick together. If one of us falls, the rest of us will be there to pick them back up." The conviction in her voice and generous propensity for kindness makes my throat raw again.

It's then that I realize Hawk's new clothes are something Charlie would wear. Charlie must have offered some of his own small wardrobe to help out my brother. My heart warms and aches in kind. I guess Melody's right. As I sit contemplating all the things I'll need to replace and what I've lost, Charlie sneaks up behind me and places my .45 and holster in my palm. He winks and moves silently to the doorway to lean against the frame with arms crossed in order to watch the hallway.

"What's going on out there?" I ask in the silence that follows.

Melody huffs and braids her hair over one shoulder as she begins to talk. "Nothing good, I'm afraid. The Spartans have effectively locked down the area around the field office. The werewolf boy that led the attack is dead. Genna killed him. The berserkers you took down are missing."

Alarm bells ring in my head and I sit up straighter. "What?"

"We searched where you had your tussle, found all the destruction and a few curious neighbors wondering what was going on, but the berserkers had disappeared. Found the bloody stump you had impaled one on, though. His mate must have helped him free and they fled." My expression must look pretty alarmed because she adds as an afterthought, "But don't worry. The Spartans will find them."

"They're sticking around?"

"Until they're called out to another emergency at least. Other agents are coming to help contain the situation."

Hawk scoffs and rolls his eyes before wandering towards the window muttering, "*Contain.* Right."

I glance in confusion between them. "What's going on?"

"They've locked down all the werewolves in town," Hawk growls and plants his hands on his waist. "They're restricted to their homes and work places as a precautionary measure. No one's happy about it."

"How long is that supposed to last?"

"We don't know," Melody answers before Hawk can say more. "But clearly the situation is getting more and more out of hand. With the attacks in Europe and now here, it's making people worried."

She doesn't need to elaborate for me to get the picture. People aren't just worried in general. They're worried about werewolves. Hawk and I make eye contact but he quickly looks away, his cheeks reddening.

"But enough doom and gloom for tonight," she says. "We should all get some sleep, you two in particular. It's been a long day."

Understatement. Although I'm exhausted beyond belief, my body aches, and my head throbs, I know I won't be able to sleep for a while. No one's come with any update on Jefferson again. That thought alone is enough to keep me up through the rest of the night.

When none of us make a move to go to bed, Melody rummages in her duffle bag and pulls out a DVD case. "But, if anyone didn't feel like they could sleep, I have the perfect movie. *Pride and Prejudice*. I watch it when I'm having a bad run and it never fails to cheer me up. Any takers?"

The boys look less than inclined but I certainly won't say no to a distraction. In short order, and a little assistance from one of the clerks up front, we jury rig the television mounted on the wall and start up the movie. Although Melody and Charlie make a show of watching it, they still keep to their positions by the window and doorway.

Hawk helps me out of my wheelchair, my legs smarting fiercely, and up onto the edge of the mattress. We sit side by side, me in my hospital gown and him smelling faintly of Charlie's woodsy cologne in our friend's clothes. The movie manages to distract me if only a little. Charlie's snide comments about the movie and Melody repeatedly snapping at him to shut up or correcting him on historical nuances also help. As it rolls on, Hawk wraps his hand around mine on top of the starchy hospital sheet beneath us. Maybe we're not one hundred percent okay but that act alone tells me Hawk is ready to move past our earlier fight. So am I.

When the credits roll, Charlie goes in search of a nurse for an update on Jefferson's condition. He comes back to report things are looking up. With that comforting hope, sleep finally starts to tug me under. Hawk says he wants to keep Genna company and leaves. Charlie disperses shortly after but I catch him passing the doorway now and again with his nose in a book. I fall asleep to the thrum of the air vents and the steady beep of medical equipment nearby.

I'm woken the following morning by sharp pain in my

legs and a dull throbbing ache everywhere else. I sit up in bed and find Melody already up and working on a laptop cross-legged on her bed. The doorway stands open and Charlie passes by every so often still reading a book as if he never went to bed. Who knows? Maybe he didn't. Hawk appears a moment later. We swap subdued "good morning"s and I get out of bed on my own. Shooting pain goes up my shins at each step but I already hate the wheelchair and don't want to use it. Assuring Melody I'm fine on my own, I get dressed in the attached bathroom into the clothes she bought for me. They're nothing special but they fit and are comfortable so I can't complain. I brush out my tangled mess of blood-red hair and when my shoulder aches too much to put it in a ponytail on my own, Melody graciously offers to braid it for me.

Having some semblance of normalcy back in jeans and a t-shirt, I walk out of the hospital room ready to at least try to face the day. A nurse finds our group and lets us know that Jefferson is awake but shouldn't have too many visitors just yet. Genna's sitting with him and he's resting. We share a collective sigh of relief.

At that happy bit of news and a fresh round of pain pills, we head to the cafeteria. Hawk acts as my escort and offers his arm. My legs ache and I take slow steps, so slow that Charlie comes round to my other side and the boys offer to carry me chair-like to the dining center. I can't tell if they're joking or not. Scowling at them both, I refuse but do take Charlie's offered arm as well to have support on both sides. Stupid legs.

The cafeteria isn't a particularly large room but big enough to seat twenty people comfortably. Most of the seats are empty—only three staff members in colorful scrubs are here. A counter lines one wall bearing various bowls of cereal, oatmeal, fruit, jugs of milk, and other breakfast foods. I ease into a chair and Hawk gives the other two a meaningful look. They hurry off to the food bar and take their time picking out breakfast for the four of us.

Hawk takes the seat beside me and clasps his hands on the tabletop looking apprehensive. There are dark shadows under his eyes and he looks years older than nineteen, stretched and worn. I know I must look the same.

"I'm sorry," he says quietly and draws slow circles on the table with his conjoined hands. "I . . . reacted pretty strongly about the whole Ashley thing. I know why you did what you did, Phoenix, I really do. You were trying to protect me like you always do. I just—" He runs a hand through his hair and finally meets my gaze. "I want to be able to decide my own fate, good or bad. By doing what you did, you only dug yourself into a hole next to me."

"Hawk—"

"I'm the werewolf, not you. No matter what I do, that burden is always going to be mine alone to bear."

"It doesn't have to be," I say softly. "One day—"

"That day isn't here yet, and pretending the rest of the world and all of its problems don't exist until that day isn't going to work." He shuts his eyes and pinches the bridge of his nose. "I can't ignore what I've done. I also can't ignore the state the rest of the werewolves are in either. Then lying to Ashley just made it feel a thousand times worse."

I pull my shoulders in and bow my head. "I'm sorry."

"It's not you. It's—" He chews on his lower lip and throws an eye around the room as if searching for the answer. "I was mad about the situation. I was angry that I couldn't tell Ashley the truth and that you lied on my behalf. I'm angry it happened in the first place. This isn't the life I would have chosen if I had a choice, you know."

"I know," I say automatically even though I don't know if he's referring to being a werewolf or the whole of it including becoming an IMS agent. As for myself, I can't imagine doing anything else with my life. Stopping monsters and saving the world is quite the day job.

"I want us to be okay again," he says. "I don't want to be angry with you."

"I don't want you angry at me either. You're kind of scary."

His lips twitch upwards. "I'm the scary one? I've seen what you can do."

I shrug, happy that we're back on terms of teasing each other. It makes everything else a little more bearable.

"And you have a nasty habit of crashing cars," he adds.

I roll my eyes. "Yeah, whatever. Laugh it up."

"Speaking of cars, the Green Monster survived the destruction."

"That'll make Jefferson happy."

"It's a bit dinged up though."

"That won't."

Hawk shrugs and straightens in his seat to survey the dining room with the ghost of a smile lingering on his face. He's in one of Charlie's shirts again, the same navy button down he had been grazed in when we chased a vampire. I can even see the small meticulous stitching on the shoulder where it was carefully mended. It's a little big on Hawk but he still looks more stylish than usual.

"You look nice," I tell him to keep the good mood going for as long as possible.

At that moment Charlie and Melody return with trays bearing cereal, a handful of fruit, oatmeal, cups of milk, and even some waffles.

"It's all in the shirt," Charlie says and scoots the tray with waffles and fruit towards me. He gives me a careful smile that I return.

"That's true," Hawk says. "And since I look nice all the time, you really meant to say I look *handsome*."

"My apologies, ginger-dork," I say and take a big bite of the waffles slathered in syrup and crowned with blueberries. After I swallow and Charlie gives me a questioning look, I mime a toast in his direction at his choice of breakfast which seems to satisfy him. "Did anything else survive from the field office?"

"I was able to salvage a few things," he says. "But not much."

"I want to see it for myself."

The other three share worried looks and Melody speaks for them. "I don't think that's a good idea."

"Why not?"

"You can't walk well for one."

"I can walk well enough. I need to see it."

Charlie holds out a hand towards his mentoring agent. "There's no harm in taking a short trip."

"Yeah," Hawk puts in. "We can swing out and then come back to visit Jefferson once he's up to it."

We settle our plans and after breakfast we walk into the parking lot, the boys helping me along again. I notice Jefferson's 442 parked on the edge of the lot with some dings in the roof and paint job. We'll have to spruce it up somehow before Jefferson sees it again. That'll make him feel better . . . I hope. Melody drives us to Soldier Road in her SUV, Charlie riding shotgun, and we pass a guard of agents at the end of the driveway before being let through.

The sight of the Moose Lake Field Office breaks my heart. The cabin is a scorched pile of charred beams and rubble. The barn hardly looks any better. Only one corner is left standing but the rest has completely caved in. I had really started to think of this place as home. And now it's gone.

A few agents loiter about the place to keep an eye on things and sift through debris. Hawk points out that the electronic equipment has already been hauled off for security reasons. In the house, after Charlie helps push aside some splintered wood joists, I find the tattered remnants of my *Go Fire Sprites!* sweatshirt. Holding it in my hands, I take a seat on what's left of the bed frame and bow my head.

Charlie stands before me looking auspicious in his tailored black jacket in the midst of ash and destruction—although he managed to accumulate some gray dust on the front of it in his attempts to help me uncover what's left of my things. Hawk remains busy digging through another section of our former bedroom.

"You okay?" Charlie asks.

I worry my lower lip. "My friend Celina got me this sweatshirt the year the fire sprites won the aetherball tournament. I've got a lot of fond memories tied up in this thing. Now look at it." I hold it up to display the charred holes with half the letters missing so you can't even read it anymore. "I never had much and what I did have had sentimental value, you know?"

He nods and tucks his hands into his pockets. "Your memories didn't burn up, though, and you can always buy new things."

"Yeah, I guess," I grumble.

Hawk stiffens and slowly rises holding up a ball of burnt leather. "Phoenix."

The ache in my chest deepens as I realize he's found the remnants of my mother's old bomber jacket. I had hoped that somehow it had managed to escape the destruction but of course that was a futile hope. The only thing left of her now is her .45 and Hawk and me. It doesn't feel like enough. I fight the prick behind my eyes and sniffle back the start of a runny nose. Why does this fight always have to be so personal?

But in the midst of the chaos and destruction, I sense the bright spots of magic buried beneath the ruins.

I sniffle loudly and run my hand beneath my nose. "Can I have a moment, guys?"

The boys nod and leave me alone to brood. Ever so carefully, I dig down through the charred floorboards and rescue Scholar's still hidden pendants. Once secured, I tuck them into the pocket of my jacket with plans to hide them somewhere safer when I can.

I shuffle out of the wreckage of the house, leaving the scraps of the jacket and sweatshirt behind, and return to the SUV having seen enough. I'm ready to return to the hospital and get some good news about Jefferson. This place is depressing.

We ride back in silence and enter the hospital foyer where the Spartan leader finds us to let us know Jefferson is awake and taking visitors. As a group we move for his room but I fall behind as my legs bark in protest. The others slow down and the boys offer to help me once again but the Spartan leader waves them off.

"Go on ahead," he says. "I'll help Junior Agent Mason."

Instantly suspicious, I squint at the Spartan who stands at about Charlie's height over my head. He's a bit intimidating with his black commando gear, square jaw, ragged scar running along one side of his face, and silver hair cut marine style. He's all brawn. There's no presence of magic in his blood so at least I know he's not a shapeshifter trying to lure me away from the safety of my companions. The others hang back but I nod letting them know it's okay and they move on. Hawk drags behind, casting glances over his shoulder until he rounds a corner and disappears.

It's just me and the team leader. He holds out his arm for support and I take it feeling awkward. I don't know him and he doesn't know me.

"I surveyed the area where you fought those berserkers," he says. "There was a lot more destruction than I would have anticipated."

"Oh?" I think I know where this is going. This Spartan is clever and probably knows I couldn't have made those swaths of devastation by myself.

"Is there anything you want to add to your report?" he asks and looks at me sideways. "Is there anything my people need to be worried about that's unaccounted for?"

I stare evenly back. "No. There's nothing else to be worried about." Which is true. Scholar is no threat to the Spartans. "If there was, I would have said so."

He nods and doesn't press the issue—in fact, he seems to respect my silence on the matter. I guess he understands that certain legendary creatures value their privacy, dragons more than most. Whenever there's an incident, they don't want to be overly involved. If I say there's not a threat, then he must take me at my word. That sense of trust makes me feel better about the situation.

We finally make it to Jefferson's room where everyone has gathered around his bed. Genna remains steadfast at his side as always and smiles are shared all around. Jefferson himself is propped up halfway into a sitting position with a mound of pillows. Tubes and wires run from him, his face has cuts scabbing over, but of course the worst of the damage is hidden beneath his hospital gown and gray blanket pulled up to his chest. He's paler than I've ever seen him with bruise-like shadows under his eyes. The Spartan leader excuses himself politely and marches out of the room. I watch him go for a moment, conscious that I don't even know his name and ought to thank him later. Then my focus redirects and I limp to the side of Jefferson's bed.

"Hey," he croaks.

"Hey old man," I say with a smile.

He has his hand wrapped around Genna's resting on top of the blanket and his thumb draws slow circles on the back of her hand as if needing constant reassurance she's still there—not that Genna looks the least bit inclined to be anywhere else.

"I'm glad to see you awake," I say. "You gave us a right scare."

"Needed to keep you on your toes," he says gruffly.

Genna growls and says, "Never. Do. That. Again."

"What, try to save your life?"

She blinks quickly and her lips become a thin quibbling

line. After seeing how strongly she's handled everything else, she shows just how vulnerable she is when it comes to her family.

He motions her closer with his other hand. "It's okay, baby girl. Come here."

Genna leans over to give him a careful hug. The rest of us of back up a step to give them a little space. This is what I need—to see Jefferson doing better and Genna having her happy reunion with him again. They've already been through so much pain and separation, it would be heartbreaking for them to endure more.

The relief and happiness of the moment is cut asunder like a hot knife through butter as I sense a presence draw near. I know the exact moment Draco arrives at the hospital. Anxiety clamps on my spine and I automatically swivel towards the doorway in apprehension. If the Spartan leader shared the details of what he found and his suspicions, then there's a very likely chance Draco knows as well. Draco, the dragon that had Terra poisoned, forced Eris into hiding, and hunted Scholar for what she knows of the truth.

I spin about when someone puts a hand on my elbow.

Hawk frowns at me and whispers, "What's wrong?"

I swallow and shake my head. "Wait here."

The weight of everyone's eyes falls on me as I limp out of the room towards the force of that presence, the power of a majestic class dragon. I hardly make it halfway down the hallway before Draco sweeps into view like a dark storm. The tails of his black suit swing behind him as he takes the corner forcefully and marches towards me. I halt and wait as I brace myself. He might not know what the Spartan leader suspected. He could be here to check in on us for all I know, though I doubt it.

But I don't hold that awe for him like I used to despite now realizing the full uncompromising strength that runs through his veins and comes off him in waves as if he needs to shed it or he'll internally combust. Maybe I had felt it all along and that's why my eyes always drew to him in a room. He is the definition of power.

And from the cold glint in his eye, I know without a doubt exactly why he's here.

Fear crawls over me.

"Phoenix," he says tersely.

"I wasn't expecting to see you here, Draco."

He tilts his head downwards, never breaking eye contact. It's unnerving. "I heard there were some unusual circumstances."

Playing the innocent card, I say, "Well, the werewolves seeking retaliation wasn't entirely unexpected."

"That is not what I am referring to." The air around me starts to feel heavy. The pressure of the energy rolling off him pushes against my ribs and my legs ache.

I realize in an instant that I'm wearing Scholar's pendant and have her trinkets in my pocket. Even though they're out of sight, if Draco can sense magic like I can, maybe he can sense there is something different about me. Could he recognize her magic? What about Hawk's blood pendant? I have to do something.

"Then what are you referring to?" I say. My words are a bit stilted as my focus is split between playing innocent and latching my own energy onto the pendant and trinkets, suppressing the magic and mingling it with my own to hide it. The concentration it takes and Draco's presence make my palms sweaty and perspiration breaks out on my forehead. I can only hope he doesn't take notice.

"The level of destruction in the forest was . . . curious."

Focus, focus, focus. "Oh?"

"I didn't know you possessed such abilities."

He can't say outright what he's looking for. No one knows why he would be hunting Scholar. He could make an excuse, come up with a lie, but if anyone else came across Scholar while assisting in his search, she could tell them the truth. That's why there is no official search for her. Draco will need to find her on his own to cover up his tracks. And me? Well, I could very well end up a loose end, couldn't I? For the moment he still needs me since Dasc will only talk to me. But how much longer will Dasc even be of use? My only protection is Draco's own cover up of the truth. If I lie about Scholar, how can he say I was in the wrong if she hasn't committed any crime except for knowing the truth?

"I can project my strength," I say. "I've been working on focusing my abilities to prepare for the trials."

His gaze has the force of fire and my skin burns under it.

"I am glad you are able to harness your strength with such catastrophic precision. You will be quite the agent and valuable asset to the IMS."

"Thank you, sir."

He clears his throat and says a little louder, "Has your assignment born any fruit? Is it your belief that Genna may be connected to this latest attack? What of her cohort, Rosalyn?"

My face draws into a frown at the accusation. "Genna and Rosalyn weren't involved. There's no possible way either of them would have helped hurt their families."

"Very well. I trust you will continue to keep an eye on them and give your usual updates."

I open and close my mouth a few times, not sure how to respond. What's the point of watching them any longer? They fought hard against their attackers and Genna's distress alone after her father was injured is proof enough of her innocence.

"Get some rest," he says. "I look forward to your performance in the trials."

He sweeps back the way he came, nurses and agents alike moving out of his path. A couple of the Spartans loiter farther down the hall and give me sideways looks. I'm sure it's pretty peculiar for a majestic dragon to show up out of nowhere, let alone carry a discussion with a junior agent. I turn away from their stares and return to Jefferson's room.

The atmosphere is distinctly different from when I left it only moments before. All eyes press in on me. Melody and Charlie are the first to look away, averting the tension building. Hawk looks angry again, Genna seems resigned, but Jefferson—the intensity of his glare almost knocks me off my feet.

It takes me a moment to understand why. They heard. They heard everything, and I realize what Draco just did. When I refused to give him the answers he wanted, he struck an underhanded blow. None of them knew about my mission to watch Genna and report on her behavior. Those were my orders—keep it under wraps. Draco knew what this hurtful secret would cost me.

"You've been reporting on Genna to Draco?" Jefferson says hoarsely. His voice almost cracks and my chest seizes up at the sound.

"Jefferson, I—"

"She hadn't been through enough? You couldn't trust her?"

Genna puts a hand on his arm. "Dad."

"No!" he shouts and then recoils in pain. I feel a different kind of pain in turn. "I trusted you to help protect my daughter! But you've been telling on her to *him*? What did you tell him? That she's a pawn under Dasc's thumb? That she was going to betray us?"

"No," I manage to squeeze out through my constricted throat. Everything inside me is twisting up. "No, I—I had orders to keep an eye on her, that's all. And I never—well, I—" I can't say I never reported on her because I did. I told Director Knox about when she held a gun on me. They almost hauled her in. And then again when she ran off to tell James' parents about his fate.

"After everything, they still don't trust her," he wheezes and is clearly struggling to breath. The heart rate monitor beside him beeps in a fast rhythm—much too fast to be good for him. "You sided with *them*. After everything I've done for *you*."

And he has done so much. Kept my secret. Kept Hawk's secret. Became our mentor. Became a father figure. Put me in touch with Scholar. Gave us a place we could call home. Came to my rescue whenever I needed him.

"Jefferson, *please*," I plead and can't stop the tears this time. "Please just listen—"

"I don't want to hear anything from you," he snarls. A

couple nurses rush in and Genna slips out of the way while Jefferson grimaces in pain. I start to back away from his rage. No. Not like this. I'm shaking my head without even realizing it and the others are deathly quiet.

I wrap both hands around my throat. "*Please.*"

"*Leave*, Phoenix. And don't bother to come back."

Crushed, and knowing there were no words I can use to sway Jefferson when I have so clearly crossed a line when it came to his daughter, I flee from the room leaving pieces of myself behind.

22

Even after four weeks of being careful and taking it easy, my legs continue to pain me. I sit on the bottom step of the stadium in Underground with the flickering orange and blue lights of the fire sprites for company as I massage my lower legs. The discoloration and most severe pain is gone but they still ache, especially after the runs I've been doing trying to get back into shape for the trials only a few days away. Accepting there's not much more I can do at this point, I pull on my calf compression sleeves and content myself with an easy walk around the track.

Other junior agents filter in as the morning grows older. I've been the first one out here every morning for the last two weeks, even beating out a few Spartans that are currently staying in Underground to judge the trials. I can't stand to stay in the Roman apartments for long. By some twisted design of fate, with all of the agents coming in for the trials and the lack of space needed to house them all, they put Hawk, me, Charlie, and three other junior agents in the same apartment. Maybe it wouldn't be so bad if Hawk wasn't still angry at me and three strangers weren't privy to our silent aggression. Charlie had bravely attempted to act as peace keeper but gave up after a week of getting no progress from either me or my brother.

Then, to make matters even worse, they moved Jefferson to Underground for security reasons along with Genna. Rosalyn and Deputy Graham elected to remain in Moose Lake but there are now a contingent of agents watching them and the city for signs of trouble. And where did Jefferson end up getting placed after given leave from the medical ward? The lower level of the Roman apartments. I swear, Draco has his hand in it or I'm a pixie.

There have been no further chats with Dasc to distract me, no missions, no planting gardens with the Barneses, no watching movies with Celina since she's away in Faunus, and no pranks with my brother who remains angry with me for not telling him my orders. I've managed to match his anger, though. If none of them can understand that I had orders I couldn't refuse and couldn't reveal, then fine. They can be angry. I'll be angry too. At least Hawk will hang out and be pleasant enough as long as the subject isn't brought up.

I blow out an exasperated breath, plant my hands on my hips, and watch a group of fire sprites leap from brazier to brazier on top of the tall poles playing a game of tag. I can sense their bright spots of magic along with the constant swirl of energy that perforates Underground. Their playfulness makes me wish I felt playful.

Surprisingly, Genna has been the one who accepted my actions without deference. She agreed that given the circumstances she would have been disappointed if they didn't have at least one person keeping tabs on her and reporting in to headquarters. She's also the only one who seems to understand that despite everything she did, the IMS did not come to collect her because of my efforts to dissuade the director and Draco from otherwise locking her up.

If only Hawk and Jefferson could agree as well.

Charlie's been indifferent about the whole thing and doesn't understand why the others are so upset about it. Orders are orders, he said. At least he respects me for trying to do my job.

As I complete a loop around the track, he enters the stadium and ports over to my side to keep my pace. I startle only briefly. I've gotten accustomed to him teleporting here and there and everywhere. He seems to enjoy giving other people a good scare, and ports for simple things like moving a single spot down the sofa to reach his book without having to get up by normal means. I get the sense he wasn't able to do it a lot where he was before. Our gifts have to remain hidden from the rest of the ignorant world but here in Underground, where we're surrounded by the extraordinary, we can be ourselves.

Moments later, Hawk comes in but swiftly starts a run around the inner ring without bothering to even come over to say hello. It'll be one of those mornings I guess.

"How are the legs?" Charlie asks.

"Better. Not good enough." I frown at my shins as we continue at an easy walk. "They're going to be a problem during the trials I think."

Charlie shrugs and starts to stretch his arms. "You'll be fine."

"Is that your expert medical opinion?"

"You're stronger than you give yourself credit for," is all he says.

We carry on in silence and he remains by my side despite everyone else running or jogging on the track. He should probably be doing the same but doesn't. There's no possible way I can express my gratitude enough for his friendship. I've discovered that once Charlie's loyalty is won, he's a diehard friend. He's become so much easier to get along with since neither of us feels inclined to argue or bicker anymore. It's a refreshing change. In fact, it's rather amusing watching him be frosty to other people now that his anti-social behavior isn't directed towards me. He's got some remarkably biting retorts that tend to make me laugh and yet feel sorry for his intended victims at the same time. But we certainly have shared some harrowing and soul-bearing experiences together. I've discovered such things either push people further apart or form strong bonds. I'm glad we went the way of the latter.

I keep an eye on the other junior agents around us preparing for the trials. I haven't really made any attempts to get to know them despite the fact we'll have some team tests to do together. Charlie and I have mostly kept to ourselves. There have been a few meals and activities hosted for the junior agents to get to know each other, but I've attended them more out of a sense of obligation than actually wanting to participate. I usually ended up on the sidelines sitting next to Charlie and we'd people watch. He might not have noticed the number of girls batting their eyes in his direction but I certainly did. Hawk on the other hand has made numerous pals already but I don't think anyone knows he's a werewolf yet. I have a feeling their friendliness will dry up the moment they do considering the way they treat Genna when she's around.

I can tell the moment she shows up in the stadium. She's like a magnet for the attention of the junior agents on the track. Heads turn in her direction, eyes narrow or avoid contact, and they move a little closer together while keeping Genna in their sights. She's a pariah given all the werewolf attacks. I've even caught gossip about what should be done about the "werewolf problem." Things have started to get hostile and all those old prejudices against the werewolves have resurfaced in ugly ways. There are a few places Genna and Hawk can no longer go in Underground at the right of the business owners to refuse customers. It only fuels my anger and theirs.

"I'll be right back," I say to Charlie. "Keep going without me."

He nods and kicks up his pace until he's running on Hawk's heels around the outer ring. I walk off the track and head over to Genna where she sits on the bottom seat of the stands tying her shoes. As usual, Witty sits in his wheelchair beside her. They've formed an odd sort of bond since Genna took up a more permanent residence in Underground. She apparently finds electronics fascinating and he finds everything about her funny and amazing as if she's made out of sunshine and rainbows. I guess both feeling like outcasts has brought them closer together too. Witty watches the runners with envy and a touch of desperation. I wish I could help him but there's nothing I can do except continue to be his friend.

"Hey guys," I say. "What's up?"

"She wanted to get some track time in," Witty answers on behalf of Genna, tipping his head in her direction.

She finishes adjusting her shoes and gives him a warm smile. "I made a bet with him and he's here to watch me smoke the field."

"What bet?" I ask.

Witty rocks the wheels of his chair back and forth anxiously. "She said she could beat every person on the track in a race. I said she couldn't so she bet she could. I didn't think she was actually going to come out here . . ." His eyes jump from runner to runner as if they're going to mob him at any given moment.

"So the winner of this bet gets what exactly?"

Genna stretches her fingers to her toes and folds in half with her forehead touching her shins. With her short hair hanging down to her ankles and her face pressed against her legs, she says, "He has to show me his oh-so-sacred comic book collection if I win."

"And if you lose?"

"I have to play that stupid computer game with him."

"It's not stupid!" Witty says and slams a fist on the arm of his chair for emphasis.

I smirk and cross my arms over my chest. "Oooooh, *that* game. He still plays that?"

Genna straightens and smirks. "All the time."

Witty makes a grumpy face. "Super-Kart is a classic."

"Keep telling yourself that, Witty. Although I might

have to come watch Genna kick your butt on your own game if she loses."

"I'm *not* going to lose," she says.

Having run with her plenty of times before, I don't doubt it. She walks to the track and I follow while Witty remains behind. Genna calls to him, "Time me!"

Once we're out of hearing range, I lean in and ask quietly, "How's Jefferson doing?"

"Better. I wish he'd stop being stupid about the whole business with you, though." She runs a hand through the front of her hair and draws the loose strands out of her face. "I know he misses you guys. He has this glum look every time he thinks I'm not looking."

"I've tried to apologize."

"Oh, I know. I was in the kitchen when you came into the apartment that day. That was unbearable."

I don't say anymore because there's nothing more I can say. Genna already knows how torn up I feel about it all and how much I want to mend that bridge with Jefferson but he won't listen. He either shouts me out or ignores me completely. It's painful even being in the same apartment building as him let alone the same room.

We stand on the edge of the track and Genna watches for a moment to gauge when's the best time to start lapping everyone.

"Good luck," I say and start an easy pace around the outside of the track.

She laughs behind me as she gets into a ready crouch in the outer ring. "I don't need luck."

Yeah, that's true. The next second, as soon as Hawk comes level with her, she takes off at a blazing speed. I grumble to myself wishing I could push myself out there along with the rest of them as the other junior agents realize Genna is showing them up. Only Hawk manages to keep pace with her but after four laps even he starts to lag behind. She's a terror unto herself as she grins viciously at everyone she passes.

She wears a different face out here when the world is watching. To them she's a fearless machine without any self-doubt or regrets. She's the terrible black wolf that'll gobble them up if they aren't careful. But I've seen the other side. I saw her panic and despair when Jefferson was injured. I've caught her staring off into the darkness by herself on the apartment balcony. I've overheard her whispered conversations with Hawk about how she regrets having to kill the boy werewolf who had been so bent on killing us all. Genna—the remorseless nightmare and the girl who smiles at daisies. There's so much more to her and the rest of the werewolves that everyone seems to forget in the face of the horrible actions of a few.

As expected, Genna outstrips everyone on the track and then jogs back to Witty with a huge smile. They share a high-five and laugh as the other junior agents sullenly slink away to other exercises. Hawk is at Genna's side seconds later to see what's going on. I make my way towards them and Charlie teleports next to me out of breath.

"I could have had her," he says without preamble. "I could have ported to the finish and beat her."

I raise an eyebrow. "But you didn't."

"Yeah, because I'm a gentleman. I just want it to be known that I *could* have beat her if I wanted to."

"But you didn't because you're such an upstanding guy. If only you were cruel and diabolical, Charlie, the world could be yours."

He shrugs and makes a face. "Meh. Maybe later."

"Why not right now?" I wrap a hand around his bicep. "We can still beat them to breakfast."

"What, teleport?"

"Yeah."

He looks down his nose at me, those pale green eyes of his catching the light. Although a bit sweaty and flushed, he manages to look handsome as always. There's no doubt why several of the junior agent girls have been batting their lashes at him. Too bad for them he doesn't seem to notice.

"That would hurt, you know," he says. "Porting with someone else."

He's bound to find out sooner or later if we get into a tricky situation during the teamwork portion of the trials. He doesn't remember what happened after he teleported me last time but I sure do. "Try me."

"You sure?"

"Hold on a sec." I cup my other hand around my mouth and shout to the others. "Last one to Old Man Two's pays for breakfast!" I shake Charlie's arm. "Go, go, go!"

Genna and Hawk immediately sprint for the tunnel of the stadium but Charlie and I are already there in a whoosh of magic. It's disorienting and my brain doesn't want to accept that I'm in a different place than I was a moment before. Squeezed through time and space, my skin tingles but even the small burst of pain I had felt the first time is gone. There's just a buzz of magical current flowing through me, balling around me and spitting me back out as Charlie steps forward, porting us yet again to the end of the tunnel and out the other side of the stadium.

We stand breathless together for a moment as the loose wisps of my hair fall back into place as if they had been lifted by a rogue wind. He stares at me wide-eyed, shocked, and then examines me as if he's discovered some extraordinary specimen. I must be the first person ever to not crumple in agonizing pain after being carried along on his teleports.

The footsteps of the others thunder out to us and I squeeze his arm again.

"Get us to the restaurant," I command. "I'll explain there."

His eyes narrow and his lips part as if he wants to argue, but then he turns his gaze to the center of Underground and we vanish. It takes three more ports along the outside of IMS headquarters and through the colonnade—scaring up a group of water sprites in our wake—to reach the outside eating area of Old Man Two's restaurant. There are only a few patrons here, veteran agents by the looks of them. They startle at our sudden appearance but then quickly resume their meals, rolling their eyes at us flaunting our powers and disturbing their quiet breakfast.

Charlie holds onto my elbow as if I might vanish on *him*. "But you—I—that didn't hurt you? Not even a little?"

Apart from sounding awed, it actually sounds like he's disappointed there's someone that doesn't lapse into extreme pain under his power.

"Nope."

"How?"

I trust Charlie but not that much. I can give him a little explanation though. "When you teleported me inside that mansion to save my brother, it hurt but nothing near what Hawk said it would feel like. I'm not sure what it is, but now all I feel is the pressure and that's it. No pain. Pretty cool, huh?"

"It's a first, I'll tell you that much," he says and continues to stare at me with his hand wrapped around my arm.

I raise an eyebrow as if this is nothing and shouldn't garner so much attention. "What?"

He lowers his gaze. "Nothing."

"Then can I have my arm back, please?"

As if burned, he quickly relinquishes his grip and clears his throat.

We're saved from any additional awkwardness by the arrival of the others. Together we commandeer a table and I immediately start up a conversation about what we might expect in the upcoming trials to distract Charlie. Old Man Two eventually comes over and serves up scrambled eggs, toast, orange juice, and fried green beans. While we dig in we swap stories and crack jokes as if there's nothing overshadowing us, as if the last several months never happened, and there are only good times on the horizon. I craved this—no, *needed* this. And it isn't until my side is splitting from laughter that I realize just how much.

The rest of the restaurant fills with junior agents, veterans, fauns, giants, centaurs, and elves so we finish up and dart away before we get absorbed into the stifling crowd. We have time to spare before the trials and by all means we plan to enjoy it. We start to wander aimlessly until Genna brings up the bet again so we converge on Witty's place in the bastille-styled apartment complex two rows down from ours. We pass through the massive wooden doors, nod in greeting to other agents we pass in the stone hallway, and eventually reach Witty's place. He turns red as he fumbles with his keys and finger-combs his dark hair in some attempt to make himself presentable. I don't know why he's so nervous, but maybe it's because he's got a crew of friends ready to barge into his home.

Witty eventually gets the key in the lock of the metal lined door and pushes it open with a lackluster "ta-da!" to his apartment. Hawk and I spearhead the way in since we've been here before. As usual, wires salvaged from old computers hang from shelves like odd tentacles, empty computer cases and internal components stack the edges of the stone floor, and thick black rugs decorate the living room. He's upgraded the space since the last time I was here with faint blue lights that run in strips along the edges of the room to give the place a peculiar glow. It's pretty cool, actually.

"Impressive setup," Charlie comments offhand as he swivels on his heel and starts to inspect the large collection of movies lining the wall near the door. "So what is this video game I've been hearing about?"

Hawk immediately plops onto the sofa in front of the large television and picks up the remote. "I'll show you."

"Careful," Witty says and looks like he wants to rip the remote out of my brother's hands as if he's nervous the other boys are going to break his precious electronics.

Genna nudges his shoulder. "Hey, you owe me a peek at that comic-book collection of yours."

He lets out a defeated groan and wheels away from

where Hawk and Charlie are starting up his game console. I follow him and Genna through the rows of metal risers stuffed with miscellaneous computer parts until we reach the back wall which he clearly dedicates to his hobbies. It's covered in posters of dragons of various breeds, from the noble class to the terrenes like Scholar. The center of the collage is dedicated to the majestics with copies of famous paintings I recognize by the Japanese artist Tatsu, a well-known noble class dragon who devoted himself to the arts.

I study the artwork while Witty unlocks a cabinet beneath the collage. I've seen all of this before but it has new meaning for me. I've actually met and worked with a majestic class dragon. Before, Draco was just a distant legend to me, but now the heroic deeds he's praised for have been dirtied by Scholar's tales. I know the real truth, not the one perpetuated by Draco himself that everyone else believes. His portrait sits in the middle of the majestics as a sign of importance—their self-designated leader. The shadow of his true form is like a rising inferno over the small figure of his human self at the bottom of the artwork.

Genna comes to stand beside me inspecting the images.

"Those are ink wash paintings," Witty says and carefully slides out a glossy box from the cabinet. "The originals anyway. Mine are copies. Obviously."

"They're beautiful," Genna murmurs and leans closer towards the wall.

Above Draco's picture is Caelum, the Master of the Skies up in the clouds. To his left is Jangwa who barely fits into his frame with his impressive rocky hide, and Eris the trickster in her lithe, serpentine form twisting around her portrait. Below Draco is Ryūjin swimming amidst a typhoon.

Lastly, on the right is Terra, her shape akin to her terrene brood, standing amongst pillars of stone. Of course one majestic is missing from this group. The one no one knows about. Echidna, mother of monsters. A shiver goes down my spine. Genna's eyes shift to me for half a moment before she's distracted by Witty opening his box.

His comic-books aren't your average, run-of-the-mill superhero stories you can buy topside. No, these are books from Tatsu himself who decided to dabble in the popular art form.

"These are *manga*," Witty stubbornly corrects me when I mention as such. "It's totally different. Be careful with those! Those are first editions!"

The booklets he passes to me and Genna are of the same ilk as the paintings of the majestics. In fact, the comic-books—excuse me, *manga*—are about the majestics and other dragon classes as well. The first several pages have lengthy descriptions of each of the majestics as they pose like action stars and Tatsu goes on and on about how amazing they are. It's clear they've found a fan in him. The Japanese Kanji I can't read is translated in subtext below.

I page through, looking more at the images than reading about the dragons themselves, when something catches my eye and I freeze.

The image of Terra stares at me down her long snout, the frill around her face like a series of fans on display. I quickly scan the translated text in search of the word that had grabbed my attention.

A terror to her enemies who burned at her touch, the monstrosities cowered beneath her and named her the Demon risen from hell to smite them.

My heart skips a beat and my mouth drops open.

Demon.

The Demon.

There's only one person I know who's been called that by her enemies. The lamia had exclaimed about the Demon when they came across a pendant that burned them when they touched it.

My mind reels as the puzzle pieces fall into place.

Terra, the majestic who brought down a mountain with her power, who's magic burned monsters corrupted with foul magic, who was tricked by Draco into being poisoned with the werewolf disease, who's been in hiding ever since.

I clutch at the dragon pendant hidden under my shirt. Scholar, the terrene who's power almost brought down her own mansion, who's magical pendants burned the lamia, who has always been distrustful of Draco and warned me against him, and who's been actively hiding since the day I met her.

Terra. Scholar.

Scholar *is* Terra.

23

"**I** have to go," I mutter and push the manga into Genna's hands before turning about and rushing out of the apartment.

Could it be? Has there been another majestic under my nose this whole time? Scholar had known so much about the past conflict with Echidna, personal details of the battles, and acts of betrayal afterwards. No one else knew what happened to Terra and Eris. According to all the historical records, they vanished. Some speculated that they shed their mantles as majestics and went to live with the other dragons, others thought they died. No one, not one until Scholar, ever thought they were betrayed and went into hiding. Only Scholar knew. How could she possibly have known unless *she* is Terra or Eris. Eris is the Trickster of course and would be more prone to these kinds of tactics but the lamia called her Demon. I know it.

I have difficulty keeping my pace casual as I make my way towards the chutes to get out of here. My shins burn at my long, fast strides even though I try to walk normally so as not to draw suspicion. If Draco suspects I know where Scholar is, then I wouldn't put it past him to have me followed just in case I ever led him to her. I'll need to be careful but I also need answers that I'm not going to get here.

Bernie the guard swaps a hasty greeting with me before I rise up the chute with two other agents heading topside. Could one of them be watching my movements and tailing me? I'll need to be sure. We reach the surface and the agents make their way to an SUV while I maneuver to the trail through the woods that will take me to the Stone Arch Bridge. The spring air has started to grow hot and I begin to sweat beneath my track pants and long-sleeve training shirt. Bugs buzz past my head but fly off once I reach the strong breeze rolling off the Mississippi River that rushes beneath the bridge.

I keep my feelers out for any magic nearby in case there's a Blessed on my tail. Thankfully there's not but I know that doesn't mean I'm clear. I continue down the bridge and into downtown Minneapolis. I halt near a bus stop and use the reflection off the glass siding to check behind me. Over my shoulder and rounding the bend of the bridge I spot a man in nondescript clothes but his pace is too measured and determined for my liking. His attention glides over me and he randomly goes to a railing overlooking the river some twenty feet behind me to stare out at the water. I don't like the look of him, whoever he is. But how to ditch him? And better yet, where do I even go?

My fingers curl around the pendant underneath my shirt and I focus my power on it like I did when those berserkers attacked.

How do I find you, Scholar?

The pendant pulses twice like a heartbeat in response.

Well, what's that supposed to mean?

I wait for it to do something else as a bus pulls up to the stop and a swarm of people get off. The pendant pulses twice again. Okay . . .

The crowd disperses and the ones waiting on the sidewalk file onto the bus. I remain where I am, unsure if I ought to get on or not.

The pendant pulses in my hand two times.

I feel that familiar twinge of magic nearby as a crow cries twice overhead. The shadow of it passes over me as it lands on top of the bus. It shakes out its wings and caws twice more.

The pendant pulses twice in reply.

That pull of magic guides me to the bird. The crow has magic?

The last in line for the bus climb on board and the driver moves to shut the doors. With a sudden start, I make a dash for the bus doors and slip inside before I can be left behind. When the bus pulls away, I see my suspicious man glaring at me through the windows as the bus picks up speed. If he's clever, he'll follow the route of the bus to the next stop. I need to get off and head in a direction he won't expect.

No one makes eye contact as I shrug my way to the back and watch the road behind us through the rear window. The bus slows and stops for an elderly woman to exit. As we sit and wait, I nearly jump when something taps on the window directly beside me. The crow hovers outside the window and pecks again. A young boy sitting a few rows in front of me turns around to watch the odd bird but no one else pays any mind. I quickly unlock the window and slide it open so the bird can hop in and settle on the bench seat.

With it directly beside me, it's clearly not a crow given its size but a raven. Its glossy feathers puff out for a moment and it makes a low squawking sound as if miffed about something before flattening out and staring pointedly at me.

"Uh . . ."

It nudges my hand with its beak. Unsure what I'm doing, I hold my hand out palm up in expectation. It lifts a clawed talon and drops a chunk of change into my hand.

"Bus fare?"

It nods once.

"Where am I supposed to get off?"

The raven leans precariously to one side so it can lift its talons again and holds two aloft.

"In two blocks?"

It nods again and then leaps for the open window, gliding out of sight.

Well, that was different. I look up and the little boy is watching me wide-eyed, his jaw hanging open. I give a tentative smile and wave. He swallows and lowers himself behind the backrest of the seat until only the top of his head is visible. He then immediately tugs on his mother's arm and points at me. The woman snaps her head in my direction.

The bus moves another block as the mother keeps an eye on me and I pull on a cord nearby to signal the driver I want off. I hustle to the front, drop the fare into the receptacle, and dash off the bus onto the sidewalk. Now what?

That tug of magic and the raven's caw guides me along the sidewalk into a busy section of businesses spilling over with people moving to and from coffee shops, hair salons, banks, and law firms. I feel a little out of place in my exercise clothes wandering through a group of well-dressed people probably heading to work. The raven continues to fly overhead in looping circles guiding me ever deeper into the crowds. As I shrug my way through the bodies, I consider just what kind of bird I'm following. There aren't a lot of plain looking animals with magic, especially in this area. This raven must actually be a spirit walker from one of the Native American tribes—a member naturally gifted with the ability to transform into a specific creature. They're rare but not unheard of. Scholar must have friends all over. First the selkies and now a spirit walker.

Do her friends know her secret? The one I am becoming more and more convinced is true?

I'm nearly lost in all the turns the raven leads me along. A few people start to notice the peculiar bird spinning round and round above their heads, slowly moving in a specific direction. Eventually it flies into a parking garage and I follow after, ducking beneath the red and white boom barrier to enter the damp shadows. I blink a few times as my eyes adjust to the light and the raven caws from where it stands on a cement wall to my left. It hops along and I follow until we're deep into the parking garage. Taking a set of stairs to the next level below, the raven flies to a nearby sedan and lands on the hood.

"You want me to steal a car?" I ask and peer inside the empty vehicle.

The raven lets out a throaty, drawn-out caw as if scolding me. I spot a key already in the ignition. This must have been sitting waiting for me. Wow, how thought out was this plan to get me to Scholar? Clearly it wasn't done at the moment I called to Scholar using the pendant. She must have been waiting for me to come find her.

I open the door and the raven flies in to settle into the passenger's seat before I get in and start it up. Before I pull out I take quick stock of the vehicle. It's a normal sedan with no hidden pockets or compartments for weapons like most IMS vehicles. It'll be perfect for blending in when I drive out of here and mingle with traffic.

"So, where are we going?" I ask.

In response, the raven opens the glove compartment and yanks out a small handheld GPS system with directions already input. It leads out of the Twin Cities to basically the middle of nowhere in farm country. The trip out and back will easily take two hours.

"Well, I guess it's a good thing I already ate," I mutter and set the GPS in the center console where I can see it. The raven looks rather peculiar as it nestles into the front passenger seat. "I take it you're going with me all the way?"

The raven gives a single croak and stares straight ahead, its head angled upward to be able to see the windshield. I guess I'll take that as a yes. It'd be nice to know exactly *who* I'm riding with. At least I know it's not a shapeshifter who can steal another person's face. Spirit walkers are bound solely to their particular animal form. Whatever face this raven ever deigns to let me see will be who they really are.

With a sigh, I put the vehicle into drive and wind my way through the busy traffic of Minneapolis following the rather obtuse route on the GPS. It's not direct by any means but I guess that's the point. It also takes me through some of the less surveilled areas to keep away from prying eyes and any of Draco's shadows.

I sort of ramble on nervously to the raven beside me while I drive. "But I mean, Tatsu must have known what he was talking about right? I remember Witty saying before how he likes to write about actual history with his artwork and not fiction. If he put that part in there about Terra being referred to as the Demon, that's got to be true, right? I've never heard of the nickname myself but Tatsu is a wise old dragon. He could know plenty of things most people don't know. You think so?"

The raven just tilts its head with a jerky motion like a normal bird. We've stopped at a red light and in the car beside me a woman gives me a look like I'm nuts. I guess I can't blame her as I talk to the raven in the seat beside me. I keep my eyes forward and ignore the civilian.

I fall silent after that but wonder if the others are worried about me by now. I kind of took off in a rush without saying anything and won't be back until late today. My cell phone is at the apartment so I can't call. I'm probably better off without it, though. Draco could be monitoring it.

The Twin Cities shrink around me and then the tall buildings disappear altogether to be replaced by woods. The road shrinks lane by lane until there's only one lane left going out. I don't turn the radio on as I mull over the same thoughts over and over again for the next hour. It's with great relief and trepidation when the GPS voice announces the final turn onto a long gravel driveway that winds into a thick patch of spruce trees. I ease on the gas and keep my eyes peeled as I go deeper and deeper into the woods until the sounds of cars and lawn mowers fade away. Nothing but nature surrounds me. Where am I?

The gravel road comes to an abrupt end with nothing in sight. Slightly unnerved, I shut off the car. When I exit I hold the door open so the raven can fly out. I expect whoever it is to finally transform so I know who I'm dealing with, but the raven disappears between the spruces and pines. I follow after, keenly aware of how vulnerable and alone I am. You'd think after all the close encounters I've had lately, I would have been a little smarter about this. Bringing a weapon would have been a good start. What if I'm actually walking into a trap? What if Epsilon had set this up and not Scholar, but had made it *look* like it was Scholar? I'm such an idiot.

I pause and listen to my surroundings. The magic of the raven lets me know it's not far ahead and there's another presence here. It's too familiar to mistake it for anything else. Scholar.

I push branches aside and step out into an empty meadow except for a single weeping willow. Its drooping, leafy branches create natural curtains to shield where I can sense Scholar. I stride across the open space and duck through the hanging tendrils to come face to face with my magical mentor, the raven perched on her shoulder.

"Thank you, dear," Scholar says to the raven who promptly flies up to watch our little meeting from a bough above.

She looks the same as ever—stern, sharp-eyed, and hair tied up in her usual bun at the nape of her neck. There's nothing about her appearance to suggest a dragon underneath that disguise, let alone a majestic if my suspicions are correct. But that's the point of a disguise if you've been hiding for centuries, isn't it?

"Phoenix, you look troubled," she says.

"I . . ." Now that I'm here, I'm not sure what to say. Do I just come out and ask it? I struggle with the right words and she waits patiently for me to find them. At last I say, "I'm glad you're okay."

A smile tugs at her thin lips. "As am I. Although, as you have undoubtedly noticed, my precautions against discovery have greatly increased."

"Yeah, I noticed."

"I appreciate your own discretion on the matter." Her smile fades. "I know what Draco did when you refused to even acknowledge my existence. I am truly grateful."

I swallow and try to push the memory of Jefferson's anger out of my mind. "The last time we met—well, before the berserkers—you wanted to tell me something."

She nods. "However, from the state you are in, I believe you may have already discovered it on your own."

So there it is. There's no more hiding it, no more third-person stories, no more keeping to the shadows. Scholar's ready to tell me her grand secret.

"Are you Terra?"

Silence falls in the wake of my question and the air feels heavy. It's as if the earth itself waits in anticipation to hear that a lost majestic has returned at last to save it. The raven overhead sits so still it could have been mistaken for a statue.

Scholar closes her eyes for a moment of vulnerability. "Yes."

My heart thunders in my chest and I take a step closer to truly study her. A majestic class dragon. A hero from legend. A legend long thought lost.

"So it's true," I breathe.

She opens her eyes as green dragon slits. "You know it to be true. You can feel it if you reach deep down. Go ahead."

I tentatively latch onto her power and feel the essence of pure magic pulsing. I reach through that shield of magic until I find a hold of bitter darkness at the core of her energy. Buried beneath all that natural magic is the tell-tale sensation of the same twisted energy that flows through Dasc's veins, through my brother's veins. The werewolf disease.

I hastily draw back with a gasp. She's hidden it well and buried it so deep that I doubt even another magic detector like me would know it's there.

"But your magic, it's—"

"Not nearly as powerful as what you felt in Draco's presence?" she says and raises her eyebrows. "Of course not, dear. I have been decimated by the foul, twisted disease that runs in my veins. My abilities are severely limited by the strength it takes to hold the disease at bay. It consumes it, battles against the poison in my blood until what is left is very little indeed. I have not been able to transform into my true self since that day. I have been forced to wield the crumbs of what I once held easily in my grasp."

I don't know if I'd go *that* far. The strength of her shockwaves is deadly enough. But to think what she could do if the werewolf disease wasn't poisoning her and holding her back . . .

That's when I finally realize what the training and the tests and the experiments with my blood have really been about.

"You want me to cure you," I murmur.

"It is a selfish hope that I have clung to for centuries," she admits. "That one day I would find a soul able to heal mine. I believe you are that person, Phoenix. The answer to the end of my suffering. All these years I have endured and feared what should happen if ever I encountered Dasc again. There is no telling if his command over the disease would be able to influence and corrupt my thoughts in the same manner he controls werewolves."

A majestic needs *my* help. It's unfathomable. Granted, learning Draco poisoned Terra had been unfathomable at the time as well. No wonder she took so many precautions to have a face-to-face meeting with me.

"Who else knows who you really are?" I ask.

"You. Our friend here." She points to the raven in the tree above us. "The selkies suspect, I am sure, although they choose to believe I am an acolyte or herald for Terra, as it were. Draco may suspect but I have hidden myself well. And Eris, wherever she may be now."

"You don't know?"

She smiles. "A person cannot spills secrets if they do not know them. We decided that hiding in isolation from each other would benefit us both. I must say I have missed the company of that dear friend."

Forced to hide because of Draco. The rest of the legendary world knows him as a hero. So few know the truth.

"I work for him," I mutter. "I work for Draco. How can

I possibly become an agent with a clear conscious knowing who's at the top of the ladder?"

"He is not wholly evil as neither am I wholly good. Each of us makes our choices for good or ill, in moments of strength and weakness, acting on whims of emotion or logic. My own personal feelings aside, I am not above admitting Draco has made great strides in ensuring the safety of the magical community. After the war with Echidna, he founded many of the hidden cities to protect our people from the spread of monsters intent on killing them in retribution for Echidna's downfall."

"Places like Underground, you mean." A place I've considered home for as long as I can remember. Draco did that. He gave me and my brother a safe place to call home. He saved us when Dasc had murdered our parents. We would have gone into the foster care system or something equally unpleasant otherwise. No, we were nurtured and cared for in Underground.

"Precisely. Many of the cities are protected by fonts of magic Draco instills there himself. Those wellsprings permeate the surroundings. Surely you have felt it during your time in Underground."

"I have." The way the city feels alive and is saturated with magic. If there is a font there and magic spills from it, then I know exactly where the point of origin in. "The arch in the middle of headquarters. That's the heart of the font."

"And therein lies the portal."

I blink. "The what now?"

"Why do you suppose it is an arch?" she says. "It is a gateway, dear. Do pay attention."

I think back to when I had spotted Draco standing in

the middle of it and lightning flashing around him. Had he just used the portal to go somewhere? "Where does it lead?"

"It is my understanding that the portal may lead to anywhere if given proper direction. But we have gotten sidetracked, dear."

"Right." Draco. Evil. Good. A mix somewhere in between. "So you still think I should be an agent even after what Draco did to you?"

"I think that the function of the IMS is necessary. As long as you realize that, I see no reason why you should not continue your training and become what you have wanted for so long."

I think her words from months before finally make sense. "The difference between arrogance and wisdom."

"Precisely."

She clasps her hands together behind her back. "I confess I had another reason to meet with you. I have conducted my own investigation into the attack in Moose Lake, and the berserkers yielded some interesting knowledge."

Well, I guess I know why the Spartans didn't find the berserkers. Scholar had taken them to be interrogated. I don't know if I can take many more revelations today.

"What did you find out?" I ask. "Were they connected to the other attacks in Europe?"

"In fact, I discovered the opposite."

"What?"

"The berserkers working alongside Genna's former comrade were as in the dark about the recent attacks as we have been. I do not believe werewolves were behind the other attacks at all despite certain eyewitness reports that have claimed otherwise."

"But that's—" Genna had also claimed the attacks didn't make sense if perpetuated by the werewolves under Dasc's thumb. But if there is a war and Dasc has been preparing his army, then the other side could be doing the same and using a clever tactic to dwindle Dasc's numbers before the real fight even starts. "Someone else was pinning it on the werewolves, turning everyone's attention to them—"

"And making them blind to everything else. A tactic that also effectively weakens the strength of the werewolf forces by using the IMS to their advantage without having to do much themselves."

Them. They. We both know who we're actually talking about. "You really think Echidna's back from the grave?"

Her face falls. "From what I have been able to gather from my sources, there is little doubt on the matter."

I gulp. "Well, the IMS ought to attack now before she can gain momentum. And we should fix the werewolf situation while we're at it."

"I'm afraid that both scenarios are not possible. For one, I have no information to indicate where Echidna might be. Secondly, I have no proof that some force of monsters is attempting to use the werewolves as patsies. I have nothing to disprove that werewolves were at the attacks."

"But—"

"This is a fight we cannot win at this point in time. We are not ready. You are not ready."

"Will I ever be ready?" I say louder than I mean to in my anger and throw up my hands. "Everyone keeps telling me that it's going to take time, I need to be patient, my blood needs to mature. The longer I wait, the longer the world suffers!"

A pulse ripples from Scholar and my breath catches as it passes through me, its essence tangible and solid.

"Do not forget how long I have waited for the opportune moment," she growls. "Do not suggest that your suffering for lack of patience compares to what I have endured for centuries."

That shuts me up fast. My face burns and I avert my gaze, unable to meet her eyes any longer. Of course she would understand being patient better than anyone. She's had to wait this long for a chance of being cured of the werewolf disease. I can't even begin to imagine what she's been through.

"So what happens now?" I ask quietly.

"Now you must pass the trials and become an agent so you may receive the training and experience you will need to survive the days to come."

I've been training and looking forward anxiously to the trials for months. Now that they're almost here, the excitement has drained out of me to be replaced by trepidation.

"You said it would take some trickery for me to get past the blood test," I say.

Her smile returns with a hint of mischief. "Indeed."

24

I feel like a monster when I inject the serum into Hawk. My hand trembles as I grip the auto-injector and hit it to my brother's thigh to inject the savior for so many but poison and suffering to him. He couldn't bring himself to do it so I had to be the one to start his pain. He sucks in a sharp breath and then quickly excuses himself to the bathroom in the apartment.

The difference is plain to me. He holds himself rigid and says little to the people around us as we, along with all of the other junior agents in our uniforms, make our way to the med ward for the first bout of testing. On an ordinary day, he would be cracking jokes and making comfortable small talk with the people waiting impatiently in line. Today Hawk is not my brother. He fidgets and curls his hands repeatedly into fists and then relaxes his fingers, curls then relaxes, curls then relaxes, like some sort of meditation to keep himself in check and not let the pain show.

It's difficult to keep myself restrained and focus on what I'm supposed to be doing. I don't dare interrupt the effects of the serum in case that somehow screws up his own test. He needs to show up with the proper dose in his system, and I can't divert my attention any more than it already is. I'll need to pass my own stage of testing if I want to avoid Draco's attentions.

Charlie enters ahead of us and takes a seat on one of the beds to have his blood drawn. I wish I could feel as carefree as he looks. This is nothing for him. They'll test his blood and discover he is exactly what he appears to be—a boy who can teleport through space and time. Simple really. If anything about this can be simple.

I watch as a certified non-magical nurse preps a blood collection kit and ties off his arm above the elbow. I note that all of the nurses and physicians taking blood samples are regular humans. They don't want any magical assistants accidentally contaminating the samples. There are at least seven of them drawing blood, escorting junior agents in and others out, and keeping the lines moving. There's got to be a hundred people here hoping to pass the trials. I nudge Hawk with my shoulder and hold my hand out to the side. It takes him a moment to realize what I'm doing but then he gives me a low-five that manages to settle my jitters. We're going to be okay. I know we will.

Hawk goes in after Charlie is escorted out to enter the next section of testing. I try to keep my eyes on my brother as one of the nurses comes for me next. Hawk nods to let me know he's going to be fine and I focus on the task

Scholar set me to. As the nurse ties the band around my arm and swabs the inside of my elbow, I close my eyes and focus on the currents of magic running through my own veins. This time I'm not trying to stop some monster from attacking. I'm trying to manipulate my own magic.

"Are you okay?" the nurse asks.

I don't even bother opening my eyes but nod. "I'm great. Go ahead."

She takes two vials worth of my blood. As she starts to package them up, I latch onto the energy that has now separated from me. I've been practicing on my own in the last couple of days but this is it. This is my true test. I tug at that magic, twist it by feel and thought alone. Scholar told me manipulating my own magic would be easier than anything else I've done, and she's right. I take part of the magical essence and draw it out of the vials and back to me until all that remains in the samples is what makes me strong. When they go to test that blood, they will know it is mine and strength is all they will find.

"Are you sure you're okay?"

I open my eyes and smile, taking measured breaths. "Yes. Everything's fine. Thank you."

She finishes capping my samples, seals them into a sturdy little container, and labels it with my name and ID number. She escorts me out and another junior agent is led in to take my place.

I did it. I can feel it. A spring enters my step.

I join a throng of other recruits heading towards the stadium. A sparse crowd has gathered to watch our progress for what little of it is open for observation by the public. The IMS will close off certain portions but at the beginning it's sort of a spectacle. I remember watching the beginning of the trials each year, which is the unofficial start to the midsummer celebrations leading to the aetherball tournament. It's finally my turn on the opposite side of the crowd and I feel a rush of pride despite Draco and everything else.

Two men wait at the entrance to the stadium and hold up each junior agent before allowing them in. One is a mousy little man holding a clipboard and checking a list. He might not look so small if not for the goliath standing next to him. My mouth drops open as I realize who the other man is.

He stands a good foot over his assistant and probably has enough muscle power in his huge biceps to probably take on monsters single-handedly. I can see resemblances in his long nose and chiseled facial features to Director Knox. They also have the same bearing of a man who has power and knows how and when to wield it. Although the director keeps his head shaved, this man has a short covering of hair and a respectable beard speckled with gray. A legend, a Spartan commander, and Director Knox's brother—Spartan Samson Knox.

Hawk jogs up behind me with a look of awe and manages to not look so pained if only for a moment. He nudges me in the ribs with his elbow. "Do you see him?"

"Of course I see him. How can someone *not* see him?"

"It's him!" he says excitedly under his breath. Spartan Knox has been one of Hawk's heroes for years. Not only is Spartan Knox an incredible man in his own right, he also— as it happens—is a werewolf. Hawk has looked up to him as a man who overcame the prejudices of being a werewolf and made something of himself. As the story goes, Spartan Knox was a former Navy SEAL who was infected overseas while protecting a contingent of refugees. He was nick-named the Frost Wolf since his other half is a pure white arctic wolf. He's so cool that I get excited too.

We pause together in front of the clipboard man.

"Names?" he drones.

"Phoenix Mason," I say and my brother says his name at the same time so it all comes out in a jumble. We try it again but end up doing the same thing in our excitement to meet Spartan Knox. *Pixies*, now we look like idiots.

When we try again, the Spartan holds up a hand to silence us. "Phoenix and Hawk Mason. I've heard of you."

"You have?" we say in unison.

He smiles. "Some angry stories from my brother as well as more impressive work lately." My face burns. He stretches out a hand and we each shake it in turn. "It's a pleasure. I'll be one of your judges and supervisors during the trials. I make it a point to meet each of our junior agents before the trials begin to get a feel for who is appropriate for certain future careers."

Well, we probably seem fit for target practice after our first impression as bumbling morons.

"I look forward to your performances," he says and crosses his arms over his chest again to stand like some Greek god from the old myths.

The clipboard man sighs and points to the stadium entrance with his pen. "Phoenix Mason, head to the right and join the other Blessed for magic performance testing. Hawk Mason, join the junior agents on the left."

We share an apprehensive look, give Spartan Knox

awkward good-byes, and walk down the tunnel entrance. At the end we split left and right to join the groups already formed at the bottom of the stands. I guess they don't need to test Hawk since werewolf abilities are already well known. I don't like the distinct separation though. Charlie waves to get my attention and pats the seat beside him. We sit together as the rest of the junior agents filter in.

The class ends up getting split in half—those granted magic from a dragon and those not—or a werewolf. There aren't a lot of werewolves in this class and I can see the others glancing in Hawk's direction trying to figure out what he is as if he might have a helpful sign on his forehead.

On the far side of the track we have a burgeoning audience and I swallow back my stage fright. Director Knox is there along with Draco, numerous other agents I recognize from around Underground, and fauns and centaurs from the council. There are other bystanders as well that have wriggled their way in. They aren't technically supposed to be here but no one forces them out either. This is going to be a show, for sure.

In the center of the track the fire sprite podiums have been replaced by a multitude of dummies, sparring circles, and slabs of stone standing in a circle like some miniature Stonehenge. The designated combat arena is guarded by no less than fifteen agents walking the track and standing by the sparring rings.

When the last stragglers arrive and split into their appropriate groups, Spartan Knox comes in followed by his assistant and silence falls across the stadium. He walks onto the track and stands equidistant between our two factions with his arms clasped behind his back. The intent stare he levels at us reminds me eerily of the ones his brother, the director, has cast in my direction on more than one occasion.

"Welcome to the start of the trials," he thunders to be heard by all. "From this moment on, everything you do or do not do will be a test. You will work alone and you will work in teams. Your strengths and your weaknesses will be revealed. This is the time when we weed out those of you who have the strength to face a hydra head on, who has the brains to attack from the flank instead, and who will let fear overwhelm them and get their teammates killed."

The junior agents glance around as if hoping to discover for themselves the weak link, or avoiding gazes because maybe they think *they* are the weak link.

"The life of an IMS agent is not glamorous. Your heroic deeds will be hidden from most of the world. Your acts of bravery and personal sacrifices will go unnoticed by the general public. But they are necessary. A hard and unfortunate truth many of you will quickly learn or have learned already during your time shadowing field agents."

I certainly know what he's talking about, but I'm ready to prove myself because this job is necessary despite the dark secrets I've learned lately about some of its leadership. Even if Draco has done horrible things in his past, the core of the agency isn't him—it's the people around me ready to do the hard work, the unthanked labor, and make the greatest of sacrifices. There are a lot of monsters out there and not enough of us.

"You've all had your blood collected to be analyzed for safety purposes," he continues. Oh, really? Is that what we were tested for? Interesting. "Now we will assess the abilities of each Blessed so we know how to incorporate everyone safely in the team exercises. If we are aware of each other's abilities, we can learn how use those strengths to our advantage. You will be called one at a time to perform what abilities you have out in the rings." He gestures to the center of the track field. "This is not a scored test but is used rather for assessment. Don't be afraid to use the height of your power."

He gestures to the clipboard man who takes over and calls the first name. A pretty girl with enough curves to strike out a batter strides forward when he calls up Amanda Fry. She stands in the sparring ring nearest our group and settles into a stance like a boxer about to fight even though she stands ten feet away from the closest training dummy. Her hands suddenly glow fiercely bright and she does a one-two punch at the dummy. Balls of fire fly off her hands and strike the dummy like missiles. Flames engulf the thing. She walks towards it slowly as she raises her hands and the flames become a rising inferno. The heat washes over me even at my distance.

My heart skips a beat as I'm reminded of the Blessed werewolf boy that destroyed the Moose Lake Field Office and nearly killed Jefferson. I clench my hands into fists in my lap and notice the sideways look Charlie gives me.

Murmurs and gasps meet her performance and when she snaps her hands out to either side like she's pulling a string taut, the flames poof out of existence leaving nothing but charred, crumbling remains behind.

I clap along with the rest as she gives an overly dramatic

bow. In the distance where a few braziers remain lit on the upper tier of the stands, flames shoot up like fireworks and the screams of hissing flames applaud her abilities. Well, clearly she's won over the fire sprites.

She moves off the field and the next takes her place. Each Blessed shows off their abilities in a wild show of destruction. Some clearly aren't as powerful as others but they can each do something beyond the ordinary. One boy walks up and stands before Spartan Knox before proclaiming that the Spartan previously had three broken ribs on his left side. There's a moment of confusion as we attempt to figure out if he can read thoughts or something before he announces he has x-ray vision. A shifting occurs through the crowd as everyone visibly adjusts to try to protect themselves from his wandering stare, turning sideways in their seats or crossing their arms over their chest. I fight the urge to dull his ability when his gaze sweeps over me. Is that creepy vision of his on all the time or only when he wills it?

When Charlie's name is called, he doesn't walk up like everyone else. Of course not. One second he's sitting beside me, the next he's beside Spartan Knox with his hands in his pockets as if he doesn't have a care in the world. The Spartan startles only for a moment before turning a sharp eye on him. Charlie vanishes but I caught his eyes lifting upward so I know to turn around and spot him at the very top of the stands where the fire sprites sprinkle him with sparks. The junior agents gasp as he ports around the stadium—to the top of the stone pillars, to behind the judges, and back to the Spartan's side—and interject with cries of "there he is!" as someone discovers where he went next. At last he gives a short, respectful salute to Spartan Knox before porting back to his seat beside me. I feel the tiniest movement of wind as he displaces the air around him.

I discreetly hold out my fist towards him and he gives me a fist bump while trying to hide a smile. I glance to the judges and find Draco staring intently at Charlie, one hand massaging his chin in thought.

One girl walks out, shrugs, and slaps her hands to her sides. Everyone waits in anticipation for her to disappear or do something miraculous but she stands there looking irritated before finally saying, "I repel bugs. Sorry, no bugs to demonstrate." Then walks back to her seat. I bit my lip to keep from laughing, more at the girl's reaction than her actual ability. The judges shake their heads and make notes on their clipboards or whisper to each other.

"Phoenix Mason," the assistant calls.

I swallow and walk stiffly to the ring of stone pillars in the very center. This is it. This is my time to shine—but, you know, not shine *too* much. I can't very well make a display of controlling everyone else's powers around me even if I could. Even if right now I want to. Something coiling inside me wants me to break loose, wreak havoc, siphon off a piece of that magic radiating from Draco just to spite him.

But I can't. All I can do is show them what they need to see. A girl possessing immense physical strength.

I plant my feet and concentrate the surge of my power through my arm, synchronized with the momentum of my own body as I punch forward into the closest stone pillar. The stone shatters with an almighty crack and the pillar explodes into a thousand little pieces as if a bomb had gone off. There's not a clean fist hole through it or a dent—no, I projected my strength the way I've been practicing, the way I told Draco I could—so that the energy dispersed through the stone itself and obliterated it. Dust billows and little bits of rock plink on my head as they rain down. I draw back and inspect my knuckles. They're abraded and sting but not so much as they used to. Instead of letting that be the last of it, I quickly roll to the next pillar, rise, and swing with my momentum to destroy another one of the pillars. I move in quick succession, channeling that build of power inside me for each punch and narrowing it into an explosive force at the singular point of contact between my fist and the stone.

The debris and dust settles as I stand amidst the wreckage of the stone pillars that are now nothing but piles of pebbles. Silence falls. Should I bow like some of the others have done? Walk away without a look back like those deadly heroes in the movies? Do I say a clever one-liner even though none come to mind?

Someone starts clapping loudly and lets out a big whoop. Hawk stands up from his seat with a huge grin and nudges the person next to him, saying proudly for everyone to hear, "That's my sister."

Equally embarrassed and happy, I beam at my brother and walk confidently to my chair.

Charlie stares at me for a moment before leaning in to whisper rather angrily, "And you tried to punch me in the face that one time?"

I stifle a snort and pat him lightly on the back. He flinches as if I'm going to smack his internal organs clear out of his chest. The others nearby look terrified that I could do that very thing to them so they give me nervous smiles and thumbs up even though they haven't bothered to even acknowledge my presence until now.

When I look up, I find Draco's narrowed eyes on me.

My destructive display is probably the most explosive but not nearly the coolest by the end of the assessment. A girl manages to make clones of herself that spread around the arena, shake everyone's hands simultaneously, then poof like clouds of smoke into thin air. Then a stick thin boy lifts the destruction of the pillars with nothing but the power of his mind. He moves his hands and directs the pebbles until they form a moving cloud of stone shaped as Draco in his dragon form. The stone dragon flaps his wings twice then the pebbles fall lifeless to the ground with a deafening crash. The boy walks back to his chair and winks at me with a smug smile as if in challenge.

What a suck up.

The last of the Blessed finishes her performance by zooming around through the air with the ability of flight. After she takes her seat, the judges give a polite smattering of applause and Spartan Knox takes over again.

"You have a short amount of time to talk amongst yourselves while the judges and I decide if there are any appropriate safety measures we need to take. Feel free to move about but remain in the stadium."

He and his clipboard assistant meet with the judges on the other side of the stands while the regular junior agents, werewolves, and Blessed mingle to eagerly chat about each of the powers displayed. A few more demonstrations are requested of the pyrokinetic girl and myself. While Amanda

Fry is more than happy to set more dummies alight to the excited applause of her fire happy friends, I'm distracted by Hawk standing off by himself and Charlie being mobbed by people wanting to be teleported with him. In fact, a few girls are cozying up to him despite the flat stare he's giving them. I'm sure nobody is listening when he tells them it'll hurt like mad if he tries to port them.

I walk over to my brother first as he hangs back from the crowd. He tries to smile but doesn't put too much effort into it.

"You okay?" I ask.

"Yeah, I'm fine," he says in a tone that makes him seem anything but fine. "Word got around. Everyone knows what I am."

The elation in my chest from earlier sinks like a rock in my gut. "Hawk, I'm sorry."

He shrugs. "I'm fine. I think he needs some backup though." He nods in Charlie's direction who is giving everyone around him the look of death.

"You sure you're okay?" I ask.

"Go help Charlie before he ports someone off the top of the stadium."

He pretends to be intensely interested with a speck of dust on the front of his junior agent uniform so I take that as the signal he's done talking. I turn about and march through the crowd closed in around Charlie. When the others see it's me pushing them aside with my face set in stone, they quickly back away to give me space. I reach Charlie right as one of the girls asks him, "Could you teleport me somewhere romantic?"

Seriously?

"Sure, how about the moon?" he says dryly. "Where you can suffocate and I don't have to hear you ask me anymore."

While the girl looks taken aback, the others laugh and seem to think he's making jokes. As I know from personal experience, Charlie is trying to make them back off. Or maybe they're trolling him on purpose. Before he can follow through on any of his violent comebacks, I hop to his side and thread my arm through his.

"Hey, this one's claimed," I announce. "Back off you vultures."

"Claimed?" The closest girl rolls her eyes. "What, you two are a thing?"

"Oh, I'm not so modest. We're dating and passionately in love." I smile sweetly at Charlie who's face turns a bright shade of red and I rest my head on his shoulder. "And remember, I can rip your arms out of your sockets if you keep bugging him."

They appraise me doubtfully but stop crowding Charlie except for the fire girl. She winks at him regardless and looks me up and down as if not impressed.

I glare at her and grab Charlie by the collar. "Come on. Let's go make out."

He startles but I nod my head in the direction of Hawk who's still standing off by himself near the stands. He wraps his hand around mine and we teleport next to my brother. Keenly aware of the eyes on us, I fake some terrible pain and double over before straightening.

Confusion is written all over Charlie's face. "I thought it didn't—"

"I'd rather not have people know about that just yet," I

say and avoid looking in Draco's direction entirely. "Keep it a secret for me?"

"Why?"

"Just—please?"

He shakes his head in exasperation. "Fine, whatever. It'll probably come in handy during the team trials though."

"Well, I'll deal with it later."

"Fine."

"Fine."

Hawk glances between us and rolls his eyes.

"I guess I should say thanks," Charlie says. "For saving me back there."

I cross my arms over my chest and scowl at him, disappointed. "You're not embarrassed?"

"No. Why?"

"That's sort of why I did what I did. I thought I'd get you back for embarrassing me when you pulled the same thing at my high school." I narrow my eyes. "Are you sure you aren't embarrassed? Not even a little?"

He laughs under his breath and ignores me as Spartan Knox approaches our little group. Despite Charlie being tall himself, he's nearly dwarfed next to the Spartan.

"Junior Agent Mason," he says. He's looking at me so I know I'm the Mason he's referring to. "If we could have a word for a moment."

Well, that doesn't sound good. The boys nudge me on when I hesitate to follow Spartan Knox to the group of judges talking quietly amongst themselves. I cross the field through the debris left behind from the showing of the Blessed and come to a halt a good five feet away from the judges. Draco has his back to me but slowly turns around to face me like a predator stalking prey. I do my best not to gulp or give any indication that he intimidates me.

"Mason," Director Knox says. With him standing next to his brother, the family resemblance is plain. "There have been a number of Blessed to have passed through the trials possessing varying degrees of strength like you demonstrated. However, some of them were not able to control their strength in normal engagements. While I believe you have shown on numerous occasions that you are more than capable of reining in your strength, the rest of the judges would like a simple demonstration as a guarantee for safety purposes."

I blink and struggle against the urge to make a face. Really? Do they think I've gone through life accidentally pulling every door off its hinges, smashing glass when opening windows, putting holes through floors when I walk around? This is ridiculous. I want to tell them they're a bunch of idiots but instead go with, "Sure. What do you need me to do?"

"Just a moment." He gestures to someone over his shoulder and I see the clipboard assistant hurrying into the stadium bearing a small crate in his hands. When he comes to a stop before me, I realize it's a crate of eggs.

"Do you want me to juggle?" I quip but no one laughs. I clear my throat.

"Merely crack one open without smashing the whole thing to bits."

"That's it?"

He nods so I pick up one of the eggs, knock it lightly on a knuckle until a crack forms and then split it open, holding it over the crate to capture the yoke. The other judges murmur to each other.

"Satisfied?"

The director nods again. "You'd be surprised how many times we've seen others make an egg explode. You have remarkable control."

Curiosity hits me and I want to ask more about these others that have possessed such amazing strength before me. Did none of them have the control I do? It seems so simple to me and absolutely normal. My strength doesn't arise unless I make it, until I need it, or in a fit of raging emotion. Then again, I doubt any of those other people could manipulate magical energy the way I can. Maybe that has something to do with it.

"So, what now, sir?" I ask.

"The trials can continue. All the Blessed will be cautioned about using their powers sparingly and carefully while in the team portion. I would have you keep that in mind as well." He looks down his nose at me as if I'd do it on purpose. I don't take it personally. I probably would. "But for the moment we'll head into our psychological testing. Spartan Knox, if you would."

The Spartan nods to me and I tag along behind him to rejoin the others. Everyone's mashed up into one large group no longer separated by magic and no magic. There's a palpable energy amongst the junior agents. We're ready for the trials to truly begin.

"While physical challenges are a major component of our work," Spartan Knox says, "mental competency is even more important. If you shy or break down in the face of monsters, how are you going to protect someone let alone yourself? For your first trial, you'll be facing your own fears and guilt to see if you can conquer them. Follow me. You're going to be introduced to the penitent cells."

A shock of dread goes through me and I spit out, "What does introduced mean?" I add as an afterthought, "Sir."

"It means you're each going to sit in one and then we'll see what we make of you."

25

The other junior agents are fidgety and nervous as we walk along the pristine white halls of the penitent cells. They've all heard of the penitent cells but few have actually seen them. Except for me. I remember the cries and shouts of agony from the monsters locked away in the lowest level. What will I endure when I sit in a cell of my own? What victims will cry out to me and let me feel the pain I've inflicted? My shoulders slouch and my heart flutters.

As we walk we pass a few centaur sentries and gargoyles. The centaurs nod in my direction and I acknowledge them in kind. The gargoyles just stare. The other junior agents quickly pick up on the interaction between the guards and me. Charlie frowns but doesn't comment. On my other side Hawk hardly seems to notice anything around him and keeps his eyes glued to the floor, his hands curled into fists.

We come to a stop outside a row of white doors with a big seven painted in blue on the wall. The rest of the judges are already here and waiting as well as some faun nurses I recognize from my various stays in the medical ward.

Spartan Knox clasps his hands behind his back and faces us. "If we are to use these cells as a form of punishment, it is important that we understand what the punishment entails. The penitent cells are infused with the magic of the fauns." He gestures to the nurses behind him who bob their heads. "It will force you to live the emotions of those you have wronged, have harmed, have killed." His eyes pause on me for a beat. "There is a saying that to understand someone else's life, you must walk a mile in their shoes. These cells are meant to give enlightenment and make monsters face the true consequences of their actions."

He moves to the closest door, puts a palm to a scanner beside it, and the barrier on the door vanishes to allow access. He pushes it open but remains in the entrance.

"You will each spend five minutes in the cells to get a taste of the punishment that as agents you will subject others to."

Spartan Knox gestures to his clipboard assistant who starts to call names. One by one, subdued junior agents take reluctant steps to their assigned cells. When Charlie is called, he draws up his shoulders and marches into the cell to face his fears without hesitation.

"Well, this ought to be fun," I hear him say as he walks in and the Spartan shuts the door behind him.

The rest of us wait in silence with nothing but the rhythmic beat of the guards marching through the halls to keep us company. Hawk's chest heaves as he breathes fast and his eyes dart around like a wild animal trapped in a corner. I lay a hand on his arm and he twitches.

"Hawk?" I whisper.

He doesn't say anything and shakes his head. The next five minutes pass painfully slow and when the doors are finally opened to let the junior agents out, they all look shaken, some more than others. Charlie braces both hands against the wall when he exits and hangs his head taking deep breaths. His shoulders quake. I want to go comfort him somehow and find out what has shaken him up so badly. However, he and the others fresh from the cells are herded over to the faun nurses who escort them out.

The next batch of unlucky souls are chosen. When Hawk's name is called, he shudders but marches to his cell. Spartan Knox calls my name next and I take a deep breath before moving forward. Draco moves at the same time to meet me at the door. We stand tersely for a moment staring each other down before I step into the cell and turn around to watch Draco be the one to shut the door. His dragon-slit eyes are the last thing I see before he locks me inside.

My heart thunders in my chest and my breath mists before me as if it has gotten suddenly cold. Darkness swallows the room and adrenaline courses through my veins as I swivel on my feet looking for an attacker. Equal parts fear, anger, and bloodlust surge through me. But these feelings are not mine. Despite the magic permeating the room like a poisonous gas, I know whose emotions they are. A vampire from the warehouse in La Crosse, Wisconsin. Moments later, dread and a mounting panic take hold as horrible pain stabs through my chest. I grasp at my sternum and the imaginary blade through my heart. Then I can see it, feel the slip of its cold metal through my skin and the blood pouring out of my chest. That wretched girl did this. That red-haired devil!

The blade and blood and pain vanish and I bend over breathing hard, bracing my hands on my knees as I suck down air, the phantom blade impossible to dispel from my mind. I truly felt that vampire's fear and pain as if it were my own until his memories and my conscious couldn't be separated. That wretched girl, the red-haired devil, was *me*. I put an end to that monster's life and in doing so, some part of me became the monster too.

The vampire's death isn't the only horror I'm forced to endure. More vampires follow it, the one I beheaded with a shovel, the countless others ended by my retractable blade. Then I feel Zeta and the hollow burn that filled her body when my power took over hers before Scholar ended her life. Next a handful of burning bullets penetrate my chest and I'm filled with surprise and horror from Dasc. Other small offenses I've committed come to haunt me like disturbed ghosts—Nessa when I punched her in the face, people I roughed up during school, and others I didn't even know I had wronged. The ones that felt slighted. The ones that felt trust was broken. Jefferson's pain from my betrayal through his eyes. Ashley's anger and grief caused by my lies and acts to bury the truth. They flood through me like a storm and it feels like hours, days even, pass instead of five minutes.

Then I feel it. The simmering kettle of anger built upon a life of rejection and unwarranted prejudice. The growing feeling of incompetence and worthlessness. The frustration. The hurt from trust being broken and choices being made for him.

Hawk.

I drop to my knees and forcefully try to push the thoughts and emotions away but I can hardly separate myself from my brother's pain—pain that I caused. All the times I held on too tightly, made decisions for the both of us, or acted without his knowledge or consent, that hissing kettle of rage or frustration grew as he felt his own freedom to act dwindling.

I did that? All this time and he's said nothing. Until recently, he's never made mention that what I do to keep him safe has felt like smothering him with a pillow.

I start to cry without realizing it. The deaths and the broken bones and shattered trust I can overcome but this . . . this destroys every part of who I thought I am and what I am to my brother.

Something inside me breaks. The power in my core is a churning storm that burns itself out until it's nothing but vapors on a high wind. I feel empty and cold and heartbroken.

When the door finally opens, I don't stand.

"Mason?"

I turn my blurry gaze to Spartan Knox. He extends a hand and waits for me to rise to take it. I stare at it for a long moment as I kneel there, defeated.

Not sure how I manage it, I get to my feet and take his hand. He pulls me out of the wretched cell and the dark swirl of emotion vanishes but leaves scars behind. I nod dully without any resistance as one of the faun nurses guides me away from the unlucky junior agents still waiting their turn. She whispers encouraging things to me that go in one ear and out the other without leaving any sort of impression.

My brother must hate me. It's the only thing I can think about.

The faun leads me out of the penitent cells and to the stadium where I join the other shell-shocked junior agents that have already experienced the nightmare of the penitent cells. Some of them are talking to each other trying to find comfort while others are spread out not wanting any sort of contact at all. I spot Charlie by himself at the very top of the stands brooding. I decide, even though I'm curious about what he experienced, that I'd rather not interfere with his clearly private thoughts. I might screw that up anyhow considering how well I've done with Hawk.

I search for my brother but he hasn't come in yet. I wait near the tunnel entrance on the bottom row of seats with my knees tucked up to my chest and my chin hidden in the collar of my uniform. There are no words to describe how awful I feel.

The clatter of hooves and heavy, plodding footsteps alert me to another arrival. I stand to find Hawk's face blotchy and his shoulders drawn in tight as if to protect himself from further harm. He comes to an abrupt halt when he sees me. The faun beside him murmurs something I don't catch before she goes back to escort the next round of people put through the wringer.

"Hawk," I croak and then find I'm unable to say anything else.

His whole body sags as if gravity itself intensifies. "I need some time. Alone."

My lower lip trembles and I turn away before I start to cry again. *Pixies*, I need to pull it together, but I don't know what to do. I don't know how to even start making this better without inadvertently making it worse. First Jefferson, now this. Maybe I should take up Charlie's shtick and push people away before I can hurt them or they can hurt me.

I remain by myself and study my feet while the remaining junior agents file in. I hope for some sort of break but no, they keep right along with the trials. After Spartan Knox informs us there will be counselors available to talk at the end of the day if we need it, he sets us to doing push-ups, jumping jacks, sprints around the track, and various other mind-numbing exercises. I don't think we're necessarily being critiqued at this point except to see who can keep going after hardship and who can't. There are a few junior agents that look like they want to curl up and die in a corner somewhere. I can't say I wouldn't join them if they did.

But I fight because that's all I know how to do, apparently. I fight through the pain of my brother most likely wanting nothing to do with me and power through the exercises. It gives me something else to focus on for a while at any rate.

We break for a very quiet lunch before getting right back to it. We pace our fastest mile on the track, do pull-ups, complete a circuit of lunges and burpees, and finish off the day with a race.

Charlie, Hawk, and I walk to our shared apartment in silence, that dour cloud hanging over us as we change out of our uniforms into pajamas. We take up various positions spaced out from each other to brood. Our three other roommates stop in to change but vanish almost immediately after. Genna swings by to see how things have been going but once she senses the atmosphere, she excuses herself as well. I can't say I blame her.

None of us says a word but eventually I feel compelled to seek out some sort of comfort, even if it's merely distracting myself with someone else's problems. I wander over to find Charlie out on the balcony. He sits on top of the railing with his back and head resting against the wall of the apartment. The air circulation is on full blast and ruffles his hair as if a fair wind had crept into Underground. I pause on the landing and watch him, unsure what to do or say next.

"Are you just going to gawk or do you want something?" he says dully.

A little fire returns to my veins. "Sorry, I can't help myself. You're just really, really ridiculously good-looking."

He blinks. I stare. Neither one of us laughs.

"I can't tell if you're mocking me or telling the truth," he says.

Deigning not to answer, I walk forward and scoot his feet out of my way so I can hop up on the small bit of railing beside him.

"How are you holding up?" I ask and dangle my feet.

"How are *you*?"

"Ah, misdirection. I guess you don't want to talk about it."

He shrugs and stares off towards the glow of the fire sprites at the top of the stadium in the distance. "You didn't answer the question either."

"Okay, fine." I chew on my lower lip for a moment and consider how I am. "I feel . . . exposed."

"You *are* sitting up on a railing."

I nudge his leg with my elbow. "You know that's not what I mean." Unable to say the words face to face, I study my toes. "The penitent cells cut me open and revealed all the horrible things inside, some I didn't even know existed. I can't hide from what I've done."

When I dare to meet his eyes, his gaze clashes with mine.

"What have you done, Phoenix?" he asks quietly. "What could possibly be so horrible?"

I cock my head. It sounds like he's bitter about something that was brought up in those cells. Clearly he thinks my bad deeds can't be enough to match his from the tone of his voice.

"I've been hurting my brother for years and never realized it. I had only been trying to help him," I say. "I've killed my share of vampires and helped take down a lamia. I nearly killed Dasc."

"That doesn't sound so bad at all."

I narrow my eyes. "It certainly felt horrible reliving their deaths and pain."

"That's not what I mean." He leans forward to rest his forearm across his upraised knee. "Those things you listed off? They sound justified. You tried to help your brother. You knocked off some monsters."

That's not all of it but I can't tell him the rest—I can't tell him how I betrayed my friend Ashley and hid the secret of her dog's demise from her. I can't explain that I let Jason be carted away where the bad werewolves go even when I've lied to keep my brother hidden.

"You aren't a monster yourself," he continues. His tone is the steadfast rock I need, the one I clung to in the storm before when he helped me deal with my gun issue. A voice of reason when perhaps I don't want to hear it. "I've seen the things you've done. You do them out of necessity. It's not like you go looking to murder anybody. Do you?"

I think about it for a moment, then say in a small voice, "No."

"Good, because otherwise you'd be a psychopath." That actually manages to solicit a laugh, if somewhat subdued. He smirks. "I mean, we all have to be crazy on some level to do this job but we aren't *crazy* crazy."

"Well, *I'm* not crazy crazy. I can't speak on your behalf, however."

He holds a hand over his heart as if greatly offended. "Hey, I am not the one that prefers movies to books."

"I never said that!"

"Actions speak louder than words. How many books have you read as opposed to movies you've watched?"

I wave a hand dismissively at him and rock back and forth on the railing. "Am I supposed to have read as many as you? Because I'm pretty sure that's impossible. You inhale books."

"Best kind of air there is."

We smile at each other, at the light teasing each of us is able to manage despite everything that's happened today.

I nudge his leg with mine. "Hey, I'm glad you're not such a stick in the mud anymore."

"Oh, gee, thanks." He rolls his eyes and looks sour but I can see past his facade. He's good at his poker face but I know underneath that cold sass is someone who wants a loyal friend. I'll be more than happy to be that for him. I certainly owe him for the help he's given me.

"So, what about you?" I ask.

"What about me?"

"What did you experience in the penitent cell?"

His veil of brooding returns and he rests his head against the wall once more. A deepening silence surrounds us while we linger in the dark as the rest of Underground falls asleep.

"You don't have to tell me," I say quietly. "I get that it's personal. I just want you to know that if you want to talk, I'm here. I'll listen. If you need a friend, I'm around."

He raises a solitary eyebrow. "Even if I'm a stick in the mud?"

"*Used to be* a stick in the mud. You've gotten better." After remembering his interactions with the other junior agents, I add, "With me, anyway."

"Well, you did make it to the mystical rainbow island of friendship."

I choke on a laugh then realize I can't stop laughing and am forced to cover my mouth with both hands. He looks astonished and raises his hands up to shoulder-height.

"What?" he demands. "That's what you and your brother said."

"But hearing it come out of your mouth—I can't even—" I keep laughing until my stomach hurts while he crosses his arms over his chest and shakes his head despite an exhausted smile lingering on his face.

When the fit finally subsides, he claps me heartily on the back and says, "Remember to breathe."

I wipe the tears from the corners of my eyes. "Wow, I really needed that."

"Yeah, I could tell. Glad to have been of service."

The creeping darkness has been banished at least for the moment. We sit in comfortable silence a little longer before I hear Hawk pad through the apartment. He pauses in the opening to the balcony.

"What was all that laughing about?" he asks as he wrings his hands. He sounds timid which is strange for him. He's never the timid one.

I look at my brother with new eyes to see the hurt and damage I've caused underneath that confident attitude of his. He felt I had been stripping away his freedom of choice. The pain that causes me is worse than what I felt from those monsters.

"Charlie said something funny," I say.

The awkward tension rises as Charlie clears his throat and looks around for an exit.

"Can I talk to you?" Hawk asks.

"Yeah. Sure."

Charlie coughs into his hand. "I should . . . I should go. Over there." And he does. One second he's on the railing, the next he's inside the apartment and hurrying into the kitchen to noisily make himself a sandwich.

I get off the railing and meet my brother in the middle of the spacious balcony. I wait for him to begin but he says nothing and eventually meanders over to the railing to rest his forearms on it. I join him and wait for the painful conversation to begin. What did he experience in the penitent cell? Did it only serve to remind him of all the things I've done to him? What if he says he doesn't want to be around me anymore? Anxiety crawls up my spine and sits like a rotten apple in my stomach.

"We haven't really seen eye to eye lately, have we?" he says. "I've gotten so frustrated with you and angry about everything that's happened."

I bite my lip and keep the raw emotion building at bay. This is it. He's going to say he hates me, isn't he? I would die for my brother without question or hesitation but would he do the same for me?

"I'm sorry, Fifi, for everything I've done."

My breath catches and I lean away. "You—what?"

"I felt your pain in that cell," he keeps on. "For the pain I've put you through in keeping secrets, for the sacrifices you've made for me, for that time I actually attacked you when we were kids."

"But I—I was going to apologize to you!"

"What?"

I grasp his arm. "I felt you, too. I thought you hated me. *Pixies*, Hawk. It just about killed me thinking of what I've done. I had no idea. I've been trying to protect you all this time but really I was just . . . maybe I was afraid I'd lose you and held on too tight."

His expression melts and he turns to face me. "Phoenix, I could never hate you. You're my twin. You can't be replaced. And I get why you did what you did."

"But you still felt controlled."

He massages the back of his neck. "Maybe. Maybe I've been too stubborn to realize your precautions and lies were keeping me safer than I would have been on my own."

"It doesn't sound much better like that," I grumble. "Look, I want to do better. I don't want to suffocate you or push you away. You're the only family I've got, too."

"I think we both need to do better. Agreed?"

"Agreed." My knotted muscles untie and I sag with relief.

Hawk chuckles and stretches out his arms. "Come here. We need to hug this out."

I wrap my arms around my brother and hold on—but not too tight—knowing that he doesn't hate me or want to lose me. The terror that had been seeping into my soul leeches away.

"We're going to be okay, aren't we?" I murmur.

"We'll always be okay. Sometimes it just takes us longer to get there."

We hug it out for a long time, probably longer than most hugs are acceptable, but I'm tired and he's tired so we don't move away. This feels more like us. In fact, we stay that way until the smell of popcorn reaches my nose and we pull apart at the same time to ask in unison, "Popcorn?"

Charlie walks onto the balcony carrying a bag of paprika smoked popcorn. I hadn't even noticed he left.

"It was getting so melodramatic over here I figured I should intervene," he says drily.

Yeah, right. Like he'd intervene. He waited until we had settled things before coming to join us.

"Popcorn?" Hawk says with scorn. "That's your method of intervention?"

"Well, it worked, didn't it?" Charlie shoves a handful of the popcorn into his mouth and talks around it. "You two eat everything. I figured food was a good bet."

I roll my eyes. "Thanks, Charlie."

He swallows loudly and holds up one hand in innocence. "Sorry, I'm not supposed to say that kind of stuff to a girl, right?"

"Do I look like I care?" I say. "Give me some of that."

The three of us fight over the bag until we consent to passing it one way and then the other as we lean against the railing and watch the few people out for a late night stroll. A couple of fauns and centaurs trot along, some agents coming in late from missions, and Genna goes by talking quietly with Witty. Hawk's eyes narrow in on them but when he catches me smirking at him, he pretends not to be interested in what they're doing in the least.

When the bag is empty and the night is getting on, Charlie rises. "We should get some sleep. Things are bound to only get worse tomorrow."

"Such an optimist," Hawk says. "Say, is the glass half full or half empty?"

"I'm more upset about who took the other half in the first place. It was my freakin' cup of water."

I snort and get up to stretch my arms before heading into the bathroom while the boys disperse to their assigned sleeping spots. After I brush my teeth and drag my feet to my bedroom, I hear Charlie whisper from the couch.

"Do you really think I'm good looking?"

I would have laughed if not for the earnest curiosity in his voice, as if he really is unsure if anyone could find him as such. "If the girls throwing themselves at you weren't evidence enough, perhaps you should try consulting a mirror. It'll fawn over you too."

"I didn't ask if they do. I asked if you do."

I pause in my doorway unsure what he's really asking. "Goodnight, Charlie."

He murmurs goodnight as I shut the door and flop onto my bed.

As I study the ceiling overhead and consider all the horrible pain and anguish I experienced in those five minutes, I remember what Draco told me and what I witnessed firsthand. The penitent cells don't affect Dasc. He sat in one of those tormenting cells and smiled. I shudder. What kind of monster have I been dealing with?

26

Thankfully for us, Charlie's ominous prediction about the following day being even worse is proven wrong. We excel at the next series of tests, and by excel I mean trample the competition. It's not supposed to be a competition, per se, but with how competitive the three of us are it ends up turning into one regardless. We run the track in groups of five and, despite my legs smarting, I win my heat. Charlie and Hawk do the same but there are some real contenders on the field. Amanda Fry the pyrokinetic nips at our heels and telekinesis boy shows his plethora of skills as well.

The physical challenges provide the kind of stimulation I need. I want to feel like I'm actually doing something instead of beating myself up over what I experienced in the penitent cell. The rush of adrenaline, sweat beading on my forehead, and surge of endorphins as I tackle each challenge builds me up out of my gloomy reverie. I was made for this.

The instructors and judges split our day into physical tests in the morning and knowledge assessments in the afternoon. After we run the track, complete the obstacle course in the middle of the stadium, and go through a series of push-ups, sit-ups, pull-ups, and burpees, they send us off to the water sprite cavern. I spot Witty and Genna sitting off to the side watching us as we pass by, a sour look on Witty's face. A jolt of guilt passes through me but I keep moving with the rest.

Some of the junior agents not familiar with Underground gasp and look around wide-eyed in panic. The first part of the cavern is a spacious hall of smooth, glittering rock. A fine mist layers the floor of the cave and the air is cool and damp. We keep walking past the initial entrance and enter the rear portion where the stone ceiling disappears to be replaced by a see-through barrier that opens up directly to the river above. It almost looks as though we're standing beneath a glass dome and can watch fish swim by. Sunlight manages to pierce the depths here and there, glimmering and pale. A man next to me trembles as he stares up at that big expanse of water over his head. I try to give him an encouraging smile but he looks too terrified to notice. Maybe he can't swim?

I walk past him to the edge of the shimmering pool occupied by water sprites along the backside of the invisible barrier between us and the full force of the Mississippi River. They perk up when I come near and a lot of noisy splashing happens that gets my shoes wet. The sprites crowd up along the edge of their mystical pool that glows with its own bluish light and chatter in their wordless way, shifting into forms of fish, seals, dolphins, or small children.

I crouch to get closer to their level. Their giddy enthusiasm at my appearance certainly makes me feel appreciated.

"Your fan club?" Charlie asks behind me.

I give him a devious smile. "Jealous?"

"Nope. Dry."

Spartan Knox doesn't need to shout to get everyone's attention when he says, "Look sharp, everyone."

I stand and join the orderly rows the rest of the junior agents hurry to form. Charlie and Hawk stand to either side of me with their chests thrown out a bit. Spartan Knox paces in front of our assembled group.

"Physical preparedness is only one aspect of being ready to go out into the field," he says as he stands a foot above everyone else, hands clasped behind his back as usual. "Each monster's weakness is unique and, while our bio-mech weaponry can handle a wide array, do not rely on them. There will be times when the only weapon you have is ingenuity. Don't think fast enough and you die. Don't know how to kill something, a monster kills someone else. Mess up, you get your team killed. These aren't warnings. These are promises. Now, listen up."

He explains the next test while he paces along the edge of the pool as more water sprites come up through the water entrance hidden beneath their mystic pool. Apparently, the sprites will create illusionary monsters along with scenarios and a choice of weapons. We'll have to identify the monster and choose the correct weapon to defeat it as quickly as possible. The rest of the judges filter in beside him and one of them, a lively old faun, gives a rather terrifying anecdote of when they used to capture real monsters and unleash them on junior agents during the trials. After a staggering number of injuries and a few unfortunate deaths, they decided illusions were a safer method of testing. The faun chuckles at the end of his story but no one else laughs.

More water sprites line up along the edge of the pool and push a heavy fog outwards. The judges have us back up to the entrance of the cavern as a company of air and fire sprites dart down as birds from a vent in the ceiling to flit through the fog. They give flashes of color and light and transform the fog into sporadic images as if warming up for the illusions they are about to create. A group of earth sprites roll in through the entrance like a pack of moss-covered stones to join their fellows in setting the stage. It's not common to see all of the sprites together in one place and united for a common purpose. But the training of the next generation of agents isn't a thing anyone takes lightly around here.

As a group, we junior agents remain near the entrance as the first testee is called forward. They start backwards in alphabetical order this time. A young man I vaguely recognize walks forward to meet the judges at the edge of the pool and the fog coalesces into a thick impenetrable wall so the rest of us can't watch the test. Flashes of light and sound reach us but they are muffled and dim. Left to our growing anxiety, the rest of us are forced to wait through the long minutes. Some people share whispered conversations and swap notes on monsters to refresh their memory. It's easy to pick out the ones who are new to the life and those who have been raised in it—the former are a lot more frantic in asking their nearby comrades for advice and tips. I know the codex of monsters by heart and shouldn't feel too worried but I still manage to be.

Hawk, Charlie, and I hang in a loose triangle but eventually a few people come over to chat in an aimless fashion to pass the time. Unfortunately, Amanda Fry, the girl setting everything on fire, thinks it's a brilliant time to annoy us.

"I hope you're all ready," she says. "Abilities aren't everything, you know. If you don't know your stuff, you can still wind up dead."

"Thanks for the cheery pep talk," Charlie says drily, voicing what we're all thinking. "Let's not do it again sometime."

She smirks at him. "Sassy."

He avoids looking at her so her attention draws to me. She crosses her arms over her chest and gives me an arrogant once over. "How are the legs? I always see you wearing those compression sleeves. You have shin splints or something?"

Every time words come out of her mouth, I want to punch her. Instead of trying to explain the whole battling berserkers thing and hoping she just goes away, I say, "Or something."

"Hmm." She appraises each one of us, her eyes cold on Hawk, before moving away.

We don't say much of anything as the first testee comes out of the fog, is ushered away by a waiting faun, and the next goes in. One after another they're called until I hear, "Phoenix Mason!" from the other side of the fog.

"Go get 'em, tiger," Hawk says and claps me on the back.

Charlie gives me a more subdued nod in his stoic, encouraging way. I exhale slowly then proceed through the fog. The sheer opaqueness of it is disorientating until I emerge on the other side before the glowing pool. The judges stand spread out on either side, spectators to a one woman show. The sprites are practically invisible in the fog, shifting colors, and wavering lights.

Spartan Knox takes a step towards me where I stand in the center. "You will be presented with a monster, scenario, and choice of weapons. Call out the type of monster when you've identified it, then choose your weapon to defeat it. Complete the test as quickly and accurately as you can. Begin."

He sweeps an arm towards the pool and I face forward.

The shifting light suddenly becomes almost too bright. I blink against it until the glare around me dims and it's as if I've been transported to a different time and place. I'm surrounded by damp cement walls and low hanging ceilings. Loose, sparking cables hang from above, water laps at my feet, and flickering lightbulbs illuminate something big and ominous moving in the darkness twenty feet ahead of me. I'm all alone now in some abandoned subway tunnel like you'd find in a horror movie and the judges have vanished even though I know they're just out of sight.

I have to hand it to the sprites—they sure know how to make a convincing, super creepy illusion. But I can also see the holes in it, feel the pinpricks of energy from each of the sprites spread around and working together to set the scene.

The ominous shape in the dark slithers closer.

The hairs on the back of my neck rise as I make out the monster's silhouette. It's obviously an enormous snake with the shape of a crown on its head. A menacing hiss trembles off the walls of the illusion.

"Basilisk," I say and immediately feel dumb announcing it to the apparently empty subway tunnel. Spartan Knox said to call it though so I'm calling it.

Now for the weapon.

I take a quick inventory of the objects around me. The sparking wires will be useless. The broken metal pipe at my feet won't do any good. I could really use something reflective. A mirror or some glass could reflect its deadly gaze back at itself but there's nothing. There's the water obviously at my feet but the movement of the basilisk continues to disturb it so there's no chance I could get it to look at a still reflection of itself. I back up as it comes closer and avoid looking on it directly. Its gaze alone can kill.

My feet catch on a pile of something soft and squishy behind me. I glance down and grimace as I realize it's a pile of dead rats. The basilisk draws near and I've run out of options.

Wait a second. I look at the rats again and realize there's one right on top that isn't a rat at all but a weasel. Of course. A mirror is the most obvious choice but the odor of a weasel is a basilisk's other weakness. *Pixies*, magic can be weird. I grab the weasel's damp and smelly dead body and hurl it at the basilisk. The snake lets out a hideous shriek and the illusion disappears into a swirling swath of thick fog. I guess I passed the first test.

The next illusion forms and I find myself in the middle of snow covered woods beneath a full moon. My breath comes out as a white cloud and goosebumps pop up over my skin as the air turns chill to match the illusion around me. A shadow looms behind and I turn to find an old cabin and table beside me. A lantern sits on top of the table with a couple of knives, rope, a revolver, and a canister of salt. I guess those are going to be my weapon choices. So what's the monster?

A voice cries out from the darkness between the trees.

"Help me!" It sounds just like Hawk.

My breath catches. Hawk wouldn't be in here. I glance at the assortment of weapons. These aren't made for werewolves anyway. No, this has to be some monster that can imitate my brother's voice. That clue, combined with my surroundings, tells me what I'm up against.

"Wendigo," I say.

Something moves between the trees—a tall, deathly thin shadow with spindly fingers. I bend over the table and examine the different knives. I need a silver one but none of them appear to be. My eyes move to the light of the lantern as the shadow of the wendigo comes closer calling for help with my brother's voice. It's a nasty trick used to lure unsuspecting victims into its clutches to be eaten. I shake off the shiver that grips me and snatch the lantern from the table. It's a kerosene make which is ideal. Apart from silver weapons, fire is the wendigo's greatest vulnerability. I crank up the flame and prepare to dose the wendigo with it but I guess my actions are enough for me to pass. The illusion disappears.

Scenario after scenario forms and disappears as I face each of the monsters I've learned about and confronted personally. A chimera on the side of a volcano undone by a sword of lead. A kelpie on a Scottish moor tamed by a special bridle. A siren on the shores of a tumultuous sea that can only be defeated at the hands of a woman—lucky for me—wielding a bronze dagger. Ogres, aswangs, kappas, harpies, minotaurs, vampires—I charge through them thinking fast and running on adrenaline. The illusions keep me on my toes and I nearly mistake a chupacabra for a grindylow before realizing my mistake. When Director Knox appears, I'm thrown for a moment before I realize it's a shapeshifter and reach for a sparking wire nearby.

Despite the fast pace with which they throw each monster at me, I'm in my prime. This is what I'm good at. This is what I'm meant to do. A sort of deep-seated confidence takes over and I don't hesitate.

Then they throw a curve ball.

Hawk stalks towards me in our apartment. Another shapeshifter? No, they wouldn't do that. When he starts to transform into a wolf, I know it's definitely not a shapeshifter. A gun lays on the end table next to me with a full magazine on its side to make its ammunition plain—red bullets. Wolfsbane. A weapon meant to kill a werewolf. It's the only weapon around. My heart pounds in my ears. I don't care if this is just an illusion. I would never kill my brother. Never. The thought alone—how *dare* they.

Illusionary-wolf-Hawk charges. I bend at the knees, ignore the gun completely, and brace for impact. The wolf comes at me and I grab its feather-light weight by the skin of its throat. Keeping my firm grip, I turn my knuckles inward to perform a blood choke. The illusion lasts a few more seconds before it vanishes and the wolf in my hands puffs out of existence.

The fog fades until the sprites and judges are visible once again. I glare at them all, furious and defiant. The sprites duck their heads like bashful children caught red-handed doing something bad but Draco returns my glare evenly. Well, that makes it pretty obvious whose idea that was. I'm ready to rip into him but Spartan Knox interrupts my murderous thoughts before I can act on them.

"Well done, Junior Agent," he says. "Your scores will be reviewed at the end of all testing." He gestures to one of the aids, a faun in a bright yellow brocade, who waits for me to follow him.

Still infuriated but deciding chewing out the judges isn't going to do me any good, I march after the faun who leads me out of the water sprite cavern and back to the stadium. The other junior agents who have already finished the illusionary test are working one on one with fauns and humans from the medical staff. My guide has me join up with one of the nurses that took care of me during my med ward stay after taking on the lamia. I push the thought of shooting Hawk out of my mind as she sets me in front of a dummy on the ground next to an open med-pack. The nurse makes notes on a clipboard as she has me perform various forms of emergency aid like CPR, bandaging a cut, treating a burn from the acid spit of a hydra, and injecting fake anti-dote for a miscellaneous poison.

The nurse informs me that my skills are sound but I should be careful about how tight I wind my bandages. She makes a few more notes on her clipboard then informs me I am to receive my next instructions from the head doctor on the other side of the stadium. I wander over and realize that the doctor in charge of the assessments is a wulver. Not just any wulver, but Dr. Lyall from the Vaults in Scotland. He gives me a sharp smile as I approach.

"It's good to see you again, Miss Mason," he says.

"Dr. Lyall." I shake his furry hand. "I had no idea you were here."

"Yes, well, I make the rounds from city to city during trial testing. I would like to think it's because of my expertise but I dare say it's also a point to see which junior agents react adversely to my appearance. For psychological reasons, of course."

Yeah, I suppose he seems like an oddity even here. "I'm glad to see you're all right. I tried to message Spartan McDonnell about the attack on the Vaults but never heard back."

His ears flatten against his head and he readjusts his glasses. "I imagine she's been rather busy. After that nasty business, she rejoined with her team and has been hunting the assailants ever since."

Assailants. Werewolves? Or someone casting the blame on werewolves as Scholar suspects?

"Do you know if they've had any luck?" I ask.

"None that I'm aware. Rather curious circumstances, I should say."

"What do you mean?"

"When one thinks of a werewolf attack, one would naturally assume there would be werewolf victims. However, no one was bitten during the attack. I suppose we ought to be grateful but I feel more inclined to be suspicious."

"Oh?"

"A werewolf's bite is its deadliest weapon. It begs the question why it was not used in such an assault." Dr. Lyall's nose twitches and his ears perk up once more. "I spoke with some of my colleagues at the other sites and they reported the same. No infection of the werewolf disease."

Curious indeed. Perhaps the reason no one was bitten was because there weren't actually any werewolves at the attacks. After the Vaults, two other facilities in Prague and Tokyo were attacked. It's the reason the tension between werewolves and everyone else is so high right now.

"Are you all right, Miss Mason?" he asks after I muse on it overlong.

"I'm fine," I respond automatically. "You've just given me a lot to think about, that's all."

"Rightly so." He tugs at the lapels of his white lab coat to straighten them and clears his throat—a sound somewhere between a growl and a dog hacking up its breakfast. "I suppose you came over here for instructions so I should give them. I will be reviewing everyone's progress and will submit my recommendations to the board of judges. Your score will be reviewed at the end. For the remainder of the day, I suggest you rest up. You will be heading to Camp Ripley tomorrow for the next bout of testing. Carry on, Miss Mason."

"Yes, sir."

"Oh, and Miss Mason?" I pause and he gives me a toothy grin. "Well done so far, lass. Nose to the air, eyes on the ground, you hear?"

I smile. Wulvers are curious creatures, aren't they? "Yes, sir."

Doing as Dr. Lyall suggests, I head out of the stadium and pass my brother on his way in. We swap a low-five and carry on our own business. I stake out a table at Old Man Two's to wait for the rest of my friends to show up and order a Red Kola. I sip at the brightly colored drink and people watch. Many of the other junior agents that have finished today's trials have found their way here and discuss the illusion test which is the hot topic of the day. They compare notes and gossip about how they think others did. Apparently a couple of boys almost failed the siren test—they went for the bronze dagger instead of the earplugs before remembering only a woman can kill a siren.

I glance up at the old clock hanging from the apothecary across the way every so often. Hawk sure is taking his time, isn't he? And Charlie for that matter. Witty is nowhere in sight, Genna as well. Although, those two are probably together somewhere talking about comic books or something. Bored, and feeling the urge to move about, I take my Red Kola with me and wander aimlessly through the market square. The smell of paprika-smoked popcorn draws me towards the arcade area.

Familiar voices pull me out of reverie.

"They're creepy." It's Genna somewhere.

"That's sort of the point." And there's Witty. Big surprise. But where are they? I round the popcorn stand, enter the arcade zone, and find Witty counting out a string of tickets Genna feeds him lazily. She's laying on the hard floor with her hair fanned out around her, legs crossed and one hand tucked behind her head as she watches the gargoyles on the roof of the emporium nearby.

I hang back to finish off my Red Kola before interrupting their conversation.

"Do they actually do anything?" Genna asks.

"Sure they do. If there's a threat to Underground, they protect the city." He counts off the tickets under his breath with a frown. "Thirty-five, thirty-six . . . They can plug holes in the structure of Underground too if they need to. The whole morphing into stone thing and all that. They're a backup in case the outer shielding ever fails. They can hold up the walls long enough for the residents to escape. Thirty-eight . . . no, wait a second. Where was I at?"

"Thirty-six last."

"Oh, right."

A hand grabs my upper arm and spins me about to bring me face to face with Jefferson. I gasp and accidentally dump the remnants of my Red Kola on the floor. His beady eyes fix me with a glare that could melt metal. In the weeks I've been avoiding him, his beard has grown out and gotten a bit scraggily. A grimace lingers under his ferocious anger and he clamps one hand to the side of his chest where the bullet wound is still healing.

"Haven't you done enough spying?" he growls.

"What? No, that's not what I was—"

"Waiting in the shadows and keeping tabs on my daughter?" His voice rises and a few fauns passing nearby halt. "All that time you spend together, do you keep notes? Make sure she toes the line, doesn't slip up? You're just waiting to put a noose around her neck."

I rip my arm out of his grip and he staggers backwards. "Jefferson, enough!" The injustice of his accusations dig deep, bringing out equal parts bitterness, sadness, and rage. I desperately want to hit something.

"Yeah, that is enough!" he shouts back and presses both hands to his weak spot. "I trusted you! After years of not trusting anyone, I trusted *you*. Then you stabbed me in the back."

With a roar of rage, I pick up my dropped cup and hurl it towards the cement wall where it shatters and pieces imbed in the stone.

"Do you think I wanted any of this?" I thunder. "Do you think I asked for that assignment?"

"Did you?"

The gusto in my chest leaves me a sharp exhale. "How can you even think that?"

"I don't know what to think anymore."

"Then think on this." I step forward until our noses are inches apart and I drop my voice so the number of curious onlookers can't hear. "Consider the number of times Genna gave the IMS cause to haul her back here but they didn't. Why do you think that is? Or why she was even allowed to go home in the first place? I want you to remember that month we spent in Scotland tracking her, the month I spent having to play nice with my parents' murderer to find her. I want you to remember the deal I made to get her back. I did that for *you*. So don't you dare think for a second that I would ever have wanted to rip away what happiness you finally found. I know what family means to both of us. So don't you dare."

He leans back and is silent for a moment. Genna has gotten to her feet and stands not far to the side looking hopeless.

At last he says, "I didn't dare. You did."

Still grasping at his wound, he stalks away through the gathered crowd and vanishes between the buildings, taking my hope of ever mending that bridge with him.

27

My shot goes wide of the mark. The target I'm supposed to be peppering down the Camp Ripley firing range hardly looks hit. There are a few holes on the edges but it's not even remotely agent qualified precision.

Jefferson's words ring in my ears. *After years of not trusting anyone, I trusted you.*

The next shot goes so wide that I lower my weapon seeing how pointless it is as the rest of the class continues firing. Hawk's target to my left has a nice, clean grouping through the middle. He's one of the top marksmen in our class of junior agents and Charlie is right behind him in skill level. I set my gun on the counter in front of me and wait.

Haven't you done enough spying?

I press a fist to my forehead wishing I could push Jefferson's anger out of my head. I haven't been able to focus on anything since yesterday and my score is suffering for it. A true agent wouldn't let something like this get in the way of their job. I have to do better. If I don't, I won't be getting a badge pinned to my chest.

The line of shooters finally empty their magazines, set their guns down, and shout that they're done. Spartan Knox walks slowly along the line to inspect the targets and give pointers to each junior agent. As he takes his time, Charlie moves around from his partition to put a hand on my shoulder and lean in close.

"Hey," he murmurs. "You having the jitters again? Did you read that book on breathing exercises I gave you?"

"Yeah, it's—it's not that." Embarrassed, I keep my eyes on the gun laying on the counter in front of me. "This is different."

"It doesn't have to be. Just remember what I told you, okay? You're in control."

I can't help but give a heartless laugh. "If I feel like lying to myself, then I'll be sure to repeat that mantra."

He frowns. "What's gotten into you? This isn't the girl I know that decided to take on a pair of lamias on her own."

"Well, that girl was a real idiot."

"I'd slap some sense into you but I'd probably get in trouble," he growls. He glances back at Spartan Knox as if to make sure he wouldn't be able to get away with it. Instead, he gives my shoulder a painful squeeze. "If you want to fail, Phoenix, then by all means. Just know that it's not because of jitters or nerves or whatever's gotten up your butt. *You are defeating yourself.*"

"Roger that, captain."

Deciding to take a risk after all, he slaps me upside the head.

"Hey!" I smooth a hand over my hair and glare at him. I don't need to feel worse than I already do.

"Don't fail on purpose, you stupid berserker."

"Why do you care?"

He rolls his eyes and returns to his partition as Spartan Knox reaches us.

I stand facing my pathetic target as I listen to the Spartan heap sound praise on Charlie's accuracy and realize just how screwed I am. I can't hit a target. That's sort of an essential skill. If I don't qualify here, I'm doomed. Everything I've worked for and fought so hard to achieve will be meaningless.

"I can't say I'm not disappointed, Mason." Spartan Knox stands directly behind me, but I don't have the strength to turn around and face him. I keep my eyes downcast. "You've performed exceeding well until today. You've been distracted."

"Yes, sir," I mumble.

"If you can't handle distractions out in the field, this is exactly what's going to happen." He gestures to the hardly damaged target in front of me. "You'll have one more chance to pass this trial. If you can't hit that target a second time around, I'll have no choice but to disqualify you from field duty. Do you understand?"

"Yes, sir."

"Then take a minute and get your head together," he says. "Once I'm done going down the line, you'll be up again."

He claps his bearpaw of a hand on my shoulder and moves on to Hawk next. I meet my brother's gaze nearly by accident and quickly look away, my cheeks reddening, as my brother gets a heap of praise next. The Spartan's words become nothing but meaningless chatter in the background as another voice grows louder in my head.

I trusted you! After years of not trusting anyone, I trusted you. Then you stabbed me in the back.

I swallow and brace my hands on the counter. Something horrid is crawling its way up my throat. Everything that's happened surfaces at this moment, all my faults and failures coming to haunt me like those ghosts of yesteryear Draco talked about. I lose myself in my mistakes, the things I should have done, and find that I don't have the strength to care anymore about what happens next.

Spartan Knox continues on but what's the point waiting for my second chance? I won't be able to hit that target properly in a couple of minutes. I vaguely notice Hawk and Charlie whispering behind me before they disappear, probably heading to the next trial.

Leave, Phoenix. And don't bother to come back.

I close my eyes against inevitable tears and hang my head. For all the power I hold, the thing I most desperately wish I could change is the one thing I'm powerless to fix.

Maybe I should walk away right now and save myself the trouble. If I vanish before the next round, at least I won't have to face being heckled or having my hopes dashed a second time. Maybe it would just be better for everyone if I wasn't here at all.

A familiar melody plays behind me on the tinny sound of a small speaker. Drums join the notes and the lyrics are sung. It's not any old song. It's my parents' song. *My* song. The one that built me up when I felt weak. The one that always let me know I wasn't alone even when I felt so lost. I open my eyes and turn around to find Hawk standing behind me holding a phone that's not his own. Charlie's there too and they watch me as if ready to jump to my rescue if I start to keel over.

I blink rapidly and continue to listen to the song. Hawk steps forward and puts his free hand on my shoulder.

"You can do this," he says. "I know you can."

That depressive hole in my chest doesn't want to argue or insist he's wrong or rally up the courage to face that target again.

"Maybe everyone's been wrong about me," I say at last, defeated. "Maybe—"

"Phoenix, we've all been wrong about you," he says sharply and punctures the last bit of breath in my chest. But then he keeps talking. "Dasc thought you would be easy to take down but you stopped him despite everything he threw at you. The lamia thought you would be easy prey but you broke out of those chains and came to rescue me. Director Knox underestimated both of us for years and now look at you. He actually smiles at you. And I—I did something really stupid and thought the worst of you after the whole Genna spying situation. But I was wrong. And Jefferson's wrong too, even if he can't see that yet. You have *always* been more than expected, Fifi. Don't sell yourself short now."

I hiccup back a sob of relief and throw my arms around my brother.

He cups the back of my head and plants a kiss on the side of my hair. "I'm sorry."

There are no words for the relief and joy Hawk has just given me. It's taking everything in me not to start crying much less say anything. I hold tight onto my brother and work my breath into a steady pattern. When I finally calm myself and open my eyes again, Charlie gives me a thumbs up and mouths "good job." I manage a smile and he returns it in kind.

My brother and I pull apart at the same moment and he shakes my shoulders. "Now, are you ready to go kick some butt out there?"

I shrug and nod. "Yeah."

"*Piping Pan*, we need a little more gung-ho enthusiasm than that." He shakes me again. "Eye on the prize. Aim for the center. Go make me proud like you always do."

"Thanks." I run a hand under my nose, square my shoulders, and take a very long, deep breath.

"Better?" Charlie asks, bemused.

I nod once. "Better."

"Then go get 'em."

The rest of the class files away to the next stage of the gun course as I wait behind with three others that displayed subpar shooting skills. I shouldn't even be with this group but I've failed myself. I can do better. I know I can. I must.

Hawk and Charlie make to walk away with the rest but then hang back and wait for me on the sidelines as I move up to the shooting alley again. Their stalwart presence helps. Not everyone has lost faith in me. I can't lose faith in myself. There's nothing I can do about Jefferson. I consider that for a long moment as I load the magazine and slide it into the handgun. The reality of it sinks in. No matter what I do, I can't hang my life up on not being able to change someone's mind about me, even if it is someone dear to me. But I can change this. This part of my life I *can* control. I am in control here. And despite what I told Charlie, that isn't a lie.

It's not over yet.

Spartan Knox calls out for live fire and I do the practiced quick draw, snapping the gun up, narrowing down the sights, and leaning into the kickback as I empty the clip into the target. The gunfire drowns out everything and when the three of us call out that we're done, Charlie and Hawk let out a whoop from where they wait on the outskirts of the range.

A tight grouping of bullet holes decorate the center body mass of my target. It's not my best but it's certainly not my worst. Passable.

Spartan Knox gives unfortunate news to one of the junior agents who still failed the test on the second try. The poor boy is escorted away by one of the aides. The next receives better news and when the Spartan reaches me next, I already know what he's going to say.

"Much better," he says and gives a nod of approval. "Go join the others."

I can't help but smile wide. It's difficult to walk at a normal pace as I make for Hawk and Charlie. Both of the boys give me a round of applause and clap me heartily on the back. As a team, we hurry to the next obstacle ahead of us.

As if fresh blood has been pumped into my veins, I move into the next trial with gusto. Now that I've passed the basic firearms test, I join the others on the live fire obstacle course. One by one, each of the junior agents run out at the sound of a bell and make their way as quickly as they can through a field of targets that pop up in an old building set piece. Some accidentally shoot a cardboard faun acting as an innocent caught in the crossfire. It's a test to not only hit all the targets but to know exactly what we're firing at. You don't pull the trigger unless you know what you're aiming at.

Hawk shakes out his arms and stands at the line waiting for the bell. The second it goes off, he blazes forward and has the first target down within two seconds. Pop, pop, pop—he navigates the course like a pro without slowing. He dances around the faun and gets the vampire behind her without missing a beat. By the time he takes down the last target and slides through the finish, it's easily been the fastest time on the course so far.

Then it's my turn. I stand at the line and shake the tension out of my arms and focus on taking deep, even breaths.

I find Charlie's hand on my arm.

"You've got this," he says. "Clear mind, fast trigger, nothing but instinct. And don't shoot the faun."

"And don't shoot the faun," I repeat. "Got it."

He steps away as I hunch into a ready stance. The bell rings and I enter a world where I've got nothing to worry about except myself and survival. I know this world. I've been here enough times to be comfortable with the rush, the drive of instinct. Cardboard and steel cutouts are nothing compared to thirsty lamia, vicious werewolves, and packs of angry vampires. I hurtle through the course—don't shoot the faun—and sprint through the finish with the satisfaction of knowing that I didn't miss a single target. Spartan Knox gives me his nod of approval and I move onto the next chance to prove myself.

When I realize the next trial is emergency driving competency, I can't help but smile. *This* ought to be fun.

"You'll do great!" Hawk says as we wait for our turn. "There aren't any semis here."

I slug him in the shoulder and he winces.

The squeal of tires and smell of burning rubber makes me hyper. I'm fidgety waiting for my chance to get behind the wheel. You'd think that being in two car crashes would have shaken my fondness of driving fast but it's only made me more determined to face it head on. Besides, it's so much fun.

At last it's my turn to get into the seat of one of the standard issue SUVs and buckle up. The wild grin I give my passenger seat instructor must make him nervous because he automatically clutches onto the handle in the door to brace himself. It's a good thing, too, because the next second I hit the gas and floor it through the maze of orange cones and cardboard cutouts of vampires. The tires squeal and the engine roars as I whip around the corners, slide past a fake faun that pops up, zig-zag through portions of a fence, then hit a cardboard villain with the side of the SUV as I yank on the emergency brake and then hit the gas to power slide through it. I let out a whoop as I straighten the SUV out and gun it down the last stretch of test track. At the finish I hit the emergency brake again at just the right moment, skid across the pavement, and slide to a stop parallel parked in front of the line of other SUVs ready for testing.

My instructor exhales loudly, clears his throat, and gives me a thumbs up. "Excellent work. I trust you don't drive like that normally, though."

"Of course not." Although I certainly wish I could. Best not to mention that I think.

"Oh, good."

He gives me the okay to head onto the next event of training. I join the throng of junior agents driving a wide array of vehicles from sedans to trucks to large commercial semis to prove we can handle any vehicle in a pinch if need be. You never know when you're going to have to commandeer a vehicle and give chase after a monster. Driving the high-powered muscle car at the end is my favorite.

As soon as I finish the driving portion of the trials, I hustle to the large dining hall for lunch. The junior agents congregate in the center and a few national guardsmen sit off to the sides. Camp Ripley is temporarily closed to the usual police officers, national guardsmen, and soldiers that come here to train until the IMS junior agents finish up their testing. The few that remain know about the other half of the world the general populace is ignorant of.

I take my tray of grub and sit near the other junior agents but far enough away so I don't have to mingle. Hawk comes in shortly after followed by Charlie. The two of them join me and we have a moment of silence as we focus on eating and not talking. I catch snippets of conversation from the other junior agents discussing where they were previously stationed for their field training.

"I was up in the boundary waters," one boy says. "Like absolutely nothing happened except for a couple of werewolves going missing. Seriously boring but the view was nice, I guess."

I swallow and meet Charlie's eyes. "Is he talking about what I think he's talking about?" I ask in an undertone.

He nods. "Probably. Half of my office went up to help look for those werewolves while we were dealing with vampires, remember?"

"Yeah."

"I was sort of reminded of it during the emergency driving trial," he says and offers a grin which I readily return.

"I bet you passed with flying colors."

"Of course," he says and scoffs. "We both survived the real life version didn't we?"

"Yeah, and made it on the news."

Hawk laughs and holds up a hand for a high-five. "Way to go, Fifi."

I give him a careful high-five and Charlie gets one as well.

"Did I hear you right?" a girl nearby asks. The three of us look up as she leans towards our group. "You guys were in a car chase?"

"Hold on, let me check my BS meter," Charlie says, looks at his watch, and then nods thoughtfully. "Yup. Pretty sure that actually happened."

I nearly choke on my food and have a coughing fit. As expected, the girl looks extremely irritated at his reply. Taking pity on her, I hastily swallow and say, "Yes. We were in a car chase."

The man across from her asks, "What happened?"

Charlie speaks up again and says dryly, "Troll stole a dump truck."

"Really?"

"No."

I guess he's in a particularly fine mood today. His defensive tactics are in full swing. I wonder why.

"Vampires," Hawk cuts in and proceeds to slice his

chunk of chicken delicately as if this whole conversation is boring. "They were being commanded by a couple of lamia. The three of us were involved in stopping a state-wide slaughter."

A silence falls over the table until the girl says, "I think you ought to check your BS meter again because you're full of crap." She returns to her food muttering under her breath, "Werewolves."

I do my best to ignore her rudeness but I accidentally bend the metal fork in my hand. I hide the evidence in my fist as I work the utensil back into its original shape with my thumb. Charlie stares at the girl as if he'd like nothing more than to strangle her but Hawk keeps cutting his chicken as if nothing's been said. Although, he does shift his foot to crunch my toes as a way to keep me in check. I don't need help. I'm fine reining in my anger. Pretty sure. Maybe.

The other junior agents at the table exchange glances as if they too share the girl's sentiment. Only a few don't. Amanda Fry, the spirited pyrokenetic, twirls her fingers and the girl's meal catches fire. The girl shrieks and shoves her fiery tray away from her. With a snap of Amanda's fingers, the flames die out.

"That wasn't very nice," Amanda says. "And you're an idiot. It was in the feeds. It didn't identify the junior agents involved though. Good work you three." She nods in our direction and spares a wink for Charlie. He turns red and focuses intently on his peas. I can understand her sticking up for Charlie—her flirting hasn't exactly been covert—but I'm surprised she stood up on behalf of Hawk. Maybe I judged her too early as a stereotypical, arrogant jerk.

The conversation picks up again and no one else asks

about the car chase or vampires or lamia although I do catch several people staring at us curiously before ducking their heads when they meet my hard gaze.

The second half of the day has us split into groups for the first of the team trials. We run through the basics of effective teamwork—communication, reliability, competency, trust, and adaptability. In essence, we have to show that we can play well with others. I guess as my own personal test, they put Hawk, Charlie, and me on separate teams.

I end up in a group of five that includes Amanda Fry and the girl with an attitude about werewolves. Amanda and I are warned against using our abilities for the safety of our teammates before throwing us into one of the set scenarios. We have to breach a building filled with civilians and take out a ghoul without arousing suspicion. Our first go isn't pretty. Amanda and I butt heads on the best route to take and attitude-girl, whose name I finally remember is Cassie, decides she doesn't want to listen to either of us and heads off without waiting for us. The next several minutes involve tripping the alarms, getting spotted, and having the illusion of the ghoul eat an office worker.

Spartan Knox isn't gentle in his assessment. We get a scalding review, are told to get our heads out of our butts in colorful language, and ordered back into the scenario to try again.

We gather outside the rear entrance to the building in black swat gear complete with helmets and bio-mech guns in the form of replica assault rifles.

"We need one leader," Amanda begins immediately. "We decide the leader and then they call the shots. If we're all running around we're going to look like idiots again."

"Yeah, and who's going to be the leader?" Cassie says in a snippy voice. "You?"

The two guys on our team mutter something under their breath and roll their eyes but don't bother to assert an opinion.

"*Pixies*," I say sharply and finally snap. "You'd think we're in high school with the amount of drama we've got going on. Are we trained junior agents or aren't we?"

Cassie puts her hand on her hip. "Oh, because you're perfect?"

Deciding that leadership is the best way to go and Cassie is obviously never going to follow the orders of a werewolf supporter, I put my pride aside and say, "Amanda. I'll follow your lead. Can we all agree on that at least?"

The boys nod but Cassie says nothing probably because I'm the one that suggested it.

"I'll take lead," Amanda says firmly and Cassie finally nods in agreement.

Although I'm not a huge fan of Amanda's plan, I go along with it because, if I want to be a team player, then sometimes I have to follow. We storm up the stairwell and kick open the door at the landing. Civilians—acted by actual field agents and teachers—gasp and startle at our appearance. One even screams.

"Police!" Amanda shouts. "Everyone on the ground!"

Chaos ensues and while some of the civilians do as they're told, some refuse and others panic and start running away. Since I'm one of the fastest, my job is to round up any panicked runners and get them to safety while the rest of the team either secures those that are cooperative or goes after the ghoul at the rear of the building. I sprint past my team and grab the arm of a lady making a beeline for the area our ghoul is supposed to be hiding. I talk her down and when she fails to listen, I more forcefully set her on the floor so she'll stay put before I track any other runners.

When I hear the pulse of a bio-mech gun, I put a hand on her head and push her even lower. "Stay down," I warn. "Get under a desk and don't come out until we tell you it's safe."

"But what's going on!" she yells.

This agent is a good actor. She almost looks like she's going to cry.

"Security breach," is all I say in response before converging on another runner before he heads right into danger.

Teamwork wins out on this go. After one of the boys and I get the workers safely out of the building, we cover the exits while the other three surround the ghoul and take it out. A bell rings to signal the scenario is over and the illusion of the ghoul disappears. Swapping smiles and high-fives, we exit the building as a team.

It's a good moment before it's interrupted by Cassie making a snide comment to me. "So was that ghoul as imaginary as your lamia?"

My hand curls into a fist but I bite my tongue as I'm conscious of the judges' eyes on us. Fortunately, I manage to hold in my anger but Amanda slaps Cassie upside the head, unafraid.

Spartan Knox intercepts us and directs us to hang up our gear and organize the bio-mech guns to close out our day. We do as directed and change into our junior agent uniforms before sorting the gear and putting the bio-mech rifles in their assigned compartments. Instead of heading to the mess hall for dinner, we hang back to watch the last two scenarios of the day—Hawk's team and Charlie's.

The judges sit in an office outside the building where the scenarios take place. Video monitors fill one wall and audio booms through the room. We hang around the rear of the office, allowed in by an irritated clipboard assistant, but since we aren't in the way, the judges don't seem to mind our presence.

Charlie's team goes up first for their last scenario of the day. For a moment it looks like the team isn't doing anything. Then the fire alarm gets pulled and I see Charlie port from the alarm to the door behind which the ghoul is hiding. He secures the door while the rest of the team barricades the door behind which they hide, forcing the office workers out the other exits before the team rushes in and bring down the ghoul. Clean and efficient. Impressive. When the team marches out, Charlie gives me his biggest smile.

Spartan Knox gestures to the group. "Well done. Stow your gear and weapons and head to the mess hall."

I manage to give Charlie a high-five as he walks by with his team before I return to the room to see my brother's team perform. It takes them a bit to get ready before they too attempt a tactic similar to one my team managed to pull off. One teammate—an anti-werewolf sort—gives Hawk the cold shoulder throughout the entire exercise but the rest of his team doesn't seem to have a problem working alongside a werewolf. They complete the task and file out of the building. After Spartan Knox gives them the same orders to stow their gear and weapons, I wait outside the armory for my brother.

Hawk comes out with a faint smile and we walk together to the mess hall, the rest of his team chatting behind us. I'm glad things have gotten a little friendlier between everyone. It hurts me physically when they shun my brother, to the point I'd like to hurt *them* physically but somehow manage to restrain myself. On the way to the mess hall, I consider pulling some harmless pranks out of spite.

"Where's Charlie?" Hawks says when we reach the dining center. Our friend is nowhere to be found.

Amanda Fry stalks past just then with a tray in her hands. "Draco pulled him off to the side for a chat. Guess who's teacher's pet?"

A jolt goes through me.

I grab her arm in a sudden panic before she can move away. She glares at me and her arm becomes too hot to keep ahold of. I quickly let go. My fingers are red and the sleeve of her uniform sizzles.

"Don't touch," she says with a note of warning in her voice.

I shake out my hand, the pain inconsequential. "Where did they go?"

"Why? Worried your boyfriend is going to leave you in the dust?"

"Yup. Sure. Let's go with that. Where did they go?"

Her eyes rake me with suspicion. "I don't think I should tell you."

Energy surges down my arms and I almost risk punching her. "Pixies, I was actually starting to respect you too," I snap and rush out of the mess hall.

Hawk stays on my heels as we run and scan the surrounding area.

Charlie doesn't know what he's walking into. I know of Scholar's warnings, I know of Draco's past, I know the dark truth behind the bio-mech guns and werewolf serum. Junior agents with promising and unique abilities have gone missing during the trials. Heck, that's what I've been trying to avoid this whole time. I've been so focused on getting myself through the trials that I didn't even consider who else could be snatched up.

If Draco has targeted Charlie for his rare teleportation ability, he could be the next missing person to slip through our fingers.

28

There's no sign of Draco or Charlie, and the guards patrolling the perimeter of the camp don't want to tell us anything.

"I don't see them anywhere," Hawk says and gives a hopeful sniff at the air.

Our eyes and his nose aren't our only options though.

"Give me a second," I say and close my eyes to focus. I stretch out my tethers and in the distance near the firing range I sense that overwhelming powerhouse of energy that can only be Draco. Guided by that power, I open my eyes and gesture to my brother. "This way."

He raises an eyebrow but jogs after me as I hustle towards the rolling hills of Camp Ripley. We pass the mess hall, the armory, the barracks, and the rest of the buildings until we crest the first hill and see Draco in his human form talking quietly to Charlie. There's no one else around but Charlie certainly doesn't seem in distress in any way. I heave a sigh of relief but don't let my guard down. I'm going to stay right here until Charlie is safe away from Draco's grasping claws.

"You really can sense magic, can't you?" Hawk asks quietly as we spy on the majestic dragon and our friend. I nod. "Can you sense me?"

"Yup."

"What can you sense from me?"

A bitter dark swirl of malevolent chaos, but that's one secret I'm going to keep to myself for as long as possible. Hawk doesn't need to know the reality of the poison in his veins.

I shrug. "Energy."

"Huh. Does that have a smell or something? How on earth do you sense that?"

"I don't know. It's just *there*."

"Magic is weird."

"You're preaching to the choir."

Charlie nods at something Draco says and the two look like they're about to turn our way.

Hawk grabs my arm. "Come on."

Before we take even two steps, Draco's eyes lock onto me and I'm pinned to the spot under that focused intensity. Hawk and I remain where we are—my brother quickly dropping his hand from my sleeve—and wait for the two of them to reach us. Charlie could have ported the distance if he wanted but he walks step in step with the majestic dragon.

"What perchance has brought you two here?" Draco asks the pair of us but his gaze never leaves me. It's clear who his question is intended for.

"We were just looking for Charlie," I say, which is true.

"Oh?" His eyes morph from human eyes to the slits of a dragon and back again. It's an odd reflex, like a cat twitching its tail as it watches its prey. "Such concern for his well-being?"

The air between us grows heavy and that pressure rolling off him pushes against my chest, tightening my lungs until it becomes difficult to breathe. I tear my eyes away from him to look at Charlie and it's like taking a deep breath of fresh air after being under water for too long.

"Charlie," I say on a long exhale. "What, er—what's going on?"

He studies me with slightly narrowed eyes. He knows something's up. "Draco wanted to talk to me about some job opportunities."

"Oh? What kind of jobs?"

I can feel Draco's eyes boring into me but I keep my focus glued on Charlie.

"Just some stuff," he mutters. "Hey, are you okay?"

"Me? Yeah, I'm great. We were just—we . . ."

"We were saving you a spot at the mess hall," Hawk says, coming in with the save. "They were going to serve pudding. We wanted to make sure you didn't miss out."

"Oh. Thanks?"

Well, I don't think Charlie or Draco are buying this pathetic little charade. Time to make an exit.

"We should get going," I say. I finally meet Draco's gaze

again and instantly feel that pressure pushing against my lungs. "If that's all right, sir."

"Of course. We are finished." He gestures to Charlie but continues to stare at me. "I got what I needed."

On that ominous note, Draco turns with a flourish and strides away into the growing darkness of the gun range. We don't move or speak until he's retreated so far away that there's no sign of the majestic.

"Are you okay?" I ask Charlie once we're free to talk without being eavesdropped on.

It takes him a long time to respond during which I realize how tense he is, how tightly he holds his jaw, and the ghost of a frown haunting his face. What on earth did Draco say to him?

"We should get back to the mess hall," he says at long last which isn't the sort of response I want.

He sticks his hands into his pockets, his shoulders droop a fraction of an inch, and he walks calmly towards the dining center. Hawk and I exchange a look and I'm glad to see that I'm not the only one who noticed Charlie's change in demeanor. We hurry to catch up with his long stride and return to the mess hall a silent trio.

Conversation is minimal at best as we eat our meal and head to our bunks. In the morning, the atmosphere between us and Charlie hasn't changed. He avoids eye contact but I catch him studying me when he thinks I'm not looking. He remains tense as the teams get switched up and we're paired together for the next bout of team exercises. He's all business as we clear a building, lay a trap for a harpy, lure out a kelpie, and then join the rest of our class for hydra combat simulations. Even though he continues to sit with us during each of the meals, he hardly speaks a word and looks so freaking conflicted about something that I'm dying to ask. I try bringing up his meeting with Draco again but he dismisses it as if it was nothing despite it being so obviously clear it was anything but.

After another three days of teamwork trials, we move onto learning how to rappel out of helicopters, skydive safely into a city, set up zip-lines between buildings, drive through treacherous terrain, and use diving equipment. Charlie warms up to us again but we're all so focused on learning and passing the trials that his most recent attitude and its implications get put on the back-burner.

The last week of the trials comes upon us and the long hours of training have visibly taken their toll on a few people in class. One boy actually oversleeps one day and gets chewed out by Spartan Knox. Some people are sporting injuries from the rougher patches of testing and others hardly talk to anyone anymore as it's clear they may not pass the trials after their poor performances. Charlie, Hawk, and I have done well and Amanda Fry is probably at the top of the class as well. The divide between those raised in the life and those introduced to it later on becomes wider and more obvious. There are some of us who were made for this life and others that still don't know if they want any part of it.

The longer I'm among the other junior agents, the more I pick up their own reasons for being here. While many are Blessed and have been raised in various hidden sanctuaries, others stumbled across our world while on the job such as a couple FBI agents and a handful of police officers. Everyone has their horrifying or traumatic experience that drives them—Hawk and I can relate. Some had family members killed, others had friends go missing, while a few survived attacks from hellish monsters. Every story proves Scholar—Terra—right about the importance of the IMS. There's a reason we're here and doing what we're doing. As a majority, the class is composed of good people wanting to make a difference. It makes enduring Draco's relentless attention more bearable.

I can feel his eyes on me always as I run through obstacle courses, tie knots, set explosives, wield retractable blades, fire a phase-repeater, and rappel down the side of a building. It's annoying and puts me on edge. It becomes distracting to the point that I almost flub the crime scene test where I'm supposed to be identifying what monster killed the bloody dummy lying in a cellar.

"Those claw marks are *not* from a wendigo," Spartan Knox growls as he stands over me with arms crossed and frowns at my fumbling. "You know better."

I swallow my anxiety and crouch to get a better look at the dummy. "I—yes, sir. You're right. Let's see. These claw marks . . . are . . . are from a—"

Draco's rippling energy washes over me from the other side of the room.

I grit my teeth. "These claw marks are from . . ."

"Head out of the clouds, Mason."

"A harpy," I announce and rocket to my feet.

He gives a single approving nod but says, "You've been letting your scores slide. Whatever's got you off kilter again, fix it. Don't disappoint me now, Junior Agent."

"Yes, sir," I say with as much conviction as I can muster,

which is dimmed by my embarrassment and frustration. I'd love to be able to fix the problem of a majestic dragon breathing down my neck but I really don't think that's a task I'm up to.

Thankfully, after passing the crime scene analysis and technology tests, I don't have to worry about Draco's influence affecting my scores anymore as the trials come to an end. It's with fevered anticipation and excitement that our class gathers in the stadium back in Underground. We stand in orderly rows in the median of the track wearing our junior agent uniforms for one of the last times. The judges stand in similar rows before us with Spartan Knox at the forefront. Spectators have come to fill the stadium seats.

Spartan Knox gives a speech about how proud they are of us, to enjoy the midsummer festivities while the judges review our trials and decide our fate with the agency, and that we'll be called to headquarters in a week or so to hear their verdict.

"You've done well," he concludes. "Now enjoy the festivities before the real work begins."

The junior agents, myself included, let out a great whoop and cheer before scattering or forming groups to chat. Charlie, Hawk, and I give each other enormous smiles and walk out of the stadium together. In the tunnel on the way out we meet up with Genna and Witty who have apparently been waiting for us. Congratulations are exchanged all around and as a merry gang we debate how to celebrate an end to the trials.

We pause on the fringe of the market to survey the colorful decorations assembled for the start of the midsummer festivities. Bright red streamers line the front of shops along with bouquets of flowers and birch branches frame the doorways. Everywhere there are intricately carved pedestals that hold bowls of burning oil which the fire sprites leap between, leaving trails of sparks through the air. Air sprites circle overhead in an interweaving dance to keep the smoke drifting up and away in smooth spirals to the vents overhead. Music can be heard from every corner of Underground—flutes, drums, harps, anything the musically inclined can get their hands on.

Light, life, and music surround me.

"Where do we start?" Genna asks. Witty squeaks his wheels anxiously beside her, rolling his lips and frowning at every nearby junior agent. He seems like he's in a foul mood but Genna looks eager to participate in everything around her.

"Dancing!" Hawk exclaims. He grabs her hand, then mine, and pulls us towards the loudest sound of merry making. We jog to keep up with his pace to the faun fields in front of the apartments. There's already a crowd gathered of centaurs, fauns, giants, nymphs, and agents. A halo of fire sprites circle overhead showering everyone with flashes of changing colors. A band of fauns play an upbeat tune on their flutes, oboes, harps, and even one electric guitar while a giant pounds on the largest drums I've ever seen.

"Oh, heck no," Charlie says as he comes to a stop beside me. "I don't dance."

"You mean won't," I correct.

"The difference is?"

"Anyone can dance. Only the scared won't dance. You're not scared are you, Charlie?"

He levels a flat stare at me as Hawk pulls Genna to the front of the crowd, the pair of them giggling the whole way.

"I think I'll just . . . sit over here," Witty says. His frown deepens and he starts to wheel away.

"Witty!" I call after him. "You do a great robot, come on!"

He waves me off over his shoulder and heads to the edge of the field.

Charlie starts to walk after him. "I think I should—"

"Oh, no you don't." I grab his arm and haul him up front before he can port away.

"Phoenix," he groans.

"I'll make you a deal," I say without letting go of his arm. "You stay and dance for a while and I'll take you on a trip to a bookstore."

He heaves a sigh but stops arguing. We zig-zag through the dancers until we reach Hawk and Genna grooving directly in front of the band. A group of elves beside them perform their own well-rehearsed routine.

Charlie shouts in my ear to be heard. "I can't dance next to them. I'll look like an idiot."

"Oh, I can help with that."

I start flailing my arms and move in jerky, spastic movements that are in no way with the beat. It's my best impression of an octopus on dry land. Charlie chokes on a laugh.

"There!" I announce and do a very terrible robot. "Now you won't look dumb." He still doesn't move and glances between my seizure-like moves and Hawk twirling Genna. "Come on. Show me your moves, Jaeger."

He leans from one foot to the other in a gentle sway

without moving his arms or anything. His helplessness makes me want to laugh but I bite back my smile. Taking pity on him, I stop my horrible dancing and lightly grab his wrists. I position his arms into a loose bend at his sides before mimicking his pose.

"Okay, easy side to side," I instruct. "Just follow me."

I step side to side while jogging my arms to the rhythm of the beat. Charlie's brow draws together as he studies my pose and does his best to copy me. His concentration and dedication to something so simple tickles a laugh out of me.

"Sorry," I say. "Your intensity is adorable."

His head snaps up. "I'm not adorable."

"Shut up, you big teddy bear. Watch me."

He frowns but keeps mirroring the steps as I teach Charlie a few simple dance moves. Eventually he starts to loosen up, especially when Hawk and Genna join us and we form a square. We throw in more moves and Charlie starts to smile and laugh—I don't think he even realizes he's doing it.

I don't know how long we stay there being innocent and carefree, laughing and working up a sweat in our junior agent uniforms. Thirst gets us after what feels like hours and we disperse from the field in search of refreshments. We find Witty sulking around Old Man Two's so we eat a quick meal and move off to the arcade to challenge each other to pinball and Donkey Kong. I haven't felt this carefree in ages. Even when it starts to grow late, Underground remains alive with energy as everyone stays up to enjoy the weeklong celebration. We catch a movie, head to the stadium to watch a display put on by the fire sprites, and then wander our way to Witty's apartment to watch him and Genna duke it out on his video games. After she scores a victory, Witty passes the controller off to Hawk who's demanding a chance to beat her at Super Kart.

Witty rolls off into the darkness of his apartment and disappears into the racks of old computer equipment. There's a significant hunch to his posture that drives concern to the forefront of my mind. I slip around Charlie sitting on the floor and find Witty unscrewing a part from the open skeleton of a computer. I lean against the table facing him and brace my hands on the edge behind me. His eyes slide to me briefly but he doesn't say anything.

"Are you okay?" I ask. The others remain oblivious as they jeer at each other loudly and the sound of squealing tires in the video game fills the living room.

Witty takes his precious time pulling what I think is a hard drive out of the computer and starts unscrewing its casing. "Yeah, I'm—I'm good. I'm fine. Yup."

"You're a really terrible liar."

With unexpected force he slams the hard drive onto the desk and curls his hands into fists as he stares at the hunk of metal and circuits. Surprised and unsure of the reason behind his reaction, I remain perfectly still as he slowly uncurls his fingers and hangs his head. He lets out a long, deep sigh that sounds like his very soul is leaving him.

"We've been friends a long time, haven't we?" he asks quietly with his head bowed, forehead nearly touching the desk.

"Yes, we have," I say in equal tone. What's going on with him?

He lifts his blue eyes to me and I notice bags under them.

"If I could use my legs and run around with you guys, would you have liked me better?"

Stunned, my mouth hangs open as I consider the thoughts he must harbor behind such a loaded and sensitive question. I can't imagine being in his position. I've never been incapacitated in such way, so limited in physical ability. So many things I take for granted are things out of his reach that he will never be able to experience. My face burns as I think of how obsessed I've been with my own abilities and being discovered for being too powerful when Witty all this time has just wanted to lace up his shoes and take a walk.

"Witty, I—"

"It's okay," he says too quickly and grabs parts around his desk to shove into a pile with such force I'm pretty sure he's going to break most of them.

I grab his arm to stop him from demolishing his precious electronics and make him look at me. "Witty."

"What?" he snaps.

"There is not, and never has been, anything wrong with you. I would have liked you just fine even if you had no limbs at all and the face of a gargoyle."

The darkness in his expression lifts and his arm becomes limp in my grip. His whole body sags in his wheelchair and he says so softly I almost don't hear, "We'll always be friends, right?"

"Of course we will, Aaron."

Instead of seeming happier or appeased, he nods to himself, wheels away into his bedroom, and shuts the door. I take a moment to digest what just happened before walking numbly back to join the others. Genna's eyes follow me and I know full well that she heard everything. She's not the only one. While Hawk diverts his attention purposefully, Charlie studies me like an interesting specimen. I get the feeling that every time I do anything, he finds it grossly unexpected or intriguing like a scientist testing lab rats. Since it's attention I don't want or need, I duck out of the apartment with my head bowed.

I wander aimlessly but find most of Underground too lively with the festivities. In search of a quiet spot—not the apartment with the other roommates and the possibility of running into Jefferson—I eventually turn into the water sprite cavern. It's dark here but bluish light glimmers from the water sprite pool to cast a mesmerizing display on the damp walls of the cavern. I creep to the darkest shadows and take a seat against the cold floor, tucking my knees up to my chest and letting the roar of the river and the sprite lights hypnotize me into oblivion.

Witty's sentiments won't leave me be. The trials must have been the catalyst for this outpouring of frustration on his part. How can I blame him? I hate being on the sidelines and he's been doing it his whole life, *forced* to by terrible circumstances. We both lost our parents but he also lost a part of his freedom. Guilt chews away at my insides. I haven't been the best friend I could have. I should have tried to include him more or do something to right the wrong done to him.

But who am I kidding? I can't fix anything nowadays. I tilt my head back against the rough cavern wall and close my eyes.

I startle when someone takes a seat beside me. I open my eyes expecting it to be Hawk but find Charlie settling on the floor, his long legs stretched out and hands clasped very relaxed on top of his abdomen. He doesn't look my way or even acknowledge I'm there but watches the lights on the opposite wall and ceiling as I had.

"What are you doing?" I grumble.

He turns his head and looks shocked. "Oh, I had no idea you were here."

"Right."

"I came to watch the lights. Obviously." He gestures to the wall.

I roll my eyes. "I don't want to talk."

"Shhhh, I'm trying to watch the spectacle," he whispers. "I also enjoy comfortable silence."

He remembered—at the hospital I confessed I didn't want to be alone and he stayed with me. He hasn't forgotten. I bite my lip and watch the lights hoping the darkness can hide the furious blush on my face.

I don't know how long we sit there as the water sprites continue to play in their pool and practice for the aetherball tournament tossing around glowing glass spheres that are the source of the light. It ends up being too long because my legs and back are now freezing from the cold walls. Charlie shifts uncomfortably next to me as well but doesn't say anything.

"Butt numb?" I whisper.

"Well, gee, that's sort of a personal question."

I choke on a laugh and hide it behind my hands. "We should probably get up and move around before our limbs start to fall off."

"I couldn't agree more."

We get up stiffly, offering each other a hand and rising to our feet on wooden legs. Together we exit the water sprite cavern and walk to the colonnade where the cherry trees are illuminated by the sleeping embers of fire spirtes in pedestals lining the walkway. It's beautiful here.

"I gotta be honest," I say. "I'm surprised you followed me."

"Well, you sort of left me alone with Genna and Hawk," he grumbles. "I certainly wasn't going to stick around for that awkwardness."

"Feeling like a third-wheel?"

He gives me a sideways look. "You don't around them?"

I shrug. "Haven't thought about it much."

"Huh."

Before this conversation can veer further into the study of Hawk's personal life and obvious crush on Jefferson's daughter, we walk into the market and are sidetracked by new merchants setting up for the following day. Underground usually becomes stuffed with creatures coming in from the outlying areas to watch the aetherball tournament and partake in the festivities. It's pretty late but they continue to prepare their stands, colorful tents, and boxes of goods. While Charlie stops to peruse a nymph's partially setup book stand, I continue to amble along the line of tents being erected along the backside of the square.

A peculiar gray tent tucked behind the others garners my attention. There are no displays being put out or anything to invite customers in. A single old woman, hooded and cloaked, bends over a washing board as she works on a long tangle of white linen stained with splotches of red. Blood.

No one else in the vicinity pays any attention to her. In fact, their eyes seem to pass from the purple jumbo tent on her left to the food stand on her right without giving her a passing thought. Intrigued, my feet carry me towards the washer woman. She scrubs and scrubs at that thing, heaving a sigh between efforts. The task seems too much for her as she hunches over and takes a stuttering inhale as if fighting off sobs.

"Are you okay?" I ask. The woman freezes with her large hood hiding her face in its depths. "Do you . . . do you want some help with that?"

Her sigh reverberates through my bones with the heaviness of it. "That is kind of you, dear child, but there are none that may help me." Her words are thick with a Scottish accent.

Pale, luminous eyes shine dully in the shadows of the hood and she runs a wrinkled finger along the back of my hand. I don't move. There's something very strange about this woman apart from her appearance. The aura of her magic is like a spider's web, latching onto everything around her with strands snapping off and latching onto new things. No, not things. *People*. I feel the gentle touch of her magic from where she touched my hand and left a tiny thread behind connecting her magic to me.

"What are you?" I breathe.

"I am the washer. I am the weeper. I am the twist in the threads of fate."

A memory from my time in Scotland surfaces, about a strange creature that lived there, and my hands tremble. The woman returns to scrubbing at the blood stains in the linen.

"What are you washing?" I ask hardly above a whisper.

"Tis a burial shroud for a poor soul soon doomed to die."

I know what she is. Tawnee had told me about her. Genna had searched for her at the Castle of Eilean Donan. Dasc wanted her for information. The lamia had tried to capture her.

The washer woman from Scotland who knows who's about to die.

It's the bean nighe.

29

The world flits around us as if we're in a different dimension or another universe as I watch the old woman wash the stained burial shroud—for someone soon doomed to die. Is that the reason I'm the only one who seems to be able to see her? Is it because I am the one doomed to die? Or is it someone close to me? My brother. Or a friend.

I remember Tawnee mentioning that if you're kind to a bean nighe, they'll give you information. I need to remember all of my manners and then some if I want the answers I'm terrified to have.

"You were born in a thunderstorm," the bean nighe says as she takes a respite from scrubbing. "An omen some might call it that you were brought about in the wrath of a storm. Perhaps it was only meant to foreshadow your life." She turns her eerie luminous eyes to me. "Or perhaps a spark of that storm lingered in your veins to draw the storm clouds around you."

A frown forms on my face without consideration. Do powerful magical beings have to speak in riddles all the time? Can't they say things plain every once in a while?

Crap, I'm being crabby in my head already. Be polite, Phoenix. Politeness will win answers.

"I didn't know I was born in a storm," I say, the only thing I can think of. Stringing words together isn't my strong suit.

"Your brother as well—the two magnets that push and pull, that drive the storm onward."

That sounds ominous. "Oh." I wring my hands as she takes another pass at the shroud. I can't take my eyes off it. Who is it for? Unable to stop myself, I say, "I'm sorry, but I don't understand. Could you repeat that, please?"

She cackles and wrings out part of the shroud. "Most of those I talk to seeking wisdom nod and bow in fake pretense of understanding. Too proud to ask for clarity. Too scared to ask too many questions. They leave and spend the next week thinking they know all the answers until the friend they thought *wouldn't* die falls off a cliff or drowns in a bathtub."

I blink and recoil in my surprise.

The bean nighe cackles some more but the sound changes from the harsh rasp of an old lady to the harmonious laughter of a young woman. When her strange eyes pin me again, her entire face has changed as if she pulled off a mask. The deep wrinkles, paleness, and signs of aging have disappeared. She's beautiful with rosy cheeks and long curls of golden hair to frame her soft features.

"I think I like you," she says, the voice stripped of its years to a youthful tenor. She draws a stool around from behind and sets it before me. "Come. Sit with me."

Entranced, I numbly take the offered stool and sit across from her. She draws back her hood to unleash the rest of her golden curls and dries off her hands on the edges of her dark cloak. Magic sure is something, isn't it?

She stretches out a hand to lightly grip my chin unabashed and studies my face as she purses her lips.

"Such a strange creature you are," she murmurs.

I could say the same but—manners. "I, uh, thanks? Thank you. That's kind of you."

"Yes. Very strange."

"May I ask you a question?"

"You may," she answers with a dip of her head and releases my chin to curl her hands together in her lap.

Okay, now we're getting somewhere. "Why are you here?" The last anyone knew, the only bean nighe seen recently was in Scotland. She's come a long ways from home. There must be a reason for it.

"I felt you at Eilean Donan. I felt your storm, saw the threads that bind you. I knew that I must speak to such a lass."

So she *was* at Eilean Donan, the very same bean nighe Genna had been seeking to find out how to kill Dasc. Cleary she had been able to escape and follow me here somehow. With her knack of only being seen by those she wishes, as I presume, I'm surprised Genna or the lamia thought they'd be able to find her at all.

"Is there something in particular you wanted to speak to me about?" I ask and a swell of dread roils through my gut.

A creature who knows death is not someone I want interested in me in particular.

"Death comes, dear child," she says. "It rises on alabaster wings and will sweep across the world. It will drive you, it will shape you, it will break you. Out of the ashes you will rise, my Phoenix, and become wrath and ruin. Such spirit. Such a strange, unrelenting thing, you are."

Death will make me. It will break me. Not words I want to hear. Not words I can understand. Words that drive fear into the heart of me.

"A storm comes," she continues. "And by the end, the shrouds of the dead will cover these halls."

"I thought you said I was a storm—or I draw the storm or—" I whisper as I voice the fear of my comprehension. "You don't mean . . ." She can't possibly be saying that *I* will be the cause of such death.

She doesn't reply. Her creepy eyes bore into me. I swallow.

I'm so distracted by trying to solve her riddles and figure out if I'm going to be some whirlwind of destruction that the gift of the bean nighe nearly passes me by. But it's an opportunity I can't afford to pass up.

"Can you please tell me the fates of a few people?"

She smiles but it's not a warm sort of thing. It's like death itself acknowledging my foolishness in seeking things I shouldn't know. "I would caution you against fate. Such knowledge can be your undoing if you let it consume you. Knowing the future before its time is a dangerous burden."

"But I need to know. Please."

Blinking rapidly, silent tears slip down her beautiful face. Compelled by such sadness, I reach out and grasp her hand to comfort her. It's what Hawk would do. She lays her other hand on top of mine and leans in closer.

"Knowledge of the fates you seek would only twist you onto paths you are not meant to follow. It is not by your hand that vengeance shall be redeemed."

"I don't under—"

She clenches onto my hand so tightly it actually hurts. Those luminous eyes plead with me as she hurries on, "Listen to the Worldly Queen. She is not wrong about the deaths in Faunus and elsewhere but such animosity sprung from those acts breeds desperation. And desperation spawns reckless ventures. The children of Lycaon will not sit idly by."

"Wait, are you saying—you mean the attack at Faunus, at Paris, at the Vaults—those weren't the werewolves?" So Terra—Scholar, the Worldly Queen, whatever else she's known as—was right in her suspicions. Someone else is behind the attacks and casting the blame on the werewolves. But the werewolves aren't going to "sit idly by" while they're thrown under the stampede. They're going to act.

"But what are they—" I begin but am cut off once more.

"Remember this," she says and yanks me forward so our faces are mere inches apart as she whispers, "Some sacrifices are too monstrous to bear but bear them you must. When the water rises, remember who saved you and who must be saved. Only you will be able to open the way."

Flabbergasted, I lean away trying to wrap my head around the nonsense coming out of her mouth. It sounds deeply profound and also goes right over my head.

"But I—you—water—*what?*"

An abrupt and loud commotion in the market square

makes me swivel my head. The second I take my eyes off the bean nighe, I feel her grip on my hand disappear. When I look back, she, her tent, the washing board and shroud, have all vanished. I stand and the stool I had been sitting on vanishes too.

"No," I plead on a sharp exhale. I spin in a circle but there's no trace of the bean nighe anywhere. Angry, I shout to the emptiness around me, "I don't understand!"

"Phoenix?" From between the tents, Charlie jogs over with a look of concern. "I've been looking everywhere for you. Where did you go?"

"I—I was . . ." I want to gesture to the tent to explain but I can't since it's gone.

"Come on." Without warning, he slips his fingers through mine and we're teleported to the edge of the square where a crowd has gathered. All eyes are on a television mounted above a plaque bearing the names of agents killed in the line of duty. It only comes on during emergency broadcasts from the IMS. Seeing it broadcasting is a very bad sign. Instead of some news reporter like you might see in an ordinary report, a Spartan—made obvious by the black matte armor and gear she's currently wearing—sits in front of the camera holding a piece of paper in her hands. She's a familiar face, and I realize she was the pilot from the Spartan team that came to our rescue in Moose Lake.

Whatever she's saying, the crowd doesn't like it.

"What are we going to do about it?" someone yells and drowns out part of the Spartan's report.

"Shut it!" another replies. "I'm trying to listen!"

Agreeing with the second opinion, I drag Charlie along with me closer to the front of the crowd in order to hear the rest of the emergency report. They'll no doubt put it on a loop to make sure everyone hears this important message—whatever it is.

I pick out the sound of the Spartan's report above the angered and fevered murmuring of the agents, elves, unicorns, centaurs, fauns, and other creatures gathered.

"It's important that we remain calm," the Spartan says. "Security measures are being put in place temporarily until the situation can be resolved. More updates will follow as we get new information." The message ends and the Spartan is replaced by a revolving image of the IMS symbol.

"We'll be next!" a deep baritone thunders.

A clamor rises around me. "I'm getting out of here!"

"Now, just hold on a moment—"

"You heard her!"

I grab Charlie's arm and bring my face close to his in order to be heard. "What's going on?"

"I'm not sure. Hold on."

I don't know if he means literally or to wait for him. Apparently he does mean literally because he ports us out of the middle of the crowd to a group of other junior agents gathered on the outskirts. Amanda Fry swivels in our direction upon our sudden appearance.

"I take it you heard?" she says and her eyes are hard on me, not glued to Charlie for once. I don't take that as a good sign either.

"We didn't actually," Charlie says. "What's going on?"

"They'll be replaying it. Just wait for it."

None of the others care to elaborate either. I'm thinking of the worst possible scenarios in my head without anyone to give me the truth. I just had a bean nighe indicate that I might be the cause of a multitude of deaths. What if that broadcast had something to do with me? The way Amanda and the others are staring or avoiding looking at me, I'd say that's a pretty solid guess.

Charlie and I stalk away from the ever so unhelpful junior agents.

"Well, we aren't going to hear over that," he says and gestures to the angry mob in front of the emergency broadcast system.

"We can catch it at Witty's," I say and keep ahold of his arm. "His equipment will be picking it up."

Without another word, we vanish from what had moments before been an area of festive cheer but has turned into a mad house. What on earth is going on? I've already got enough confusion running through my head with what the bean nighe laid on me. But perhaps this is all connected?

We make it back to Witty's apartment in record time thanks to Charlie's particular ability. Without even knocking on the door we barge in to find the others gathered on the couch and glued to the television. The video game has been replaced by the Spartan's announcement. I catch the last few lines as the message ends again. Hawk and Genna are stony faced but Witty looks fearfully to us.

"Did you hear?" he whispers.

"No. What's going on?" I ask.

Witty waves us in without a word and we stand next to him as the message queues up again. The Spartan reappears.

"This is Spartan Alona Ravenspell with the Special North American Taskforce," she begins. "Two hours ago we received a code black from the Winnipeg Division in

Canada. Spartan teams responded and cleared the area. The division had taken heavy damage from explosives and we are still confirming those injured or killed in this action. However, the assailants left a message behind claiming responsibility for the attack. They have been identified as the same splinter group of werewolves that had previously assaulted Faunus and facilities in Paris, Prague, Tokyo, and Edinburgh. They also left indications that they plan to attack other facilities in the near future. Therefore, we are urging residents at all secured sites to keep alert and report any suspicious activity to your local IMS. It's important that we remain calm. Security measures are being put in place temporarily until the situation can be resolved. More updates will follow as we get new information."

The message ends and the tension is palatable in the silence left behind.

Witty is the first to voice what I'm sure we're all thinking. "What kind of security measures?"

His question is answered by a well-timed knock on the door. When no one moves to answer it, the knocking becomes insistently aggressive. Witty is half way to it when the door flings open and Jefferson storms inside. As usual, his eyes go immediately to his daughter. There's a backpack slung over his shoulder and he's as taut as a bowstring.

"We're leaving," he says without preamble and waves his daughter over. Genna rises and meets him halfway across the room but doesn't leave even with him tugging on her arm.

"Dad, what's going on?"

"I'm not going to let them take you away from me."

"Woah, woah," Hawk interrupts and springs to his feet.

All of us gather around Jefferson in fear and confusion. "Who's coming to take Genna?"

Jefferson gives my brother the dagger eyes. "I don't have time for this. Genna, let's go."

She continues to linger and resists his attempts to drag her out of the room. Before anyone can move anywhere, a force of IMS agents stream through the open door into Witty's apartment until the place is much too cramped. Our group of friends bunches in together, Hawk and Genna wordlessly being shoved into the center for their own protection. This looks bad. This looks *real* bad.

The IMS agents—carrying unholstered bio-mech guns I notice—part to allow someone to enter the room. Draco rounds the door with a flourish of his black coat and his focus hones in on Genna behind Jefferson's partially outstretched arms as if to shield her. The blood freezes in my veins as his waves of energy push against me relentless and cruel. I don't know why the IMS agents are here. They aren't needed with Draco around.

"I'm here to collect you," Draco says and it's unmistakable his words are meant for Genna. He hasn't taken his eyes off of her or spared anyone else so much as a glance since he entered the room.

"You aren't taking her anywhere," Jefferson growls. Despite the fact that Jefferson's threatening one of the most powerful beings on the planet, I actually feel Draco should be afraid. Jefferson practically hums with suppressed rage. Out of the corner of my eye, I see Genna place a hand between her father's shoulder blades. Whether to comfort him or herself, I'm not sure. Perhaps both. Even though a majestic dragon is coming to "collect her," whatever that means, Genna looks resolute and unafraid. I can't say I don't admire her for it given the fact my own heart is racing.

Although my typical reaction is to fight, everything in me is screaming to flee. My hands tremble as adrenaline takes over. Hawk's fingers slip through mine and I hold on to him. If they're here for Genna—if they're going after all werewolves—then I have to be ready to fight for him in case they want to take my brother too.

"It wasn't a request," Draco says and takes menacing steps forward until he's nearly nose to nose with Jefferson. When Jefferson doesn't move aside, Draco gently extends a hand and, easy as you please, slides him out of the away as if he were moving aside a curtain.

I don't make the smartest move. Before Draco can reach Genna, I step between them so the majestic dragon is a mere breath away from my face. I look into those frosty eyes that I had once held in awe, once revered as a storm of righteous power. Now all I see is bitterness, rage, and not an ounce of pity. What happened to him during Echidna's reign broke him and he pieced himself back together in all the wrong places. He's supposed to be a force for good, not a terror unto himself.

"What little leverage you have, Phoenix Mason," he says hardly above a whisper, "is of no use to you here."

"Why are you taking her?" I ask and refuse to be intimidated. What a stupid instinct. Of course I should be intimidated.

"I don't have to answer you."

"So you just waltz in wherever you want and take

whatever you want without reason? I thought the IMS didn't work like that."

His eyes narrow but the agents surrounding us swap glances. At least my words seem to resonate with them if not the angry dragon in command.

"I'm instituting safety measures," he says in a flat tone that suggests he really, *really* doesn't want to be cowed by me. But he's a leader. The agents look up to him. The agency wouldn't be anything without him. He has to maintain his image if he wants to keep us under his thumb with the pretense of a benevolent leader.

"And taking Genna is a safety measure?"

"If you want further answers, speak to the director, but she will come with me regardless."

Jefferson joins me in a barricade between Draco and Genna. It's the first time in what feels like ages that we've sided together as a team, but Genna herself pushes past us.

"I'll cooperate," she says. "As I always have. I don't want to cause trouble."

"What noble intentions," Draco says with the slightest bit of a sneer.

He leads the way out of the apartment and Genna follows. The rest of the agents trail after them, forcing us to wait until they've cleared out before we can follow.

"I'm not losing her again," Jefferson says.

"You won't. Not if I can help it. Hawk—"

"On it," my brother says without even knowing what I'm about to ask. He jogs with Jefferson after Draco and Genna heading towards the penitent cells while I tug on Charlie's arm.

"Let's go to the director," I say.

He hesitates. "You can't just barge in on the director whenever you please."

"Trust me. He'll let me in."

Witty rolls to a stop beside us. "What about me?"

"Find out whatever you can about these 'security measures' and what Draco's up to."

"Okay," he says in a small voice and doesn't argue.

I grab Charlie's forearm and we port the distance from the apartments to headquarters in the space of two seconds if that. I've gotten used to jumping around with him so I don't need nearly as much time to reorient myself but it still takes a moment to take in the black walls suddenly before me.

There's a commotion here as well. Another crowd has gathered as residents bombard the agents with questions about what's going on, if Underground is going to be hit next, if they should leave to a safer area, what *is* a safer place. There has never been a frenzy like this before. They must be scared with the last attack having been so close.

Thanks to Charlie, we manage to circumvent the crowd entirely and port inside the open door to the foyer. It's not much better here. Instead of civilians in a panic, there's a swarm of agents moving to and fro, rushing down hallways with fresh intel, others heading to the armory, and a few Spartans I recognize already geared up and running out to their transport. Charlie and I squeeze up against the wall to let a group by.

The receptionist snaps her fingers and waves a hand over her desk to get our attention. Her face in grim and her hair frazzled. "You two! What are you doing here?"

"I need to speak with Director Knox," I shout over the noise of a group of talkative agents hurrying past.

"He's in an emergency council meeting. You'll have to wait for news like the rest."

"But—"

The phone at her desk rings and she makes a shooing motion at us before picking up the call and ignoring us.

Charlie leans in to be heard. "I told you."

"I need to talk to him. Now, before they do something stupid."

"Seriously? How big has your ego gotten that you think you can order the director and IMS around? They know what they're doing. They aren't going to do anything *stupid.*"

I glare at him. He can be such a jerk sometimes. "Because I have information about the attack, about them all."

"How?"

"I just spoke with a bean nighe, that's how. Remember when you couldn't find me at the market?" I gesture wide to the door behind us and nearly hit another agent coming in. "That's where I was. It told me the truth about the attacks and the IMS is about to hunt down the wrong people. If we don't get in there now, we're going to be too late."

At my final words, something changes in his face. The doubt disappears and his eyes grow hard.

"I'll never be too late again," he mumbles under his breath, takes me by the arm, and we move through space and time to land next to the black arch in the middle of headquarters to look on the chaos in the building through the windowed hallways.

The second I catch my breath I say, "The council meetings are held over—"

"I know."

We vanish a second time, and a third, and a fourth, until we're on the opposite side of headquarters and head down a slanted tunnel to the level beneath the arch and its courtyard. As expected, the massive iron wrought doors are guarded by no less than four agents hefting phase-repeaters. They spot us and one immediately makes to head us off. We can't very well teleport inside the room because Charlie doesn't have a direct line of sight. I'm not sure what to do. The guards make it very clear that we are in a restricted area and not allowed entrance. I try to plead with them and end up causing a ruckus as we have a row. I'm pretty sure we're about to be arrested when one of the massive doors cracks open and a centaur sticks his head out.

Charlie leans to the side to get a look into the room, mutters, "We're so getting arrested for this," and we port past the guards into the heart of the council chambers.

30

The conversation taking place a second ago dies in an instant as we appear in the middle of where we're not supposed to be. We stand at the center of a great circle table made of the same stone as the portal arch in the courtyard above. Scattered across it are urgent memos, classified documents, aerial surveillance photos, and numerous laptops cracked open in front of the four council members seated before us. A ginormous collection of televisions covers the far wall where even more startled council members join in from wherever they are remotely. Fauns, centaurs, elves, a few unicorns, a single giant, a gryphon in gleaming armor, and two nymphs stare at their uninvited guests that have rudely interrupted this private council meeting.

Director Knox wheels about from where he stands in front of the screens to find Charlie and me still grasping each other's arms after having teleported inside. I have no words to adequately describe the anger on his face.

"What is this?" the elf council member for Underground squeaks and stands up in his chair to plant both hands on the tabletop. The centaur and faun delegates seem equally as perplexed by our presence. Director Knox on the other hand looks ready to kill us.

The guards burst in a second later with their phase-repeaters pointed at us. I tighten my grip on Charlie's arm and he does the same to me as we consider our options.

"You better have a darn good reason for trespassing in here," the director says in a barely restrained voice. "Regardless, you'll both be spending some quality time in the penitent cells."

I gulp. Charlie gives me a flat stare as if to say he agrees with the director. I can't say I blame him. He took the risk of bringing me here. I owe him.

"Sir, I have urgent information about the recent attack and the ones in Europe," I announce loud enough for everyone—including the remote link council members—to hear.

"News that you somehow learned this very second after Genna Barnes was put in custody," he says sharply. He doesn't believe me, does he? He thinks I'm fabricating a story to help her out.

Unable to stop myself, I level a glare at him. "I just spoke with the bean nighe."

"Excuse me?"

Despite his clear mistrust, several of the council members on the screens behind him lean closer to the camera. The unicorn's monitor flashes to alert everyone that he's entering a comment which appears beneath his image—he can't speak it himself as unicorns speak with telepathy and that's a little difficult to do through a monitor.

I want to hear this, is the unicorn's message. The other council members nod and the faun in the room points it out to Director Knox. Still scowling, the director crosses his arms and gestures reluctantly for me to continue.

"Genna had been tracking one in Scotland, remember? Well, apparently the bean nighe saw me at the Castle of Eileen Donan and followed me to the States to deliver a message. I just spoke with her in the market like fifteen minutes ago."

"Why you?" One of the nymphs with green hair and paler green skin folds her hands under her chin wherever she is remotely. "Why was the bean nighe so intent on speaking with *you*?"

The bean nighe's words ring in my head. *I felt your storm, saw the threads that bind you. I knew that I must speak to such a lass.*

"I—I'm not sure. I guess because I've been so involved with everything going on, with Genna, with the werewolves, with Dasc."

Charlie's grip on my arm tightens painfully and I wince before he lets his hand finally drop to his side. I keep my grip on his upper arm to ground myself. It's intimidating facing the entire United Council while trying to keep secrets at the same time. I want to know I'm not here alone.

"And what did she tell you?" the nymph asks.

"She confirmed that the attacks weren't by the werewolves. That someone else was setting them up to take the blame."

"Who?" the nymph asks at the same time Director Knox says, "Confirmed? What do you mean confirmed?"

"Well, uh . . ." The bean nighe had confirmed the suspicions of Scholar—Terra—a majestic class dragon betrayed and in hiding. A huge bomb of a secret if ever there was one. Think, Phoenix. You can sell a lie better if it has a twist of truth in it. "Genna didn't think the attacks made sense if it was werewolves. She didn't think they were behind the attacks."

The director steps to the edge of the table and plants his hands on top of loose sheets of paper. "And who, exactly, is behind the attacks?"

I lick my lips and prepare myself for a bad reaction. "Echidna."

After gasps and shocked murmurs from the council members, a heavy silence drapes the chamber and starts to smother me. My cheeks burn hot as I realize they don't believe me. Echidna's an old dead myth, a monster smote and gone. It's like I'm heaping whatever sleights I can on an imaginary ghost. I have to prove myself somehow but I can't reveal what I've learned from Scholar. I need to protect her. But I have to do *something*.

"Genna said a war was coming with Echidna," I continue in the void. "When we first brought her in, she said that was what Dasc was preparing them for."

Director Knox pinches the bridge of his nose and lets go an irritated sigh. "Was there ever a bean nighe, Mason?"

I blink. "What?"

"I realize you're just trying to protect your friend but—"

"*No!*" I shout. I find Charlie's hand on my arm again, reeling me back in. "I'm telling you the truth. The bean nighe from Scotland came here to warn me that death was coming and the wrong people were going to be blamed!"

"Then you were lied to."

"Why would she lie?"

"Mason, we have some of the assailants in custody."

My breath catches. "What?"

"The Spartan team got there in time to capture a few stragglers making a break for it." He jabs his pointer finger at me. "And the *only* reason you are learning this is so you stop this ridiculous nonsense. This information does not leave this room. Do I make myself clear?"

"Yes," I say in a small voice and Charlie repeats me in equal tenor.

"They were werewolves. In fact, one of them was Dr. Rosewell, one of your missing persons from Moose Lake if I'm correct."

Ice crackles in my veins. No. That's not possible. "But the bean nighe—sir, it said that pinning the blame on the werewolves would make them desperate so they must be retaliating!"

"*Enough!*" he thunders and swipes a hand through the air like he's physically cutting my argument in half. "I have a city to keep from panicking, a population of werewolves to rein in, and people to protect. Whatever leverage you think you have, Mason, you don't. I'll deal with you later. Now, *out!*"

He gestures over our shoulders and the guards surround us. Realizing that it's useless and not a soul is going to listen to me, my shoulders droop and I crawl over the top of the table to meet the guards. Charlie and I don't teleport this time. I think they might shoot us if we did. So, like captive criminals, we're escorted out of the council chambers. One of the guards radios for some jailers to come pick us up. We wait with heads bowed as a gargoyle and centaur arrive to escort us to the penitent cells. I start breathing hard just thinking about those cells and run my hands through my hair in agitation.

"I'm so sorry," I whisper to Charlie. "I didn't mean for this to happen."

He's quiet for a long time and I'm afraid he hates me. Again. We walk along and I try to avoid eye contact with the crowds gathered outside headquarters and the patrols we pass on our way to the cells.

"You didn't tell them everything, did you?" he says softly. "The bean nighe told you more."

At least he's not questioning if I actually talked to a bean nighe, not like the director and council members. I'll take solace in that.

"She said the shrouds of the dead will cover these halls. And I—" I worry my lower lip and avoid looking at him directly. I can't possibly tell him everything but there's a part of me that wants confirmation that my fears are unjustified.

"Phoenix."

Our eyes meet.

"I'm scared," I whisper. "I think it's going to be my fault."

His eyebrows knit together and cast shadows over his pale green eyes as we step into the entrance of the penitent cells. "Why would you think that? Did she actually say that?"

"Not directly, no, but *you* try talking straight with a bean nighe some time." I cross my arms over my chest as we wait for the guards to exchange words and open the doors for us. "Stupid things have to be so freaking cryptic about everything."

"But you know for sure that she was saying the werewolves weren't behind the attacks?"

Do I?

"Of course," I say without hesitation regardless.

The doors part and I walk in, not as an interrogator or friend of the director, but that unruly child I had been years ago—except this time I'm getting a much worse punishment. We follow the centaur and gargoyle past the interrogation rooms I've become so familiar with and towards another set of doors leading to the active penitent cells where the horror of their magic will be unleashed on us for trying to do the right thing.

A door slams open, angry voices bicker back and forth, and a group shuffles into the hall behind us. We momentarily pause to witness the commotion as a couple of guards haul Jefferson out between them. He shrugs them off with a few choice swear words, straightens the collar of his shirt, and then spots us further down the hall.

"What's going on?" he says loud enough for everyone to hear.

One of the guards, a burly looking man, puts a hand on Jefferson's arm. "That's none of your—"

Jefferson yanks out of the agent's grasp. "It *is* my business, now get off me."

He storms away from his escorts against their protests. There's no sign of Hawk or Witty anywhere. Did they get kicked out too? Or are they under house arrest like Charlie and me? The knot in my stomach tightens. Where are they?

"What are you two doing here?" Jefferson asks in his usual gruff manner.

"Got arrested. You?"

He startles. "Genna's being interrogated. What do you mean you were arrested?"

"I thought you didn't care."

Something changes in his dour expression—if he hadn't been chewing me out for the last month, I might have guessed it was regret. But no. That couldn't possibly be.

"Why were you arrested, Phoenix?"

"Because I was trying to protect your daughter and the rest of the werewolves."

He stares wide-eyed.

One of the guards helpfully interjects, "These two trespassed in the middle of an emergency council meeting. Come on."

I turn away from Jefferson to follow the centaur into the area of cells where poor souls go to have every wrong they've committed shoved in their face. The doors swing shut behind us leaving Jefferson and his own escort behind.

Tremors start in my hands so I take a slow breath and momentarily close my eyes to prepare myself for what's about to happen next. When I open them again to face the consequences, I find Charlie preparing himself in the same way. He catches my eye and we both nod to each other. We can take this. We did the right thing and we'll get through this. The centaur leads me to the first open door and the gargoyle has Charlie enter the next one down. The door closes behind me and traps me in the white room. The familiar, bitter taste of magic sinks its claws into my subconscious and I take a seat against the wall, curl my legs in towards my chest, and brace my head between my knees as the torments of my past come back to haunt me.

I don't know how long I remain curled up there telling myself none of it is real—even though everything was very much real to someone at some point—before the door opens. I expect the guard but instead find Draco in all his black fashion glory.

Without preamble he asks, "You spoke with the bean nighe? It was here?"

I rise to my feet, shrugging off the horrid sensation of a sword going through my chest again, and step closer. "I did. It was."

"And?"

"And I passed on the warning it gave me to the director and council."

"What did it tell you, precisely?"

His slit dragon eyes emit a faint glow with the force of the gaze he levels at me. That, along with the echo of the penitent cell's magic, make me shiver.

"Does it matter?" I say. "No one believes me."

"I am not them."

What is he looking for? I'm sure he would want to find the bean nighe himself to have a chat with the strange creature—but he didn't ask where it was. He wants to know what it said to *me*.

A breathless question escapes me. "Why?"

"Because you mentioned Echidna to Director Knox."

I swallow. "I did."

"And because I take the safety of my charges very seriously. The people of this city are under my protection."

The ghost of a sword through my chest comes at me

again and I clutch at my sternum. Draco notices and makes a wide gesture to the open door. I quickly escape the nightmare room and the phantom pain bleeds out of me. I take several deep breaths to free my lungs from the iron grasp they had been in.

Draco shuts the cell door and then practically pins me up against the wall of the hallway.

"What did she say?" he asks again.

Surely telling Draco won't hurt if I leave out any mention of Scholar. She herself said that he's not wholly evil or good. He did found the hidden sanctuaries and has kept the legendary world safe for centuries. I believe him when he says he takes the safety of this place seriously. So do I.

"She said a storm was coming, that these halls would be filled with the shrouds of the dead, and that the werewolves aren't behind the attacks."

"Despite the evidence we discovered at the location in Canada."

"I told you no one believed me," I grumble. "She said the werewolves would retaliate. Maybe that's what happened in Canada, I don't know."

He straightens to his full height and takes a single step backwards to give me space. "I believe you."

"You do?"

He clasps his hands behind his back. "And she said Echidna was the one orchestrating the attacks?"

"Well, not in so many words. But if you put two and two together from what Genna said when we first found her and what's been happening now—"

"I see."

He focuses on the wall beside me and falls silent but

doesn't move off. I clench my hands together as turbulent waves of magic roll off him. I don't want to stay here not only because of the penitent cells, but I have an irrational fear that if I stay in Draco's proximity for too long he'll discover my secrets.

"Am I free to go?" I ask.

In answer, he holds out a hand to the next cell down. The dragon barrier drops and the door springs open under his silent command. Moments later Charlie staggers out looking disheveled and his hair's a mess like he's been pulling at it.

"You may go," Draco says and strides down the hall without a single look back.

I hustle over to Charlie as he braces himself against the wall with both hands and bends at the waist like he's about to puke. Worried, I lay a hand on his back and try to see his face.

"*Pixies*, Charlie, what happened in there?"

He shakes his head vigorously, makes a sound like a strangled cat, heaves a few times, then straightens and nods as if he's perfectly okay, which he clearly isn't. I feel awful.

"I shouldn't have asked you to help me," I say and hold tight onto his arm, somewhat fearful he's going to collapse on me. He's so pale.

"Nah, I'm great."

I roll my eyes. "You're insufferable."

"Berserker," he shoots back.

"Unicorn."

My attempt at a smile to lighten the mood twitches into a frown and I choose to ignore the awkwardness by tugging him away from the cells.

"Come on," I say. "We need to figure out what's going on out there."

"Yeah, let's get the heck out of here. Hang on."

With my hand still on his arm, he ports us through the hallways at a dizzying speed, porting past the guards and all, until we're completely clear of the penitent cells and in the main hub of Underground. The second we're free and clear of those horrible cells, my first thought is to find Hawk. He had gone along with Jefferson after Genna but there had been no sign of him back there.

"I need to find my brother," I say.

"Phoenix."

"Yeah?"

He runs a hand through his hair. The color is starting to return to his face but he's still much too pale. "Even if someone else is setting up the werewolves, they struck back. They aren't innocent in this."

I round on him. "So you agree that condemning them all for the actions of a few is the right thing to do?"

"That's not what I'm saying."

"Then what *are* you saying, Charlie?"

"That maybe you're blind to all of the possibilities here." He plants a hand on my shoulder and I have the urge to shrug him off. We had been in this together and now he's switching sides? "Look, I like Genna. I do. And your brother's great. But werewolves aren't human."

"Neither are we. Not really."

He sighs and withdraws his hand. "Dang it, would you just listen to me for once instead of arguing? There's more to them than we'll ever understand and that darkness inside of them can never truly be contained."

I take a step back. "You think my brother would hurt the people here? Hurt you? Hurt me?"

He's silent a long time which is answer enough.

I shake my head. "I can't believe this. Ten minutes ago you had my back jumping into the middle of a freakin' council meeting to help the werewolves. Now you're ready to cage them up? What happened between then and now?"

His eyes narrow. "I just got a reminder of what we're actually dealing with."

"What did you experience in that cell, Charlie? What's messed you up so badly that you're ready to chuck your friends into the meat grinder?"

"And how can *you* possibly forget what one werewolf managed to do to an entire city?"

My face burns. "I can't do this with you. I'll find Hawk on my own."

"Phoenix—"

I shove past him, knocking my shoulder into his as I move angrily past. I hear his footsteps stumble but I don't look back to see if he's okay. My heart is pounding in my ears. I can't believe what Charlie said. Then that other part of me can't believe what I said either. Is he right? Is he wrong? When did the lines become so blurred?

Maybe it doesn't matter. The only thing I care about is finding my brother because no matter what he is or what he may or may not do, he will always be my brother and I will always protect him.

I trot to the market square which is in an uproar. I shrug past fauns gossiping in groups and centaurs being as stoic as ever as they watch the emergency monitor fire up the same report over and over again. Old Man Two at least gives me the time of day to let me know he saw Hawk and several other werewolves being shepherded to the living quarters area. I thank him and sprint away to our apartment.

Junior agents, elves, and some unicorns loiter between the rows of housing. The festivities in the faun fields have all but been abandoned. No music plays, no sounds of laughter or joy. No, the news of an attack so close to home has shaken everyone.

I burst into the marble apartments and take the stairs two at a time until I reach ours. I find the three other junior agents that had been staying with us huddled in a group outside the door talking in whispers. They don't talk quietly enough because I catch talk about "the werewolf problem" again. When they see me, their conversation dies and they step aside to let me through the door. The apartment is the same as ever even though in my mind I feel like the furniture should be upended, glass smashed, and the walls destroyed. Our lives and world are unraveling.

"Hawk?"

He emerges from his bedroom and I heave a sigh of relief. He's okay. They haven't hauled him off like Genna.

"How'd it go?" he asks.

"Badly. We need to talk."

He gestures for me to enter his room. Well, it *is* a disaster in here with clothes strewn all over as well as empty chip bags. Hawk comes in after me and shuts the door for some privacy. I take a seat on the edge of his bed and run both hands through my hair. What a nightmare this is becoming.

My brother sits beside me and I explain the meeting with the bean nighe, the failed attempt to persuade the council, and stint in the penitent cells. I don't bring up Charlie's insinuations. There's no need to add that burden to Hawk's shoulders.

"That's a lot to take in," he says and mimics my posture of holding my head in my hands. "Can we get a limit on life-altering revelations or something? This is getting ridiculous."

"I know. I'm sick of it too." I rest a hand on his shoulder to ground myself. "What about Genna? Any word what's going on?"

"Well, they took her into the interrogation wing then kicked me out immediately. They asked all of the resident werewolves to return to their homes and remain in lockdown for our safety as well as everyone else's."

A dangerous first step. They're drawing a line and outlining villains by setting the werewolves apart.

"You know, this is exactly what the bean nighe warned me about," I say. "Animosity breeds desperation. She said the werewolves wouldn't sit idly by while their kind are being treated like this."

Hawk doesn't say anything in reply but clenches his jaw, the muscles under my hand tense, and he stares at the far wall as if he could burn a hole through it with his eyes. His reaction tells me everything I need to know.

Hawk won't sit idly by either.

31

I'm used to the noise, lights, and surge of spectators heading for the stadium in Underground at the start of the aetherball tournament each year, but the guards posted at every entrance and exit, loitering in the halls, and casting suspicious glances at any werewolf in the vicinity is new. It certainly throws a somber shadow over what's supposed to be the most exciting event that takes place around here.

Hawk sticks close to my side. The werewolves are being allowed to forgo their temporary lockdown in order to enjoy the games as long as they go where they're told and endure the steady gazes of the security detail stationed everywhere. I want to shield my brother from it but there's nothing I can do except support him however I can.

We move slowly into the stadium with a throng of people. Just ahead I spot Jefferson walking hand in hand with Genna. They let her out the same night they came for her, but there's a guard shadowing her five feet back wherever she goes. They didn't have any proof she knew of the most recent attack but no one wants to trust anyone.

When we finally reach the inside of the stadium, we clamber into the stands a few rows behind where Genna and Jefferson sit. I notice our section is comprised of a majority of werewolves and is being given a wide berth by many people except for, you know, the security guards. Figures. Doing my best to ignore the present circumstances, I divert my attention to the middle of the stadium.

The track and center field have been completely taken over by a blacktop arena surrounded by ten foot high acrylic glass to protect the crowd from the mayhem soon to take place. Enormous lights hang from the cement ceiling to illuminate the playing field with a spectacular glow so none of the action will be missed. Four nymphs stand on upraised platforms on each of the four corners of the field. They've partway shifted into trees to root themselves to the ground but their upper bodies remain decidedly human and female in their green-skinned glory—the referees.

It takes forever for the stadium to fill but fill it does. Then Draco himself walks into the center of the arena to announce the start of the tournament. The crowd gives him a deafening cheer and he holds up both hands to acknowledge them. I clap politely with the others but don't cheer for the dragon that stripped Scholar's freedom away. I haven't forgotten what he's done and the grudge he's been holding for hundreds of years against the werewolves, a grudge that affects my family personally.

I ignore most of his short and pointed speech about how we need to come together in this time of crisis. I look around for my friends. Normally Celina and Doocan would be sitting with me and Hawk during the tournament but as far as I know, they're still in Faunus. Witty should also be here but I don't see him. Weird. He loves these games. I don't think he's ever missed a tournament. I spot Charlie off by himself further up the stands looking as grouchy as ever.

Cheering erupts around me and I refocus on the game about to commence below. The fire sprites enter through a glass gate on the closest side while a line of rocky boulders roll in on the opposite end. The first match is a bout between the fire and earth sprites. One of the nymph referees walks into the center of the playing field and deposits a single glowing sphere of luminescent glass. The sprites line up on either side, the nymph exits, and at the sound of a gong rung by Director Knox, the game begins.

I want to cheer along with the rest as the fire sprites nab the sphere and make a fiery rush through the earth sprites but my heart's not in it today. Normally the aetherball tournament is an adrenaline fueled frenzy for me. It's a game of power and amazing control as the sprites duke it out without damaging the glass sphere and score goals through their opponents' posts. Earth and fire collides, dust fills the air, and the stands rock with the sound of thunderous cheering. But the section I'm in, the one occupied with werewolves, sits subdued. It's hard not to let that stillness overcome me and I can't find the energy to cheer along with the rest as the fire sprites make the first goal.

The swirl of magic wraps around me and for the first time attending one of these tournaments I can really *feel* it like Scholar taught me. The whole of Underground pulses with energy, pushing and pulling, and thrumming with life. But there's something else. Something . . . wrong. It's not the bitterness of the werewolves surrounding me but something even further off and coming closer. My eyes wander over the stadium as I try to pick out what it is. I rise part way out of my seat to see past the stands and spot a red light on the wall of Underground flare to life. Moments later, a number of the security agents notice as well or touch a finger to the comm link in their ears. The rest of the audience is too absorbed in the game to notice.

I nudge my brother with my elbow. "Hawk."

He sits up straight and follows my line of sight. "That's the proximity alarm."

It's not a usual occurrence to see that light come on. It means something dangerous has tripped the outer perimeter and gotten too close to this hidden city. Whatever it is might not know Underground is here, but it's close enough to rouse the guards.

"Something's coming," I say. "I can feel it."

"You can feel it?"

I nod and stand. My blood runs cold as the weight of bitter magic presses in on me from above. Whatever it is, it's got the same corrupted magic running through its veins as all of Echidna's monsters but it's *powerful*—and directly over the city. I have to warn someone or do *something*.

As if sensing my own increased distress, the red light on the wall starts to flash and an intermittent alarm blares through the city. The sprites carry on for a little bit longer, too caught up in the game, before they come to a standstill as everyone freezes to listen. Dawning panic is reflected in the faces around me as they realize what that sound means.

There's been a breach.

Two seconds later, the power goes out.

Cries and screams of dread fill the stadium around me as the only light comes from the team of fire sprites in the middle of the stadium. I automatically reach out to grab Hawk's arm so we don't get separated in the darkness. A tremor passes through my feet and a sound like thunder rumbles through the air. Metal groans and cement grinds as something assaults the very walls of Underground. If that something manages to break through and get past the protective barriers keeping the waters of the Mississippi River at bay, this whole place will be swept away.

The shrouds of the dead will line these halls.

In the midst of the chaos and despair of the reality of what's happening—that Underground has become the next targeted magical sanctuary—a golden light blossoms from the far side of the stands. White hot fire stretches out like tendrils through the air until the entire stadium is lit with its light. Draco stands with a single hand outstretched towards the wreath of fire to illuminate the darkness—the Firestorm of Europe.

"Agents to your posts!" he commands with the deep growl of a majestic dragon. "Protect this city!"

Men and women hurry out of the stadium and call to each other to organize in the midst of the attack. The enemy is unknown, the size of the force unknown, but one thing is certain. There's a nasty monster hovering in the waters overhead. I'm still at a loss how they cut the power. Underground has its own source of energy. The only way to turn off the power is from inside.

Which means they're already in the city.

"Everyone remain calm!" Draco shouts. "Remain inside the stadium unless ordered to evacuate. In such an event, follow emergency protocol to leave through the exit in the water sprite cavern."

I want to help, not sit here like a troll in the mud. There must be something we can do. That's when I notice several people attempting to wake a man slumped over a few rows down.

"Oh, no," I breathe as I realize who it is. Keeping my brother in my grasp, I push my way through the mob in the stands to find Jefferson unmoving on the bench. Two other agents are attempting to rouse him. "Is he . . . ?"

"He's got a pulse," the female agent responds. "Not sure what happened. Could have gotten knocked out accidentally during the excitement."

The two agents keep checking him over in the dim light offered by Draco's web of fire but there's an obvious person missing from his side. A person who would have been frantic and demanding assistance if anything had happened to Jefferson.

I turn to my brother. "Where's Genna?"

His eyes widen and we both stand as tall as we can to look over the heads of those closest to us. There's no sign of her. No. No, no, no. This can't be happening. The only reason Genna wouldn't be at her father's side and making sure he's okay is if—no, she wouldn't have. What possible reason would she have to knock Jefferson unconscious?

Only one, truly horrible thought comes to mind even if I don't want to believe it. It doesn't matter if it's werewolves or Echidna's forces attacking. This is a prime opportunity, while everyone is distracted, to break into the penitent cells.

Before I can convince my brother to go with me to search for her in the lower levels, a horrendous crack rends the air and I'm peppered with pebble-sized chunks of cement from above. I hold up a hand to protect myself and blink away the drifting dust to find a massive crack spreading through the ceiling.

"Sweet majestics," a werewolf breathes behind me as the roof starts to collapse.

A thousand tons of cement, steel I-beams, and water comes tumbling down in a tumultuous roar. My only thought is to clutch at my brother as our home collapses to kill us all. There is no escape or running. No one can possibly move fast enough to clear the doom falling for us. Screams of dread ring in my ears. This is it. One fell swoop and a city falls just like that.

A burst of light blinds me from the chaos and destruction. I close my eyes against its intensity and hunker with my brother, each of us with arms thrown around each other in a final embrace before the end.

The groan of steel beams twisting and cement rocks grinding against each other comes to a slow halt. I carefully open my eyes to find a powerful shimmering barrier holding the fallen ceiling and rushing water at bay. The barrier's light feeds from the center of the stadium where a massive scaly hide can be seen through the settling dust.

Scales like smoky granite cover powerful muscles straining against the use of magic, plates of bone line a long back and tamper off down a thrashing tail, and two jagged horns jut out of the back of an angular head. Teeth bared, blue slit eyes glowing, and two massive wings spread out to either side with the tips trembling at the strain of projecting the barrier that's keeping the whole of Underground from collapsing.

Draco's majestic dragon form is unveiled in all its glory.

"Move for the cavern exit!" Director Knox thunders from somewhere. "Go now!"

A stampede ensues as all of the residents of Underground scramble out of the arena while the majestic dragon holds his ground in the very center to give us time to escape. Draco, who poisoned Terra and hunted her for years, doing his utmost to save the people of this city in a deadly gambit. Should that barrier fail, the ceiling and Mississippi River will take him.

Hawk grabs my hand and pulls me down the steps to join the panicked throng making their way out. I stop next to Jefferson's unconscious form as the two agents try to pick him up without great success. I sling him up into a fireman's carry across my shoulders and continue to make my way out of the stadium in the wake of my brother's footsteps. As we go, there's a great rustling of wings and I catch glimpses of the gargoyles of Underground surging towards the massive hole in the ceiling to help Draco patch the damage.

How did our enemies find us? Underground is warded in a number of ways with safety protocols reaching out in a five mile perimeter. Nothing like this should have ever happened. But then I guess the darkness throughout the city answers that question. The power couldn't have gone out without someone on the inside. That same person could have disabled certain safety measures if they wished. The main perimeter alarm is the last alarm before breach. Any threat should have been detected well before that.

With the power out, the darkness only adds to the chaos. I'm slammed into from every side as everyone runs for it and I nearly lose Hawk before grabbing onto the back of his shirt to keep him with me. The fire sprites come to the rescue as a flock of brilliant birds that string out from the exits of the stadium and light the way to the cavern escape route. I suddenly find Old Man Two beside me who parts the crowd around him and holds out his arms.

"I can take him, young one," he says. "Hurry now."

He and Hawk help transfer Jefferson off my shoulders onto Old Man Two's back. It's an unusual honor to ride a centaur, even if Jefferson is too unconscious to realize it. It only goes to show how dire the situation is.

"Thank you," I shout over the screams and shouts around us. Then it's not just screams but roars and snarls of beasts. Something overhead—most likely the thing I felt before—makes a sound like a very angry whale. What on earth is it?

The air around us waivers with the pulses of bio-mech guns and it's clear the battle has commenced although I can't see where. Old Man Two trots ahead with Jefferson safely on his back and we hurry along after him. But where's Charlie? Where's Genna? Where's Witty?

Hawk jerks to a halt and just about collars me as he pulls on the back of my shirt. "Phoenix, look."

He points and I see a figure dart through the crowd.

"Who was that?" I ask.

"Rosalyn."

Oh, no. The only reason she could be here is if she's with the attackers. Then it must be the werewolves retaliating again—and no doubt seeking to free their lost leader.

"She must be heading for the penitent cells," I say.

In an instant we change directions and shove our way through the crowd after her. A moment before we're clear of the surging crowd, an agent grabs me by the arm to stop us.

"What are you doing! This way, come on! I don't care what valuables you think are worth your life going back for, just move!"

"You don't understand!" Hawk shouts. "There's going to be a breach in the penitent cells!"

"What are you—AAHHHHHHHHH!"

Five claws stick out through his chest, red and dripping with his blood. His shriek of pain ends suddenly as the claws retract and he slumps to the ground. Standing in his place is a woman wrapped in a trench coat with a hood pulled up to hide her features. What's visible of her hands is covered in small feathers and the blood of the agent she just killed before our eyes. Those terrible long claws on each finger glisten as they curl and flex for another attack.

The immediate crowd around us pauses as they realize what just happened. The woman grins and lunges for me. Her hood falls back in the fast movement revealing volumes of dark hair and the start of black feathers that run up her throat and end below her ears. A harpy. Her claws flash towards my chest but I drive my arms up to deflect her attack, leaving her midsection exposed. I kick at her stomach and she lets out a huff as I drive the air out of her lungs and she folds over. I twist to her side while grabbing her wrists and flip her over onto her back with the motion. Hawk slides on the floor to the dead agent, whips up the bio-mech gun, and puts the harpy down with a rapid series of pulses. The moment we're sure she won't be getting up again, we converge and face the crowd defensively in case there are more enemies hiding.

"Harpies? Really?" Hawk says. "What on earth are we dealing with?"

After seeing Rosalyn, my first thought was that this was a werewolf coordinated attack but now . . . I mean, they've worked along shapeshifters on a few occasions but harpies?

"Come on," Hawk says and tugs on my arm to get me moving.

We race away from the crowd fleeing the crumbling city. There's no sign of Rosalyn anymore so we come to a halt and Hawk sniffs at the air. After a few moments, he jerks his head towards headquarters and we continue on. As we near the looming black building, I realize we should be seeing people coming out of here too. We should see agents, bookkeepers, secretaries, *someone* heading for the exit. Surely they haven't all managed to leave already.

The screams, cries, and roars become faint as we enter the side entrance to headquarters. The door stands ajar and bodies litter the hallways. Oh, no. We move separately to a man and woman face down on the floor to check their pulse. By some miracle they're only unconscious and not dead as I fear. Is this the work of the traitor that sabotaged the power? Darkness breathes like a living thing deeper in the building where there are no lights to guide the way and the light from Draco doesn't reach here.

"Hold on," I say and dig into my pocket for my cell phone. Hawk does the same and we turn on the flashlight function to lead the way into the creeping dark.

We move as quickly as we dare. There's no telling

what's in here or if there's a trap waiting for us but we follow Hawk's nose to lead us along Rosalyn's trail. Where on earth was she going? If she was going to help break out Dasc, wouldn't she have made for the penitent cells? Why come here?

Our flashlights reflect off plaques on the walls as dust shakes from the ceiling while the battle continues elsewhere, rocking the entire city. We pass records and I automatically look through the opening to the courtyard where I feel that hum of power from the arch in the center. Despite its all black surface, the arch is clearly visible in the middle of the courtyard by the glowing golden letters etched on its surface. Eerie as it is, it also reminds me of something else.

"Wait," I say and catch my brother's arm. "Back here."

I turn around and run my hand along the wall until I find the door to the inconspicuous "cleaning supplies closet." Bursting inside, I slide my hand across the back wall. Golden dragon script blossoms in the darkness and the wall splits in two to allow entrance to the penitent cells.

"Draco's private entrance," I explain to Hawk over my shoulder and descend the stairs that glow after my feet touch the first step. "How the heck would Rosalyn even know about this? Even if Genna has a part in this, she didn't know about this door."

"Do you really think Genna could have done all of this?"

"I don't know what I'm saying or what to think."

"Let's keep moving."

We reach the bottom and after passing through another of Draco's hidden doors, we step into the white walled hallways of the penitent cells. I expect there to be no light and all the doors smashed open, but the bright fluorescents dazzle my eyes and I have to blink to adjust to the brightness. The penitent cells must be on their own power system.

There's no one in sight and it's eerie with the sound of the monsters still crying out from their cells. I gesture to Hawk and we move lightly on our feet along one wall towards Dasc's cell. We're about to round the corner when I hear voices and throw out a hand to stop my brother.

"It was right where you said it'd be." It's Rosalyn.

"And the message I asked you to pass along?"

My chest aches as I recognize the second voice. No. After everything, it can't be. Hawk tenses beside me and we share a look full of heartbreak and betrayal.

"She heard it," Rosalyn replies. "She was on my heels so I suspect she's here by now."

"Good," Genna says. "That'll buy us time."

I signal silently to my brother and countdown with my fingers. We're going to end this right here. At my signal, Hawk rounds the corner with the bio-mech gun drawn. I'm hot on his heels ready to join the fight but the second we show our faces we find a phase-repeater pointed at us held in Rosalyn's hands. Genna and Dasc are already making a run for it. Hawk tries to take a shot anyway at Rosalyn who's closest but she dodges and lets off her own pulse that knocks the bio-mech gun out of Hawk's hand.

By the time her attention shifts to me, I'm already close enough to do something. The gun points in my direction but I grab the barrel and aim it towards the ceiling. The pulse knocks out ceiling tiles and showers us with white dust. Rosalyn's unfazed and is quick to retaliate but this fight isn't going to end like our last one. After everything we've been through—rescuing her and Genna, bringing them together with their families, sticking up for them at every turn—I can't believe it's come to this but I will do anything in order to stop Dasc from escaping.

She sweeps at my legs with her foot but I twist my stance to keep my balance and wrench the gun out of her hands to toss it to Hawk. He catches it in a single smooth motion as I use my might to fling Rosalyn into a nearby wall. She hits it with a solid thud and groan before sliding to the floor. Hawk hits her with a single pulse to make sure she stays down.

"You'll thank me later," he mutters at her.

I'm already in pursuit as Genna and Dasc vanish around a corner up ahead. This is straight out of my nightmares. Dasc escaping from Underground and being unleashed upon the world once again. Except this isn't a dream. I'm not slipping on the ground in the chase. The walls aren't shrinking in around me as he vanishes. They are *not* getting away.

My energy flows and builds up in my hands ready for the confrontation. I keep on running with Hawk catching up from behind echoing my pounding footsteps. Genna and Dasc slip around corners just as I enter the next hallway after hallway. Either they're racing without a clear objective or they know exactly where they're going. I can't tell which. We keep running until we're at the far end of the penitent cells. Around one last corner, I finally catch up to Genna and Dasc as they run right into a dead end. They must realize it too, because Genna swings about and fires her bio-mech gun at me.

I stretch out a hand and knock the force of the pulse aside as if swatting a fly. The discharge ricochets and makes a dent in the wall. The disbelief on Genna and Dasc's face is momentary as I charge headlong at them. Genna fires again and again but that spark in my veins ignites and I deflect each pulse until my hand clamps around the barrel. My strength overpowers her own and I rip the weapon out of her hand. Her reflexes are terrifyingly fast in turn. She snaps her foot up to kick away my hand before her fist collides with the side of my face.

Our movements become a savage dance of limbs—block, deflect, strike, kick, dodge. Despite my strength, the fight feels impossibly even. Whenever I head in with a powerful blow, she manages to dodge around me, always circling around so she's at my back. Everything I throw at her she deflects or uses my own strength against me.

In the midst of our struggle, I spot Dasc doing something by the wall. I try to lunge around Genna but she hooks my foot and I nearly fall on my face. I catch myself before I hit the white tile and kick out with my other foot. She slips around me as usual and aims a punch at my face. This time, instead of evading her attack, I take the sharp hit to my cheek at the same moment I pummel my fist into the floor. Genna stumbles from the force of my strength creating a shockwave of demolished floor in a ring around me. I take the moment to roll away from her as well and give myself distance.

Where on earth is Hawk? I thought he was right behind me.

Genna crouches, breathing hard, and places herself between me and Dasc who's still doing something at the wall. Scholar's pendant around my neck pulses as my every trepidatious thought, doubt of Genna's intentions, and character are confirmed in the worst possible way. The stolen girl, the Whisper, Jefferson's one and only child—still in Dasc's pocket after all this time.

"What are you doing?" I pant and grimace against the pain throughout my body from Genna's vicious offense.

There's nothing of the girl I know in that cold, hard mask. "What I have to."

I take a step towards Dasc and she mirrors my movements to make sure she remains between us.

"Why?" I roar. "How can you protect him after everything he did to you? What about your father, Genna?"

"As pleasant a chat as this is," Dasc cuts in, "I really think we ought to get going, don't you?"

"You aren't going anywhere," I snarl.

"Oh, I dare say we are."

He straightens and I see he's left some sort of device against the wall. A bomb. How the heck did they get a bomb down here? If they blow that, the cells will flood. We're on the outer wall of Underground, no longer in the riverbed itself, and the magical barriers have come down. But that's the plan isn't it? From Dasc's hand several breathing masks hang. They're going to take the river out of here.

"Genna, please," I plead with her. "I don't want to hurt you but I can't let that monster go free. Remember what he's done—what he did to your mother, what he did to James."

Dasc has the audacity to laugh. Where the heck is Hawk? I could really use some backup. I spot the bio-mech gun on the floor but it's near Genna's feet. I won't be able to reach it in time. I'm going to have to really hurt Genna if I want to make it to Dasc.

"What I did to James?" he says and puts a hand on Genna's shoulder. "I didn't do anything to James. Genna here is the one who killed him."

My blood runs cold. "No."

Genna's face is stony and she doesn't correct such a horrible lie. No. She couldn't have. She even went to comfort James's parents about his passing. Or . . . or maybe it was to assuage her own guilt.

"Everything you've done, everything you've said since you've come home—it's all been a lie?" I ask, unable to accept this truth.

It takes her only the space of a moment to reply. "Yes."

"I trusted you!"

Rage burns through me and I slam my fist into the ground. The force of it shatters the tile around us, drops down part of the ceiling, and blows back the walls on either side of it. Genna teeters on her feet and in that breath of opportunity, I lunge for the bio-mech gun. My fingers wrap around its cool surface and I bring it up to take them both down.

A pulse reverberates through my back like a giant's fist hitting me from behind. The bio-mech gun slips from my grasp before I can fire and I fall face first into shards of tile as the world darkens around me.

Seconds, maybe more, pass before I blink away the haze. Wheels roll uneasily past me on the broken floor.

"It's done. The security measures will kick in any second."

I know that voice.

My body is loath to acknowledge my demand on it to move but I manage to raise my head just enough to find Witty looking down at me. A bio-mech gun is held in his hand. He shot me. He shot me in the back. Dasc stands beside him as a comrade.

No, it can't be.

I recall the last conversation Witty and I had. He acted so oddly and expressed some deep-seated grievances he's always had about his condition. Then the way he's been following Genna around. Only someone with intimate knowledge of Underground's systems could have tampered with the security alarms and turned off the power. Someone who's been working the systems since they were a kid.

"You betrayed us," I say hoarsely. He doesn't shake his head or look affronted at my accusation. No, his face turns bright red and a tear slips down his face. "Why? How could you ever help that monster?"

"I *am* in the room, Phoenix," Dasc drawls.

"He's going to heal me," Witty says weakly.

I try to rise only to find my hands are tied behind my back—it must have happened during those brief dark moments of unconsciousness. My strength is returning too slowly to rip apart my bonds.

"You mean he's going to turn you into a werewolf," I say.

My lungs feel two sizes too small. Witty had mentioned before how fascinated he was with Dasc's healing abilities. I never even considered that Witty might be so interested because he's been looking for a way to heal his legs. To walk again. The one person no one ever suspected was the most dangerous one of all. The means to make Underground so vulnerable that freeing Dasc could actually be possible.

Rosalyn steps into my line of sight next having come to already. Where's Hawk? What's happened to my brother?

"You brought the monsters here?" I ask as the rest of the puzzle falls into place.

She smirks and becomes the same girl I met at Eileen Donan. "Certain information was passed along to bring Echidna's brood here."

"Genna's idea." Dasc looks to his protégé beside him with pride the way a father might look at his daughter. "That's my girl." He pats Genna on the shoulder as I roll onto my side fighting the fog in my brain. "They provide quite the convenient distraction if I do say so myself. Why waste your own resources when you can make someone else waste theirs? It's the same method they've been using to turn the IMS against my wolves. I suppose it's backfired on them this time."

There's a loud boom that rocks the penitent cells.

"And that's the bell!" Dasc says cheerfully. "Well, class is over and we really must be going."

They step over to the wall and my eyes glue to Genna, pleading with her. There's no pity in that cold face. The Whisper.

I wrench my bonds asunder as my strength returns. "You're not going anywhere."

Rosalyn's foot comes out of nowhere and collides with the side of my head. Dazed and with pain reverberating through my skull, it takes an effort just to get air into my lungs again.

"You're going to be a little preoccupied to stop us, I should think," Dasc says. The girls put on their oxygen masks and pull Witty up out of his wheelchair. "Rosalyn knew a certain someone had been keeping an eye on her and Genna since their arrival at Moose Lake. Her conversations were being monitored so she dropped some hints that your life would be in imminent danger."

He takes a step closer and smiles. "Did you really think I didn't know a certain dragon was residing in the Moose Lake area?"

The breath leaves my body in a gust. I've been so distracted by the circumstances before me that I've given no heed to the pendant pulsing around my neck. Scholar's pendant. A warning of danger.

"She kept her distance and I played ignorance, but if Draco ever came looking, I would have used her as a decoy. He certainly knows how to hold a grudge doesn't he?"

"What did you do?" I breathe.

He glances at the watch on Rosalyn's wrist. "I think that explosion we heard will be dear Terra looking for you at the portal where she thinks you are currently being swept away to Echidna for sinister purposes. And Draco? Well, let me think."

Another explosion shakes the walls and this time it's punctuated by a ferocious roar.

"Oh, dear, I do believe they've found each other," he says. "And by the sounds of it are doing more damage than Echidna's baby leviathan!"

So that was the presence I sensed. I manage to get to my feet only to find Dasc has leveled a bio-mech gun at me. He fires without preamble so I'm not quite ready for it. I manage to disperse part of the pulse but I'm still hit square in the chest. My own power fights it but I'm knocked to the ground, winded yet again.

"So, now you have a choice before you," he says. "You either stop me and abandon your friend to Draco's wrath along with the rest of Underground. Or you let me go, and hope you're fast enough to save Terra before Draco rips her apart. Your choice."

"I like option C," I pant. "Stop you and save Terra."

"Well, that'll be a little difficult considering."

"Considering what?"

"This."

He holds up a trigger in his hand and presses a small button on top. The block of cells around us explodes in a hail of cement and white tile. There's a tremendous groan as the side of Underground buckles and the force of the Mississippi River comes rushing in. Ringing fills my ears before I'm swept away by the water. I slam into the emergency doors that close if ever there's a breach. I can't see or breathe as the river fills up every space. The pressure against my body feels like it's going to push the bones right out of my body and I nearly black out.

In the midst of getting creamed by the river, I feel the spots of bitter magic from Genna, Rosalyn, and Dasc slip further and further away. They're escaping. I have to stop them. I don't care what it takes—I have to do something.

With my back pressed tight against the emergency door, I realize there's a gap between the upper and lower doors. It didn't close all the way. If the water keeps on going through that hole, the penitent cells and Underground will flood. Curse it all!

A pair of hands snake through that gap and grab me under the shoulders to force me through that tiny space. I feel like a cork trying to hold back a dam until I finally surge through and splash into the watery corridor, coughing and sputtering.

Hawk pants as he drags me out of the geyser of water trying to break apart the emergency door. We press up against the wall and watch the water take over the penitent cells.

"We have to close those doors!" Hawk shouts over the roar. Water comes up past our knees. "I need you!"

Still dazed from the water and getting stunned by the bio-mech pulses, I stagger with him towards the side of that gap.

"Where were you?" I shout at him.

"Witty got me," he growls and looks furious. I guess I'm not the only one Witty shot in the back.

We wade through the water, hands searching for purchase on the side of the emergency doors as we move closer to our goal. Once close enough, I manage to grab one of the handles near the lip of the lower door and find why they won't close properly. Somehow in the midst of my battle with Genna, the track of the door was dented. I almost lose my grip as the current rips at me and my head goes under.

Hawk pulls me back up as he hangs onto the handle next to me.

"Just get out of here!" I shout at him. "I've got this!"

"I'm not leaving you!" He circles one arm around my waist to help keep me upright. "You might try doing something stupid like going after Dasc if I leave you on your own!"

The thought crosses my mind. If I could just close this door on the other side . . . The more time we waste, the more distance Dasc puts between us and him. My chest heaves as I stare at the water flooding the cells. I think of the bean nighe as it rises and rises. She said that some sacrifices, no matter how terrible they are, need to be made. I have to let Dasc go for the sake of Underground and Terra no matter how much I hate to.

And when the water rises, I have to remember who had saved me and who needs to be saved.

Energy courses down my legs as I plant my feet and out to my hands as I tug on that handle with everything I have in me. The door screeches as I force the dented metal to slide in a way it doesn't want to. The pressure of the river is insanely strong and doesn't want to be stopped. My arms quake and every muscle in my body is pushed to the edge. I let out a roar as I haul on the door. It moves inch by inch until the flow of the water thins into a powerful jet, then a smaller one, smaller and smaller. The doors latch, a mechanism inside rumbles, and a barrier snaps across the doors to seal it for good.

Hawk and I slump into the waist-high water. My muscles reel from the strain and I let myself float for a moment before I get my feet under me and scream as loud as I can at those doors. Underground's salvation. Dasc's assurance of freedom.

"They're gone!" Hawk shouts. "There's nothing we can do!"

We were too late to stop Dasc. We were too blind to stop Witty and Genna. But this fight's not over yet.

"There's still something we can do," I say and turn away from those doors to face the hallway leading to the exit. "We have a majestic dragon to save."

32

Blood burning and heart pounding, I take the stairs two at a time up Draco's secret flight to headquarters. I have to brace a hand against the wall as rumbles threaten to knock me off my feet. Wherever Scholar is, she's putting up one heck of a fight. And there's a baby leviathan somewhere, I can't forget that either. That must have been the thing that brought the ceiling down. *Pixies*, if a baby was able to do that, I never want to meet a full sized one.

I don't have time to anguish over Witty's betrayal and Genna's return to her kidnapper. This is going to break Jefferson and there's a shadow growing over me filled with doubt and rage that I can't shake. Who else will betray me next? I never saw it coming, any of it.

We burst through the upper door just as the wall separating us from the courtyard is blown asunder and a wave of insufferable heat rolls over us. We bunch up behind the door to avoid the worst of the destruction and then peer out to witness the battle unfolding.

An entire section of headquarters has been reduced to rubble and dust fills the air. I hold the edge of my sleeve over my mouth and nose and blink away what tries to get in my eyes. Hawk does the same as we inch forward ever so quietly to see what we're facing. Through the gap in the wall, I glance to the breach over the stadium. A shimmering barrier holds back the flood of the river as gargoyles crawl over it like a hive of bees, slowly settling in and forming a solid stone wall that will keep the city from collapsing until repairs can be done.

The pendant around my neck pulses like a frantic heartbeat echoing Scholar's, wherever she is. It's hard to see much of the courtyard itself through the cloud of debris and fire. The dust and flames part for a moment as a shockwave splits the air to reveal a sight both despairing and awe worthy. Scholar slides across the rubble strewn floor in her small—relatively speaking—terrene form as the ground trembles and rises to her aid. A looming shape that I catch only briefly hovers above Scholar—a great angular head so large it could easily take Scholar in its jaws lined with vicious teeth and snap her in half. Draco roars, terrible in his wrath, and his eyes glow with sparks and fire. There's nothing of the man in the black suit in that looming visage. He is power incarnate, rage unchecked, and he's focused entirely on turning Scholar into charred meat.

Flames lick the ground and punch through the air as Draco attempts to blast Scholar into cinders but she's lithe and dodges and just barely manages to redirect the fire with her own shockwaves. As graceful as Scholar is, it's clear she's using everything she has and is still losing the battle. One of her forelegs has nasty burns down its length and her frame heaves with every breath.

How on earth can I possibly help? The power Draco is tossing around is on a level I can never contend with. I have the feeling that the only reason Scholar is still alive is because Draco is holding back so he doesn't accidentally tear Underground in two.

Hawk wrenches me behind the secret door as some of Draco's flames come too close and singe our hair.

"What do we do?" Hawk shouts in my ear to be heard as the mingling roars of the dragons and screams of monsters deeper in the city reverberate through the air.

The bean nighe wouldn't have told me what she did if the only thing I could do is sit by and watch. She told me some sacrifices had to be made to save another. I made that sacrifice. I let Dasc go along with Genna, Witty, and Rosalyn. I grit my teeth. That can't have been for nothing. I peer out from the door again as the two dragons battle around the black arch. Scholar skids and slides and ducks but she doesn't run away like she should. Scholar could make a break for it if she wanted but she keeps charging forward as if that's going to do her any good. Draco is also doing his best to block her advances.

Oh, I'm so blind.

I grab Hawk's arm. "The arch. She's trying to get to the arch."

"Why?"

"It's a portal," I say and duck into cover again as a wreath of fire comes far too close. "It'll get her out of here but she can't reach it."

"So how can we get her there? You want to run into the middle of that?" He gestures to the courtyard crumbling to pieces. If we ran out there we'd either be burnt to smithereens, obliterated by shockwaves, or crushed from bits of headquarters falling. It's a miracle the city hasn't collapsed with the ruckus they're making.

"We need a distraction or something."

"And what could possibly distract *that* long enough for Scholar to get out of here?"

One of Scholar's shockwaves sends a rumble directly into the stairwell and we're forced to leap out as the ceiling above us gives way. We hunker behind one of the hallway walls and can only hope we aren't spotted by Draco. If he knows we're here, I won't be able to pull any special stunts to help Scholar without him realizing it. The bean nighe said I was the only one who could open the way. Did she mean that by my own distraction Scholar could slip away? That would mean exposing myself and showing Draco exactly what I can do. That would mean *I* would be his next target.

But something has to be done. He's going to kill her.

"Hawk..."

"Don't you dare think about running out there," he snaps. "You want a distraction? Fine. You wait right here and don't you dare move."

"No, you can't!"

He sprints away but not towards the intense battle in the courtyard. He shifts partway along the hall before he disappears heading towards the exit. What on earth is he doing? As much as I want to run after him or headlong towards Scholar, I wait. I have to trust my brother. He's going to find me a distraction and then I'll make my move. What move exactly? No idea.

I cover my head and have to move twice to avoid parts of headquarters caving in before Hawk comes back. He races through the hallway at full speed and barks twice at me before flying past. Snarls follow in his path and shadows paint the hallway with sinister shapes illuminated by Draco's fire. Hawk barks once more before my senses return to me and I chase after him deeper into what's left of the building. I have to crawl through some tight spaces that make me nervous before I find Hawk hunkered down and panting as a wolf in one of the hallways that has managed to stay mostly intact on the first floor. Blood drips from his mouth.

What did he do?

When I crouch low next to him, he places both paws on the rubble I just crawled through, pushes against it, flips his tail once, and nods at me. I get back up and brace both of my hands against the crumbled black stone. I give it a good heave and manage to block that way so whatever Hawk has trailing him can't follow us. If they try to find another way around, they're bound to run straight into the pitched battle in the courtyard. I can only hope Hawk's idea of a distraction doesn't hurt Scholar more than it helps.

Hawk nudges me with his muzzle and stalks to a hole in the wall where a window has been blown out. We step carefully around the shards of glass and stay low to get a new view on the battle in the courtyard. Scholar has curled up on the ground with yet another leg scorched and a shield of perpetual shockwaves forming a bubble around her but her attempts to keep Draco at bay are weakening. She's not going to make it much longer.

This is my fault. Rosalyn drew Scholar here because of me. She came to save *me*.

It's my turn to save her.

A hideous shriek echoes from the other side of the courtyard. Draco doesn't even look up from trying to smother Scholar in flames until the shriek changes to laughter. The flames die for only a moment as he whips his head around and I push up higher on my toes to see what's drawn his attention.

Oh, of all the distractions Hawk could come up with—

It's the lamia with white hair that nearly killed me in Scotland. The one that now has a bloody bite mark on her leg.

Hawk turns to me and gives me a wolfy smile, canines red. I fight the urge to smack him upside the head.

It had been bad enough when Epsilon had gotten a taste of Scholar's blood. I don't even want to consider this lamia getting her fangs into Draco's power. Then Underground really will come down.

But she's not alone. Oh, no, Hawk managed to attract a whole slew of monsters to join the battle. Harpies, vampires, a freakin' chimera even surround her like bodyguards. It's not them that worry me though. My fears are confirmed when a second later a piercing scream shatters my thoughts and rips through my skull. With a baby leviathan here, I'm not surprised this lamia took a bite of its power in order to raze my home. I fall to my knees with both hands over my ears and Hawk shakes his head violently as if trying to get the sound out. Draco roars in response to the leviathan scream and no sound comes from Scholar at all as if she's too weak to cry out. I have to get her out of here. *Now.*

I can feel the bitter magic that's issuing from the lamia like a cloud as it spreads its poisonous scream to us all. It's so very difficult to concentrate when I feel like my head is about to explode but I reach out to grab that cloud. To my astonishment, I actually take hold of it like my fingers have wrapped around a fine invisible mesh. I give that blanket of magic a sharp tug as if yanking a cloth off a table. The screaming in my head stutters to a halt and I try to steady myself while keeping a tight grip on that magic.

The lamia screams in response to my silencing of her powerful spell. Hawk staggers on all four paws and I feel a sense of gratification of what I was just able to do. And to think, back in Scotland all I could do was suffer such magic. Now I'm able to pull it right out of the lamia and throw away the magic she had stolen.

Such victory is short lived as I feel a hand wrap around my throat from behind. The cold fingers tighten and I'm lifted right off my feet. The iron grip makes it impossible to breath and my toes dangle in the air as I claw at the hand suffocating me. Hawk snarls and lunges for whoever it is behind me but I can sense dark bitter magic. Some monster managed to find us.

I'm thrown to the side and my shoulder slams into the hallway wall creating a Phoenix-sized dent but the grip on my throat is gone. Coughing and wheezing, I push myself upright to find Hawk in a tangle with pale limbs and long dark hair. While they struggle, I hear the rush of flames and the lamia screams in the courtyard. The remaining monsters snarl, hiss, and shriek as Draco sets upon them. Now would be a wonderful opportunity to get Scholar out of here if not for Hawk in serious peril.

I pick up a rod of bent steel framing, rush forward, and whack it across his attacker's back. The woman lets out a groan and loosens her hold on Hawk long enough so he's able to slip free of her encircling arms. He skids over to me. When the monster woman raises her head, I see my fear reflected in her dark eyes.

Epsilon.

How many freakin' lamia are here?

I raise the rod again with all intentions of crudely severing her head from her body but she ducks under the blow and comes up directly into my face. I see her fangs stretch wide before Hawk slams into her from the side and they go tumbling once more.

A desperate, throaty cry from behind splits my focus. It's Scholar crying out. Then there's Hawk, fighting for his life. In the midst of his struggle, he looks to me, jerks his head towards the courtyard, and gives a vicious bark. I know what he's telling me to do but I don't think I can do it. Leave him and save Scholar? An impossible choice.

But only I can open the way.

Curse it all! I reach out towards Epsilon and find that thread of magic keeping her alive. I clench my hand to strangle it like she did to my throat. Clenching tighter and tighter, her movements become stiff and jerky. Lamia aren't alive, not really. They have to have magic from other creatures in their veins to keep them sustained. If they don't have it, they wither away. Hawk gets his jaws around Epsilon's throat and thrashes. I've given him the opportunity he needs to gain the upper hand. Turning away from the bloody scene, I stagger over to the blown out window to find Draco tossing the dead chimera aside and advancing on Scholar once again. She's only ten feet away from the arch but it's too far. With both of her back legs badly burned and a majestic coming upon her, she'll never make it.

So I do the only thing I can think of and reach for the power of that archway. I can feel its electric current, smell different air, glimpse different sky as I wrap my hands around its threads like I did with Epsilon and pull.

The response is immediate and unexpected. It's like trying to hold onto molten lava. I nearly scream as the power of the portal put there by Draco himself burns me away. It's too much. Magic fights magic and I'm a small insignificant thing compared to what's stored in this archway. My clenched fists shake trying to hold onto that power and something deep inside my fingers and arms splinter.

But still I tug and pull to make that magic inch closer and closer to where Scholar lies prone on the ground with Draco's shadow over her. Neither of them see me in the shadows of the ruined hallway trying to move that portal towards my friend.

This isn't at all like stopping lamia or Scholar's shockwaves. This hurts like nothing I've ever felt before but still I hold on. I'm so close, so very close.

Hawk gives a sharp whine behind me before I find those horrid fingers closing around my throat again.

No, no, no, *no*.

"Pathetic," Epsilon whispers in my ear. "Worthless."

I struggle for air and my entire body trembles as I move that mountain of power to Scholar inches away from death.

"I thought you had more fight in you," Epsilon sneers.

She's right. I do have more fight. And I'll always keep fighting because that's who I am. I've nearly given up a few times but I've struggled on.

I was born in a thunderstorm and a spark of that lightning lingered in my veins.

The magic fracturing my bones takes a sudden twist and light blossoms from the archway. The light spins like a whirlpool in the center of the arch but I can see where I've stretched that magic out like an elastic cord towards Scholar. The light follows the path I've tugged and then—just as Draco realizes something is amiss—the tendril of light touches Scholar's foreleg.

Epsilon and I are blown backward from the force of the portal's ignition. I have a brief flitting thought of someplace safe and far away—of a castle on an island where three lochs meet—before the light explodes and Scholar disappears.

The lamia and I fall in a heap on the floor. My hands and arms continue to burn even though I've released the magic of the portal and that stupid iron grip remains around my throat. But the light of the portal is gone and the air sucks in towards the arch like a rubber band snapping. Draco stands alone in the courtyard bewildered for a moment before he lets loose a roar that threatens to level what remains of headquarters.

Hawk whines somewhere beside me and Draco's head swivels about on his long neck to pin us with his gaze through the broken window. The grip around my neck vanishes and I collapse on the ground as Epsilon flees from the wrath of a majestic dragon no longer distracted by the target of his centuries' old pursuit. Hawk and I are left to lie breathless and in pain on the floor of the hallway.

Scholar escaped. She's safe. I did it.

Draco turns back to the arch as if desperate to follow her through but the portal's magic is depleted. He'll have to store up magic until it'll open again, I'm sure.

Shadows creep into the edges of my vision and I try to blink them away but I have no strength left. I reach out blindly to the side and wrap my fingers in Hawk's fur. His panting and steady heartbeat reassure me that I haven't lost everything today. A burgeoning silence stretches on with the battle finally at its end. There are no more screams or cries for help, no hisses or snarls of monsters, no gun shots or dragon roars.

The silence reverberates in my pounding skull until a voice calls out in the growing darkness.

"Genna! Where are you?" It's Jefferson. He must have come to and made his way back in the middle of the disaster to find his daughter.

As my heart breaks, I let the darkness sweep me away.

33

I stare out over the Mississippi River from my hospital room on the fourth floor. The sun shines on the trees in bloom and leaves trails of gold on the water. Cars rev their engines and honk their horns like it's a regular Tuesday afternoon in Minneapolis. All those people out in the ordinary world are worrying about grocery lists and being on time for work—none of them know that the "explosion at the power dam" was my world collapsing in on itself.

In the distance I can make out the yellow dozers and cranes and all manner of construction crews sorting out the mess topside. The work beneath the surface will be far more extensive. I watch it with heavy bags under my eyes and a glum disposition about life in general. I've been up here for three days but haven't felt particularly inclined to leave my room unless it's to avoid the persistent visitor that keeps trying to see me. I can't face that conversation.

So, I sit at my windowsill and occasionally walk through the halls watching the ordinary doctors and nurses check on their patients. There are several in the know about my world but most are just saving the regular world every day. All of the injured humans from Underground were shuttled here since the nearby hidden sanctuaries are flooded with creatures that would be a little conspicuous out in public. Underground is restricted until the repairs are finished so that means the fauns and giants and centaurs and unicorns are crowded in secret tunnels and bunkers throughout the Twin Cities. It's an uncomfortable situation for everyone, some more than most.

I sense Draco somewhere in the building doing his usual security sweep. He's been hovering over everything and everyone in a foul temper. As far as I can tell, he doesn't know the role I played in getting Scholar safely out of his clutches. I've heard rumors from some of the other agents that he keeps going back to the arch and staring at it as if wondering how it could have betrayed him.

There's a light knock on my door and I know it's my brother by the particular series of knocks. He's gotten into the habit of using it since I don't open the door for most everyone, especially since I'm trying to avoid a certain someone.

Hawk slips inside wearing normal street clothes like your average teenager but he's got a large white bandage on the side of his neck where Epsilon tried to rip out his throat during their tussle.

He holds up a laptop in his hands. "You've got a call."

I don't move from the window. "Great."

"Phoenix, come here." He sounds so stern that I slink

over and take a seat on the hospital bed. I keep my arms curled in towards my body in their white casts. I've got fractures throughout my hands and forearms thanks to trying to wrangle a portal. Last time I ever want to do that. At least I was able to blame my wounds on attempting to close the emergency doors against a raging river. No one doubted me.

Hawk takes a seat next to me and opens the laptop on the sheets between us. The screen comes up with a video chat I'm very familiar with. I raise an eyebrow at my brother but he ignores me and accepts the call. A face nearly hidden beneath bushy red hair takes up the screen.

"Oi, lassy, you look terrible."

"Tawnee, that you?" I say. The Spartan looks to be in good spirits despite last I heard she was tracking the assailants from the Vaults attack.

"It's me."

"I had no idea you'd be calling."

She smiles. "Well, I wanted to catch up and say thank you."

"Thank you?"

"For that present you sent us."

Present? I didn't send any present. I frown and she gives me a knowing stare. It takes a moment for it to click what she's telling me as I remember that final moment when the portal activated. I meant to send Scholar far away where she'd be safe and the castle at Eileen Donan just popped into my head. I must have been telling the portal its destination without realizing it.

Tawnee gives me an encouraging nod when my frown lifts. "Yeah, the packaging was in bad shape—you ought to be more careful—but it's all right. We'll be sure to take good care of it."

"We? As in—"

"The selkies and me, of course. It was such a generous, thoughtful gift. It'll be in safe hands here."

I heave a sigh of relief. Scholar made it to the selkies, the very same who had made it their mission to protect her before. So she really is safe.

"And how are you?" Tawnee asks. "I heard the fight was rough."

"We'll live," Hawk answers for me as I feel like I can't speak anymore. I roll my lips and study my wrapped hands. "Any luck on the hunt?"

"No, unfortunately. Those wee devils can run but we'll catch up to them eventually."

Dasc and his followers. At large once again. One of my greatest fears realized. He's managed to evade the whole of the IMS searching for him and his elusive werewolves. I let him go. I let Genna and Witty and Rosalyn slip through my fingers. I have to find a way to live with that but it's proving difficult. Werewolf restrictions have gotten even tighter as fears of what Dasc will do on the loose rise.

"Stay frosty and chin up," Tawnee says and promises to touch base again soon before the video chat closes.

Hawk and I remain motionless where we sit for a long time. We don't have words to share. It's been a long few days for both of us. Our friends betrayed us, people lost their lives, and now more than ever I don't know who I can trust.

There's a knock on the door and it cracks open to reveal a nurse in her scrubs. "Excuse me, but your visitor is back."

I swallow. "Can you please tell him I'm asleep and not to be disturbed?"

"Of course." She closes the door silently behind her.

There's a beat of silence before my brother asks quietly, "When are you going to let Jefferson in?"

"I can't. I just—I can't face him."

"What happened with Genna wasn't your fault."

I blink back a prick behind my eyes. "Do you really think that's going to matter? He's going to hate me. I let her go, Hawk. And now she's back with that psychopath."

"I know, but I don't think you can avoid him forever."

"I can try," I grumble. "I'm tired."

He frowns. "Yeah, I can tell when you don't want to talk anymore."

Scooping up the laptop, he slides nimbly off the bed. "I'll be around if you need me, as always."

I nod and curl up like I'm going to take a nap on the bed. The door clicks as he leaves and I'm alone again. I stare out that window and wish the sun would glare at someone else for a change.

I don't leave my room or allow any visitors for the rest of the evening. The nurse brings in dinner but I sit and gaze out my window as I relive that day over and over again. Surely there's something different I could have done to have stopped Genna's departure and Dasc's escape. A different choice I could have made, a different tactic I could have employed, *something*.

The familiar beat of knocks sounds on the door but softly as if afraid I'm asleep and not wanting to wake me. The door doesn't open.

"Come in, Hawk," I say without turning around.

The door clicks but the footsteps only come in so far. I sigh and glance over my shoulder to chew out my brother for being annoying.

Jefferson stands in the open doorway. I instantly get to my feet but remain where I am by the window. My breath catches and my heart thunders painfully in my chest. Neither of us moves for what feels like ages, each of us too wary to test the waters. I haven't seen Jefferson since the day Genna disappeared again and I haven't wanted to. After all that work and heartache we went through to find his daughter, I let her slip away.

"You've been avoiding me," he says.

Yeah, that's true. I remain silent.

"I've been meaning to say a few things."

He takes two steps forward and I hold out a casted hand to make him stop. "Please, don't."

"Phoenix—"

"I can't."

He takes another step. "Can't what?"

I blink rapidly forcing that sign of weakness back. "I—I can't tell you how . . . how *sorry* I am." I suck in a sharp breath as I fight against a sob working its way up my throat. "I know I've disappointed you and I *tried*, Jefferson. I really tried but I failed. I know I did and I'll never be able to make that up to you. I understand if you hate me s-so—I—"

I break down and hold my pathetic, stiff hands to my face trying to hide behind the casts.

Jefferson strides forward with confident steps and I find myself wrapped up in a hug. His smell of pine needles and coffee wraps around me along with his arms. He cups the back of my head as he rests his chin on the crown of my forehead. My sobs stagger to a halt in my shock.

"It's okay, baby girl," he murmurs. "I've got you."

That endearment, more than anything, cuts me open and I collapse into a sobbing mess in his arms. Jefferson hangs on and gently rubs my back as I weep into his shirt.

"I t-thought y-you *hated* me," I force out between sobs.

"I should be the one apologizing, not you," he says. I wrap my stiff fingers in his shirt as if trying to hold onto the old Jefferson—my cranky adopted uncle Jefferson, the one who vouched for me and came to my rescue. "I've been such a troll," he grumbles.

The relief and insanity of it all manages to elicit a laugh from me.

"You were right," he continues. "And I was so blind I couldn't see everything you were doing to help me and my Genna. I'm so sorry for what I've said and how I've acted."

"Me too," I say in a small voice.

"I don't blame you. I don't blame you one bit and I want you to know that. I forgot what you did to bring her home but I promise never to be so stubborn ever again."

My sobs slow and I sniffle. "Don't make a promise you can't keep. You'll always be stubborn."

"Yeah, you're right. But so will you. I'm sorry it took me so long to come around. Family isn't just blood, you know."

I wipe my cast under the bottom of my nose and cling tighter to his shirt, finding a bit of home that has found its way back again.

34

Underground has certainly seen better days.

Construction scaffolding is everywhere. Earth sprites and gargoyles help hold up the walls while workers maneuver cement and steel beams into place. The barrier left behind by Draco glimmers against the force of the Mississippi River visible through cracks in the repairs. Water sprites rush to and fro scouting out leaks and squeaking to each other when they've found one. Air sprites shoot up and down the lift tunnels to move the air since a lot of the vents overhead have collapsed. The remnants of colorful banners from the midsummer festivities lie trampled and discarded on the ground. I toe one with my military boot and think morosely of happier times.

Hawk nudges my shoulder with his own. He looks like a true professional in his junior agent uniform, hair combed neatly for once, and even an impressive battle scar disappearing into the collar of his shirt. I'm dressed likewise but feel less intimidating with the compression sleeves that reach from my knuckles to halfway up my biceps. At least they took those stupid casts off.

"Ready?" he asks.

"As I'll ever be, I guess."

"Oh, I'm sure it won't be so bad." He wraps an arm around my shoulders and we walk forward together. "It's just a room of judgmental council members staring at us, poking holes through our story, and questioning everything we've ever done in our lives."

"You really should never become a motivational speaker."

"Believe in the power of change!" he announces loudly with a sweeping gesture, drawing the attention of several construction workers nearby. I roll my eyes.

His excessive joking clues me in that he's nervous and we have every right to be. We're going to explain our side of the events directly to the council. I can only hope that we rehearsed our stories well enough to hide the truth about our hand in helping Scholar escape. I sincerely doubt the council would believe us if we told them the truth about Draco and Terra's past.

We walk past the rubble of headquarters, which still has extensive repairs to undergo, and make a right for the penitent cells entrance. It's the very last place I want to go but it's where they decided to setup the administration until things get back to normal—if they ever can. We're allowed in by the sentries and the director's secretary appears to escort us to one of the conference rooms. At least they aren't putting us into an interrogation room. It's a small comfort.

The double doors open to the black oval table I'm used to and find all of the Underground representatives and Director Knox seated around it waiting for us. There's no sign of Draco, thank my lucky stars. He's probably already out hunting Scholar and Dasc. I hope the selkies and Tawnee are good at keeping secrets and hide Scholar well enough.

"We'll speak with Hawk first," the director says without preamble. "Phoenix, wait outside."

No pleasantries then. Okay, fine. My brother and I share a low-five before I retreat into the hallway and lean against the wall as I wait for my turn. Unfortunately for me, the doors are sound proof so I don't get a chance to hear how it's going. I close my eyes and focus on breathing in and out, calm and steady.

"Well, I'm glad to see you took that book I leant you to heart."

My eyes snap open and I push off from the wall to find Charlie directly beside me. I nearly jump. He must have ported there. I didn't hear or sense him coming at all. I clamp a hand over my heart and glare at him for a moment before walking to the other side of the hall and resuming my previous pose.

"Is there a reason you're avoiding me?" he asks and leans on the wall opposite me, mirroring my posture.

"I'm not *avoiding* you."

"So not letting me in to see you at the hospital wasn't your idea?"

I purse my lips and try to cross my arms over my chest but they hurt so much that I ease them carefully back to my sides. All the while Charlie's eyes study me in that way he usually does like I'm an interesting specimen.

"I didn't want to talk to anyone," I say quietly and clear my throat. How about a diversion tactic? "What are you doing here? You getting interrogated too?"

"No, they wanted to give me a medal actually." He pats a shiny silver pin above his heart that I hadn't noticed.

"Oh. Right. Of course."

I shouldn't be surprised. I heard about what he did during the evacuation. He was porting all over the place making sure everyone got out safely. Even had a few close calls, almost getting creamed by falling cement, but he kept going until he about passed out. He's a hero, no doubt about it. Me on the other hand . . .

"I'm sorry," he says softly. "About Genna."

I stare at his boots, eyes unfocused. "Why apologize? You were right."

"Doesn't mean I'm not sorry about it."

I meet his gaze. "Could I have done something more?"

"You mean try to reverse fourteen years of brainwashing, stop a mad man from being mad, or heal a cripple?" he says drily. "There was no winning scenario, Phoenix. Everyone made their own choices. You made yours. Sometimes you just have to live with the consequences."

Then maybe someday I'll just have to be strong enough to create the winning scenario.

The door to the conference room cracks open and we both stand at attention. Hawk slips out looking a bit flustered but he gives me a thumbs up. No one's putting him in handcuffs or escorting him to a cell. That must be a good sign.

"Phoenix, come in," the director calls from inside the room.

I take a deep breath and march for the door. Before I go in, I turn and look back at Charlie and Hawk in the hallway. They both give me encouraging nods and their support is something I know I can rely on to face this and every other day to come. I offer a timid smile before heading into the room.

The door shuts behind me and I take the empty seat at the end of the table opposite Director Knox. As soon as I settle in, they ask me to explain the story of Dasc's escape and the attack. I'm able to stick to the truth pretty well until I get to the part about Scholar. As Hawk and I practiced earlier, I say how Hawk and I became trapped by a group of monsters that suddenly came in and we dared not interfere with the battle taking place in the courtyard. We did what we could to help, we took on Epsilon when she surprised us, and that's it. End of story. We survived. Epsilon fled. Dasc escaped. Genna, Witty, and Rosalyn disappeared with him.

Then the questions come. They poke and prod at my story, question why Hawk and I didn't run for help, how did Hawk manage to be disarmed, why did Epsilon target us, blah, blah, blah. I sputter now and then as my face grows hot under the pressure they lay on. I mean, I get it. One of the biggest bads they ever captured has escaped and I was always good friends with Witty. I was at the center of the investigation around Genna. Dasc had only wanted to talk to me. I can't give them good answers. I don't know half of why everything happened to begin with. But they never seem satisfied with anything I give them.

"But why didn't you give chase after Dasc?" the faun asks.

I level a flat stare at him. "That's the third time you've asked that."

"Phoenix," the director says with a note of warning in his voice.

"Look, not to be rude, but if I had gone barreling after him—as I sure as heck wanted to—the entire penitent cells would have flooded along with the rest of Underground. I didn't 'give chase' because I valued the lives of everyone still fighting in Underground. I made a choice and I have to live with the fact that my parents' murderer is out there somewhere free. So you can ask me again and in different ways but the answer is always going to be the same. I traded his freedom for the safety of those in this city."

The faun at long last finally falls silent and the others follow suit. The tension simmers until Director Knox clears his throat.

"Despite your disregard for the chain of command," he says, "you've proven to be a capable and loyal agent time and time again. I don't doubt your loyalties or the fact you would have gone after him if you had any other choice. If the council is satisfied with their findings, I suggest we dismiss Junior Agent Mason from this session."

There's a general murmur of agreement and the director gestures that I'm free to leave. I ease out of the seat, arms and hands smarting, and take my leave.

Hawk and Charlie are waiting for me outside.

"How'd it go?" my brother asks the second I'm clear.

I shrug and wince at the movement. Stupid arms. "About as painful and irritating as I expected."

"Well, I know a cure for that."

"Don't try to hug me."

He rolls his eyes and presses both hands to his heart. "What kind of horrible person do you think I am? No, I was talking about ice cream."

Charlie laughs and we walk together out of the penitent cells to the market square. We join a throng in line for food at Old Man Two's restaurant which has reopened to feed the construction workers and agents that have remained in the city. We sit in a group and I can't help but feel the void of Genna and Witty's absence from our group. I thought we had all bonded, that our friendship had meant something.

"Everything's different now, isn't it?" Charlie says and contemplates his ice cream as if greatly saddened by its melted state. "And it's just a couple of days before they place us in our careers."

I groan and sink further into my chair. "Pixies, I'd nearly forgotten about that, you know, with all the—" I gesture vaguely to our surroundings and Hawk makes an explosion sound. "Exactly."

Hawk talks around a spoonful of chocolate ice cream. "Well, wherever they put us, we better keep in touch." He gives Charlie a very meaningful look after saying this and I snort a laugh.

"Oh, how very dignified," Charlie says and points his spoon at me.

I nudge his chair with my foot and he quickly grabs the table with both hands to keep from tipping over. We laugh and continue to joke with each other like we used to, as if we aren't down by two of our number by means of betrayal. But for now, I'd like to at least try to enjoy this moment.

A couple days pass and then the junior agents are summoned back to Underground. Headquarters has been whipped into shape—well, half of it anyway. The director's office has been cleared out and fixed along with that side of the building but the sound of heavy machinery and equipment fills the air as the rest is repaired. I stand in line with the other junior agents outside as we're called in one by one for our face time with the director where our future will be decided. Once a junior agent goes in, they don't come back out the front so as not to get our hopes up with gossip about certain job opportunities. Not all of us are going to be field agents. Some of us will have to do office work or otherwise sit on the sidelines.

Charlie and Hawk go ahead of me as we're called alphabetically. They pass through and I don't get the chance to see them before it's my turn. I walk the familiar path up to the director's office but pause in the hallway to look out over the courtyard and black arch siting dormant in the middle. Beneath stands Draco in his usual human appearance and black suit, one hand resting on the side of the arch and gazing upon his creation as if asking what had happened. I can only hope he doesn't get the answer he seeks.

The door to the director's office stands ajar so I enter and he has me close it behind me. I take the seat before his desk as he sits with his fingers templed together. He looks tired but that's to be expected. I'm sure he's had his hands full with the attack, trying to put this city back together, and hunting down a number of fugitives.

"Well, hasn't this been an exciting year," he says with all the signs of fatigue.

"Yes, sir."

"You stopped the alpha werewolf, interrogated him, stopped a war from breaking out with the vampires, fought a pair of lamia, found a kidnapped victim which led to finding a whole host of kidnapped victims, fought yet another lamia, survived your second car crash, and—well, you obviously know the rest of it." He flips through a couple papers on his desk before leaning back in his chair. "You were a troublemaker, always have been."

"Yes, sir," I say quietly.

"And now . . . well, now you're something of a hero, aren't you?"

I blink. "Sir?"

"You've made mistakes, some more grievous than others, but you haven't let that stop you." He studies his papers. "I've received numerous commendations on your behalf from Spartan McDonnell, Agent Boyd, and Agent Barnes. I see even Spartan Knox has endorsed you."

I swallow, surprised by such an outpouring of people speaking on my behalf. I can only hope they've been saying good things.

"I've obviously cleared you for active field duty as soon as you've healed." He gestures to my arms before folding his hands on top of the paper. I'm not sure if I feel proud or exhausted. "You need a better appreciation for the chain of command but I believe—as do others—that with the right training, you could make a very fine agent indeed."

He does? "Thank you, sir."

"And with the commendations from your peers, the majority have recommended you for the Spartan program."

A ringing fills my ears and I almost stop breathing.

Thankfully, the director keeps talking in my own absence of words or thought.

"Of course, you'll have to apply and pass through their extremely rigorous training program, but I believe you have what it takes to become a Spartan. You could start as soon as you complete the application process and are fit for duty again. The only question is if you want it."

I sit stunned for what feels like ages. What do I want to do? Be accepted into the most prestigious group of fighters on the planet? They're the most selective and hardcore group of agents in the IMS. Could I really make it? What about Hawk? Did he qualify too or will he work a position like Jefferson?

"I—" I open and close my mouth a few times but can't get any further words to form.

"A decision doesn't have to be made on the spot, Mason. I would suggest you think this over but don't wait too long. As soon as you've made a decision, return to headquarters and someone from records will help you with the proper applications."

"I—yes. Okay. Yes, sir."

"Good. Then I'll give you this."

He starts to hand over a piece of paper when someone knocks violently on the door. Without waiting for a response, whoever it is bursts into the room. The director and I launch to our feet in unison at the intrusion.

Jefferson storms into the office. He stops beside me but his focus is entirely on the director.

"Agent Barnes, what do you think you're doing?" Director Knox demands.

"I just heard you're putting together a team to hunt

Dasc," Jefferson says without preamble. "I want to be on that team."

"You don't barge into my office and make demands of me," the director says and plants both hands on his desk. That's a very bad sign and an angry posture I've seen directed at myself numerous times before.

"Genna will be hunted along with him, won't she?"

Director Knox lowers his head a fraction. "I'm sorry. She made her choice."

"Then put me on the team."

"You're compromised on this, Agent Barnes. I can't risk putting you on that team."

A muscle flexes in Jefferson's neck and he shifts his jaw. "David, I'm asking you as a friend. She's my baby girl."

I feel small and insignificant as I see my two mentors at odds on the worst of situations, but I already know what the director's going to say. I'd wring my hands if they didn't hurt so much.

"I can't. You know I can't."

Jefferson nods and runs a hand over his mouth and beard. "Okay. I understand." He reaches into his back pocket, pulls out his IMS badge, and sets it on the desk. Then he unholsters the bio-mech gun at his waist and puts it on top. "Then I'm doing what I should have done the last time around."

The air leaves the room.

Director Knox closes his eyes as if pained. "Jefferson, don't."

"I stayed with the IMS when I lost her before because I thought they could help me find her. Now I see they're only going to get in my way."

"Don't do this."

"Consider this my official resignation. I'm going to get my daughter back." He stretches out his hand and the director takes it with reservation. "It's been an honor, sir. Take care."

Jefferson turns to me next as if the director suddenly doesn't exist anymore, and he smiles.

"I hope he gave you my recommendation for Spartan training," he says.

I nod automatically but can't string together any words for this moment. He's leaving. A terrible ache forms in my chest.

"I'm so proud of you, Phoenix," he continues. "We've had a hard time of it but it hasn't been all bad."

"Jefferson . . ."

"Come here, kid."

He opens his arms wide and I step forward to embrace him. If ever I knew my father, I imagine his arms around me would feel this way—strong and safe and caring.

He rests his cheek against the top of my head. I just got my Jefferson back. I can't lose him twice.

"Take the training, Phoenix," he says quietly. "Learn to protect yourself. Train so you can take on the world. Do more good than I ever could. You've got fire in you. Don't ever let it go out."

I roll my lips and wish I could say something as poetic in return to express what he means to me. I can only hold on tighter and whisper, "Thanks, Dad."

He plants a kiss on top of my head and draws away. With one last smile and nod, he walks out of the office and vanishes down the hallway.

The words he leaves behind give me something I haven't felt in a long time. Hope.

I've got fire in me. I am a storm. Death may shape me. Death may break me.

But I will rise.

I turn back to the director. "Where's that application you were talking about?"

ABOUT THE AUTHOR

Bethany Helwig lives in a small town in Minnesota. When not working as a paralegal, she writes fantasy novels, composes music, tries her hand at art, and enjoys the madness that comes with participating in various fandoms.